J

Jude Cook lives in London and studied English literature at UCL. His first novel, *Byron Easy*, was published by Heinemann in 2013. He reviews fiction for the *Guardian*, the *Spectator*, *Literary Review*, *New Statesman*, *TLS* and the *i* paper. His essays and short fiction have appeared in *The Stockholm Review*, *The Moth*, *The Tangerine* and *The Honest Ulsterman*, among other publications. In 2017, he was longlisted for the RA & Pin Drop short story award, and in 2018 he was shortlisted for the Leicester Writes Short Story Prize and longlisted for the Colm Tóibín International Short Story Award. He is an editor for The Literary Consultancy and teaches creative writing at the University of Westminster. *Jacob's Advice* is his second novel.

www.judecook.com
@judecook_

JACOB'S ADVICE

ADVICE

JUDE COOK

unbound

First published in 2020

Unbound
6th Floor Mutual House, 70 Conduit Street, London W1S 2GF
www.unbound.com
All rights reserved

Text design by PDQ Digital Media Solutions Ltd.

A CIP record for this book is available from the British Library

ISBN 978-1-78352-913-1 (limited edition hardback)
ISBN 978-1-78352-899-8 (paperback)
ISBN 978-1-78352-900-1 (ebook)

Printed and bound in Great Britain by Clays Ltd, Elcograf S.p.A.

1 3 5 7 9 8 6 4 2

For Samantha and Benjamin

The greatest evil perpetrated is the evil committed by nobodies
— Hannah Arendt

ONE

My cousin, the well-known pharmacologist Larry Frost, always maintained his three favourite Americans were Jewish men: Bob Dylan, Saul Bellow and Woody Allen. Out of a nation of 300 million, it was this triumvirate with which he most identified. 'Of course,' I counselled him, being older by seven years, 'liking them doesn't make *you* Jewish too.' But he was convinced that somewhere, deep down, he *had* to be. There had to be a reason for his strong sense of empathy. He loved the output of all three unreservedly, even the later, unfunny, unlistenable or unreadable works. By some accident or mix-up in our family lineage, he insisted, there had to be a reason for his overwhelming feeling of consanguinity. He was a philosemite extraordinaire, if not one of the Chosen People. Obsessed with the notion. Absolutely in thrall to it; which was, and is, his nature. This conviction reached an apex of what I considered almost mystical grandeur and absurdity when he moved to Paris in the autumn of last year and found himself a Jewish girlfriend. Ariel, almost twenty years his junior, and so pretty she broke men's hearts at thirty paces as she approached them on the dust-blessed, pollen-laden Parisian streets. *Where has she been all my life?* they would ask their secret souls – me included, when I finally met her. On the kind of sunny morning when the air still breathes Flaubert's famous exhalations of 'love and intelligence', Ariel was unstoppable. Her luminous face, with its languorous mouth, peeking from under a felt cloche hat clamped to a crown of shimmering black hair, was an engine of attraction. Add to this a formidable mind and an even stronger will, and she was devastating. But I'm getting carried away... I must first let you meet Larry, and explain how and why I came to be living in Paris myself.

I should establish straight away that we are both doctors, but of different kinds. Larry, to his new colleagues, is Dr Lawrence Frost, a visiting neuropharmacologist at the Institut Pasteur on the rue de Vaugirard. And I, to my students back home at Birkbeck, am Dr Newman – Nicholas Newman, a research fellow specialising in the history of Revolutionary France and the Napoleonic era. I've published widely on the First Republic and the Jacobin cause, and was once asked to be historical adviser on a romantic comedy set at the time of the Terror – not much of either genre to be found there, I argued; so in the end I said no. I'm only Nick to my closest friends (and Dad to my son, whom I won't be seeing for a while now I'm resident here). Larry, by contrast, is Larry to everyone after a first encounter. He's even Larry to the *directrice générale* of the Institut. He has that kind of effect on people. In fact, I've always thought there was something Promethean about Larry: not in his suffering – I rarely see any of that – but in his daring; his intrepid, principled force. Though nicely berthed at the Department of Neuroscience since October (and at the palatial Place des Vosges apartment of Ariel's parents, no less), he has always held adversarial positions. Against everything, it seems.

A true contrarian. Ever since I've known him as a 'grown-up' he's been something of a crusader against the monstrous $600-billion pharmaceutical industry, with its shabby regulation, its market-driven misdemeanours, its academics sucking at the lucrative teat of the drugs manufacturers. After graduating from medical school, followed by a stunning doctorate in cellular function from King's, Larry seems to have made a career from his Cassandra voice, penning articles everywhere from the *BMJ* to the broadsheets. Maybe I should revise 'well-known' pharmacologist to 'notorious'. He's a one-man revolution; a corrector of consciousnesses, and conscience.

All this is congruent with his big, slightly un-English personality. Maybe this is where all the Jewish stuff originated – though he insists our grandmother's background has something to do with it. Larry's always been exuberant, opinionated, scalpel-sharp. An eager, garrulous, indiscreet man with wild, dark curly hair and mobile (even manic) eyes the same colour as my own, he often appears shorter or squatter at a distance – as if he's carrying a bit too much weight for his height. At the café on the rue Saint-Jacques where we've met virtually every morning since I arrived mid-March, one might almost mistake his seated figure for that of a fat man – an overweight sports correspondent for *Le Figaro*, say, with his tanned dome-brow rippling with fissures. A weathered traveller's face, too. Larry spent much of his early thirties seeing the world. He has a complicated theory of freedom; its many roads, its many price tags. I'm rather envious of his adventures, as I spent my thirties in a university office whose single window offered a great view of a brick wall. As well as lecturing everywhere, my cousin would bang out his articles at café tables from Honduras to Malawi, and eventually the Australian Outback, where he'd perch his laptop on the makeshift desk of an oil drum. 'A surprisingly good writing surface,' he informed me. 'If your subject is global profiteering, an oil drum will keep you on-message throughout.'

Then there's Larry's repertoire of hand gestures. Off-putting at first, if you don't have long acquaintance of him (and this goes for the French too, amazingly), in full spate he really is a sight to be seen. Combining a whirling right with a wringing motion involving both, then a sudden drumming with his fingertips on whatever surface is available, he has a whole orchestra of emphasis at his disposal. The entire band is often unleashed when he has advice to give. Larry was notorious for this in our family, and my own father would occasionally sit passively and be lectured by his ten-year-old nephew. Yes, a great adviser of everyone from friends to multinational corporations ('who never listen, anyway'), he thankfully takes a philosophical view of its usefulness. A wonderful old saw is often at hand once he realises his words have fallen on barren ground: 'The thing about advice, Nick,' he would say in his slightly high, cajoling voice, 'is that fools seldom heed it and wise men don't need it.' So why, I would demand, do you always give it? 'Because I'm Jewish, man!' And there we'd be, back at the beginning.

I once asked him to name a favourite work by each of his three heroes. Naturally, for an aficionado it was never going to be the obvious, canonical stuff. You weren't going to get *Herzog*, *Annie Hall* and 'Like a Rolling Stone'.

'For Bob – and trust me, this changes on an hourly basis – it has to be "Sara".'

'Expand, please.'

'For its minor-key melancholia. For the depth of Bob's grief over his divorce, the separation from his kids. It's masterly – not just for the restraint of emotion, the generosity of spirit, but for the Arabic-influenced singing. The melody and its melismas are… exquisite!'

'Just give me a title for each. I don't have much time.'

At this his brow rippled in concentration, like the effect of wind on a sand dune.

'For Saul…' (he always used first names, as if he were a close personal friend of them all) 'it would have to be the short story "What Kind of Day Did You Have?".'

'And Allen?'

'For Woody,' – and he gave me his joyous smile which unfortunately resembled a wince – '*Bananas*.'

'*Bananas*? Really? But I recall that as lightweight. It's like choosing a Leonardo sketch over *La Gioconda*.'

'Yeah, but it's a masterpiece of visual comedy.'

He once told me that he first got into Woody Allen at twelve. Before he understood what the films were really about, he said he just loved the music and the sight gags. There was one of which he was particularly fond – in *Play It Again, Sam* – where the newly-in-love protagonist, played by his hero, walks the sunshiny streets of San Francisco, backslapping men who sit on a ledge overlooking the bay. On the cut, he slaps a newspaper reader on the shoulder, who promptly topples over the edge. Woody just walks on, oblivious.

'How do you feel about the accusations?' I asked him. 'They're pretty serious.'

Here Larry paused for a long while, not something he was given to do when answering a question. 'I'm torn, Nick, I really am. How would you feel if someone you loved and admired was accused of something appalling? I mean, you wouldn't want them to be capable of such things. Ultimately, though, I believe a person is innocent until proven guilty in a court of law. There's no rule that says Woody has to stand trial in the court of social media. So, until then, I'm going to enjoy *Bananas*.'

I didn't bring up the matter again.

Larry became a Dylan nut when he found himself in a school friend's bedroom at fifteen, trying to form a band. His friend lowered the needle (still in use in the eighties) on 'Subterranean Homesick Blues' and it was all over. As for Bellow, this came about as a result of Larry's peripatetic wanderings. He was turned on to the novelist by a girl he was seeing in Mexico City. But not because she was a fan. 'She really disliked him and his writing,' grinned Larry, 'so I just *knew* I had to try him.' And so he read *Seize the Day* (a very Larry title), and from that moment he was smitten. 'But why was I destined to discover an affinity with Bellow, and not, say, Updike or Fitzgerald?' he'd ask meaningfully. 'Answer me *that*.' And then he'd be off, on to current advances in molecular biology, or corruption within clinical research organisations, and I'd lose him again.

We all know brilliant people. They're quite frightening, really. They upset our equilibrium with their energies and outpourings – they're like grown-up children, and we're tenderly protective towards them, with the added poignancy that we can't effectively extend that protection. We encounter them, so to speak, in a state of nature. Voltaire so terrified the French king and Frederick's German court that he ended up banished to the Swiss border for the last years of his life, wearing nothing but a dressing gown and silk slippers. The brilliant are on their own in the universe, just as we are, the stupid or dull. Not that I consider myself such, even on a bad day, but certain people do blaze brighter than others: like supernovas they announce their significance by the sheer size of their emanation, mental in Larry's case.

And sometimes fulminatory. Like all only children (I confess now that I am one too), my cousin has a terrible temper. As do I. It's because we were never socialised properly and made to share with siblings or peers. We think the world is our own, but we're forced to face the fact that it isn't, and on a daily basis, all the way through adult life. Understandably, this leaves us angry.

On certain days, Larry's occasional anger even seems to echo the city's. In January, Paris underwent the seismic attack on the offices of its notorious, though well-loved, satirical paper, *Charlie Hebdo*. Two Islamist militants gunned down nine cartoonists and journalists, a bodyguard, and a maintenance worker. In the resultant convulsion, two police officers were killed, one of whom was a Muslim, while another gunman murdered four Jewish hostages in a kosher supermarket. The world was up in arms at this flagrant assault on free speech and the Jewish people, with '*Je suis Charlie*' on everybody's lips. Even now, in May, the *Charlie* tags are still clearly visible on the sides of Haussmann apartments, or the bulky kerbside rubbish bins; though not so many *Je suis Juif*, ironically. The city is ostensibly back to business as usual, with only the sight of armed soldiers three abreast to indicate anything ever happened. However, the paranoia, anger and unease still run deep, though Larry rarely refers to *les événements de Janvier*.

All of which – the political situation, Larry's intuitions about our ethnicity, his short fuse – make his current aura of calm expansiveness more extraordinary. Given his rages, his brilliance, his abandoned enthusiasms, it's stranger still that Larry's father was an accountant. A man with the very un-Semitic name of Colin. My father, Tom – once a history teacher at the delightfully named Blue School in Wells, Somerset, near where I grew up – never took to Colin Frost. Larry and I are related on our mothers' side, the irrepressible Macmillan sisters. They're very similar – could even pass as twins – although my aunt Beverley never boasted my mother's slightly Gallic beauty; the delicate ears and echoing curves of chin and lip. There's a photo of the two of them from the early sixties: my mother Natalie, the elder sister, in a high-piled beehive; lipsticked, laughing, and bristling with the efficiency that would make her an excellent company PA in later life. And next to her is Beverley, under the lights of what appears to be a fairground carousel. Why are funfairs such a mid-twentieth-century phenomenon? The art of the fifties and sixties is infested with them. Perhaps Austerity Britain saw them as updated versions of the Vauxhall Pleasure Gardens. If they couldn't have bread, there were at least circuses. Places of licence and danger, too, especially for young women like our mothers, with their transgressive pull, their hazardous whirling machinery, their transient leather-jacketed men. Indeed, behind the girls are the shadowy goons I presume were their boyfriends at the time, men whom our fathers most probably despise to this day. Lacking my mother's sparkle, and with all the signs of the hypochondria that would later become a pathology, Beverley is trying very hard, but failing, to enjoy herself. I should say now that both sets of parents are still alive. Mine happily retired in my home village of Chewton Mendip (a place name my ex-wife Cassie ridiculed mercilessly. I can hear her Bostonian vowels tearing *Tchew-tarn* to pieces, like a cat with a carcase of chicken). And Larry's still live in his childhood house on the noisy Northolt Road, Harrow-on-the-Hill – or *on-the-Hell*, as he predictably came to call it, the place being the most boring, suburban black hole in the universe, according to him. Not many polymaths originated there, I have to agree. I always found the area, and Uncle Colin himself, hard work on our many visits. Unlike my family, who drove every summer down through France, via Paris, and on to the glorious Midi, instigating my rabid Francophilia, Larry's folks almost never ventured abroad. Bournemouth was as far as they got. No wonder Larry became such a globetrotter. And Uncle Colin, taller than my dad, but less robust, always had the air of the boffin or mathematician about him – a bone-dry man, with little humour or urbanity. He was as boring as accountants are traditionally held to be (though my current guy, a rogue by the name of Barry Gallagher, with whom I am entangled in a legal dispute, could hardly be described as such). Careful, punctilious, well-spoken, though disguising his jagged north

London accent for much of the time, Larry's dad had the look of a man who spent many hours in dank offices, frowning over figures. A committed smoker, the endless packets of Pall Mall greyed his skin and broke up the lower registers of his voice. He was a dark horse, too, on the romantic front, as we later found out, much to everyone's surprise, but all that can wait.

The place where I grew up was called Spring Cottage: one of two solid-looking, Grade II-listed houses on the main road into the village, with stone-mullioned windows, a red pantile roof, and a cool atmosphere from the uneven stone slabs on first entering. The front door, still the original wonky planks from the eighteenth century, was hung with holly in the winter, and, in summer, hidden by an intense explosion of lavender growing wild on the grass verge. Inside, my father made sure a well-stocked wine rack was the first thing you encountered; the kitchen and through-lounge occupying the whole ground floor of the house. Naturally, this would once have doubled as a bedroom, with alcoves for beds still scooped into the walls, which my mother filled over the years with tallboys or dressers tumbling with crockery. Unlike Larry's house, ours was full of books, in rickety, leaning cases, or in stacks that grew from the floor. Dad made a point of leaving tomes on de Gaulle, medieval France and Matisse lying around, and Elizabeth David's cookery books were on prominent display next to a rustic chopping board. Outside on the road sat the red, box-like Renault 4 with its clattering engine, a car that still managed to take us to the Massif Central and back every year.

My father was, and is, an admirable man. I resemble him in many respects, though with the way things have gone in my life, there's less to admire. We have always liked each other. It's long been a source of puzzlement for me when men have confided they disliked, or were never understood by their fathers – Larry, for instance. We've always been more like friends, albeit from different generations. We share the same interests, anticipate the same ironies. As soon as I was able, we were having discussions on a high level; initiated by him, like the father who can't wait to kick a ball about with his son. He had a thirst for advanced discourse – the major questions of the day, politics, ethics, philosophy. I remember him trying these subjects on Larry's dad a few times and getting frustrated. On the Frosts' rare visits, I recall our fathers talking together over wine in the summer dusks; candles on the slatted table in our big garden, plagued by flies. Larry would have been too young to have comprehended a word, though the general tone must have osmosed into him somehow, given how he turned out. Our dads would be there late into the night, arguing heatedly but good-naturedly about socialism or monetarism or Kant's categorical imperative – things nobody bothers with now. And, when we were alone, my father would think nothing of bringing Hegel's *Phenomenology* or *The Social Contract* into what now seem like Socratic dialogues for a ten-year-old to be having. At mealtimes, too, he would show off his knowledge, though it never seemed as such coming from his mouth. This was stuff everyone should know, he indicated.

A solid, bull-chested man, Swansea born, Thomas Newman had failed as an academic, but had become a schoolmaster instead. A more respectable profession, some would say. In fact, my mother met him when working in the admissions office of

Exeter University where Tommy, as he was known then, was a dashing postgrad with dreaming Welsh eyes and a slight curl to his hair. My mother, no slouch in the looks department herself, had, as I said before, the French look of Simone Signoret or Claudine Auger. 'She had one of those beauty-spot moles – you know the type,' my father liked to rumble, Welshly, at the dinner table. 'The type you paint on with a pencil. Everyone was in love with her!' Causing my mother to retort: 'Why didn't I have more fun, then?' This was never spoken in the spirit of recrimination. They were a happy couple, I can see that now, with all the mystery of connection that lies at the heart of happy couples. How had they made it work while my romantic life had bordered on farce? Maybe it was down to my father possessing those masculine qualities I always undervalued. Sure, he was linguistically and intellectually adept – his degree was combined honours, French, Spanish and Russian, before European history turned his head – but he could also put up shelves and dig a plot. He had overhauled Spring Cottage when they moved there in the late sixties, with shovel and spirit level. Perhaps it was that Welsh earthiness, the connection to the land: he was simply physically skilled in ways that I'm not. He kept a kitchen garden for his speciality, authentic Provençal ratatouille; he fixed the Renault when it became *en panne*, which was frequently; and he put up a tent with competence. All those manly virtues and capabilities you take for granted at the time, until you have to demonstrate them yourself in front of a sceptical wife and son.

It's hard to square such quotidian upbringings with the lives Larry and I ended up leading. Not that they've been particularly glamorous or extreme – more that they have been outward facing, publicly engaged. The Macmillan sisters produced two passably successful academics, both still the right side of forty-five; only just, in my case. I suppose I've been particularly lucky in terms of publication – I've never been the archetypal dweller of ivory towers, knee-deep in dust, content to confine his knowledge to obscure academic journals. I've put out three books – not a bad tally for someone yet to be honoured with a professorship. And from fairly humble beginnings too. After a postgrad from Birkbeck in the early nineties, I stayed on when they offered to co-fund a doctorate (not a college chosen at random after Cambridge, either – I wanted to haunt the squares of Bloomsbury). Its dissertation, *France 1789–1804: From Ferment to Torment*, made it into print via the CUP, as many an unready first thesis will. At the time I was twenty-five, loving London and reading for England, or rather, for France: Balzac, Zola, Hugo, all the lengthy masterpieces a history degree will prevent you from visiting, but tantalisingly keeps mentioning. I was also falling in love with the first in a longish line of brilliant, opinionated women, the last of whom I married. Two decades on, after innumerable articles and monographs, I'm still at the rock face of the Revolution – 'It's an industry, like any other!' Larry would often holler. 'You should've chosen a discipline worthwhile to humanity.' Maybe, but then so are the Tudors and Hitler and October 1917. And unlike pharmaceuticals, the investigation of currents in history is not saturated with shame and exploitation. At least in theory.

The French establishment appears to like me, too, at a safe distance. After my surprise pop-history hit, *Misers and*

Moralists: French Literary Life up to the Bourbon Restoration, they made me an *Officier dans l'Ordre des Palmes académiques* – for 'services to French culture'. The youngest-ever foreign recipient, apparently. I was flushed with intolerable pride, as were my folks. In contrast, Larry's parents have never been that impressed with his achievements. On occasion, they've even seemed a touch embarrassed. A doctor son reading from his own work on Radio 4, and they act as if he's a failure. I suppose some people are never satisfied... My latest book is a work in progress tentatively entitled *Elysian Fields* – with the rough subheading, *The French Revolution in Perspective*. The long perspective, covering two centuries of global change, the scouring of two world wars; from the Enlightenment to the Age of Information. It follows the thread of sedition from the First Republic up to *les Événements*, through Fukuyama's premature end of history, and so on, to France's non-involvement in the Iraq debacle and the recent Arab Spring. It's ambitious, certainly, and I'm not sure how to proceed with it most days. But, to mark the Académie's *promotion violette*, the Sorbonne have generously awarded a research stipend that may well last me until the end of the next academic year. How could I say no? It was more than the publisher was offering, anyway. To be perfectly frank, I was glad to be out of London, for reasons I will expand upon later.

Larry once suggested I only became a historian because it was my father's subject at a provincial secondary school. Not so, cousin! It was almost English lit. When it came to the history versus literature contretemps, I had begun on the side of Edmund Burke – a man who has unfortunately become a cipher for a certain mealy-mouthed Tory posture, and who is perhaps long overdue rehabilitation. Surprisingly, Burke thought that art revealed the essence of man's nature: 'Art *is* man's nature,' he said. There's a story of Burke and Charles James Fox ganging up on the Duke of Richmond in an argument over the relative merits of the two subjects. As with Sidney, who thought poetry represented the Golden World, Burke insisted that poetry told the truth about humanity, not history. On this I was in hot agreement. It's become a truism to say history only gives us *the* Mark Antony, whereas Shakespeare gives us a *particular* Mark Antony. However, as I got older, I began to favour the accuracy of the record, not the poetic distortion. I was siding with Plato here. If you want art, make up a bunch of characters, stick them in a room, and then claim it shows how human beings operate in a sophisticated civilisation. But don't claim facsimile as reality. When it came to history, like Aristotle, I felt myself to be an eternalist. Time and nature were one, and we have a responsibility to tell the truth. He was the first to notice that dolphins breathed air, for example, and didn't have gills like fish. This didn't stop other primitive biologists classifying dolphins as fish rather than mammals for thousands of years. Like my father used to say, at some point we have to face up to the reality of things. No, the reason I stuck with my subject, *au fond*, was because I felt I was more interested in the human than the average historian. I might have become a biographer, but I felt it was the human material behind the political events that my books had been examining all along. Who wouldn't want to peer a little closer into the life of Denon, Napoleon's extraordinary director of the Louvre, or that slippery traitor, Talleyrand? Balzac, too, a novelist impossible to separate from history, was enmired in the human reality; the morality morass of day-to-day transactions, not dates and so-called facts. So I can admit art and history are more than just first cousins. Everything's okay as long as you keep them at a decent distance.

The Sorbonne also gifted me a fifth-floor apartment on the boulevard Saint-Michel, looking west over the Jardin du Luxembourg. I'm in the *cinquième*, the Quarter, but on the borderline with the legendary sixth. Literally on the border – the wide pulsing thoroughfare of Saint-Michel marks the division between the two *arrondissements*. Some evenings from my balcony, stubby Kronenbourg in hand, a salmon sunset behind the eternal *Tour*, I can just make out, through the foliage of the park, the bejewelled one-time haunts of Hemingway, Joyce, Fitzgerald. La Coupole, Café de la Rotonde, Le Select. Still trading in tale-tellers, no doubt, but without the sawdust on the floor. To come clean, I never fell for that co-opted romanticism of Paris in the twenties. Being poor is never glamorous, even if you have the pont Neuf to gaze on every day. Old Papa jazzed up life in the Quarter for *A Moveable Feast*, but Henry Miller and Orwell told the bitter, gritty truth. Having visited the city every year for what seemed like a decade as a boy, it's never been that exotic for me. I've always felt Paris was in my blood. Nevertheless, even I have been seduced afresh this time around. When I open my shutters in the morning to feel the gentle spring sunshine on my frazzled face, I seldom fail to feel like the Young Man in Caillebotte's painting. Even from the fifth floor one can detect the good bakery smells from the street below at 6 a.m.; intensely nostalgic for me – and pleasurable even if they weren't. Along with bread, and the tang of gasoline, comes the burnt-sugar odour of *crêpes beurre-sucre*, assailing my nostrils like the call of the past. For me, the waft of the *crêperie* is the authentic aroma of childhood. When I was a boy, the fact that such a divine gift should be readily available on street corners, and all over Paris, was a never-ceasing wonder. Bristol didn't have anything to compare. Just recently, I've stood transfixed at first light, inhaling the early air, watching the sun rise over the place Edmond Rostand like a slice of molten peach. After a few moments, the beams begin trembling through shutters and keyholes of rooms where I imagine many novels have been written. Finally, after a full five minutes, with the green street-cleaning vehicles below still hosing the pavements with frothy water, I've witnessed Apollo grandstanding and overturing down the great boulevards; flaming in the leaves of meshed trees, transforming the zinc roofs of Montparnasse into stretches of copper, bronze, essential gold.

Disappointingly, for much of April, the weather hasn't been up to much. But in early May, that great foliation of life and beauty unique to the capital is underway – a kind of vibration or anticipation of better things; the wide boulevards basking in springtime splendour, the blossom confettiing on passing heads. About time, too. We're all yearning for better things. My days are spent largely at the Sorbonne's Maison de la Recherche, or sitting dazedly in the Jardin, a book in my lap, watching the old couples and *jeunes filles* crunching up the gravel paths; the intimate wind of early summer shifting the high walls of foliage in a solid mass. Sometimes, if the sun's up, this tableau can resemble a trance or dream, like finding oneself in a scene from Resnais' *Last Year in Marienbad*. I like the connection with the pastoral in the Luxembourg – rarer to find in Paris than in a city like London. Haussmann didn't plan on much greenery. There are tall planes, chestnuts, copper beeches; the soporific trickle of the fountains. Really, I have everything I need. The apartment is fine too: one bedroom, but with a large living space, white-painted, and a good Wi-Fi connection. Luckily, like most blocks in Paris, there's a reliable lift. In this cramped space, I sometimes encounter the splendidly sour concierge, Mme George, along with her black cat, who I'm certain is her familiar. I speak French with her most days, despite her being so disobliging, even monosyllabic. On street level, next door to the entrance hall, there's a kiosk for the English papers, which I still like to buy despite being able to read them all on my phone. There's also a good grocer, and a *boulangerie* two doors down that does an excellent *tarte aux pommes*, slices of which I keep in my room for famished moments, which usually fall late in the evening. This bakery must be responsible for the enticing waft of baguette that wakes me every day. Apart from Larry, and a couple of Sorbonne contacts from the old days, I keep to myself. Why fill up the mental tank with the wearying gas of endless socialising? There's nothing I like better than an evening alone on the balcony, especially now the warmer weather has arrived. You can buy a kilo of tomatoes for a couple of euros, some Pont l'Évêque cheese, a good *saucisson* and never miss the inside of a restaurant. Like I say, I have everything I need, just about. I have my research, unsurpassable galleries, and twenty cinemas within walking distance. I want for very little.

Apart from the newly clement air, I also like the fact that my *appartement spacieux* has a bit of height. There's nothing like a high elevation for raising the mind. Not great height, where you are literally in the gods, too high to see the detail of the street, but just high enough for the mind and soul to be taken upwards. Here, in the fifth *arrondissement*, my thoughts can fly again. At home in Bloomsbury, I rent a first-floor flat from the University of London: 10–12 North Mews, behind Doughty Street, where the delighted tourist will find Dickens' first London address still going strong. Unfortunately, my stake in it is a gloomy little pad facing a residents' concrete yard. Housed in an art deco block that has been gentrified over the years by the annexation of a keypad-entry carport, along with new mirrors at the top of every staircase (putting one uncomfortably in touch with the ageing process, I find), it's killing to the spirit. Still, it's round the corner from both Birkbeck and Cassie, and my son Ed, so I suppose I should be grateful. Relations with my ex-wife have been a little strained of late, to say the least, and that's one of the reasons I needed to get out of town. Since our divorce, they live in one of those high red-brick mansion blocks at the bottom of Rosebery Avenue, near the mouth of the busy Exmouth Market. Cass, Boston-born, from a wealthy academic family, can't stand the place. I always found it pretty agreeable in the short time I shared it with them – she needs to see some of the London hovels I wrote whole books in. On the eighth floor, it certainly has some elevation. But Cass found it intolerable from the start.

What can I say about my ex-wife? I'm still unable to see her clearly without emotion. Small, with a dark bob she's always pushing behind her ears, she's an outboard motor of forceful energies and imperatives. Quite daunting if you're not used to her. She has one of those open, oval, ingénue faces, which darkens the more it disagrees with you. We met at a UCL Christmas party at the end of the last century (I love telling people this, it makes us sound like biblical ancients), where she still teaches courses in modern American literature and feminist criticism. Cassie Corvino had just arrived fresh from Harvard when we first chinked flutes of slightly warm University of London fizz; she about to publish her major work, *Gender, Ideology and Freedom*; me already semi-established. It was only a number of years later, when we were unhappily married, that I let slip (as these things will) that I'd never finished her book. Which was a lie. I'd never even *started* it. We always save the most wounding remarks, I find, for the most heated exchanges, even those of us who come from placid families who stayed together, like Larry and me. Never having witnessed such bust-ups first-hand, we must learn it from TV or the movies. It's only when you're at the peak of a blazing adult row that you get to see, paradoxically, what kind of children you both once were. We save atavistic traits, too, for moments of high emotion. A wilful, spoilt girl, quite probably; pushed by her parents to be creative, when, as she told me, she 'didn't have a creative muscle in her body', Cass could be vicious in verbal conflict. Notice the use of 'muscle' in the idiom, not bone? No, I didn't at the time either. Of course, from an early age she was a voracious reader – Brontës, Austen, the rest – and had a highly developed discursive faculty by the age of ten. She's living proof of the dangers of reading Plath before your thirteenth birthday. She soon moved on to the gentler, more lapidary stuff; her countrywomen, Wharton, Cather and Emily Dickinson, courses in which she still teaches. It was also Cass who introduced me to these writers, for which I'm grateful. And for loving me once, which I know she doesn't any longer.

Anyway, now that we're divorced, she's always threatening to take Ed back to the States permanently. Boston being a Harvard town, she sees the institution as her spiritual home. This, as you can imagine, is my greatest fear – to be parted from my son not by a few streets, but by thousands of miles. Cass's biggest fear, however, back at the mansion block, is merely that Ed will tumble from a great height when she takes her eyes off him for a nanosecond. I tell her not to worry so much. Boisterous and curious, like boys should be, with the most beautiful glossy dark hair and Italianate brows, he's a wonderful kid. Small of physique, inherited from his mother, he loves sliding in his socks on the flat's parquet flooring. My ex tells him he will break his neck doing this, an admonishment I unhappily know it easier to stay silent about. Infect a boy with a motherly timidity about life, and you never know where it may end: in the bedroom, probably. 'He's *ten*, Cass,' I found myself shouting at her when I went to visit last Christmas (the temper, as I told you). 'He knows not to hurl himself from an eighth-storey balcony!' But that didn't seem to convince her. 'A fool!' she began shaking her bob from side to side, upbraiding me in front of Ed. 'A holy fool. I can't believe I married a holy fool.' Naturally, I didn't want our son to witness a row, sitting there with his party hat on, expectant, at any minute, of his grandparents. But it was too late. So easy to wound a young life. You think they're not being wounded, but they are. They sit there staring back at you – you, their supposed parent and protector – with those seemingly inviolate, innocent eyes blinking into your own, and the damage is manifest. Cass thinks our split hasn't made any difference to him. Well. She would say that – me *marrying* her didn't seem to make any difference to her. She never took my surname; par for the course as a published academic, I suppose, but the result is that Ed is now Ed Corvino. His name was originally Edward, after the grandfather Larry and I shared, but she changed it to the Sicilian Eduardo. So now my son has the admittedly grand, but gangsterish, full name of Eduardo Corvino. Try getting that through passport control at JFK. It's strange how the smartest people misunderstand the simplest psychology – it's almost a rule in academia that the brightest minds have the emotional intelligence of fleas or water buffalo. Extremely organised, efficient, perspicacious – slightly chilly, yet Americanly charming on first meeting – Cass nonetheless hasn't the slightest idea of what's going on under her own mental roof. I could see from the start that Ed had been deeply affected by his parents' separation – that he was confused, agitated, annoyed by it; alive to any undercurrents of discord between us. But Cass thought everything was business as usual in his soul, to the extent that she was exercised by the subject. I felt it my mission to minimise any disharmonious incidents. Why I fucked this up by shouting at his mother on Christmas Day, I'll never know. He'll remember *that* one, that's for certain.

To get back to Larry, and his life in Paris...

Last week, on 1 May, *la fête du Travail*, we went for a *cinq à sept* drink at Le Pantalon on the rue Royer-Collard. I'd been trying to get a proper evening audience with him for a few days, but he was perpetually out, investigating the restaurants of the Marais with Ariel, and, of all people, her ex, Rube. Rube is Rubens Xavier, a black DJ and artist who had been Ariel's first proper boyfriend, and it's to Larry's credit that he tolerates the very idea of his presence. Maybe he's trying to demonstrate the magnanimity that comes with being thirty-seven, but I doubt it. He's in Rome, so he's doing as they do. To counteract any residual chemistry between Ariel and Rube on these nights, Larry's been bringing along his buddy from the Institut, Professor Singh (or one of his buddies, he appeared to make friends with the whole faculty after five minutes). The four of them have been meeting up practically every evening, and I've begun to feel slightly ostracised. I've met Nadir Singh a couple of times; a lovely, quiet, sanguine man of fifty, with shoulder-length hair, admittedly grey. Long hair is something I always like to see on a professor, but then Nadir is one of Paris's tiny minority of Sikhs, so he doesn't have much choice in the matter; France having banned the turban along with the hijab in the classroom a decade ago. Yes, Larry was being elusive, and our quick *express* at the zinc counter every morning on the rue Saint-Jacques wasn't sufficient. There were certain urgent matters I needed to talk to him about.

That day I had spent most of the afternoon in the Sorbonne's grand Serpente library. The rococo splendour of the Louis Quatorze furnishings always made me feel like I'd eaten a whole box of marshmallows. I'd been looking up several papers relating to Chateaubriand's *Le Génie du christianisme*, his work notes in effect. I needed them for the section of my new book that explored how religious revivals always follow revolutions. As if a beaker of God has to be imbibed after the secular intoxication of sedition has worn off. I took the scenic route to Le Pantalon – a backstreet café a stone's throw from my apartment; one of those dark dives that accepts only cash, and where the Pernod drunks still prop up the bar all day. It was a place I had found myself in sitting alone after long hours straining my eyes. Walking down the boulevard Saint-Michel in the warm air of late afternoon, watching the horse-chestnut candles quiver in the trees of the Luxembourg, imagining what Ed was doing in that exact moment, I wondered, as I often did, why I had ever chosen to live anywhere else.

Once through the doorway, with its incredible life-size paintings of naked goddesses winking a welcome, I found the tiled interior warmly lit and already almost full. And no sign of Larry. Lateness is something we're supposed to tolerate with the brilliant, but my cousin takes tardiness to virtuoso levels. Irritated, I sat down and ordered *un demi* and tried to gather my thoughts. I should declare an interest here, as the saying goes. Or reveal, rather, why I have felt the need since March to be more proximate to Larry than I have in the past. For the first time, I felt I needed his advice – and I was prepared to listen on this occasion. It's what I consider the real reason for my being in Paris. After all, why would I separate myself from my only son for what was shaping up to be a year abroad when I could've probably looked up Chateaubriand's notes on microfilm at Senate House? Well, for a number of years – since turning forty, in fact – I haven't been in the best of health. Let me explain. Four, almost five, years back I was seeing a consultant at University College Hospital for a prosaic urology-related problem, which I won't go into now. Finding the standard antibiotics ineffective in clearing up the infection, my man Dr Decker – as dependable and brisk a physician as one could wish for – prescribed me a more potent antibiotic from a broad-spectrum group known as fluoroquinolones. The 'fluoro' prefix, which I didn't register then, refers to their basis in fluoride, the friendly ingredient all children know from their daily toothpaste. Thinking no more of it, I dutifully started on what I hoped was a cure, worried only by the fact the first pill made me slightly dizzy and dyspeptic, as these medicines often will. Seven days into the course, holed up in my flat one lunchtime, researching new documents relating to the Hundred Days, about to sit down to some halloumi cheese I had just grilled, I had an experience that can only be compared to a mini-stroke... I won't relate the details, suffice to say it put me in hospital, and that its fallout affected me most profoundly, and probably will for the rest of my life. I had suffered an adverse reaction – a bad one, but not as bad, I subsequently found out, as many in the States had suffered. It seems absurd, given that research is my line, that I hadn't looked into this particular pill before I put it into my body. Perhaps it was Dr Decker's plausible, martinet manner that prevented me. Or outright stupidity, as Cass somewhat heartlessly suggested. Larry's reaction was the strangest of all. When I phoned him a week afterwards, his first words were a compassionate but firm, 'Bad luck.' Was that all he could offer? A neuropharmacologist? His specialism was the effect of medication on the functioning of the central nervous system. In fact, his response troubled me for a long time. We expect medics to immediately offer suggestions of cures, exotic courses of treatment, second opinions. But no, just 'Bad Luck, old man...' It's only recently, after our in-depth conversations about the world of Big Pharma, that his words have made more sense.

A cursory look online would have told me fluoroquinolones were linked to a whole host of gothic side effects. Only on the market in the US since 1987, they were just beginning to be promoted to front-line use in the UK. To my horror, my first Google search revealed that my particular pill was issued with a black-box label in the States, courtesy of the Food and Drug Administration, warning consumers and doctors of potential tendinosis and tendon rupture. When I asked Larry why the British packet carried no such warning, he rolled his eyes and said, 'Check the leaflet that comes with every medicine. Even with aspirin, they warn of every side effect known to man in order to cover their arses legally... At least the FDA are *trying* to protect their citizens.' Tendon rupture was the least of my worries, as I soon found out. The class of drug to which my pill belonged was associated with irreversible peripheral neuropathy, fatal liver and kidney damage, fatal hypo- and hyperglycaemia, toxic psychosis, spontaneous rupture, not only of tendons, but also muscles, ligaments and cartilage. If that wasn't enough, testimonies and forums revealed a raft of related symptoms, many of which I found I was suffering from, as I stared blankly at my laptop screen: head pressure, muscle tremors, chronic muscle and joint pain, blurry vision, eye floaters, snow-vision, rapid weight loss... The list appeared endless. Some reported tinnitus, which I was happy to have avoided, as I love music beyond almost anything; especially, just recently, Mendelssohn. Practically all sufferers claimed to feel they'd aged fifty years in one night. A week after my reaction, I could vouch for that, too. Climbing the stairs of the Birkbeck main building, I felt I possessed the knees of a sixty-five-year-old. If I had to identify my main symptoms, the principle was a deep numbing ache in both legs, combined, paradoxically, with a constant feeling of laceration of the skin from the knees downwards, as if I had just walked through a brace of stinging nettles – a prickly deep-freeze. I later found out that this was what a peripheral neuropathy felt like, the peripheries being, poetically, your hands and feet. Added to this were fasciculations in the most unpredictable of places – muscle-twitching everywhere from the belly to the eyelids to unreachable places in the back. It was like having an army of rodents under the skin. Finally, sharp shooting pains in the tendons of the wrists and ankles. In the early days, peeling a banana felt as if I were putting critical strain on my hand.

Of course, I hoped and prayed all these symptoms would go away. But they didn't. I have what's known as irreversible nerve damage, coupled with a high risk of tendinosis. Larry helpfully explained that the tendons weren't like muscles, which repaired over time, but more like ropes, which frayed, eventually snapping like a line of old rigging. Thanks, cousin! This particular visual image makes doing anything more strenuous than walking perpetually worrying. In the past five years I've seen neurologists, rheumatologists, acupuncturists, even homeopathic quacks who cost me a fortune, all to no avail. I've lost over two stone in weight, and can't do any exercise harder than the walk from the Sorbonne to Le Pantalon. Admittedly, there are worse scrapes to be in health-wise, and a number of my contemporaries back in England are battling cancer, but living with chronic pain presents a unique set of challenges, many of them psychological, I have since discovered. There are good days and bad days. But what can't be cured must be endured, as the old saying goes. In the absence of any aid, one question still persists – how could a legally prescribed drug, available all over the world, be allowed to continue on the open market when it has damaged so many? It was for this that I needed close conference with Larry. How had I, a reasonably well-informed academic in a modern, technologically connected society managed to trade a mild short-term medical problem for a serious long-term one? (The Americans have even invented a verb for it. I'd been 'floxed'.) Ah well, there lies the rub, as my cousin frequently told me. He was an education, and is educating me still.

When Larry finally did turn up at the bar, almost a full hour late, it didn't take him long to get into his stride.

'Distorted evidence,' he announced brutally. 'All science is built on the bedrock of evidence – once you distort it for financial gain, you get rubbish science that's worthless to everyone, especially to poor old fellers like you, Nick…'

I smiled. Larry never wasted an opportunity to point out our age gap. We were at a cramped table next to the smeary, green-framed window; jostled by early evening drinkers, straining to make ourselves heard. Before me stood my third *demi* – in front of Larry, a carafe of *vin rouge frais*, his favourite.

'Granted,' I found myself shouting over the din, 'you've been through this many times before, but I still can't see how, with all the regulations in place, drugs like fluoroquinolones are still on the market.'

Looking into Larry's close-set but terrifically avid eyes, I realised that, deep down, I still secretly wanted my cousin to cure me. It must be a very old impulse, that faith in the physician, the veneration of Hippocrates.

'*Fuck* regulation!' roared Larry. Both his arms were in the air now, and I feared he would knock a drink out of someone's hand. 'The pharmaceutical industry effectively regulates itself, or knows how to get around government interference. These are trans-national companies! The big beasts of the jungle. The apex predators. Listen, it starts with the drugs trials. When a trial produces a result a corporation doesn't like, under the current ruling they're legally allowed to withhold the findings from doctors and patients alike. It's crazy.'

'Then the law needs to change.'

Larry rolled his eyes. Tanned, slouched in his ochre polo shirt, with two days' stubble on his square chin, my cousin sometimes resembled a ticket tout. Now he became like a parent attempting to explain a painful fact of life to a small child. Always with a charismatic wincing smile, however. That was the thing about Larry – he had a winning charm, attractive to women, undoubtedly. I had always been naïve about money, but Larry – innocent as he was in other respects – was nothing if not a realist when it came to the wider world.

'Drug companies *are* the law! They are perfectly entitled to run ten trials but only publish the one positive result. Selective publication has distorted science irreparably, and nobody's doing a damn thing about it. They've stuffed formerly esteemed journals with biased junk-data you wouldn't believe. Any evidence that a new pill might be dangerous, or even deadly, can be hidden with ease. Statins, antidepressants, painkillers – you name it. Stuff people take every day. And this trial data is being withheld from practising physicians, and, by extension, their patients, all over the world. Most doctors haven't a clue as to what they're prescribing.'

I'd heard this damning analysis before, and it never ceased to be seductive. It made me pity Dr Decker immensely. It wasn't his fault, after all, I comforted myself, that he'd messed up my health permanently. When I went back and informed him what his antibiotic had done, his face had turned white.

'So that's why my consultant could tell me he'd been prescribing fluoroquinolones for twenty years and never had a problem.'

'Exactly,' nodded Larry, finishing off the word with a drum roll on the sticky table. 'He might not have personally encountered a patient with side effects, but that doesn't mean it's not a potentially dangerous substance. Say the chances of a serious adverse reaction are point-one of a per cent. In the States, these new hardball antibiotics have probably been prescribed to over three million patients. That's still three thousand people with irreversible neuropathies, or inoperable tendon ruptures that have put them in wheelchairs for the rest of their lives. They even give flox antibiotics to kids who are allergic to penicillin, for God's sake!'

At this I thought of Ed, and shivered visibly.

'What about systematic reviews?'

'They've been monkeyed with too,' and here he leaned forward for emphasis. 'What you have to realise is that the drugs companies are not in the business of helping mankind to get well. Oh, no. They want to sell you something new when the old potion was perfectly good in the first place. Every year they fork out billions to change the treatment decisions of doctors – in fact, they annually blow twice as much on marketing as they do on researching new drugs.'

I took a pull on my beer, noticing, with alarm, how thin my wrists looked compared to Larry's. His were thick and hirsute, mine like emaciated sticks. The weight loss had drawn the skin on my cheeks, too, and almost given me wattle under the chin. No one in the heaving Pantalon would've have guessed we were cousins.

'Why do doctors put up with it?'

'Because, because...' – and now he weighed his words – 'because thus far, ignorance is bliss. What you have to realise is, doctors learn very little after med school. Over the course of a forty-year career, they hear about what works and what doesn't through a mishmash of journals, word of mouth from colleagues, or increasingly, sales reps. And therein lies the rub.

Sometimes these very colleagues are in the pay of the drugs companies. As are certain sectors of the journals. In over forty years, medicine has changed unrecognisably, but by and large, your average doctor – from GP to neurosurgeon – is largely in the dark.'

Larry sat back, shaking his head mournfully. I studied him with care. Though we were both sombre-featured, I had my father's Welsh poetic eyes; watery and abstract, whereas Larry's pupils, the same olive stones as mine, were darting swallows. It's been said I have a melancholy face. That I can't help, but I sometimes wished it contained some of Larry's zest, gusto, relish. I was taller, too, than my cousin, and favoured the academic's uniform of linen jacket and collared shirt, while he had always been a casual, even a slovenly dresser. Rarely in a tie, he preferred sweatshirts and hiking boots. As he talked, he often worked the strong ridge of lines on his brow with his fingers. He was doing this now, but without speaking, as the bar raged behind us. A powerful, heavy-set man, pushing forty, with a proud pucker in his chin, I could see why Ariel liked him. He was *un homme sérieux*, as well as possessing a certain *gaieté de coeur*. A magical combination. What's more, Larry was all about big truths, intellectual confrontation, wide-canvas ideas. His soul was big too – some people just have that capacity for expansion, scale; love for their fellow human. I often felt diminished beside him, moaning about my divorce, or my health saga, or talking about the ant-like lives of certain eighteenth-century *sans-culottes*.

To change the subject, and brighten his mood (as I knew it would), I asked: 'How's the *idée fixe*?'

'The genealogy?' flashed back Larry. 'Just great, man!'

I loved how my cousin, a respected research pharmacologist – a doctor once invited to dine with the G8 science ministers – could get away with 'man'. I put it down to long exposure to Dylan's insinuating rumble.

'Tell me more.'

'I just need to definitively prove matrilineal descent, and we're home and dry. I'm Jewish... And, *évidemment*, so are you.'

It was my turn to roll my eyes, or at least raise them heavenward, as I found the former action painful. I had always felt it was okay for Larry to indulge his Semitic obsession himself, but when he extended any implications to me, it rankled.

'Is this really the best use of your time?'

'To tell you the truth,' he continued, slightly sheepishly, 'I've come up against a bit of a brick wall. Very dispiriting, actually.'

To make matters worse, when it came to Larry's crisis (and I realised then, after a few weeks in Paris, that proving his ethnicity *had* become a crisis in his life), I was aware my face resembled a study in scepticism. I tried to soften its features as he spoke.

'What are the Viennese records showing? You might have to go there.'

'Fairly disappointing,' said Larry, shaking his head, and pouring the last of the carafe into his squat glass. 'They only go back to 1857...'

'So we had a European grandmother on our mothers'

side, Larry. It doesn't prove a thing. All you know is she was originally Austrian and her surname was Berg. She spent most of her life in Ruislip, and ended up working in the high-street chemist's. She's as English as – as *Gentile* as – a bacon sandwich.'

'Well…' countered Larry, surprised at my outburst. 'I never knew her. She died the year before I was born.'

'And I only knew her up to age six or whatever. It was your folks who lived just round the corner from Grandpa. I was stuck in the mystical west.'

'She was just Grandma Lotte to us. A family memory.'

'Hence more of a mystery.'

Larry craned forward and tapped his right temple: 'Persistent intimations… That's all I'm going on.'

I realised my legs were stinging and biting me as I sat there, and this always intensified my temper. I wondered how migraine sufferers got through life. They must feel like snapping off passing heads.

It was true our grandmother came over to England with our grandfather, Edward, in the 1930s. Edward, a Scotsman who lived until the Berlin Wall tumbled, had been an immaculately dressed old timer with a sandy toothbrush moustache. I remember being fond, if not a little scared, of him on our visits to Eastcote from Somerset. It was one of the ironies of Larry's current adversarial stance that our grandfather was once a rep for a pharmaceutical company – in a gentler age, admittedly. It was Edward who bought his grandson his first chemistry set, securing his course for life, in retrospect. From Galashiels in the Borders, our grandfather had run away as an adolescent to work in an Edinburgh chemist's, using his steady-spoken charm to get a job for one of the drugs companies whose sales teams were always visiting the shop. Soon they were sending him all over Europe, which is where he met and married Lotte. They returned and ended up in London, off Russell Square, dodging Hitler's bombs. He worked as a fire warden during the war, and I loved to hear his tales of putting out huge blazes with only sand and buckets of water. My mother Natalie was born at the height of the city's immolation. Only when Larry's mother came along did they move to west London, to the bland sprawling suburb of Eastcote. Their years there were quiet and largely blissful. Involved, in his fifties, with developing patents for various drugs, including asthma cures, Grandpa lost everything on a bad investment and ended up running the local chemist's, Macmillan's, on the high street. Back where he started – and the pain of this sometimes shone in his eyes when I questioned him about the past; his tall frame composed in his favourite tubular-steel armchair. Grandma Lotte, as I remember, was small, beautifully preserved, with great vitality and a habit of nodding rhythmically in agreement (though this could've been down to hearing loss). She was forward and funny in comparison to the stately, sedate Edward. But Jewish? At the time, I decided she didn't *look* typically Jewish. Then I felt immediately ashamed of assuming all Jews looked a certain way. I really had no idea, and neither, I suspected, did Larry.

Our mothers confirmed grandma was from Vienna – which sounded very exotic – but the subject of her wider family was never really raised. Admittedly, Larry's research was being hampered by the fact that she wasn't from a very prominent Viennese family: in fact, it transpired they had been dirt poor, as the few stories handed down to us corroborate. Also obstructing Larry was the fact that Berg was a fairly common – and very Aryan – name. I only knew of the composer, not just through his sublime piano sonata, but by his notorious death. After falling victim to an insect sting on his back, Berg had his wife perform an ill-advised operation using a rusty pair of scissors, causing him to die later of blood poisoning, aged only fifty.

Larry was looking around the bar now, and I knew this meant he'd had enough of the conversation. It was even noisier than when we'd entered. Our window was obscured by the shadows of men leaning against it, students and manual workers who had gone out into the narrow descending street in order to smoke. He drained the last of his *vin rouge*. I realised suddenly that his quest irked me because I didn't want to be downwind from his disappointment when it was proved conclusively, once and for all, that he was wrong. That he wasn't Jewish and never had been. Would I be disappointed? Perhaps. If my cousin was correct, if Lotte *did* turn out to have been an Austrian Jew, I would be Jewish also. But I hadn't examined what this would mean on the interior – I hadn't thought about it hard enough, or put it under the microscope. God knows, I had other things to occupy my mind. Of course, I knew what Larry would say to this, and he was about to say it now...

'You're in denial.'

'That's one of those shallow psychobabble phrases,

coopted from hazy Freudian notions that most of its users know nothing about, and we both know it.'

'Doesn't stop it being an active concept, though.'

Larry's eyes had ceased their habitual movement, and his hands were at rest on the tiny circular table. I gathered I had wounded him with my resistance, and I really hadn't wanted to. He was in earnest, deadly earnest, about all of this, and maybe there was something in it after all – though I doubted it. My old instinct for realism, perhaps, in the private as well as the public sphere. Only Tolstoyan characters had the privilege of self-delusion. In the twenty-first century there was no excuse. We knew which forces were acting on us, and it was rarely denial. Plus, we had the internet. A quick google usually cleared up any factual doubts in a jiffy. But as I said, my cousin was in thrall to the notion. He had read ten, fifteen heavy histories of the Jewish race, from standard works, to Shlomo Sand's recent, controversial *The Invention of the Jewish People*. He'd studied Judaism diligently; its origins and rituals and stringencies; its calendar and culinary prohibitions. His veneration of Bellow had sent him to Singer, Zweig, Kafka, Proust and Primo Levi – and, latterly, Roth (both of them), David Grossman, Hannah Arendt and Susan Sontag. He'd even talked seriously with Ariel about conversion, whether his quest threw up a positive result or not – and they'd only been going out for less than a year. Ludicrous for an atheist! And all this from an intuition, a *hunch*.

Feeling hungry, and in considerable pain, I changed the subject for a second time: 'How's Mademoiselle Levine?'

A transformation came over Larry whenever Ariel was

mentioned: he appeared to *melt* – and his features performed this act now, his brow clearing of wrinkles. He was in love. It was obvious, and I was happy for my cousin. And Ariel, too, when I had observed them together, seemed to be in love with him.

Larry dragged his chair back over the tiles, making to stand up.

'Let's go to Le Bambou and I'll tell you all about her latest developments. For a girl of twenty, she leads a complicated life. *J'ai très, très faim…*'

Three hours later, back at my apartment, waiting for the lights to achieve their full strength, my legs on fire, I opened the mini-fridge and uncapped a Kronenbourg with a satisfying clunk and hiss. Through my window, Paris was under a seemingly perpetual dusk – *entre chien et loup* – the sky in the west still a strange pistachio, a rosy blush over the horizon.

We had walked to the Le Buisson Ardent on the rue Jussieu, opposite the university building. Le Bambou (a Vietnamese place in the *treizième* Larry frequented with Ariel) had been packed out. We had talked much about his situation, staying off the other topics, and for that I was grateful. I hadn't been able to hear myself think in the bar, and there had been much to assimilate – I'd come to Paris and left my son behind for such conversations, and felt slightly overwhelmed. Over the snowy linen tablecloth Larry had revealed a great deal about his heart – and Ariel's wealthy cosmopolitan parents, with whom he lived. We'd had the oysters and switched to white wine – a terrific Sancerre. Larry's big appetite had made him plump for the *daube de boeuf*, while I opted for the pan-fried squid. I was once a fairly strict pescatarian – I could never live without fish or molluscs – and still try to eat as little meat as possible. Cassie, suspecting all Englishmen to be latent homosexuals, took this lifestyle choice (adopted at fifteen, I should add) as damning, definitive proof of my orientation. And this from an expert in gender hybridity in modern American fiction!

It had been a wonderful evening, but I wanted to reflect now on everything we had said.

Walking over to the shutters, I yanked the handle, releasing the vertical bars, allowing the doors to swing open – a mechanical device still operational from the Second Empire. Noise and street smells assailed me boldly. The fifth-floor elevation, the alcohol, made me immediately dizzy, and I had to hold on to the cool wrought-iron balcony for balance. Steadying myself, beer in my other hand, I breathed deep of the spring night. *La Ville Lumière* glittered for miles in every direction under a delectable turquoise dome of sky. Very slowly, high in the atmosphere, winking flashes from aircraft were progressing without noise. To the south, the Montparnasse tower stood in mordant isolation; sinister and unloved, unlike Eiffel's scintillating gold needle to the west. I had come to think of them as the two poles of existence – as Eros and Thanatos – one bright, lit up at night, full of erotic promise; the other dark and threatening. The poor relation. In fact, the southern tower always put me in mind of the bland Centre Point on Tottenham Court Road, equally unloved by its city's denizens.

But what to do about Larry's crisis, his cause? Even more pressingly, what could I say to him about Ariel? Marriage had been mentioned, a startling idea, given the chasm of age, class and culture between them. Watching the traffic stream up the boulevard Saint-Michel, I felt a pang of distress for my cousin, for the future of his capacious soul. His love life had always been a disaster area: he'd never been able to sustain a relationship for over eighteen months, though he claimed his upper limit was two years. Big difference! Being a divorcee, I of course couldn't pretend to be any kind of authority, but I felt the ten years I spent with Cass ought to count for something. How had our parents managed it? We often discussed this, and indeed had talked about the steady, pigeon-mated old age of our folks in Le Buisson Ardent. Professionally, our lives had yielded higher things, but personally they were train wrecks – 'At least until now,' Larry had said brightly. It goes without saying that I loved my cousin, felt protective towards him, but there was still something wild and untamed there that led him into dangerous emotional, if not physical, territory. On his many adventurous excursions – Honduras, the Amazon, the Himalayas – some of the tales he had returned with were excoriating. He had almost lost the fingers of his left hand to frostbite on the last one. And now he was risking all for a girl who was still a student. I've often felt the principled, or activist personality was covering up for some deficit in their spiritual life. They needed to be outward-facing, *engagé*, firing on all cylinders all the time, because to look inward was to survey a barren room – a landfill of messy, unattended emotion. Larry, the great champion of other people's causes, conformed to this model in most respects, and for this I worried for him.

And what of Ariel herself? A student of archaeology and art history at the Sorbonne (though I had never encountered her on the famous steps), just turned twenty the previous November, she was confident, pert, even a little arrogant – though it was often hard to tell with some French girls. BCBG is how the Parisians would describe the tribe to which she belonged. *Bon chic, bon genre*: those sleek, connected young creatures who moved effortlessly from lush Champs-Elysées restaurants to the new, ultra-hip clubs of the *treizième*. They were Paris's new elite – an evolution from the old Bobos, or bourgeois bohemians, they wore a stamp of superiority and deep money, along with their Gérard Darel handbags (boys and girls alike).

Using her mother's connections, Ariel was doing some modelling, and Larry had in fact met her during a photo shoot in the Jardin du Luxembourg. For a while, last autumn, the Institut had put him up in a terrible place on the rue André Gide, behind Montparnasse station, so he would walk around the park most days to escape. And there she had been, under the halogen bulbs, emerging from the morning mist, with that awkward conceited beauty unique to late teenagers – a sort of potentiality in every limb and gesture. A big body with sumptuous curves, on the tall side, with a thumping vitality, Ariel was, to use my cousin's phrase, 'unreal'. Larry had been smitten. With her stunning Russian-Turkish eyes – also a gift from her mother – she was a heartbreaker. During a lighting change, Larry had wasted no time asking her out in terrible

French, and she, to his surprise, had agreed. She had been fascinated, so my cousin told me, by an older man who, at last, wasn't a friend of Papa's. Apparently, all those hounds had been after her since she was fifteen. Papa was François Levine, once a high-powered adviser to Sarko, now a minister for les Républicains. A Gaullist, though against *la droite forte*, he had never really wanted a ministerial position. I had seen him a couple of times on TV. Tall, elegant, with a superior Gallic nose and thin, infrangible, sculptured cheekbones, I could see why he had gained the nickname *l'Aigle* – the Eagle. There was something avian about him in profile. Dark-suited, severe, intense and even humourless, there was a singular determination in the fine lines of his brow. His flying cheekbones and gaunt aspect reminded me of the English painter John Piper. He was old French Jewry, with a chateau in the Loire and a sumptuous apartment on Paris's most expensive square. Ariel's mother, Rivka, by contrast, was her own creation. Larry told me she was from a poor family of indeterminate number in the Ukraine, and had basically blagged her way to Paris using her networking skills to move into the upper echelons. A forceful, professional persona, she was a senior creative stylist at French *Vogue*, and presented herself with the effortless composure of *soignée* Parisian women. I had also only ever seen her on TV, by François' side. Dark, with a low centre of gravity, it looked as if she battled with her weight, and perhaps the bottle, judging by her eyes. 'A typical helicopter Jewish mother,' Larry told me with a great grin, not meaning it to be in any way a slur. Ariel, like the both of us, was an only child, and it occurred to me, still on the balcony, the beer becoming warm in my hand, that this was why we had all got on so famously the few times we had ventured out together.

According to Larry, François was worried that Ariel would do a Carla Bruni and drop out of the Sorbonne before she was twenty-one to become a supermodel. But he gave me a cast-iron reason why this wouldn't happen. 'She's too sexy,' he had smiled over the Arctic tablecloth. 'Have you noticed how most supermodels are totally sexless? They're cold. They haven't got that warmth, that sex energy. It's all inward-looking for them when they strut about on the catwalk – just a pure act of narcissism.' It was true, I had conceded, that Ariel directed her attention outwards at the defenceless males of Paris, just as Bardot or Deneuve had. She was a head-turner. But that was another reason why I feared for Larry. As much as they loved each other in the present moment, I felt my cousin was throwing his lot in with the wrong person. At thirty-seven, Larry was just beginning to feel the pull of parenthood – I could see it in his eyes, the biological imperative to further his desperate genes. I could tell because I too had felt it strongly before Ed was born – a kind of male equivalent of broodiness. A helpless vulnerability. I could also tell, however, that he had picked Ariel as the agent for this project. This was something François and Rivka might be interested in – news to them, I felt, from what Larry had told me. As I understood it, they saw him as the customary *homme vieux* experiment every girl of twenty indulges in. Ariel's own attitude was harder to gauge on the few occasions I'd encountered her. On her recent nights out with Larry – often accompanied by Rube and Professor Singh – I got the impression she just liked the company of older people, especially men. Anyway, in Paris there were, thankfully, different rules. Things were so much looser than in London. Here you spent the evening either in good company or bad: that was the only classification, and age or class or colour didn't come into it. There were no set guidelines of what comprised cool or uncool. The BCBG of Paris could dine with their banker parents one night, then gyrate to electro with the largely Algerian crowd from the *banlieues* of the *dix-huitième* the next. It was characteristic of that scene to drift among disparate, cosmopolitan clans, picking up and discarding at will. Naturally, it was this discarding that I worried about when it came to Larry, hopeful, as he secretly was, of marriage and children.

I also questioned my cousin about the *Charlie Hebdo* attack, a subject he was understandably reluctant to discuss too frequently with Ariel. Larry had been an avid reader of the magazine, and on the day of the shootings had been at the Institut as usual; horrified along with everyone else while Paris went into lockdown. Two days later, events came even closer to home with the siege at the Hyper Cacher supermarket in porte de Vincennes. That evening, he had had dinner with the whole Levine family – an unusual occurrence – and the talk had been of the dilemma facing France's Jews. Many of François' friends were already discussing the possibility of 'making *aliyah*', of giving up on the Republic and seeking a new, safer home in Israel. At this idea, Ariel's father was loftily scornful: it would signal defeat, he had almost shouted, with uncharacteristic passion; the end of *laïcité*, of triumphant French secularism, and of the long contribution to French society by Jewish families such as his own. By 6 p.m., armed guards had already been posted outside Jewish schools and synagogues, prompting Rivka to say, 'I did not know we had so many. Now the terrorists will know their location by playing spot-the-cop.' Larry told me François was to become even more indignant when Netanyahu visited at the weekend, urging France's Jewish population to mass exodus. But at the table, all my cousin could do was show solid support and sympathy in such a horrific and constantly evolving situation. Only Ariel's comment as she finished her dessert of pomegranate and out-of-season berries drew silence from the table: '*Mais* Papa, after the war you thought we could all be French Jews for hundreds of years. Perhaps it was only for seventy years...'

Stepping back inside – reluctantly, as the balmy, teeming night was of a singular beauty – I went to rest my legs in my favourite armchair. Its contoured upholstery was a perfect fit for my frame, and I had often wondered how I might smuggle it back to London when the time came. I was paying for all the walking I had done with Larry, I knew, and the pain in my ankles was almost unendurable. Over the years, I had discovered the only things that brought relief were sleep, alcohol or a hot bath. The apartment only having a shower, the latter wasn't on the menu, and I contemplated opening another stubby, but that would have meant getting up. As I said, there are good days and bad days with my condition, and for that mercy I should be grateful. On good days, the neuropathy felt merely like someone digging their fingernails into my calves – on a bad, like two Rottweilers with their jaws clamped to my ankles. On a mild-pain night, it was akin to sitting up to your knees in freezing-cold water, on a bad – like this one – it resembled the time you fell off your bike as a kid and skinned your knees to shreds. And nobody could tell any difference from your outward appearance. It was human nature to assume that if there are no visible signs of malady then you're okay. I had compared notes with a couple of Birkbeck professors, sufferers from different strengths of lethargy sickness – ME, in other words – and they said the same. After my adverse reaction, I was struck by how quickly people stopped asking how I was. It was natural, sure, to tire of such enquiries – they had their lives to lead – but all the same, sometimes it hurt as much as the lacerated legs.

Draining the last of the beer, I decided it was the psychological reality of chronic pain that brought the hardest dilemmas. How to live your life when there is torment without end? A hair shirt we never asked for. Torment was overstressing it, perhaps – on many days I was merely in what medics call 'discomfort', but the question remained as to how to get through a life where only death will provide relief. Proust, very witty, as people rarely give him credit for, said death cured us of the desire for immortality. It cures us of all physical malady too. Proust also said of love that it was a striking example of how little reality means to us. Thinking of Larry, I found this to be true as well. We despise reality and can't wait to escape it through falling in love. But the problem of how to endure my own reality remained. The phrase 'old bones' had been unsettling me recently, because foremost in my mind was the thought that I wasn't going to make them if I had old bones at forty-four. Some days, as I said, I felt incapacitated, emasculated even. The world dictates that much of a man's being is tied up in his physical strength, his ability to 'do' – just as a woman's is in her beauty. Besides, I consoled myself, many had endured worse. Pascal lived until thirty-nine, plagued by constant headaches: there was rarely a day he wasn't in some kind of agony. I often told myself that my condition was a lesson – a kind of test. But set by whom? Who are we sticking it out for? Sure, we must endure our going hence, et cetera, but I knew a fundamental change had occurred on the interior that fateful day in my flat, the halloumi cheese going cold as I dialled for a cab to take me to UCH. I divided my life into a 'before' time and an 'after'. I realised now that I was looking forward to the oblivion of death, if that's what awaits us. At least somatic oblivion – the soul could do all the Peter-Panning it liked, as long as it didn't have to suffer chronic circadian pain. For the cessation of this, I would be eternally grateful. In fact, the permanent, irreversible condition resonates with notions of hell or perpetual punishment. You will be in pain *for ever* – for as long as consciousness lasts. If you are an atheist (and I wasn't: I was a hesitant agnostic, open to certain ideas of spiritual correspondence), this is a very grave prognosis indeed. There will be no end, no release in any kind of afterlife. You literally live forever in a hell on earth until you are stopped. Or stop yourself, the latter not being an option, not while Ed was alive, anyhow.

Indeed, the insoluble question of Ed was something that cycled, like the pain, at this time of night. The divorce settlement had given me standard access arrangements with my son – half the holidays and every other weekend. Yet while

I'd come to Paris on Larry's trail, Cass had told me to stay away. She seemed to block every attempt to make a simple plan, either for me to see Ed in England, or for him to visit me. I couldn't help but feel the boy saw this as an abandonment. He was perhaps too young to see that his mother didn't want me around, regardless of my emotions. But an absent father is an absent father, and leaves permanent scars. The whole mess broke my heart daily.

Settling on a shower rather than sleep or more booze, I stood up and went to the small but newly fitted, rather chic bathroom and turned on the jet. As the hissing of water filled the air, another malaise, one I had all but forgotten over the course of the evening, presented itself. It went by the name of Barry Gallagher – my accountant, or as he became, in the end, my financial adviser, currently being sued for eloping with my funds. All my savings, in fact, put aside during a lifetime of diligent work and successful publication. A man the French would call *un connard*.

It's almost a cliché to be ripped off by your accountant, but it happened. I had been put on to Barry by a writer friend of mine, a tolerably successful novelist, who said he knew a man who specialised in 'creatives'. As I was in the process of separating from Cass, and setting up my own website to promote my books, I badly needed someone to organise my finances. The fact that Barry suggested our first meeting to be held in a pub – the Jeremy Bentham on University Street, curiously named after a teetotal Utilitarian – should've rung alarm bells. A squashed, red-haired Irishman in a toothpaste-stained suit, he had, to use his phrase, 'The gift of the gab, squared.' As we downed Guinness, I remember thinking his face resembled an over-packed ravioli. A no-nonsense, can-do persona, with a worldly seen-it-all air, he told me that he had once managed bands before working for the Inland Revenue, but that he 'hated music'. Another warning sign. Yet he was plausible and pushy, and got straight on the phone to Newcastle to sort out a pressing on-account tax bill ('I used to work for these eejets, so I know how to get around them'). And so I took him on. Over the four years he dealt with my books, he effectively became my business manager, with access to all my passwords, eventually bundling all my investments into one portfolio when he branched out into 'asset management'. Bad move. He had been dealing from a deck of lies. And now he had absconded – for a while nobody knew where he was. Under that Irish charm there had always been a strange, undermining insolence. Violence, even. I continuously had the impression he was laughing at me, somewhere. With his equivocal, dead, Celtic eyes, hard as flints in a crumbling church wall, and his soft, fat hands, I should have trusted my instincts and said goodbye to Barry after the first pint of stout. I had been taken for a ride, like old Louis XIII by the speculator Le Barbier. But I had been under much stress, as I liked to explain away the episode to myself, and besides, I felt bizarrely sorry for him. I have a weakness for the needy, and it's something I really should've weaned myself off after all these years, but I seem to attract them. As someone who came from a stable home, I'm often a magnet for all the broken, damaged, unstable cases out there – both men and women who feel the urgent need to confess, or get revenge, or both. At first, I didn't mind any of this, but at my advanced age, the last thing I needed was individuals who required special pleading. Coming from stability confers a certain self-confidence, while the opposite scenario holds: past trauma always seems to equal present insecurity, present madness – it's an infallible equation... I should've had my eyes open when it came to Barry. He had been poor, and he had struggled back home in Galway ('We lived in a fecking barn, Nicholas, I'm telling ye!'), so I gave him access all areas. For once I should have examined the reality of the situation with more care.

Under the stinging needles of the shower I tried to wash Barry out of my hair – cleanse his interloping presence from my mind. Some people are plain poisonous, malign; contagious – you catch them like a cold and can't shake them off. Newly alert from the zinging pine of the shower gel, its emerald ooze between my fingers, I could still see my accountant's eyes, vestigially present, through the mist. At certain times when we had discussed my finances, one of these eyes would narrow – the right one, I think – and I became aware he was viewing me with utter inner contempt, the source of which I had no idea. Maybe he was cracked. Perhaps he despised my background, what he would perceive to have been an easy ride. But I doubt it. It was more like common or garden malice, evidence of a grubby soul. A cowed power freak, Barry had been full of boiling, baseless resentments that he struggled to hide – a conceited, dissipated, avaricious, bloated, corrupted, laughable man...

Nevertheless, the fact remained that I had very little money in real terms. I was subletting my mews flat to a Ph.D. student who I felt was going through a crack-up (the unstable, as I said, gravitate towards me). Totally against the London Uni rules, but I couldn't let it sit empty while working in Paris. I needed the Sorbonne's grant more than ever, and I needed to finish the book, though I didn't let on to Cass. I didn't want to give her the pleasure of gloating. Despite coming from old wealth in the States, she still asked for the full maintenance whack every month. Along with lawyer fees to battle Barry, and with all my assets – how shall we say? – liquid or non-existent, she was cleaning me out every month. Crippling, and she wouldn't let me off the hook. Having scarce funds at twenty-four is one thing, but at forty-four, all you can think is: *Not this shit again*. Tiresome in the extreme. You just don't have the energy any more to dig yourself out of the hole. And my weekly call to Ed was scheduled for tomorrow – I knew I would have to go over it all again with my ex-wife. I was in shackles. It was painful for my son, and I'd been responsible for enough of that already. Still, everybody's enslaved to something: a spouse, a job, a maintenance commitment, a dream. Nobody can call themselves categorically free – at least not until they're dead.

Stepping out of the shower, the luxurious white towel around my salved prickly shoulders, I effaced thoughts of both Cass and Barry Gallagher from my mind. Making preparations for bed, my thoughts returned to Larry. I decided I should give him a break and stop torpedoing his great quest. Perhaps, I thought, as I turned back the crisp linen sheets, I should help him a little more in his crisis. That's what cousins were for, surely? I had given him a tough time in Le Pantalon, and for that I felt less than pleased with myself. Larry was trying to establish a self, a true self, a *final* identity – something we all see as imperative in our thirties, for some reason, as if to leave it any later were never to find it. However, what most of us discover is that the true self was there all along: it doesn't come with some additional component or revelation. Larry didn't like to hear this analysis, as he felt I was pulling the rank of age, which I was, in a way.

I cut the lights. Lying there in the dark, my hair still wet, but with the pleasant heat of the shower still in my bones, my skin began to itch. At once my stomach muscles were in spasm, twitching unstoppably. This always occurred at the end of a day, as if the machine, the great musculoskeletal system that I took for granted in the 'before' years, needed to have its revenge after much stressful exertion. It put on this display just in case I was starting to forget about my condition. The cycle of these secondary symptoms had been a particular cruelty in the beginning: you think they've disappeared, only for them to return with a vengeance a day or six weeks later. Only the neuropathy was a constant – a control in an experiment that nature was conducting on my body. That lacerating pain, stoically resident in both legs from the lower thigh down to the ankles, 24/7.

But what of Jewish consciousness? Was there such a thing? Is this what Larry hankered after? A sense of belonging – to a people, a history, a cause he felt he had always belonged to. And what if, evidently, as my cousin had told me with relish, I belonged to it too? Would it be momentous to discover this, or would I merely feel a mild sense of interest; that, in reality, on the interior, it made no empirical difference? I concluded that it just meant *more* to my cousin than it did to me, and in this I should be understanding. The fact of my own ambivalence irked me deeply, and I knew it was something I would have to deal with in time. What did it mean to find out, in the midst of life, that you were something you never suspected? There wasn't much that could make a difference in a life, not at this late stage. The answers were in the ether; or out there in the Parisian darkness that, I could see, through a crack in the bedroom doorframe, had finally fallen over the city.

'Nicholas Newman,' I said clearly into the entryphone panel, before a click and a whir allowed the ancient door to yawn asunder.

Two weeks after my tête-à-tête with Larry I found myself in the marble-cooled vestibule of the Levines' extraordinary apartment. The hands of a near-priceless Louis Quatorze clock told me it was 6 p.m. It had been a glorious spring day, one of those for which Paris is justly famous. With the stirring smell of white roses in the place Paul Painlevé, under skies of gas-jet blue, it had been a banquet for the senses, and I was almost grateful for the settled calm of the hallway; the glaciate atmosphere, distilled from centuries of undiluted wealth. Drinking down the tasteful opulence, I was startled by a ringing voice.

'*Bonsoir*, monsieur Noo-mahn!'

A hustling, smiling woman, broad of behind, was making her way down the winding planes of a staircase that, I imagined, joined the hall to the piano nobile. Rivka, without a doubt. As she approached with both hands outstretched strangely, palms upward in greeting, I registered how much more beautiful and femininely compelling she was in person than on television.

'*Bonsoir*, madame,' I answered, slightly formally, stepping forward. 'Very nice to meet you.'

Before me, smelling like a million euros of *parfumerie*, she raised both palms and placed them on my shoulders to deliver the full *trois baisers*. An oddly intimate greeting for someone I'd never met, but not unwelcome.

She smiled generously, hands still on me for a second. '*Enchantée. Alors*, you must join us upstairs for your cousin's favourite aperitif – *un pastis*. Come!' and she gestured for me to follow. '*Par ici.*'

In moments I was sitting next to Larry in an identical green leather armchair of majestic depth, a glass of the promised liqueur in my hand.

The occasion was Ariel's completion of her *présentation orale* – which contributed significantly to her degree – and a celebration in one of the Marais' myriad restaurants had long been planned. The fact that the daughter had picked Chez Omar – a couscous place that no longer took reservations – had put her parents off joining us. This was certainly Ariel's intention, and something for which Larry might have been grateful. He'd been living there since Christmas, after all. Rivka, talking unstoppably, had taken me along a slippery parquet hallway, the central channel of the apartment, whose main feature was a floor-to-ceiling mirror in which a single chandelier dazzled. I had been given a swift grand tour. It was a truly incredible place – the apartment seemed to occupy the whole of the *bel étage* on one side of the square, though I knew this couldn't be the case. It just gave the impression of a never-ending series of rooms – a Versailles of the *troisième*.

And now we were sitting in a south-facing living room, the ceiling-high balcony doors open to the spring evening, the long drapes in motion from the wind outside. Occasionally a linden blossom would waft across the immaculately polished *meubles*, as Larry tried to explain neurotransmitters to (he secretly hoped) his future mother-in-law.

'... Okay, neurons are excitable cells, you see, because their surface is covered in proteins—'

'*Ah bon.*'

'And these are called ion channels, but don't worry about that for the moment.'

'I cannot help but worry!' said Mme Levine, keeping up gamely.

'And so you see, these allow smaller, highly charged particles to enter and leave the cell...'

He was gesticulating now, smarter in appearance than usual in a loose cotton shirt, engaging Mme Levine with his excitable exegesis, but losing her too, I could tell. Larry had lost me on many occasions. It was the central nervous system and its mysteries he dealt in, he insisted, and this was his main excuse whenever I asked him to commission research into my particular affliction. He claimed he had nothing to do with the peripheries, like the mechanic who says he will fit you a new piston but won't touch your tyres. His specialism was dopamine and serotonin uptake, growth areas in the pharmaceutical world, to say the least.

'*D'accord*,' smiled Mme Levine, 'so at the Pasteur, you are testing these cells and the effect of new drugs on them?'

'Yes. But we don't use real live human beings.'

Rivka laughed gaily, then asked, 'So you use animals, *oui*?'

Larry's brow deepened. 'No, no, no. We're not vivisectionists, at least not in my department.'

'But you still test…'

This was evidently not a subject that came up frequently, and I could see my cousin didn't relish it now: his eyes kept drifting to the door, expectant of his lover. Despite the presence of a low brown sofa against the opposite wall, sleek as a limousine and scattered with cushions, Rivka had decided to perch on an elegant chair very near to Larry. A silver tray bearing a decanter of yellow-white pastis, with a pitcher of water to mix, stood on its own little table next to Mme Levine's sheer-stockinged knees.

'Yeah, but testing is the wrong word. It's more an investigation – into how nerve systems communicate. We don't have the budget to patent new drugs, and wouldn't want to anyway.'

'Ariel said you were involved with researching into Parkinson's disease. A friend of François' has just been diagnosed with it…' And here she shook her coiffured head, making me notice her gold seashell earrings. '*Terrible*.'

'Sure, we do a lot with dopamine reuptake.'

'Don't get him on to post-synaptic neurons,' I interrupted with a smile, 'We'll be here all night.'

I actually wanted to question Ariel's mother about the apartment's stunning ceiling before the daughter, busy readying herself in one of the three palatial bathrooms, made her grand entrance. Above us, a splendid chandelier hung from what would be the original beams. These were finely embossed with seventeenth-century decorative patterns, along with extraordinary classical scenes; faded Actaeons and Pygmalions, unquestionably once gilt. It was the sort of living room in which one rarely, if ever, found oneself in Paris, unless one were a visiting dignitary. I took a look around – it was a fragrant, aerated, echoing space; cavernously ceilinged, the parquet flooring polished to an efficient glow. Ed would have loved a sock-slide on that. The whole place was a symphony of browns, teaks, taupes, ochres, with only a worn, but surely priceless rug for colour, its patches of regal lapis lazuli beneath our feet. Between the two glorious windows, a writing table and a Salon chair made an exquisite composition, both undoubtedly once owned by headless luminaries from the *ancien régime*.

Yet, unlike the Serpente library, there was nothing over-the-top grandiose or triumphant about it – just a sense of scuffed, elegantly preserved dignity. The exterior, by contrast, couldn't help but stun. Through the billowing drapes I took in the sweeping vista of the Place des Vosges, its brick and stone facades with their classical arcade running beneath the *premier étage*; the magisterial gardens with an inner box of geometrically clipped lime trees, a wall of brutal topiary. Begun by le Vert galant in 1605, often called the most beautiful square in Europe, everyone had lived here from Richelieu to Mme de Sévigné to Gautier and Hugo; the latter's house being a place I remember visiting as a child, my father claiming fraudulent knowledge of his books. Yes, Larry had definitely lucked out this time – though he confided he didn't see much of Ariel's parents, both being out most nights at ministerial engagements or fashion junkets.

My cousin was still speaking, and I tried to focus on the coffee table in order to get back into the conversation. Its surface was a smoked-glass plane bearing four neat stacks of couture books – the heavy format too big to handle – at the end of which perched a glass vase containing a hank of blooming yellow tulips.

'… Synaptic pathways are important. Divisions and borders too. It's all about intra- and extra-cellular biochemical reactions.'

'You've lost me now,' cried Rivka, her palms leaving her knees. I could see she had the same slightly too-small face as Ariel's – a miniature that warned you not to be taken in by it. There was a cunning and intelligence one shouldn't underestimate. She hadn't landed on the Place des Vosges by accident, after all.

At that moment, a voice from the doorway made us all crane our necks.

'*Chéri!*'

Larry and I stood simultaneously as Ariel breezed in. She was taller than ever, it seemed, and wearing what appeared to be a turquoise micro-dress and a pair of strappy Sandro zipper-heels.

'*Bonsoir, messieurs,*' drawled the girl in her famous voice. I had forgotten her voice – a beautiful low instrument, like an oboe or bass clarinet that magically spoke French.

'*Bonsoir!*'

Exchanging brisk kisses with Larry first, then me, before delivering a cursory peck to her mother's cheek, Ariel crossed the room and slumped down full length on the sumptuous sofa, as if she planned to remain there all night. Virtually horizontal on the upholstery, Ariel's legs threatened to exceed its length, so unnaturally long were they. Even though I'd seen her a few times before in various sartorial incarnations, I had to admit she looked especially breathtaking. The klaxon of her curiously carnal beauty, deafening in the sedate room, was at once a noise we all chose to ignore, or a secret we all agreed to keep.

'What took you?'

This was Larry, smiling almost uxoriously in Ariel's direction, as the wind blew her hair around her undefended, Cytherean shoulders.

'Was I that long?' shrugged the girl. '*Désolée.*'

Ah, the Parisian shrug, but never so ravishingly delivered. I tried to recall what it felt like to be twenty myself, but gave up after a couple of seconds.

'Yes, what took you, *ma chérie?*' asked Mme Levine, turning, with sudden authority, on her daughter.

Another shrug. A disharmonious note sounded in the room. Their whole relationship, I felt, was present in the slight tilt of Ariel's chin in her mother's direction. *Helicopter* wasn't the word, I decided; all the commonplaces for defusing such situations suddenly deserting me.

'You have kept these English gentlemen waiting.'

'That's quite all right,' I managed to interject.

Rivka turned to us. 'Can you believe she bicycles in this gear?'

'I can believe it,' nodded Larry, lasciviously.

'*C'est mauvais goût.*'

This was anomalous, as Rivka must have dealt with models all the time who wore next to nothing. Maybe it was the old parental trope that certain behaviours were okay as long as your own children didn't indulge in them.

Ariel sighed at the old combat with her mother. '*Bof. Je m'en fous.*'

With the motor of her youth at full tilt, her tremendous legs honouring the fabric of the couch, Ariel knew she didn't have to apologise for the way she looked or dressed. In any case, the world sanctioned it, every minute of every day.

'It's not even summer yet…'

'*Un Vélib'*, *Maman*,' she cried, petulantly. 'How else do you suggest I get around this city? It is the only way!'

'But we bought you a car for your eighteenth birthday.'

Larry had told me about her yellow Citroën, housed in a vault-like underground garage somewhere. They had been out to Fontainebleau and Giverny in it when the weather had looked up a few weeks back.

Slightly uncomfortable myself, I was sure this mother-daughter act wasn't something put on for our benefit. It was a dynamic they had fallen into early and would probably always play out. They didn't even know they were doing it. Like a married couple who have long since given up caring about keeping their quarrels private, Rivka and her daughter would always conduct open public warfare unabashed.

'*D'accord*, but I thought we might have drilled in some sophistication… After all these years.'

'*Maman*, we are meeting Ana and Delphine, and I do not want to look like an old woman, *tu vois?*'

Ariel was staring angrily at her mother: an anger that intensified the beauty of her tiny features.

Clearing his throat experimentally, Larry offered, 'Well, you are in the company of two old men.'

Now the rancorous look was directed at him, but it disappeared after a couple of seconds.

Addressing us once more, Rivka shook her head. '*Qu'est-ce que vous entendez par BCBG?*' She waited for our reply, before adding, 'No, I do not really understand it either.' And then to her daughter: '*Mais, pour ta mère, c'est pas bien!*'

She had full-spectrum dominance now, and I didn't want a domestic scene to spoil the exquisite May evening. I had enough of those back home. I looked up again admiringly at the ceiling beams. For some reason I expected Ariel to be in as much awe of the place as me, but remembered quickly that she lived there. The grand tour had revealed they even had a music room, with a gleaming Steinway, and I decided to ask her if she played, but the imperious mother intercepted me.

'Lau-raunce tells me,' she began, pronouncing my cousin's name with rolling, tigerish vowels, 'that you have a son.'

'Yes,' I said, relieved at the change of subject. 'A little boy... Edward. He lives with his mother.'

'Ah,' she smiled, indifferently fascinated. '*Charmant...*'

As a conversational gambit, this was even worse than what had gone before. A silence filled the room for a full five seconds, the wind taking the curtains like a ship's sail.

No one knew quite what to say, until Ariel boomed: 'Ok-ay. *Allons-y!*'

And we were all gratefully on our feet; Larry and I accepting the *trois baisers* from Mme Levine once again; Ariel already out the door, fuming – a volcano of Parisian indignation.

It was only as I was leaving that I noticed the nine-branched menorah candelabrum on a teak dresser at the back of the room: discreet, but prominent if you were sharp-eyed, which I rarely was. It gleamed dully but anciently among the doilies and coarse tortoiseshell brushes, and I wondered if it was ever used. It was the only indication, in fact, that a Jewish family inhabited the sweeping parlours and endless reflective corridors.

Half an hour later, under the crimson awning of Chez Omar – Ariel mellowed by the long stroll in the enchanted evening – we were relieved to find Rube and Professor Singh already there, having secured an outside table. They were in fine spirits, and appeared to have become unlikely friends themselves over the past few weeks – the one-time street-kid *tagueur*, and the immunology expert. By the time we had all queued for steaming plates of couscous, topped with coiled, humorously scatological *merguez* sausages, the *maman* incident had all but been forgotten. Ana and Delphine, I gathered, were to join us later. I had opted for the vegetable broth, and was glad to rest my legs as I took a chair in what felt like the middle of the populous pavement.

'It's a cultural crisis like no other...' Larry was saying, worked up now the wind had died down and the paper tablecloth had ceased its attempt to join surrounding diners. The meal was over and we were all a little drunk. He was prosecuting an argument he always enjoyed when in the company of Rube and Nadir; while Ariel and I were content to sit back and listen. 'I mean, you don't see evidence of it in London, riots notwithstanding.'

'Why cultural?' enquired Nadir, guiltily pouring the last of the *vin rouge* from the second of two *pichets*. 'More political, surely?'

'Yeah,' joined in Rube, '*Ici*, we have our own riots. And terrorists.'

Saturnine, strong-boned, deep black, with his formidable forehead glassy from the heat, Rube was sitting safely across from Ariel, an arrangement Larry no doubt approved of. Though her ex was more like an older brother now, rather than a love rival, I could tell my cousin was still wary of any ties between them.

'Okay, granted. But when I came here – when was it, *chérie*?'

'*Octobre*,' Ariel murmured, lounging back with her eyes closed, her legs bestriding the paving flags, her face protected from the late rays by the shade of a plane tree. I smiled at how relaxed she appeared, all of Paris seemingly streaming past, as if our table were an island in the Seine. I remembered how this al fresco dining – almost in the road – had been alarming during my visits as a boy. Now I quite enjoyed the feeling of street theatre.

'Yeah, when I arrived last autumn, I was shocked at the prominence of the far right. It was a revelation, man.'

'*Bienvenu!*' grinned Nadir. He was smiling through a full, silver beard. This matched his greying mane. He too seemed singularly relaxed, though this might have been aided by the alcohol he had given up claiming not to touch. With his purplish lips, and careful, qualified, apologetic manner, the professor had the air of a man with a deep, culturally complicated sorrow himself. Also that of a man with a lot to say if you gave him time. His spectacles were small, with unfashionably light steel frames, and his inquisitive eyes would sometimes look skyward and remain there ponderously.

'I mean, you have this socialist government that becomes deeply unpopular in the space of a year, and is still clinging on. Then you have Hollande – admittedly dignified after *Charlie Hebdo* – using the shenanigans of his former partner as cover to raise income tax for the rich to seventy-five per cent.'

'And Italy in constant meltdown,' pitched in the professor, 'Don't forget about *Il Cavaliere*.'

'Yeah, an unstable Italy whose deficit will always outstrip its GDP. I mean, they've had fifty governments since the war…'

Larry was at full throttle now; at full rhetorical tilt, employing the whirling motion with his right hand.

'… And then you have Spain, where youth unemployment is something cracked, like—'

'*Soixante pour cent*,' nodded Rube, his head to one side in a listening aspect, showing his proud nose in profile.

'… Plus, a catastrophic Greece and Cyprus, and an overbearing Allemagne, whose policy of austerity is deeply at odds with Hollande's own reforms.'

'*Dégueulasse, c'est sûr*,' agreed Rube. 'Despite Syriza and Monsieur Tsipras, Greece is still – how you say? – fucked.'

'And most of all, a euro currency that is tearing the fabric apart rather than gluing it all together.'

'So why is it a cultural crisis?' asked Nadir.

'Because, because in times of jeopardy, a nation comes together – regardless of which stuffed shirts are in government, regardless of how diverse its capital city is. We saw it three years back with our Olympics extravaganza.'

'He's right,' mused Rube, resignedly. 'Here in Paris – there is no unity.'

A testy waiter appeared and began stacking our empty plates along one arm. I thought he might react to Rube's statement, but there was nary a flinch. The man gestured towards the empty carafes: '*Encore?*'

I nodded. '*Oui. Deux, s'il vous plaît.*'

'You see, Larry,' Nadir began slowly. He pronounced my cousin's name, La-ree. 'Where I come from, to talk about a nation coming together is absurd. We had our convulsion in forty-seven. Jinnah got his two-nation solution and look where we are now. Just think how much worse it would be if Tara Singh had got his way and founded a Sikh homeland. A Khalistan next door to a Pakistan. A plot of land is nothing to the power of a religious ideology.'

'Try telling the Palestinians that. It's when the two are combined that it's fatal.'

'Maybe,' conceded the professor. 'What did Amos Oz say? "As long as the disputed territories are only a struggle for real estate, everything's fine."'

'Yeah. It's when notions of a Holy Land are dragged in that it gets impossible.'

At certain moments, I felt Larry believed, on a genetic level, that his Jewish status had already been proved beyond any doubt. In his own mind, he was already circumcised. 'Let's stay off the Middle East,' I interjected. 'At least while we're on the street.'

I took a glance along the rue de Bretagne, which ran west until it reached a complicated junction, its nineteenth-century lamps dangling like earrings over the thriving traffic. Every nation on earth seemed to be represented, though maybe this was peculiar to the Marais: Chinese, Vietnamese, Senegalese, Moroccans, old Parisians wobbling past on peasant bicycles. Indeed, every sexuality. At least a couple of men had passed holding hands, one pair even openly kissing.

'Granted. But as Sikhs, we were created to defend all religions while still believing in the primacy of our own. We are unique in that respect.'

'Since when were you observant, Nadir?' chuckled Larry, looking around impatiently for the wine.

Professor Singh just smiled at this. He knew better than to start a row about religion with a proselytising atheist like Larry. A robust man, with a chest like a tank – *costaud* as the French say – Nadir had a low, yet trembling voice. It was very definite, the words chosen with supreme care, with a resigned cadence at the end of each sentence, especially when speaking in English. Larry had told me his story a few weeks back. A pre-eminent scholar in the southern Punjab, he had brought his family to Paris in the late nineties, only to end up in the Sikh enclave suburb of Bobigny. There he had been shocked by the poverty and racial abuse. He'd been happy for a few years, despite having to commute miles to the Institut every day. But then he had taken cultural integration too far. He had acquired a French mistress. His wife, Jaspreet, had thrown him out immediately – banished him from the home, and now he was living cheaply in the same Institut Pasteur lodgings on the rue André Gide that Larry had longed to leave. This was where the complicated sorrow originated – here was a professor living like a student, separated from his beloved children, all of whom were teenagers. 'There's no place for divorce in Sikh culture, La-ree,' he had said. 'You are breaking a bond established in the presence of the Adi Granth...' And now he was lonely, hence the nights out with Larry and his knockout girlfriend. Naturally, I felt for him, being separated from my own offspring, and wanted to know him better.

'Not only zero unity,' said Rube, unexpectedly rejoining the debate. 'But no tolerance...'

Always a little morose, Rube was one of those heavy, inward personalities, who hung at the edge of conversations like the lead weights in a clock. Tonight he was unusually sprightly. He had even smiled – a rare occurrence, revealing a mixture of very long and very short teeth, all a brilliant white, surrounded by a roguish stubble. There was something of the track star about him, his hands having an impressive span. The smile had revealed a boyish, pleased side to his character, and there was a flickering sensitivity in his eyelashes when he spoke.

'*C'est vrai*,' frowned the professor, 'the amount of times I have been called a jihadist on the RER. *Mon Dieu.*'

'Because of the beard?' asked Ariel, suddenly opening her eyes.

'Because of the whole package.'

Hoisting herself up in the uncomfortable seat, newly

involved, Ariel glanced over at Rube. Racism was something they had certainly experienced, and discussed in depth, by the looks of it. Larry had told me Rube's mother was a Catholic who had brought him up in the *banlieues* of the *vingtième,* so he had undoubtedly had his fair share of abuse. Apparently, he began his teens as a graffiti artist but now created serious installations, with his own studio near the Bellevois gallery where he had exhibited a couple of times. He still spent his evenings DJ-ing, mainly at legendary places like Batofar, which was where he had met Ariel, then only seventeen. A covert churchgoer, he still received racist comments from the congregation, and, in the aftermath of *Je suis Charlie*, more than just occasionally. Most of his friends were Muslim Algerians, and they were less philosophical about the subject.

'That's disgraceful,' said Larry, always the first to take on another's cause. '*Fucking* reprehensible.'

'In a civilised society, you expect better,' shrugged Rube.

'Especially in Paris, of all places. The ancient centre of liberty and free intellectual debate!' At this my cousin's arms flew into the air, as if he had been shot.

The wine had arrived, and I started to refill everyone's glass. 'You see, I put this down to the Larousse. At least de Champlain got out of his library.'

'Who's he?' Larry asked, irritated by something he didn't know.

'Founded Quebec by starting a fur-trading colony. Of course, he christened it New France. From the mid-nineteenth century, the average Parisian intellectual never had to mix with other cultures. If he wanted to find out about the Maoris, he just looked them up. Only Flaubert got on his camel. It's become a very insular society in many ways.'

I expected, even wanted, Ariel to contradict me here, but she said nothing. She sat there dazed, the breeze blowing her sable hair across her delectable cheekbones. Then it struck me that Larry had promised an audience with François earlier, something I had been looking forward to. To allay the vibrations of partisan feeling stirring in the twilight, I asked, 'By the way, where was your father?'

Anticipating a reply detailing some impressive ministerial function at the Palais Royal, I was surprised when instead she wrinkled her nose and said: '*Avec* Solange.'

'Who's Solange?' I asked, innocently.

Larry caught Ariel's eye and cleared his throat. He was about to speak, but she answered first.

'His mistress,' murmured Ariel, huskily. 'He sees her most days. For his *cinq à sept*.'

'I see.'

From Ariel's expression, I gathered she didn't much care for Solange. Larry had told me she admired her father to the same extent that she reviled her mother. She was one of the few women, he had said, who would eventually turn into her dad. I noticed then, from the trembling emotion in her eyes, that she had a curiously expressionless face. And that she rarely laughed. If I'd been a younger man, this might have been unnerving, but at my age I could tell this was just the customary insecurity and defensiveness of twenty. She was *dying* to laugh. I hoped Larry brought this out, otherwise they were sunk.

'Tell me, Ariel,' said Professor Singh, sidestepping the sexual misdemeanours of her famous father with brilliant diplomacy, 'before the abhorrent events of January, did you ever have any trouble?'

'In what way?'

'With, how shall we say, ethnic *ressentiment*?'

Ariel sat back against the window, a pane of glass completely obscured by flyers and posters, and considered the question. Everyone at the table was watching her now, Larry especially. It was a matter that interested him intensely.

'Not much. But I remember at the gates of the Jewish *école junior*, near where we used to live, names were called out… *Mais pour moi*, personally? *Non*.'

'But surely, around here…' And Nadir indicated the street where two Hassidim were passing in their wide-brimmed black hats, their coiled locks gleaming from the newly bright neons of the bars. Though not in need of an armed police escort, they still had a haunted look they might not have carried a year before.

'Oh, *bien sûr*,' she shrugged. 'Despite everything, the shopkeepers are insulted. Every day they get called *sale juif*.'

Larry shook his head gravely. 'Try saying that in Hendon or Stamford Hill. You'd get your ribs kicked in.'

'It is a serious problem,' affirmed Rube. 'And now Marine Le Pen has taken over, she is trying to shift the focus to the Muslims.'

Delightfully, he pronounced the word 'foe-cous'.

'Yes,' said Ariel. 'Now they are the new supposed enemy within, not us. But why should it be up to us to solve things, not the government? Why should we leave our country now and live in Israel?'

Larry was getting worked up again, the sure signs of it showing in the rapidity of his eye movements. 'Yeah. And why wasn't the shooting of those Jewish school children near Toulouse defined as a pogrom?'

Ariel flinched at this, a new gravity entering the soft, placid air of the evening. For some reason I felt duty bound to drive the conversation back to less flammable pastures.

'There's been anti-Semitism here since Roman times, Larry. I mean, now they have the biggest Jewish population in Europe. There's bound to be some increased... friction.'

'I know that,' shot back my cousin.

'And all the more reason to withstand it,' said Professor Singh, with sudden conviction. 'It's the return of the old-style anti-Semitism that is so worrying.'

'I agree,' I found myself saying. 'It never went away. Like most European nations, France has a history of mass expulsions, vilification, humiliation. England's no better. The Revolution emancipated the Jews for a time, then it all came blowing back with Dreyfus.'

'*L'affaire?*' shrugged Ariel. 'That's nothing to now. It's the attitude beneath the smile that hurts. It all comes out when they're drunk. Like with that shit Galliano. Or Dieudonné and his stupid fascist salute.'

'It can be more casual, too,' I said. 'Look at Clemenceau, saying that Klotz, his post-war finance minister, was the only Jew in Paris who knew nothing about money.'

'Or,' offered the professor, 'when de Gaulle accused the Jews of being a domineering people back in 1967. He was angry with what he saw as their disobedience in going to war.' Professor Singh had the due seriousness of the old-style academic – a compactness of thought that you didn't see much any more. Unlike Larry, he always sat very still while listening to you. My cousin still listened – don't get me wrong – but he was synthesising and arguing inwardly all the time, eager to speak.

'I can't believe he said that!' cried Larry. 'Where did he stand on Germany if the Jews are suddenly a domineering people?'

'I think we all know where de Gaulle stood on Hitler, Larry,' I said, turning my chair to face him. I was also aware, out of the corner of my eye, that Ariel was monitoring him closely.

'Okay, but the rest of France weren't so fussy!'

'You can't say that,' Rube broke in, also turning to face Larry full on.

'Why not? There were what – eighty thousand Jews deported from France up until 1944? And most of those, as everyone around this table knows, were denounced by the French people themselves.'

At this, I heard the chair next to me scrape back violently. Turning, I caught Ariel's turquoise dress as it disappeared past the neighbouring tables, under the gold lettering of Chez Omar's awning, then through the restaurant's door, which slammed behind her.

A silence descended over our table. It had been inevitable, really. The second walkout of the night from his flighty *amour fou*, but maybe this one was justified. Larry was still leaning forward, arrested mid-rant, like a frame of film paused on a television screen.

'Woah,' exclaimed Rube, sucking in the air. '*Woah-whee.*'

'What?' asked Larry incredulously. 'What did I say?'

I exchanged glances with the professor, who quickly looked down at the table, which was stained with the rich red paprika and chilli from our long-forgotten meal.

'*Pour les Français,*' advised Rube, 'the subject is – *comment dites-vous?* – off-limits, my friend.'

Confident that Larry wouldn't understand, Professor Singh tapped his nose and turned to Rube: '*Il a un verre dans le nez.*'

I looked along the rue de Bretagne. With a strange serendipity, kippah-wearing youngsters had appeared in their droves, streaming past on their *vélomoteurs*, kicking up noise in the mellow evening. Knowing things were unsalvageable, and thinking of the beer I would open on returning to my apartment (which I had decided to drink while soothing my legs to Glenn Gould's *Goldberg Variations*), I addressed my cousin: 'Sometimes, Larry, a man can have too much empathy.'

One phenomenon that has preoccupied me recently, as I edge nearer to forty-five, is that existence seems to be getting stranger. It's just all-round weirder, more unfathomable, more difficult to negotiate. At an age where one should recognise some kind of earth-tenure, my feet have felt as if they were levitating alarmingly, inches from the ground. Is this unusual, or is it the promised end for us all? How to make sense of the past, of one's parents, of failed relationships, how to simply *be*, appears suddenly to confront me daily with an ever-increasing list of frightening ramifications. The pattern becomes more complex, deeper, less easy to distinguish, as Virginia Woolf warned. On luminous Paris days, when strong winds blow the *tricolore* on the avenue Montaigne, or shunt vehicle-shaped clouds behind the Haussmann skyline, I have begun to feel an insidious but tangible sense of dislocation; something that can only be described as ontological instability. The spirit of Sartre has entered me at last, after many decades of my resistance. He was right: we are condemned to choose, and keep choosing at every instant of our adult lives. It's very distressing, and a terrifically solemn business too. No, revise that – it's hilarious, or it would be, if the joke wasn't on us.

At the end of May, after Larry and Ariel had patched things up, I met my cousin at a different café from our usual one on the rue Saint-Jacques. I don't know why we changed – by unspoken consent perhaps. We talked briefly about his faux pas; the taboo subjects of the *collabos*, of the four terrible years of Paris's occupation, of Drancy and the deportations, and the savage *épuration* that followed. All of it was out of bounds still, and Larry hadn't known. Admittedly, like neurotransmitters, it probably wasn't something that came up frequently chez Levine. Dipping his brioche into his coffee, he agreed that in the future he would exercise some restraint, as hard as that was for him, 'And God knows, you can vouch for that,' he added. For light relief, he told me, he was taking Ariel out that evening to see *Play It Again, Sam* in its *version originale* on the rue Galande. He took great pleasure in telling me the translated title of the dubbed version (and only Larry would know a fact like this): *Tombe les filles et tais-toi!* Roughly: *Pull the Birds and Shut Up!* Maybe he should follow its advice, I suggested, at which he laughed. Only cousins could say such things to each other, I decided afterwards. Still, it's a great title, you have to agree.

The fact was, Larry saw no anomaly in squiring so young a woman as Ariel around the streets of the Marais. The largest age gap I'd ever dealt with was a couple of years at most – I couldn't begin to understand what a whole generation of difference might feel like. Maybe it was a two-way education of sorts – and Larry had told me this was one of its joys (among others, I should imagine). With a younger girl, you had the chance to be her first experience of many things, while you get to feel rejuvenated in return. Despite Ariel's generation having seen and done everything – being terminally unimpressed – Larry said he was enjoying 'showing her around a little'. With the noise of the café I thought he said *shoving* for a moment, but that was far from plausible, built like she was. He told me they were planning on travelling in the summer, Institut permitting, and that he was looking forward to returning to many of the places he had visited. He would reveal to her the wonders of Kyoto, of the Himalayan foothills, of Pompeii, like one of those older-man teacher-husbands so beloved of Victorian novels. Surprisingly, Ariel had never seen the classic Woody film, and Larry was taking great pleasure in 'showing it to her'. It was a work of art, he insisted, like Beethoven's late quartets, or the *Ghent Altarpiece*, or the *Oresteia*; something that would last her a lifetime. No matter what happened between them in the future, whenever *Play It Again, Sam* came on TV dubbed into French, she would smile fondly and think of Larry. I recalled seeing the movie myself for the first time in a French cinema, escaping from my parents on one of our visits. It had been screening at a cavernous place on the rue Voltaire, with only a couple of other people in the auditorium. I had laughed unstoppably, while these mysterious others had sat stonily in the stalls. Maybe, my father suggested afterwards, they had been film critics.

Before I departed for my day's research, Larry had enthused about a number of other subjects, as was his wont – one always left him still holding his coffee cup, babbling about Gaia theory or some such. He was a great believer in the fact that the earth sought to optimise conditions for life upon it. 'If we die, everything dies,' he told me once. 'Plants would use up the supply of CO_2 in the atmosphere in twelve years if the human race wasn't there to replenish it.' We were all held in a lethal balance, and what were the world's governments doing about it, despite endless G8 and IPCC summits? This time it had been telluric currents – a new one on me. Apparently, these were electric currents that moved underground or through the sea – and nobody knew whether they were a natural phenomenon or the result of human activity. 'A bit like climate change, then,' I suggested, unthinkingly. 'Not a bit like climate change!' he had jabbed back. 'You're swallowing all that bad science again. No – scratch that – *non-science* is what the climate change deniers are peddling.' Despite having a weakness for conspiracy theories, Larry was always super-persuasive. He had a strong faith in the species' ambition to survive at all costs. As a pharmacologist, he had seen this at first hand. The money spent on drugs designed to prolong life was phenomenal. 'But why,' I asked, thinking of the shooting pains in my wrists and ankles, 'do we favour prolongation over fulfilment? Longevity over quality of life?

Better to live briefly and brilliantly than to bear witness to a slow decline?' For once, he didn't have an answer to that.

Heading for the Sorbonne afterwards, I found the murky skies of the morning were bearing rain. The first in over a month. I stopped for a second at the kerb, arrested by its novelty. Just a thin drizzle, hampering the progress of pedestrians along the rue Cujas, but not unwelcome. It had been so hot recently, some days had felt like July, and I enjoyed the sappy, genial brush of fine raindrops on my face.

But I had work to do, so I crossed the street quickly, aiming north. As I walked, I passed florists arranging their displays; students on the way to exams; browbeaten workers with heavy stress etched into their frowns. '*Métro, boulot, dodo*' was the phrase Parisians used – Métro, job, sleep. Each lost in the midst of their lives, hermetically sealed. I felt suddenly thankful that I had Larry as my companion in Paris. Without him, a year-long sabbatical might have been unremittingly bleak. I didn't know what I would do come the summer, when he and Ariel went off to see the world.

Walking steadily, I felt I needed a moment to compose myself before the customary return to the 1790s, so I stopped at the place Paul Painlevé. Usually, before visiting the Serpente library, I paid a visit there, a secretive little park in front of the university's *grande entrée*, heavily overgrown now in late spring. It was somewhere I went to collect my thoughts, to be alone without interference from tourists; the opposite of the regal Luxembourg, as much as I loved it. Walking around it now, the rain delicious in the muggy, torpid air, I discovered the green benches too sluiced to sit on. I tramped the inner circle looking for any available surface. But I found none. Instead, I stopped in front of a small statue of Hebe; a smooth goddess heaving an urn, overlooked by the bearded bust of the mathematician Painlevé himself. It had always made me smile, the grizzled old prof and prime minister stern-faced atop the wonder of marble below, the bowing youthful nape offered to the sky.

Standing there frustrated, deciding what to do, I felt overcome by a spreading sense of dissatisfaction, its source unknown. I looked up into the trees, arrested by the hiss of the drizzle. They were lustreless and bleached in the drab morning. The city seemed to have lost its gloss. Growing up in the country, I once knew my trees fairly well, and, getting wet, I tried to name all the ones nearby. There were no planes here; instead there were copper beeches with their dark, defiled leaves. Also walnuts, and more exotic varieties: a tall cedrela, a paper mulberry, and what looked like a weeping elm. In the far corner, in front of the Cluny Museum, stood an even taller tree of heaven. These were spectacular when in sunlight, and I had often sat for half an hour at a time, drinking down the fecund abundance, the striking odours, the matinal vapours of the emerging year. I looked around me now with a kind of unnameable despair... No, I couldn't face Mirabeau or Richelieu or the rest of them this morning. I decided I would do something I hadn't done for years in Paris – just walk.

Leaving the park swiftly, I headed north once more: over the rue des Écoles and left onto the boulevard Saint-Germain. It was very busy. The smell of *crêpes beurre-sucre* made me nostalgic and hungry all at once, despite only having just had breakfast. Turning right into the roar of the boulevard Saint-Michel I walked fast, past thronged cafés and bookshops, all the way up to the quai des Grands-Augustins. *Tout le monde* was off to work while I was evading it. I was glad I had left the apartment in my belted trenchcoat, otherwise I might have received a soaking. My father had worn just such a coat, and, although Larry had ridiculed it earlier, I liked the way it conferred maturity, as well as covering up my weight loss and making me feel vaguely like Humphrey Bogart.

At the river, which was the colour of turpentine under the ashen skies, I made a quick patrol of the bookstalls. But I decided I wasn't in the mood, and so crossed the pont Saint-Michel and onto the Île de la Cité. Maybe I had only needed to see the water. Perhaps that had been the single source of my malaise. Indeed, the sight of the fishermen along the rangy wharves lifted the heart slightly. There they sat, in any weather, with a Buddhist patience. In my youth I had watched and waited with them, overjoyed when they hauled a flapping silvery bream from the turbid water.

Turning abruptly, I walked west, along the quai des Orfèvres, the rain horizontal now, blowing into my face along with the wind from the Seine. I was gripped with a vague sense of mission. The freeing sweep of the stone *quais* – so familiar and yet still so romantic – was drawing me inexorably to the head of the Île de la Cité, where it joined the pont Neuf at its centre.

And there, on the bridge, I came to a halt.

Looking downriver from one of the bastions that punctuate the bridge's graceful camber, I was met with a magnificent sight. All of Paris under the sultry mist of late May. Nothing more fair. With an avid attention, I took in the plane trees and the poplars along the banks. The Louvre and Tuileries beyond, shrouded in deliquescent air. Below me, churning up water, were tugs and barges, as well as the wide drifting *Bateaux Mouches*. I could see fishermen in the little park under the bridge too, with its equestrian statue of Henri IV above, its old graffiti tags, some of them perhaps by the hand of Rube... I breathed in deeply. Yes, this had been the only tonic I had needed.

Something else caught my eye as I lingered there. Along the *quais* were sentinel herons, very still, with their characteristic noble aspect. These I also recalled from boyhood – and some other location I couldn't quite place at that moment. The static birds had the power to induce in me the same trance or dream state as the trees in the Luxembourg. Watching them, waiting for them to move or fly away, which they never did, had the power to mesmerise. With their surreal stillness, their brittle legs, formed like the struts of an anglepoise lamp, they were spellbinding. The herons stirred something very deep, very essential inside me. Something very ancient at the heart's core, and it troubled me greatly that I couldn't quite put my finger on what it was.

Turning around to look at the opposing view – no less inspiring, with its broad stone ramps that led back to the pont Saint-Michel – I thought I might be succumbing to the Sartrean terrors once more, and tried to steady myself within. Things did become stranger, more unaccountable, the longer one lived. It was distressing in the extreme, as one felt some form of wisdom should have descended by now.

I bent down to grip my ankles, in an attempt to massage away the pain. The paradox was that I needed to walk every day, as I couldn't undertake any other exercise. I used to love running and squash. Only non-weight-bearing activities like swimming were manageable now, and I only got to do that with Ed, which, as you can imagine, was not very often... Suddenly angry, I decided there and then to sue Abaddon-Blix, the fluoroquinolone drugs' manufacturer that had ruined my health. I had heard from my lawyer that they were very close to retrieving my funds from Barry Gallagher in an out-of-court settlement. If that was the case, I would plough it all into taking on the multinational, as well as perhaps a short holiday for Ed and me, something Cass had reluctantly sanctioned on the phone the previous week. Larry would undoubtedly laugh at the futility of this, but what did I have to lose? He had told me that unless I *actually* ruptured a tendon, ending my writing career, it would be very hard to sue the corporation. Damage had to be measured in 'loss of earnings', in quantifiable trauma. But how can you quantify pain? Something unobservable, but prosaically familiar, to every inhabitant of Planet Earth?

Hearing the klaxon honk of the barges beneath, my brow cooled by the rain, I concluded, nevertheless, that after a certain age, freedom of choice is all you have left. I would start building a case. Larry might be tempted to do the same if he had to spend twenty-four hours in my body – if he had been floxed, as I had. In Sartrean terms, Larry was just another component in my *mauvaise foi*. I refused to allow him to contribute to the weight of facticity hanging heavy in the aqueous air. God knows, we spend our lives planning to do things we never get around to – and then it's too late. Clearly, that's what joins us as a species: having to face the same damn things as each other, and then choosing what to do about them. A daily ordeal, enough to send anyone around the bend. We always assume our fellow man is better equipped for this challenge – has read more Heidegger or Badiou, possesses more aptitude or tenacity – but, chances are, he's as lost as you or me.

However, a new legal case would have to wait until next week, as I remembered I had agreed, only half an hour previously, to help Larry with his genealogical research into Grandma Lotte. This had been arranged for the following morning, at the CDJC – the Centre de documentation Juive Contemporaine, housed in the Shoah Memorial Museum on the rue Geoffroy-l'Asnier. My cousin had wanted to spend the whole of Saturday there, and suggested we meet fifteen minutes before opening time – at *dix heures moins le quart* on the dot. I would aim for ten. After all, he was bound to be late.

TWO

'You seem distracted…'

Larry's concerned face was frowning at me atop a white lab coat.

Like the finger-click that brings one round from a long trance, his sentence had the required effect of returning me to the present. Ever since contemplating the herons along the Seine, I had been able to do little else but think about taking my revenge on the unscrupulous pharmaceutical barons. It had obsessed me day and night, and, for a couple of weeks, I had found it impossible to deal with normal life.

'I'm sorry,' I said, as convincingly as I could muster. 'I was miles away. Dreaming.'

We were standing in the main lab in the Institut's Department of Neuroscience. It was now a morning in early June, and Larry was showing me around. A long-planned visit.

'I don't want you to miss any of this, man. I don't know when I'll be able to sneak you in again.'

'I'm all ears, Larry.'

We began to walk slowly, in step, between the polished work surfaces.

'This is high-level research we're undertaking here. Measuring neuropeptides and chromogranin. We're trying to battle some of the world's most persistent afflictions. The effect of a stroke on the central cortex, for instance...'

All around was the steady whir of centrifuges and lab machinery. Humming power packs attached to huge electrolysis tanks. It was so early we had the place to ourselves, apart from the occasional post-doc assistant peering through the doorway with a clipboard.

'What are those?' I asked vaguely, pointing at a desk covered in printout stats.

'DNA multi-array studies,' said Larry, in his high, proud voice. 'We're doing a lot of electron microscopy. Looking at brain injuries. The immunohistochemistry can tell us if more neurotransmitters have been recruited to an injured cortex...'

I scratched my head, as if in unconscious sympathy for those broken brains, but understanding next to nothing. 'Are you working on new antibiotics here? I thought there was some kind of crisis on.'

'That's Nadir's department.'

'How do you mean?'

'Well, he tells me the WHO reckon antimicrobials have added twenty years to everyone's life... But now bacteria of all strains are becoming resistant to them. They estimate it's killing twenty-five thousand people a year in Europe alone – as many as die in road accidents. So yeah, a crisis that no one's paying attention to.'

We stopped in front of what looked like a bank of microwave ovens. 'But surely, this must be music to the collective ears of Big Pharma?'

'You would think so, wouldn't you?' returned Larry,

scratching his chin. His eyes, deep-set at the best of times, seemed especially embedded this morning, and the tough tanned flesh of his face was beginning to show a tropical perspiration. 'Yes, they're relentlessly trying to make and market new pills – but here's the rub. No new antibacterials have been discovered since eighty-seven. It costs up to a billion to develop a new medicine, and, for finding alternatives to penicillin, that's too expensive. They're focusing on cancer and diabetes cures now. The simple fact is antibiotics are only given in short courses. Hence, they make more money from the big beasts – the terminal illnesses that require constant medication. *That's* how cynical it is.'

'It certainly is,' I affirmed distractedly.

'Hey,' said Larry, taking my arm. 'Shall we get coffee first? You don't look so well.'

'Good idea.' I must have appeared pale, or mentally disturbed. 'I missed breakfast. You dragged me here against my will, remember?'

'No I did not!'

In moments we had repaired to the Institut's sombre canteen for bowls of dark *allongé*, with a plate of croissants between us. At least here I could let Larry talk to his heart's content about electron microscopy micrographs and not pretend to be listening.

For a full fortnight, I hadn't been able to focus on my own research, let alone Larry's stuff. We'd been to the CDJC – a total waste of time, predictably – and I'd told him about my intention to sue Abaddon-Blix. My cousin had been suitably scornful. If governments couldn't make these companies admit culpability, what chance did I have? He suggested I save the money and take Ed to Disneyland. I told him this was already part of the plan, though I hadn't envisaged Florida as the destination. 'Disneyland Paris was what I had in mind,' I said. 'Fair enough,' he had countered, 'it's all free advice. Part of the service.' I had felt like grappling him to the ground, right there on the rue Geoffroy-l'Asnier. Instead, tears had appeared in my eyes, hot and pendulous; a measure of the stress I had been under, perhaps; an indication of what a trap life could become. Certain decisions or misadventures hoist you far above the jungle by your ankles, and there's nothing you can do but watch the vultures begin to congregate in the surrounding trees.

Now, in the Institut's cafeteria, Larry's black eyes appeared close to bearing waterworks of their own. A steady realisation of this brought me out of my contemplations. He had been talking about François and Rivka for the last ten minutes, and I'd barely been listening.

'The old man is mighty strange,' Larry continued, the noise of the canteen intensifying as the morning staff arrived. 'I'm just beginning to realise the full extent of it…'

It was hard to tell whether the beaming glassiness in his pupils was a result of sorrow or a strange exultation. My cousin would only explain it away as 'Jewish emotionalism', and this deterred me from asking if anything was the matter. Plus, we were male.

'Firstly, he's banging this Solange piece every other afternoon. Actually, "tart" is what Ariel calls her – *une poule*. Sometimes she gets an upgrade to *une grande horizontale*. She's a junior minister: you've probably seen her on TV. But he still makes a point of returning on time, smelling of roses, to eat *en famille*. No, not roses, lemons. He has this *citron* cologne; maddeningly familiar, man. I just can't place it. You get a blast of it in every room... Then he's cold with his daughter for weeks, yet she still hero-worships him. I just can't work him out. He used to be a lawyer, you know. Did you know that?'

'Don't talk to me about lawyers,' I managed to mumble, an eye still on Larry's emotional temperature. We were in a quiet corner, in a semicircular booth, and maybe this was encouraging his candour.

'And not only that, but he's started to look askance at me.'

'That's because you have designs on his daughter other than just sleeping with her and introducing her to American culture.'

'What does he expect? Am I an old fart all of a sudden? First, he's so welcoming in the way only the French are – you know, ten-course dinners; making you feel part of the family. And now the cold shoulder, virtually.'

'The eagle has landed.'

'You know, he took me aside the other day. Offered to take me to lunch. Just me and him. But why? To warn me off?'

'It won't be to improve your French.'

Larry had started to employ his eccentric gestures, a sure sign of his agitation. Both hands were now in rapid emphatic motion.

'We were in the big corridor of the apartment – you remember, the one with the mirrored walls? And, as he was talking to me, he kept catching his own reflection in the glass:

admiringly, preeningly almost. Looking down his cheekbones at his own profile, but out of the corners of his eyes. Isn't that a little bizarre? For a man of his age, dignity, status? And that lemon cologne in such a confined space. Overpowering.'

'No. It's his *power* that's overpowering. His political heft.'

'You don't think it was a male moment? Between a father and a possible interloper for his daughter? He's a head taller than me, after all. He was trying to dominate me, master me.'

'That can't be easy, Larry.'

'Anyway,' my cousin added, wringing his hands forcefully, his eyes less precipitous of tears than a moment before. 'They've got a big cocktail party coming up. You're invited, by the way. Madame Levine took a real shine to you.'

I recalled that Rivka had smelt pretty overpowering too, in an ostentatious way. Maybe that's what great wealth granted: the ability to conceal animality while smelling of roses.

'I'd be delighted to come along. Maybe I'll finally get to speak to the great François.'

Larry brightened for a moment. Despite his high emotional state, it struck me that my cousin was never really melancholy, and this was all a woman wanted in a man. Which didn't mean to say he wasn't without his mental agonies or tortures – some of his enthusiasms were an agony to him, I could tell. But he was rarely, if ever, actually *down*, and this made him an attractive proposition to the opposite sex. It was where I had gone wrong my whole life, I surmised. Of course, there were many things that worked against him in matters of love. Too many to list. He'd never made it past a couple of years with the same person, remember. For some reason, La Rochefoucauld has been much on my mind, and, just recently, a few of the *duc*'s slightly conventional formulas had struck me as very profound indeed. Maybe this was symptomatic of ageing, I wasn't sure. In fact, La Rochefoucauld and Mme de la Fayette had lived on the very road where the Institut was situated. One pearl that I felt applied to us at that moment stated that the most difficult undertaking in friendship is not concealing your own faults, but making your friend see his own.

Just then, a voice put in from beyond the booth.

'*Messieurs*. Mind if I join you?'

It was Professor Singh, looking greyer than last time, carrying a breakfast tray. This was laden with little *pots de confiture*, a bowl of steaming coffee, and a heap of croissants. I'd never seen so many on a single plate.

'My friend,' said Larry, even brighter now. 'Take a seat. I was just showing Nick the labs.'

The professor squeezed in next to me, and I sensed his weight straining the Institut's wooden-bench seating. 'Ah, but you found something more interesting to talk about?'

'The Levines. They're a soap opera. No – a box set. I could see them on HBO. Or whatever the French equivalent is.'

'There isn't an equivalent,' I said, with as much irony as I could muster.

'Well, count yourself lucky,' the professor exclaimed. 'Living there in paradise.'

This was an allusion to Nadir's current digs, which Larry had fortuitously escaped.

To change the subject, I pointed at the feast on the tray. 'Are they all for you?'

'*Bien sûr...*' smiled Nadir. Despite his cheery demeanour, he couldn't help but come across as a man in mourning. There were heavy woes to go with his pile of breakfast carbs. There was a gentle unworldliness, too, of a man who had only, according to Larry, slept with two women: his mistress and his wife. Which was extraordinary, given his age. He had just turned fifty, and had spent the big day alone, banned, as he was, from setting foot in the family home and seeing his three children. And food was a great comfort to the melancholy, the lonely. I had experienced this myself. With nothing more substantial to masticate, the mind looks forward all day to what the body might eat – planning every meal in detail; one's solitary evening pleasure.

'... I need to keep my strength up, yaar. I have to give a paper this afternoon. In Chantilly.' Nadir had begun to break the croissants up, carefully buttering them, and then adding to each a heart of bright red strawberry jam with the tip of his knife.

'And what's the paper on, if I may ask?'

'Toxicology. It is a very interesting area.'

It certainly was, to me at least. Larry had told me that the chemical basis for my adverse reaction was technically fluoride poisoning. At the time I remember thinking that of all the things to be poisoned by, this benign substance was the last one would expect. I wanted to question the professor further, but my cousin interrupted.

'So what are you doing here?'

'I am just taking advantage of the *déjeuner du matin*,' Nadir admitted in his careful tones. This he said with slight embarrassment. The permanent staff ate at the faculty for free, and I was sure his wife, like my ex, was taking him for a grand ride in the Bois de Boulogne, financially speaking. I felt immediate warmth for him.

To spare him his shame over his *gratis* breakfast, I said: 'Chantilly? Really? I haven't been there for years.'

North of Paris, with a giant cream-coloured chateau decimated during the Revolution, Chantilly was where my father had once taken me on a daytrip from Paris, while my mother walked the boulevards and fantasised about shopping for haute couture. I had returned a couple of times over the years, while writing various books, but it had never been as magical as the first time.

'Come along, if you like. If you want to find out more about toxicology, this is the conference to attend.'

Larry looked across at me like a lover spurned. Despite my preoccupations, I had enjoyed the parts of the lab my cousin had shown me, though had been disappointed not to see the expected organs swimming in jars. In the end, however, one lab looks much like the next. I had wanted to see the inside of the Institut Pasteur since childhood. From the outside it looked simultaneously mysterious and dowdy, like an intelligence services building dropped onto the elegant rue de Vaugirard. But the chance to see Chantilly again was too good to pass up.

'I'd love to come along, Professor. Thank you.'

'Okay,' shrugged Larry, 'but I'm not sure when I can authorise you access again.'

'That's fine. My mind was elsewhere anyway.'

*

The following day, I decided to take my work to the Luxembourg, the weather being balmy at 9 a.m., promising heat later. But first I needed to call Cass. Descending in the lift, nodding '*bonjour*' to Mme George, frozen perpetually in her lodge, I slipped my €10 card into the slot of the payphone. It was in deference to my youthful Parisian visits that I still favoured a trusty callbox over a mobile connection when phoning home. Luckily, this old contraption still functioned, and had a hairdryer Perspex surround, which proved good acoustical protection, so I was always assured of a confidential conversation. As I waited to be connected, I thought about my excursion with Professor Singh. It had been wonderful to get out of town for an afternoon. I had come to know Nadir and his domestic troubles very well as the SNCF train shot us across the flat, burgeoning green fields to his conference. Rows of poplars, pike-straight and equidistant, had run parallel to the tracks for whole stretches, the open vents admitting a sweet, invigorating, hopeful breath of early summer. Orchards, hayfields, canals, small towns and churches had passed us under a brilliant blue sky. And Chantilly, with its stately chateau, had been as enchanting as I remembered.

Just then, Cassie's voice came on the line. 'You're early.'

'I know, I wanted to get out while I had the inspiration. How are you?'

The last thing I needed at this hour was a row. Her voice carried its familiar combative edge, and she was being uncharacteristically blunt. Usually Cass's speech was a fluent lecturer's barrage of terms and references – she was never stuck for an eloquent comparison or an apt critical term. Now she just sounded sore as hell, to use her phraseology.

'I've thought about what you proposed, and the answer's no.'

The last time we spoke I had suggested I might withdraw from my maintenance commitments, just until the end of the year, in order to provide wriggle room to hire a lawyer that could take on Abaddon-Blix. I told her not to answer immediately, but to ponder it for a week or so. This she had obviously done.

Feeling I needed to stand my ground, I said: 'I've already approached the CSA.'

'Well, you'd better un-approach them, buster!'

At this I almost laughed.

'We don't have to use such terms on each other, Cass... Is Ed in the room?'

By her silence, I took it that yes, he was. I felt a quick jolt of anger, and tried to suppress it. Nothing, I had decided, was going to spoil my morning. Holding the receiver slightly further from my ear, I let my ex have her say.

'Nick, you can continue to pay what your attorney tells you is fair, or you can leave us to shift for ourselves. I won't advise you one way or another. I can only speak my mind and give you the lowdown on how things are panning out in London town – which is still pretty rocky financially, if you must know. But it's your decision. I don't want Eduardo perceiving his father as anything other than the one capable male left in his life. Of course, he has Gramps if you want to abdicate that role. But in the end, I won't rib you or steamroll you into making your alimony contributions on time every month. Like I say, in the end, it's your decision.'

This time I did laugh.

'But it's not my decision! You're just guilt-tripping me now. It's not up to me – you have to sanction it with the Child Support people. And I know you can afford it.'

Gramps, a scion of East Coast deep money, was where she would go if I didn't cough up. Predictably, a reference to his wealth raised her temperature even higher.

'That's my business.'

'And it's your decision.'

'Yeah, but it sounds like you – while sauntering the boulevards and rereading Montesquieu – have already decided. I've got a child to bring up here. *Our* child.'

Cass habitually referred to Ed as *her* son, as if he were some kind of immaculate conception. Only when money was at stake did he become a joint venture. However, now was not the time to question personal pronouns.

'Okay,' I snapped, conceding defeat. 'Let's leave things as they are. Can you put Ed on, please?'

A second later, I heard his piping voice. It always demolished my heart.

'Hi, Dad!'

'Hey...'

'I wish you two wouldn't argue.'

'Discussion, not argument. Lively debate. How are things?'

'Dred, Dad. London is so *long*.'

I heard Ed's high tones elongate the vowel for comic effect. In my day, dred had meant cool, as in Natty Dread. Now I gathered it was just a corruption of dreadful. But 'long' baffled me for a moment.

'You'll have to speak up a bit. How's school? In fact, why aren't you at school?'

'It's an inset day. Anyhow, school is for lameos.'

I got the gist of the last word but felt we might get nowhere if he insisted on using incomprehensible slang.

'You don't have to talk like that, Ed. At any rate, I haven't a clue what you mean. I thought you liked school…'

I conceded that it was impossible to be educated in London and not speak like this. Nevertheless, I worried that his recent usage was symptomatic of the divorce. While his bed-wetting had stopped, Cass had admitted that he was returning home aggressive and swearing more often. She put this down to peer pressure, the imperative to use urban slang; all the stronger if you were white and a bit uncool. At Christmas I had been startled when he proclaimed the dinner to be 'sick', peppering his conversation with 'isits' and 'rahs'. He had spent the day talking about his 'yard', his 'garms' and his 'rents' (by which he meant us, his parents), until I sensed even he felt it was a little over the top.

In the clever way of children, he changed the subject swiftly and with a masterful note of spontaneity.

'Hey, why don't you sack those dusty books and come back here to play Call of Duty? Mum got it for me, but she won't play it.'

'Did she now? I'd love to come back, Ed, but I'm tied down with work. You'll understand that when you're older.'

This wasn't strictly true. I had plenty of time to visit. Since I'd arrived in Paris, I had been petitioning Cass to make time for me to return to London and see my son, but she had been strangely resistant. I didn't want to get into the reasons why with Ed. The fact was, I couldn't fathom the reasons for her reluctance, except for the usual obstinacy. Our separation was all the more galling, as Ed had been genuinely worried about me going to live and work in Paris in the days following *Charlie Hebdo*, thinking of the city as one of bloodshed, not of light.

'But I am older... than I was when you last saw me.'

This sentence troubled my heart as much as the mere sound of his voice. In my mind, I saw him all the time. It was hard to comprehend that I had disappeared in his eyes. He was never out of mine. I cleared my throat gruffly: 'You know what I mean.'

'C'mon, Dad, I know you'd be great. You get to destroy foreign armies with tank divisions! Isn't that what you write about?'

'Something like that... But I'm terrible with technology. I was thinking more of the zoo.'

'Oh, my days...' Ed's voice sang down the phone clearly, as if he were in the next room. This particular modern idiom I liked, finding it touchingly quaint, especially when used by crack dealers.

'What's the matter? Grown out of London Zoo?'

'Nah... It's just... it's just a bit...'

I could tell he was trying not to sound ungrateful. I had found the place unbearably melancholy the last time I had taken him there. More curious than my son about the hippos and llamas, I had spent half the time trying not to catch the eyes of all the other separated fathers doing the same tour of duty with their own kids. When I told Larry that I had taken Ed to Regent's Park, he quoted me the Bellow line about how zoo animals have no idea they are part of the divorce world. Very droll, and strangely apposite coming from a quondam anthropologist.

'Okay. Say no more. We'll sack the zoo, to use your phrase. Discussion to be continued. Can you put your mother back on the line?'

I talked to Cass for a further five minutes. I might have even punched the Perspex booth a couple of times, causing Mme George to jump in her den across the corridor. It was only when I got out onto the street that I began to calm down.

Deciding I needed to walk in order to cool off, I made my way south in the effervescent air. At the bottom of the boulevard Saint-Michel, I crossed the tumultuous traffic at Port Royal and headed mindlessly down the boulevard Montparnasse. The sun was already high in the sky; the foliage of the legendary Closerie des Lilas bursting from its green marquee. Behind this facade, Zola and the Goncourt brothers had once talked of social injustice; Verlaine and Rimbaud had debated symbolist poetry; Fitz and Hemingway the correct mixture of cognac and Cointreau in a Sidecar. On the wide pavement, young women in diaphanous dresses, wearing shades so large they almost obscured their faces, passed me like fish in an aquarium; swimming at summer's pace. But none of it was that entrancing this morning. I still had a head of steam on. *It's your decision.* Infuriating! And it always came after a long sequence of reasons detailing exactly why she felt making a certain decision was bad. And then would come her peroration, like a knuckle-duster inside a kid glove... 'But of course, *in the end*, it's your decision.' Almost the definition of the passive-aggressive stance!

And Cass had even appeared to exhibit a strange clairvoyance. It was true, I had a copy of Montesquieu's *Persian Letters* and his *De l'esprit des lois* in my battered brown-leather satchel. Along with these were my MacBook and the manuscript of *Elysian Fields* thus far – a paltry twenty-page introduction, which would need extensive rewriting. Had I mentioned my reading matter in a previous conversation? Just so she could turn it on me like a club? And that other phrase: *the one capable male left in his life*. For some reason, it had given me a strange surge of hope – for what, I wasn't sure. As I crossed the road once more, at the Vavin Métro station, in order to gain the quieter, more expansive boulevard Raspail, stretches of which ran behind the tall walls of the Cimetière du Montparnasse, I knew this pang was because her phrase referred to the vexed question of who she'd been seeing since our split. On this subject, she had been wholly inscrutable. And I had made a vow not to question Ed about it. Unless she was lying, or making a value judgement on some man she was dating, it meant she was seeing no one. Yet the very notion that she might have been sexually active since our split (after all, she hadn't taken vows of celibacy), that Ed might soon be thinking of another man as his 'new dad', caused me to writhe in despair. But what could I do? She was young, bright, successful; at the height of her sexuality. She wasn't going to join a convent just because she had a kid by her ex-husband.

Thinking of Cass in this light caused a slight unexpected stirring of arousal as I ducked out of the sun. A light wind was running, troubling the leaves of the plane trees, as I walked in the shadow of the cemetery. Physically, my ex-wife had the body type I always went for. Small, with energy that emanated from the base of her spine. Her whole torso rotated around this centrifuge. Far from shy when naked, in the early days of our marriage she would walk the corridors of my flat with no clothes on, her perfectly circular behind moving around this locus, like the two halves of an apple. Her breasts were perfect too: small, with dark, almost mahogany areolae, matching her bob. When she bent to pick up the Sunday papers, the soles of her feet dirty, you saw the mysterious cleft revealed intimately for a moment, then gone. Yes, we were well matched in the beginning – in love; thinking of bed and pleasure all through our respective lectures; delirious until we could find each other again in the thrilling gloom of my bedroom. Incredible to think it had come to this – a weekly fencing match over the phone. Now she had become what the French would term a real *abelardiser* – a ball-breaker.

And yet I had to qualify my half-hearted hostility towards Cass – I didn't want it to rub off on Ed, though some of this was inevitable. It was more her corroding disdain for me – born God knows where – that he would become weakened by. I still loved her sharp mind, the pure blade of her intellect, her range of reference. Unlike many of her peers, she was able to weave Aphra Behn and George Eliot into her subtle analyses of where women had got to today. She had pointed me in the direction of many writers myself. During our time, I had become an earnest reader of everyone from de Beauvoir to Susie Orbach, as well as hardline polemicists such as Eve Kosofsky Sedgwick. It was just her own books I had trouble with. And she seemed determined to cast herself as the archetypal American academic – purse-lipped, humourless, blind to ridicule. 'Gloria Steinem and Germaine Greer are funny women,' I reminded her once. 'By which I mean laugh-out-loud witty.' At this observation she threw a copy of *The Female Eunuch* at the back of my head.

But where did these tussles leave the three of us? Did we have any kind of future? Our break-up had coincided with Barry's overhaul of my finances – they had both seen me at my worst. Leaving the Rosebery Avenue flat for the last time, I felt my appearance resembled Grün's description of Marx: 'an unkempt fanatic unable to support his family'. Yet emotionally I felt I was fighting for the right outcome for our son. Of course, his secret wish – like all children of divorce – was that his parents would get back together and build a happy unit again. Since this was unlikely, we had to find a third way. The major thing was that I had never really imagined Cass and I would split – that, like my parents, we would figure it out somehow. I hadn't made contingency plans for this outcome, and I knew whatever expedient we hit upon would be bad for Ed. Only adults from broken homes themselves are prepared for this: they know what a lifetime of Christmases with alternating parents feels like. And when he got older, what then for him? Live six months of the year with each of us? No, Cass would never sanction that. Now he had grown out of the zoo, once I was back home, contact would dwindle to nothing until he began to think of another man as 'Dad', a scenario that brought me out in an icy sweat.

At the bottom of the boulevard Raspail – a road that Hemingway found boring to drive down but not to walk along – I stopped to rest my legs. The sun was back on my forehead again, and I was grateful for it. I felt suddenly light-headed, perspiration darkening the shirt under my arms. Ahead of me was the expansive place Denfert-Rochereau, with its defiant lion on a pedestal at its centre. Its old name – or that of the street that funnelled into it – was the rue d'Enfer. The fact of this caused me to smile for a moment. I felt I'd arrived at the correct destination. What had drawn me here I had no idea. The need to erase Cass's manipulations from my mind, most probably, before I got down to some serious work.

Setting off again on the west side of the square, I thought about what lay beneath my feet. The underworld kingdom of the catacombs. Those other streets of femurs and skulls, engineered by Guillaumot to prevent the Latin Quarter sinking into cavities opened up by mining the city's foundations for gypsum, limestone and clay. In the 1770s, a quarter-mile stretch of the rue d'Enfer had literally vanished into a gaping chasm. It was apt that the old Street of Hell, only renamed in 1879, should eventually be filled with the dead. A ghoulish pandemonium hidden beneath the bright boulevards. And a masterstroke of subterranean architecture: if the galleries ran in a straight line they would form a continuous stretch that would reach the Massif Central. There were 200 miles of morbidity threading under the City of Light. My father and I had walked them, at my insistence, on every visit to Paris. At the time I couldn't get enough of the gruesome tunnels, the ceiling-high walls of bones and skulls. The fact that all these relics had once belonged to men, women and children who had been as alive as me was what held the fascination. Also, the fact that Paris – so beautiful on the surface – had something hollow and rotten beneath it. Now, of course, I had no urge to make another visit. Paris still saw ten sinkholes appear every year, and a few people had died, but nothing like the abyss that had opened up under the place Denfert-Rochereau.

Arrested again on the street, remembering I had work to do, I sent up a quick prayer (to whom I wasn't sure), to always be kept above ground, and never be dragged below. To always remain in the light.

Twenty minutes later, sitting at a green iron table outside the Luxembourg's brasserie La Buvette des Marionnettes, my laptop open in the bucolic shade, I tried to be light-hearted about the morning's events. Let Cass have her way, damn her! The writing was on the wall as far as taking on the multinational was concerned. Any legal case would have to go on hold for the time being. I'd rather my money went to my son than into the silk pockets of some Chancery Lane big shot. The irony was that any eventual settlement might have provided big money for 'our' child. I'd entertained dreams of a modest trust fund, a nest egg. But then he had Gramps, as Cass pointed out. The old boy had probably left Ed half of West Virginia in his will. As I stirred a cube of brown sugar into my *express*, waiting for my panini *mozzarella tomates* (it was now more lunchtime than breakfast), I was aware my urge to help

Ed financially was all part of wanting to count for something in his future, in a practical sense. Perhaps it was for the best I abandoned my litigious plans. I would always count. I was his father, though Cass would rather I disappeared from the picture and just deposit money in her bank account every month.

And maybe part of my fear of Cass resurrecting her love life post-divorce was down to the fact that mine was pretty much a busted flush. And not entirely out of choice. The urology-related problem I mentioned – the one that led to the adverse reaction and a lifetime of affliction – was the delicate matter of abdominal pain, which sometimes extended to the old equipment – the testicles, to be blunt. Dr Decker had originally thought I might have kidney stones, then changed the diagnosis to an infection that could be cleared up with a powerful antibiotic. For obvious reasons, I began to refer to this as my 'Balzac', a term which was lost on my urologist, but not on Larry. When I consulted him about it, he seemed to find my plight semi-amusing. He couldn't stop asking me to list symptoms, or the many restrictions it might put on a man's love life. It was only after the fluoroquinolone disaster that the jokes stopped. It was true, I told him, there's no greater passion-killer than what felt, on occasions, like a constant kick in the balls (something a sufferer on an online forum likened it to, and a sentence I wish I'd never read). At the time, I even thought it was all highly ironic myself. I was forty, just separated from Cass, and single. There's never a good time to experience acute testicular pain, but encountering it on your release from a ten-year relationship when you find yourself a free agent once more, and inclined to do something about it, is pretty bad. I soon found out what a pain in the balls freedom could be.

A further irony was that, while Dr Decker's pill damaged me for life, I still have the original affliction, in various states of intensity. Like the neuropathy, there are good days and bad days. The result is that I'm pretty much out of the action. At first, this was both a terror and a relief – like the lifting of a lifelong imperative or injunction; that of pursuing the opposite sex. I was no longer chained to an idiot, to use Kingsley Amis's splendid phrase. It felt oddly freeing not to be razzed by lustful thoughts all day, as most men are, even the imams and clergymen. Especially them. Since my divorce, my sole romantic encounter had been with a woman who worked for my first publishers – one of the secretaries. Kath, a blonde *voluptueuse*. We had originally got it together in the nineties, before I met my wife. We had both been in our late twenties, and had pursued the kind of passionate, sex-based affair that you can only have at that age. I had tired of brilliant women, and just wanted one who, like Kath, would dress up in stockings and heels, and beg to be taken on all fours on the carpets of the many hotel rooms we booked into. Terrible, I agree. The hotels had been her idea, to heighten the sense of illicit pleasure, though there was nothing forbidden about our liaisons. Kath eventually fell in love with me, something she revealed just around the time I exchanged glances with Cass over the flutes of tepid UCL champagne, so I had to end it abruptly. Ten years later, when she heard about my divorce, she came after me. She had booked a room in an exclusive

City hotel, and, though shy at first, both of us of a different vintage, it took no time at all to slip into the old routine. It was almost as if she had waited out a decade to get me back in that room for a night of ardour – and it certainly was arduous, on old Balzac. I had explained my delicate problem to her over cocktails in the bar downstairs, but she wasn't going to let anything stand in our way. She said she would be gentle with me, a state I had almost forgotten could exist between adults, what with my acrimonious divorce proceedings. There was something sad and moving about contemplating beginning our affair again. The poignancy of two people not as young as they used to be, meeting to recreate past glories, was very intense. It showed in our every gesture; in every familiar touch of her warm fingers to my arm, or the way I tentatively brushed her breasts under her lambswool sweater in the bright lift on the way up. It was like relearning a language neither of us had ever really forgotten. I can't have acquitted myself that badly, as afterwards, to flatter me, Kath had murmured, 'That was... tantric,' referring to how long I had lasted. Yes, it had surprised me too. With dawn light showing, she suggested that maybe we were destined to always meet like this, for the rest of our lives, whoever we ended up with. It was a shattering thing to say – her childless and nearing the end of her fertility; me a divorcee with a son I wasn't sure, at the time, I would ever see again. And both of us single, with no intention of starting anything serious with the other. Unable to reply, staring at the bed, I imagined the torrid sheets resembled the wreckage of both our lives. Telling her I would think it over, I kissed her for the last time before saying goodbye. And then the real pain set in, of the physical type. Staggering to move my car from its bay before the restrictions kicked in at 8 a.m., I felt as if I'd just walked from Aberdeen to Brighton, but not on my feet.

'Monsieur...'

A female voice was at my elbow, setting down the hot, neatly halved panini. It belonged to a waitress in a uniform of white shirt, black tights and a pinny, which, I couldn't help but notice, was sleek to her skirt. Above her, the leaves of the planes murmured in the silence. She was smiling into my face, a sweep of gamine hair around her eyes. I vaguely registered she was about nineteen, very pretty. Feeling I should engage with reality again, I said: 'Ah, *merci beaucoup... et un autre café, s'il vous plaît.*'

'*Bien sûr. Un express?*'

'*Oui.*'

She smiled again, as only a young woman can smile at an older man alone at a café table, and slunk away.

I watched her walk off under the dappled, impressionist's bower that shaded the green tables from the rest of the sunlit Jardin. Well, she was something... And there it was. The old seal-bark of male lust! I was twice her age, at least, but the need to observe the sway of her bottom as it disappeared under the trees must have been hardwired into the system. Though the last five years had felt like a long, silent threnody for my old body – the healthy body – there was life in the old mutt yet. Prior to the antibiotic, I'd never spent a night in hospital, or had an adverse reaction to anything (often confused with 'allergic', I was to discover). I had always been in tip-top health, and sexually active, apart from a few lost years after university. Maybe I wasn't for the scrapheap just yet. I could still admire the goods in the window, though I winced at how Cass might react to me using such a phrase.

Glancing at the introduction to *Elysian Fields* on the laptop screen, cracking my knuckles in readiness to plunge in, I took a bite of the steaming sandwich followed by a sip of cold coffee. I had to begin once more at the beginning – throw away what I'd written. I also reached for another of La Rochefoucauld's trusty maxims. If I remembered correctly, it stated that whatever life gives us – or hurls at us – we are never as fortunate or unfortunate as we suppose.

Late June brought a breakthrough for Larry and his great quest. It was the day of the Levines' cocktail party, and he called me on my mobile to tell me, with high excitement, that his mother had made a discovery. While clearing out the loft of the Harrow-on-the-Hill house they had never moved from, she had unearthed a cache of letters tied with a pale pink ribbon, much disintegrated. These had been sent by our grandmother whenever she found herself travelling around the world with Grandpa on his pharmaceutical business trips. In a touching show of old-world courtesy, he would always insist Lotte come along for the ride, though he was engaged in business for most of the day. Lotte, most probably bored senseless in a series of European cities, would write home – and not just a postcard, but long rambling missives in a blue ink that had now turned an autumnal brown. These, Larry exclaimed, might hold the 'key'. I had been in the Serpente library at the time his call came through, and had foolishly picked up, thinking my phone was on silent. His voice had been so loud, a number of students had thrown castigating looks my way. Without replying, I had heard Larry out, then told him in a whisper that we would discuss it all later at the Place des Vosges.

Getting ready for the evening, I recalled Larry had this crazy theory that Daisy Buchanan from *The Great Gatsby* was in fact Jewish. Fitzgerald had apparently fully intended this, and it was obvious to an attentive reader from certain clues early on in the narrative. I remember him explaining it to me one day: 'Okay, firstly, Daisy was drawn to good old Jay Gatz – almost certainly a Jew before his metamorphosis. Why was she drawn? Fitzgerald doesn't explain, but it's certainly not his money. Secondly, there's a line in the first chapter that's always tripped me up. During that first dinner on the "rosy-coloured porch", hulking husband Tom is advocating the ludicrous racist book, *The Rise of the Coloured Race*. He goes around the table propounding: "After all, we're all Nordics," until he comes to Daisy. Now, here's where it gets interesting. And here I quote...' He had the book with him at the time. '"After an infinitesimal hesitation he" – that's Tom – "included Daisy with a slight nod." At this she winks at our narrator Nick... Proof positive, my friend! There in deathless prose. Daisy ain't no *Nordic*!' I told him it was an interesting theory, but that he might find it hard persuading the American academic establishment of his 'find'.

And now, with these letters, I felt my cousin was clutching at similar straws.

In the Levines' drawing room, packed with important-looking people, many of whom were former UMP ministers and their opposites in Hollande's cabinet, along with *gros bonnets* from the world of international fashion, Larry cornered me near the open balcony doors, portals that didn't seem to be allowing any air whatsoever into the calescent room. Dressed for the first time in a loose blue suit, he was in superabundant mode; an ecstatic look on his face, as if he were high, or the channel for religious feeling. This might have been down to the fact we were both drinking from flutes of the best champagne either of us had ever savoured, but I knew it was the excitement over his discovery that had charged him to full voltage.

'They're mind-blowing in their detail, Nick. There's stuff I never knew...'

'Have you read all of them yet?'

I was genuinely interested, though keeping the sceptical mask in place. Behind his back, Rivka was moving among her guests with her crocodile smile, ensuring everyone was topped up with Bollinger before the cocktails could commence. Further off stood Ariel with her unmistakable father, along with two young women in gowns, eagerly talking over each other while the daughter listened. Whenever Ariel interjected I could hear her low voice from across the room – it cut through confidently.

'No, not all of them,' blinked Larry. 'Only the ones with a Vienna postmark. Those seemed the most important.'

'When do they date back to?'

My cousin took a generous sip of champagne, a smile emerging from the corners of his mouth. 'The nineteen-fifties. Nearly all of them are from then.'

'She would've been in her forties... Where were our

mothers in all this? Surely they didn't go with her on these trips.'

Larry shook his head, very fast. 'No, no, no. They were with our grandfather's folks. They held the fort back home. And anyway, some of these jaunts were very short. A couple of days here and there, but enough to get her out of London.'

'So... did they turn up anything other than a travelogue?'

'Certainly! In Vienna, right, there were people I'd never heard of... Like her brother.'

My interest piqued, I said, 'Really? I didn't know she had one.'

'Neither did I until now.'

'That would make him our great-uncle. My mother never mentioned him.'

'And get this,' Larry continued almost proudly. 'She *hated* him. Absolutely detested him. Otto Berg was his name. A pompous old bureaucrat. And her nieces too. Ottilie und Elise. A couple of harpies in the making, according to her.'

'Well, I never...'

Thinking of Lotte's opinion of her family made me recall her with a sudden intensity. The twinkle of sedition she always kept in her eyes; her incredible vivacity and outspokenness, in contrast to our serene grandfather. I could picture her in their house in Eastcote, talking rapidly, wearing the black cashmere polo necks she favoured towards the end, on which always sat a big brooch or pendant. These held me fascinated – big pearls or amulets that might have contained Lilliputian letters or locks of hair. It was hard to stare at them for long, sitting, as they did, on the prow of her formidable bosom.

'The nieces might – just might – be still alive.'

'They'd be the same age as our mothers.'

'Well, I'm definitely paying them a visit.'

'With Ariel?'

'Of course. She's never been to Vienna.'

'That's odd,' I mused, the champagne easing my knees with the steady hand of a masseuse. 'People her age have been everywhere twice.'

'Now *you're* sounding like an old fart.'

I glanced over to see Ariel steering her father and the two young women our way. Once they had turned around, I recognised them as Ana and Delphine, transformed by their daring dresses. They had shown up very late on the night outside Chez Omar's, helping to defuse the situation somewhat. Despite not wanting to encourage Larry, I felt I needed to question him further.

'Still, it's strange Ottilie and Elise didn't come up in the records. You made a thorough search, as I recall. Are you sure they weren't there? You must have looked at the family tree of every Viennese family from the eighteen-nineties onwards.'

'Perhaps. Census reports could've been destroyed. After the Anschluss, the war, everything was chaos... This is the peril of relying on My Heritage dot-com.'

'Stranger still that Lotte didn't mention them. These relatives she despised. She couldn't resist a good gripe and a gossip, if you remember.'

Larry gave me a pained look. He didn't remember. And that was part of the problem. He was flailing in the dark, with people whose faces and histories were shrouded in a similar blackness. All he had was the radar of his intuition – his pressing intimations.

There was to be no more discussion of Lotte's letters as Ariel, her two friends and her father were upon us. After elaborate greetings – and a decision to speak in English for Larry's benefit – I began to agree with my cousin about François. He was quite the enigma. Taller than expected in close-up, he literally towered over us; not drinking, his hands clasped behind his pole-straight back, occasionally making a princely gesture. He was vain, certainly, but displayed impeccable manners. He had just returned, so he informed me casually, from meeting Hollande's current first lady, Julie Gayet, in the 'Madame Wing' of the Élysée Palace. Perhaps this visit had flushed him with a special sense of courtesy, though his airs seemed to come naturally to him. While the girls babbled and I questioned him further about his party's recent change of name and the Assemblée nationale, I too felt overwhelmed by his *citron* cologne. Larry had called it maddeningly familiar, and only when he turned away did I realise our grandfather had worn a similar type of lemon aftershave. Less expensive, naturally.

A tray passed with more champagne, from which everyone but François took a fresh glass, and I turned to engage Ariel's two friends. Feeling warmly on my way to becoming quite drunk, I became aware that Larry was showing off to Ana, and that Ariel was giving him her censorious look. I had learned on the previous occasion that Ana was studying philosophy and literature at the Sorbonne (French, English and German literature – if only our universities offered the same!), and that

Delphine was reading politics and economics. Neither of Ariel's friends were doing anything so frivolous as modelling, though they both could, by the looks of it. Ana, with her dark feather cut, shorter than Delphine, was slightly Spanish in appearance, while Delphine more resembled the way Kath might have looked at twenty, blonde and blossoming. Both were striking in their evening gowns, like a couple of thoroughbred racehorses allowed in to graze under the Louis Quatorze ceilings. While everyone listened as Larry explained the workings of the brain, I noticed Ana and Delphine had both opted for the fashionable tattoo – Ana's was on her ankle, a butterfly, just above her finely turned left Achilles; Delphine's a thin band of Maori tribal patterning across her right shoulder. As always with beautiful women, I involuntarily imagined them as old ladies, with the devastation of the years on their faces. I knew you were supposed to picture them with no clothes on first, but maybe this compulsion was a way of neutralising the over-manning, commandeering power of their looks. And how insouciant they were about it all, too. Old François must have become blind to having such divine creatures drifting along his palatial corridors, oblivious to their gorgeousness. His daughter was also dressed to kill, in a black pencil skirt that accentuated her behind to near masterpiece level. Perfection of this kind could only be found in Bernini or Raphael, I decided, as I drained another flute.

'The human brain is the most complicated system in the known universe...' Larry was saying, while Ana nodded with rapt attention.

'Not mine!' giggled Delphine, causing even François to lift a smile.

'No, seriously. It contains one hundred billion neurons.' And here Larry pointed at me. 'Even his...'

This gave the effervescent girls a chance to laugh again, at my expense.

'And here's the thing...' he continued. 'Even that number is exceeded by the number of cortical connections. There are perhaps a hundred trillion connections in every brain. We're only beginning to unravel the mysteries of consciousness. The human genome might get us there eventually—'

'I read your essay,' interjected Ana brightly. '*Sur le même sujet.*'

'Ah, in the *BMJ*?'

'No. On your website.'

'Yes, I read it too,' advanced Ariel, in her lowest of low tones.

Despite herself, I could tell she was enjoying the gentle flirtation between her man and one of her best friends. She was showing him off – just as she had shown off Rube, though with much less success in my cousin's case. The suit had transformed Larry, giving him sudden authority. As I said, most of the time he looked like the telephone repairman. And Rube had always been super-impressive to Ariel's friends, all of whom were rich and spoilt – he had been the dude who DJed in all the coolest clubs.

'Ah, I'd forgotten I'd posted it there.'

Delphine, who in my deluded state of tipsiness I felt had been eyeing me appraisingly, suddenly offered: 'But why does that make us so special? Surely other animals have *plein de connections*? The higher primates.'

'You would think so. But only in humans is the SRGAP2 gene duplicated four times – the other apes have it, but we have three more copies of it. And this all has a profound effect on the connectivity of the neurons… we're much more joined up as a species. By forty or fifty per cent. We stand apart.'

'We certainly do,' offered François, unexpectedly.

Larry was especially on form tonight. I had forgotten about his website – a forum where he posted his most controversial papers, opening up the comments thread to intense debate from around the world. Of course, the Big Pharma corporations had tried to silence him – first attempting to buy him off, then planting bogus responses in the comments by hired hacks. A popular tactic. The Wikipedia pages of the same companies and their products were similarly policed to keep them free from dissent. Go to the official page for most fluoroquinolones and you would think they were wonder drugs that had never harmed anyone in their short existence. Larry was a compulsive user of the internet and social media, while I favoured the dusty library. From the start he'd been into Facebook and Twitter. I was staggered to see he had sent over 20,000 tweets since joining up and had three times that number of votaries. And it wasn't all self-promotional waffle either – it was whistle-blowing on one corporate scam after another.

'So you're not just extracting sunbeams from cucumbers at the Institut?' I put in, the drink talking.

Larry chose to ignore me, his audience still giving him their full attention. 'The human brain is an amazingly evolved system. A meat-computer. The big mystery is the interface between the mechanical brain and the instrument that has given us the greatest works of the human imagination.'

'*C'est magnifique*,' gasped Ana.

'I wish I had stayed with science...' Delphine lamented. The canapés were passing, exquisite vol-au-vents bearing caviar and prawns, and we both eyed them eagerly.

'However,' I began, 'I have to take you up on the term "meat-computer".'

'Why? It's quite commonplace in the neuroscientific community.'

Larry had often used the phrase in our private conversations – usually when discussing how the brains of Einstein or Hawking had evolved – but I found it unsettling in the extreme, especially when thinking of the soul and the higher achievements of man.

'It's just such a depressing way of thinking about human life.'

'I agree,' said Ariel.

'Not at all,' admonished her father with gentle authority. 'We must deal with the world as it is, not as we would desire it to be.' This was delivered with a grave finality that silenced us all for a moment. There was a sense of readiness, acuity, decorum, maybe even paranoia about François. I could see he had a lawyer's poise, but also an unassailably patrician manner. I smiled to myself at the thought of Larry's forthcoming tête-à-tête lunch. He would need his pith helmet for that.

Feeling hungry, I looked about the room for the *amuse-bouches*, but they had gone. More people had arrived, the guests seemingly grander the later they showed. Unlike the living room where Rivka had first received us, this space was undeniably opulent, or maybe the guests in their black tie and gowns had conferred this, I wasn't sure.

'I am glad there are people like you engaged with scientific reality,' fawned Ana. '*Moi*? I just read Goethe and Proust all day.'

'Exactly,' Larry said, with renewed emphasis. 'I feel it's of great importance. It's all about connectivity in the end. New breakthroughs are being made all the time. It's a vital area of research.'

I pondered the notion that Larry's life had been a quest for connectivity, for hidden designs within and between nerve systems and cells. It shouldn't have fazed me that he was looking for a hidden pattern in our past. And I wasn't surprised he was showing off tonight in front of Ariel's dazzled friends. When we were younger – when Larry was seventeen and I was a postgrad in my early twenties – my cousin had always wanted to engage me in lofty conversation. Unsurprising at that age. The more advanced the better. Spinozan ethics and how they applied to science; the theories of Comte, Proudhon, Hegel, Raisson, Bergson; deconstructionist blind alleys courtesy of Lacan and Foucault. Even now, I felt we were never far away from such discussions. It pleased us both to talk at this high level, though when I was a young man it had irked and embarrassed me to engage with a teenager on big ideas.

'And what about you?' enquired Delphine, touching a forefinger to my arm.

'Me?' I said, startled. 'I'm not involved in anything groundbreaking. Just a book on the Revolution.'.

'Another book,' smirked Larry.

'Ahh,' said Delphine, her face alight. 'How far are you with it?'

'Not that far, I'm afraid. Like Larry, I'm still trying to make connections. Why history keeps producing conditions that foment sedition. Paine was big on this.'

'Go on,' Delphine smiled.

'Well, contrary to popular opinion, he was against the whole idea of 1789, of Desmoulins and his green ribbons. His big thing was to address the underlying social conditions that produce revolutions in the first place, so we never had to endure one again. He was all for an egalitarian society. I'm trying to link this to contemporary events and thinkers. The sons of Paine, if you like.'

'Ah, it sounds terrific.'

'Thank you. I just need to dig a little deeper.'

Delphine was curling a lock of blonde hair around her finger, her face flushed – as mine was, most probably, from the champagne. Despite the flattery of such interest from so young a woman, the last five years of ill health had always made me feel like Hemingway's mutely impotent Jake Barnes. In love, but unable to do much about it.

'If you'll excuse me,' said François, with an almost imperceptible bow, leaving us to talk to other, more distinguished guests.

'Well…' said Larry. 'I think it's cocktail time.'

Everyone agreed instantly to this suggestion, and we made our way over to the makeshift bar.

As I watched François' retreating back, my eyes were drawn

to two framed prints at the far end of the room. Both were in heavy gilt surrounds. It was only as I focused on the one on the right that I realised who it was by. It was a Chagall. There in all their glory were the unmistakable electric mauves, rich papal purples, sweet yellows; broadcasting their power into the summer night. Not a depiction of lovers, but a *shtetl* scene, with a fiddler and a dancing donkey. A reminder, perhaps, to Rivka at least, of just how far they'd come.

As I continued to stare, it took a couple of seconds more to realise it wasn't a reproduction, but an original.

THREE

And now, in Paris, the city was under its summer cosh. The weight of heat impeding people in the simplest of tasks. Just the suffocating humidity stopped the mind from functioning at any worthwhile level. June had melted into July, which had become a truculent and torrid August, and I found myself alone among the deserted streets and restaurants while Larry went off on his adventures with Ariel. A number of things had happened before he disappeared that had revised my opinion of him, and his great quest for proof of a Jewish identity. Just before he left for the subcontinent, he called late at night, very anxious. He was worried about many matters, it transpired – about the prospect of spending so much time alone with Ariel; about her father's increasingly inimical behaviour; about his faltering research into what he imagined was our Ashkenazi heritage. His voice had echoed in one of the Levines' cavernous guest bedrooms when he first came on the line. After five minutes, I knew I was in for the long haul, and went to sit in my favourite chair. This being near the open balcony doors, it had the advantage of cooling me down, the curtains open to the soft sticky night.

'You know, I'll always associate Ariel with Gershwin's *Rhapsody in Blue*. She used to play it all the time after we first met. That spiralling clarinet at the start! That's *her*, man.'

'What's your point, Larry?' I asked, good-naturedly stifling a yawn. 'It is very late.'

'My point is that I don't want that special romantic buzz to end. We're going to be together for six solid weeks. I've never spent so long with a woman. I've always travelled alone…'

'Well, maybe now's the time to start. You can be free and with someone too. It's one of those balancing acts. Like patting your head and rubbing your stomach at the same time. You just need to find a talent for it.'

Larry might not have been a melancholic, but he had the workaholic's unawareness of how he shut out nearly everyone emotionally – something that was just beginning to unsettle Ariel. At twenty, she wanted hot emotion from a man, especially one of Larry's age, who should have been walking over blazing coals every day to win her afresh. It was part of my cousin's exterior charm to be the long-legged fly on the stream, to be mentally up there with the skyscrapers, but it had probably impacted badly on his relationships.

'I'm trying. I might have to get a manual. You know, one of those self-help guides for emotional illiterates. How to survive a holiday with your girlfriend.'

'No such book exists.'

'You know, only last week I felt the age gap between us for the first time. Usually she's more mature than most forty-year-olds I know, but she told me something that made me change my mind. She admitted she'd never had her heart broken.'

'Lucky her.'

'No. I really think if you haven't experienced that, you haven't lived. You're not fully adult. You know nothing about human, erm, pain, or human... vulnerability.'

These concepts were difficult for Larry, I could tell. I wasn't sure he had ever had *his* heart broken. I decided to divert him from the subject, but fell at the first hurdle.

'So, she's only broken hearts herself?'

'Probably.'

'Like Rube's.'

We both knew what I was about to say: *Make sure she doesn't break yours*, but I managed to stop myself in time. The last thing he needed from me was more *conseil paternel*.

'Anyway,' Larry said directly. 'That's not the real reason for calling. I wanted to tell you about my lunch *avec* François.'

'It's happened?'

'Yes. We met yesterday.'

Despite being in almost daily contact, there was much about my cousin I didn't know. He moved through the city inconspicuously, and practised lies of omission, both of which I have never been able to master myself. Though it was way past midnight, I was intrigued to hear more.

'He took me to the Lapérouse.'

'Really? I've never been. Walked past many times, but always preferred to continue along the river.'

'Amazing place. Thank God we went at lunchtime, though. An evening table might have felt like a lovers' rendezvous.'

The Lapérouse was a Parisian institution dating from the 1760s. A wedge-shaped bistro on the quai des Grands-Augustins, it used to be notorious for its *salons privés*;

intimate, velvet-lined dining rooms, which used to lock from the inside. For a while it was famous as a clandestine spot for French ministers and their mistresses, and François had undoubtedly taken Solange there for its celebrated chateaubriand glazed with port. But I was intrigued as to why he took the man dating his daughter there, out of all the classy diners in the city.

'You had a room to yourself?'

'Yeah. Astonishing red velvet chaises longues and the original floorboards from before the Revolution. And a great view of the pont Neuf.'

'He must have wanted a very private chat.'

This was the only rationale I could find – perhaps he hadn't wanted to broadcast his family's involvement with a controversial English pharmacologist. After all, François was a public figure, recognised everywhere, especially with his height and perpendicular bearing, his profile like the sail of a catamaran.

'I wasn't complaining, Nick, I can tell you! It was fabulous. He ordered a Saint-Véran *blanc* straight away. Then a bottle of Château Grand Barrail, or something crazily expensive when the main course arrived.'

'What did you eat? Just as well you were his guest. Out of the Institut's staff, there can't be anyone who dines better. No one gets further from that abysmal canteen than you.'

'He went for the rabbit, soaked in so much lavender it smelt like a *parfumerie*. I played safe and had *le steak* Lapérouse.'

'So why the big occasion?' I asked, the curtains stirring, sending a delightful breeze across my brow. I had sweated so much during the day I felt I had lost a litre of water from my body.

'I wasn't sure at first. He asked me to name my favourite *philosophe*. As if this was the kind of talk two men could only have away from the womenfolk.'

'You're kidding?'

'No. I told him Comte. With Slavoj Žižek as a second choice.'

'I bet that went down a bomb.'

I had been dealing with Comte much in my research. In the days before Larry left Paris, I had switched to the Sainte-Geneviève university library on the place du Panthéon, as its iron-framed reading room was cooler than the Serpente. Comte's positivism had been something I was trying to connect with Paine; how it tried to remedy the social malaise of the Revolution, calling for a new paradigm based on the teleology of science. His three stages of social evolution, quaint-sounding now – even irresponsible, post-Marx – were somehow very attractive. That the search for truth had to advance from the theological to the metaphysical, to a positive outcome based on rationality, was something I was eager to explore in the new book. His letters to Mill were absorbing me for hours at a time.

'And then he asked whether I loved his daughter.'

'He *did*?'

This was startling. So old François had to take Larry for a fancy lunch before he could talk about matters of the heart. As if his Place des Vosges extravaganza didn't have enough rooms.

'Yes, he did. It threw me off course for a moment. Half the time I was trying not to be dazzled by his intensity, his public manner, his knowledge of French political manoeuvring — about which I know next to nothing. And then he flings me this curve.'

'What did you answer?'

'I said yes, of course!' Larry's roaring laugh echoed down the line from just under a kilometre away over the Seine. I wasn't sure some of it didn't come in through the open balcony doors.

Once he had quietened down, Larry said: 'I think only a French father could ask something like that, don't you? Straight out with it. They still believe in love as a viable concept, as a driving force, as a game-changer.'

'Absolutely,' I ventured, thinking of literature instead. 'It runs like a rod of jade through everything. Hugo, Dumas, Zola. The French nationalised love. They demonstrated how it can stand in defiance of tyrants, or revolutions. Whereas the English just turn love into a personal dilemma, or a sordid mental crisis... How did he react, by the way?'

'He didn't. He just kept on with his *lapin*. Just assimilated it without a flinch.'

'That may be dangerous.'

'Why would it be dangerous?' Larry asked, a quiver of outrage in his voice.

'Don't know yet. Did you sense hostility?'

'Perhaps...'

'Where did the conversation turn after that?'

'He kept on saying, "I'm interested in you La-wraance, *very* interested." Like he had me under surveillance, or something.'

'He most certainly is. What then?'

'I just rambled about Ariel, and all the places I wanted to show her in the world. I think he's glad I'm taking her off his hands. They go to the Loire every summer.'

'Maybe that was his secret purpose. He wanted to check out your breeding, your etiquette in ritzy surroundings. To see if you were fit to be seen at his big pile in the country.'

'Well,' my cousin said, with a strange sigh, 'I do live with them already. If he doesn't know that about me yet...'

I felt Larry was withholding something; that he was building up to a big reveal. I could just picture the two of them, on the creaking chairs with the sumptuous décor. The supercilious former advocate and Sarkozyste; and my yabbering cousin, tearing into his steak, giving away too many secrets of the heart. The waiting staff probably thinking it was a business lunch. Which, in a way, it was.

'You know what,' began Larry again. 'It suddenly clicked over dessert who he reminded me of.'

'Yeah? What did you have for pudding by the way?'

'*Pudding*? You can't call it that!'

'I know. I apologise.' The quaint English word had just slipped out.

'The *tarte au citron* for him, believe it or not,' Larry chuckled. 'And *rien* for me. Ariel's started to make comments about my weight.'

'You were telling me...'

'Oh yes, François and who he resembles. Of all people – my own father. It's uncanny. Perhaps it's the height, the reserve. I only just figured it out. Whenever I'm with François, I become a kid again. He has that diminishing quality, as if one's whole life project of scientific enquiry is infantile or adolescent. With Dad it was money, with François it's politics. *Real-world* stuff, they imply, with their steady gaze. Not messing about in labs with chemistry sets.'

'Maybe it's his affair that made you think of Colin.'

I always referred to Larry's father by his Christian name, never 'uncle', for some reason.

'I hadn't thought of that,' Larry said, ruminatively.

A decade ago, Colin Frost had been exposed as an adulterer when the female junior partner in his accountancy firm had arrived at the door of their Northolt home and asked Beverley if she had five minutes to speak. There, over instant coffee in the newly fitted kitchen, this woman (who went by the name of Georgia Swallow), admitted that she and Beverley's dependable husband had conducted an affair for the last twenty years. Georgia had started to cry, and, as so often in these situations, Beverley had instantly forgiven her usurper and formed a sisterly solidarity that would aim its considerable armoury against the errant male. The Frosts' marriage had barely survived the nuclear fallout. Luckily, Larry had been in the Antipodes at the time, but had fielded many furious calls from Beverley, asking him what they should do; whether he minded if his parents separated, or whether she had his father castrated with the help of the high-street butcher. Larry, uncharacteristically mature, had argued that since they had got this far, they might as well see out their golden years together. And if this minx Georgia (she was actually known as The

Minx for a while) was repentant, had in fact stopped seeing his dad and was now firm friends with her, so much the better. Plus, he liked to know his childhood bedroom would still be there when he came back from his travels. Colin – the darkest of dark horses, as I have already suggested – never spoke about the matter with my cousin, though the defeated look of the exposed criminal was always manifest on his face when I encountered him subsequently.

'So,' I began, clearing my throat, 'in Freudian terms, when it comes to Ariel, you're sleeping with the sister you never had.'

Larry didn't laugh at this. He was conflicted enough already, I knew, from the very fact of their near twenty-year age difference, though he pretended otherwise.

Instead, he became serious. 'No, I was thinking more in terms of why I feel filial towards François. He's really nothing like my dad. But do I actually want to be his son? Do I need to feel like I'm part of his clan? That's what's been troubling me...'

It was true, I was starting to believe, that Larry wanted above all things now in his late thirties to know a sense of belonging. To not just be some freewheelin' citizen of the world. He secretly wanted, in the words of Bassani, 'the inevitable quick glance of Jewish complicity' when he met a stranger from the same tribe. Until recently, he had still been hot for starting the conversion process to Judaism, until he found out it might necessitate a certain operation.

'Not the identity stuff again, Larry... It has got very late.'

Ambivalent myself towards the very idea of forging an identity around national or cultural or racial borders, my months in Paris had had the inevitable effect of sparking a reluctant interest. Maybe there was something in it after all. My combat with Cass had sent my thinking in this direction. What was my own identity based on now, apart from my job? Being a parent, yes. But what did it mean if you have children but never get to do any parenting, like me and Nadir? Are you still a parent? Or just one of the world's millions of absent fathers? Those ghost men. And then the notion of the tribe. What did it mean to find in your forties that you didn't belong to one? If you had no fierce sense of belonging or allegiance – unlike the Sikhs, the Scots, the Arabs, the Jews – who are you, exactly?

'It's not something that's just going to go away, Nick.'

'Granted, but the tribe François and Rivka really belong to is the rich. Can you really categorise the Levines as observant? To me as an outsider, being Jewish doesn't seem that important to them.'

'Oh, it is!' Larry protested, the last word echoing off the walls of his room. 'It's central to their sense of themselves. This is what I've been driving at – it's where they find their confidence. They know who they are, in world-historical terms. They also know who they are in terms of what they eat, and who they eat with; who they go out with, and who they marry. It's not about being observant or not. It's deeper than that. And it's especially relevant now they feel under attack in their own city once more. In January, the Grand Synagogue was closed on Shabbat for the first time in seventy years – since the Nazis were here! I mean, who *are* we, Nick? Who are we really?'

My cousin was sounding desperate now, and I wiped a droplet of sweat that had been hanging like a dewdrop from my upper lip.

'I'm too tired to get into this one now… And anyhow,' I said, abruptly remembering, 'you told me François had the rabbit. That's not a kosher animal, is it?'

Larry lightened up. 'There's much that isn't kosher chez Levine. But that doesn't mean their Jewishness isn't all-important to them. Okay, they only show up at synagogue on Yom Kippur, but the old boy keeps twenty handsomely bound volumes of the Babylonian Talmud in his library.'

'And Ariel? I can't believe she spends her nights trawling through those.'

'She's still finding her way, admittedly. She was bat mitzvahed at twelve, went to a kibbutz between ditching Rube and the Sorbonne. But she has all the time in the world to explore her Jewish identity. I mean, she feels more French than Jewish, understandably. After the Hyper Cacher attack, she was outraged when some Jews took to the streets to sing 'Hatikvah'. She was one of those singing 'La Marseillaise'. And again at the solidarity rally on the Sunday. You should have seen her in front of the TV when Netanyahu said come to Israel! As if it's any safer there. It's demeaning to the diaspora.'

'What about Rivka?'

'Well,' began Larry, warming to his subject, 'she's the most observant of them all, I suppose. Whenever she passes the synagogue now she sees armed guards. They're on first-name terms. She said she was afraid of them at first, but has come to like them. She feels suddenly looked after by the

Republic, whereas before she felt alone. An alien, even...
You know, she treasures this old dish they used to use for the
Passover Seder – it's practically all she took from the Ukraine,
apparently. Along with a beautifully illustrated Haggadah and
this exquisite Russian samovar. She's always telling me about
her happy childhood memories of the rituals; the four cups of
wine, or the apple dipped in honey they had at Rosh Hashanah.
And all the old dishes: the beetroot soup, the buckwheat kasha,
the blinis and knishes, and these sour-cream dough cakes. Just
the names are magical: *pierogi* and *pirozhki* and *baranki*! I'm
always asking her to introduce me to more Jewish food.'

'What does she say?'

'"You're in Paris! Enjoy what's here. You're in a gastronomic
paradise..." But then one day she relented and cooked me this
traditional dish. Nick – it was terrific. And strangely familiar –
like coming home. I don't believe Jung's collective unconscious
and all that claptrap, but it was like I'd been waiting my whole
life to taste it again. A *krupnik*. A mushroom and barley soup,
made with a mutton bone; gefilte fish on the side, and these
intriguing little matzo balls...'

'Okay. What about the Sabbath?'

Larry paused. 'True, they're not blessing the bread and
wine every Friday night, or praying at the synagogue every
Saturday morning. But then they lead these incredibly busy
lives. I've never met two more social animals than Ariel's
parents.'

There was a lull, where I became aware of the street sounds
from outside. The revving of a *vélomoteur*. Café shutters being
rattled down. The insistent bark of an outraged dog.

'Like I said, they're not substantial people, Larry. On one level, they're very superficial – Ariel excepted.'

It was hard to know how carefully to tread here. On the one hand, I loved my cousin and wanted to protect him. On the other, I wasn't about to give him a lesson in perspicacity when it came to his girlfriend's folks.

'Take the Kabbalah—'

At this I groaned. Larry had revealed the previous month that he had been 'reading into it'.

'No, it's vital to understand its importance. There has to be a reason for these persistent intimations – these clues, threads, noises in the night, so to speak. If the Kabbalah attempts to bring the mysteries of creation into – how would you phrase it – *closer proximity* to man's own experience, then it might hold the key. I seriously need to get to the bottom of the big questions here. If I am Jewish, what does it mean to be part of a people the world has seemed intent on wiping out for six thousand years? Does it mean anything, except on the interior? Granted, the Levines' sense of themselves has more to do with wealth and status, although, as I said, Ariel is the tabula rasa case in this instance. She's forming her identity, like wax newly imprinted day by day. Until recently, to be a Jew to most of her generation meant nothing more than getting insulted on the rue des Écouffes every other morning—'

At this, I interrupted: 'So it's more to do with anti-Semitism than anything in the Kabbalah? Maybe all this intuiting of ethnicity just appeals to your sense of empathy for a persecuted people.'

'Which could be seen as a Jewish trait, too. But yes, I've been doing a lot of thinking about that as well. I mean, who decided they had *no right to live*? When was it decided, man…?'

Through the open balcony doors I could see the monolithic Montparnasse tower, implacable in the black night. Flies too, had made their way into the living room, and I knew it was time to wind things up.

'Let's talk again, Larry,' I said, knowing we might not have the chance before he left.

'Certainly…' he answered, with a barely audible sigh of regret.

The next day, I walked to Au Chai de l'Abbaye, a favourite quiet café on the rue de Buci, to think things over.

I also wanted to visit La Hune bookstore, in Saint-Germain-des-Prés, to track down a new collection of essays on Saint-Domingue's revolution of 1791. It had received great reviews, and I felt I needed to read it for my book, the waters of which had properly broken a few weeks back. I'd heard some of the monographs argued that when a sense of national unity began to dissipate in Paris, concepts of *liberté, égalité et fraternité* were actually more relevant to the slaves in France's most prosperous colony. It seemed like vital stuff.

As I made my way there, the sluggish streets struck me as very melancholy, like a city after lockdown, or curfew. Like how Paris might have looked under occupation, in fact, during the intolerable summer of 1940. I'd had an unsettling dream after my talk with Larry in which people from the past had turned up unwontedly in the bars of the Quarter. I was still trying to throw it off as I traversed the dusty cobblestones of the squares. Now that all the *boulevardiers* and families had disappeared to the seaside, only mad dogs and tourists were abroad. And with it being too hot to descend into the Métro, I submitted to the punishing walk. Even Hemingway's haunts, Les Deux Magots, the Café de Flore and the Brasserie Lipp, with their empty wicker chairs on the pavement, looked sadly derelict. The site of the Flore, at the intersection of the rue de Rennes and the boulevard Saint-Germain, had once been the coolest *carrefour* in the universe. Now only irascible waiters ran back and forth, serving the sporadic customers, trying to appear busy.

At an exterior table of Au Chai de l'Abbaye, on the quiet rue de Bourbon-le-Château side, overheated (frustrated, but also highly impressed, that La Hune had sold out of my book, forcing me to order it), I mused on what my cousin had said. Why was Larry transferring his antipathy towards his own father onto François? I could see how François' sinuous social ease, coupled with his cold haughtiness, had unsettled Larry. Sartre's psychoanalyst told him the effect of never having known his father was to have no superego. He had never been taught obedience. My problem, I felt, was the opposite – I sensed the intervention of the superego all too often. Unlike with Larry and Colin, my father was never someone I felt I had to rebel against. Although we were not as close as we once were, there was a certain respect and understanding there, so rare to find, as I see now with my male acquaintances. It's almost as if my dad and I shared a consciousness. He had turned up in the dream too, riffling through the books on the *quais* – not unusual, as many of my memories of him concern the two of us in the city. My mother had been absent. One thing Larry and I were in agreement over was the fact that our mothers, having had their twenties coincide with the golden 1960s, were two of the luckiest people still alive. Though they didn't seem to think so. Unless you lived in a mews flat in Chelsea, they insisted, the sixties largely happened on television. Elsewhere, in other words. For most of the country it was 'the nineteen-fifties as usual,' to use Aunt Beverley's glum phrase.

But what of Larry's sudden efflorescence of feeling? I was trying to see things through his eyes – he was at the centre of his life, after all, just as I was in mine. I raked the memory vaults for something in his past that might have led him to his Semitic infatuation. He had always been an obsessive, that much was true. Like many doctors, my cousin was once a big smoker. Maybe with such daily proximity to death, medics needed to bait the Grim Reaper, or mock him – while most people keep thoughts of extinction at a great distance. And Larry had been an obsessive smoker, like a junkie fretting about his score. Yet one day he just quit. I remember meeting him outside the Institute of Neurology on Queen Square. Usually he would have been puffing away anxiously, but this time he was greedily eating sweets. And not M&Ms, but a brown paper bag of sticky candies, like the ones from childhood. Larry had thrown all his cigarettes away that morning and visited the sweetie shop. A quick glance in his jacket pockets revealed they were rammed with similar bags. Cola cubes, pear drops, liquorice allsorts. This was even more strange, as we were about to have lunch. 'Won't they spoil your appetite?' I had asked, meekly. 'I don't fucking care!' he had shouted, scattering the pigeons from under a bench. His cold turkey certainly intensified his thunderous temper for a while, and eventually his sweets addiction was mastered. But his obsessive, monothematic tendencies went further back. They had been cultivated in childhood. He had been a distant, withdrawn boy at first; constantly reading in his room, or building Airfix models. And then something just flipped at age seven or eight – he became a wild, tearing presence. A pain in the neck, though I didn't pay much attention, as I had still been a teenager myself at the time. Intensely precocious at maths, physics, chemistry – interested in everything – he had turned his bedroom into a makeshift lab. With Grandad Edward's chemistry set bubbling away, he became a mad inventor, conducting scientific experiments until the smell of sulphur caused his mother to throw away all his test tubes while he was at school. But even this sabotage didn't faze him – he was on to something else. Only when he discovered music did his enthusiasms start to interest me. He was forever asking me to bring him vinyl when we visited Eastcote. But very quickly he ditched the British composers such as Britten and Foulds that I had put him on to and took up with Dylan. Some of his flamboyant attractiveness was definitely formed around then. He didn't just like Dylan, collecting every album and bootleg he could lay his hands on – he wanted to *be* Dylan; to be the hip gringo standing in the dusty Central American doorway on the cover of *Street Legal*. Many of his faults were apparent by then – he was intensely competitive, preoccupied, unaware, innocent. But unlike me, for some reason, by seventeen he was also capable of inspiring love, respect, even awe.

Larry had been inclined to melodrama, but never triviality. In his conception, only the important matters were worthy of connection or address. His own name, for instance. Born Lawrence Michael Frost, he had started calling himself Larry at around ten after hearing the abbreviation on an American cop show. *Miami Vice*, most probably, given that it was 1987. His parents never went for it, and still call him Lawrence even now. But Larry hated his full name; positively cringed when he heard it; ran from what he perceived to be its pomposity, its archaic flavour. Of course, once he got the Jewish bee in his beanie, his early decision became prophetic. He proudly claimed that Lawrence, or Larry, was originally borne by Jews for whom it was an Americanised form of similar-sounding Ashkenazi surnames. The fact that it derived, I informed him, from the Old French *Lorens* didn't deter him from thinking this to be a proleptic coup. It was a sign from Yahweh himself, not evidence that his very Aryan old man had a great-grandfather with the name Lawrence.

But in many ways, Larry – like Gatsby – was his own creation. He had a Platonic conception of himself, to which he had to remain faithful. His three heroes, Saul, Woody and Bob were also self-constructed in some way. All three had changed their names – Saul beginning as Solomon Bellows, Woody as Allan Konigsberg, and Bob as Robert Zimmerman. The one fact that kept Larry's conviction alive was that he was genuinely drawn to all three before he knew – or cared – that they were Jewish. For him, he just felt a connection, an aesthetic excitement. These were artists of the last century, working at the highest level, in the newest media. Film was only a hundred years old, but Woody had effortlessly assimilated everyone from Chaplin to the Marx Brothers to Fellini to form a new comic shorthand on celluloid. The best films, such as *Hannah and her Sisters*, would remain a record of how we lived and loved back then, in Greenwich Village or the Upper East Side, just as Ibsen and Chekhov revealed so much about the same preoccupations in nineteenth-century Oslo or St Petersburg. Dylan, of course, was the academic's singer of choice, and Larry could talk for hours about the great man's relation to Emerson or his Whitmanesque ideas of personal freedom – or the rich, end-time vulnerability of his comeback *Time Out of Mind*. And once he found Bellow, the heavens just opened. He divided the world into people who loved Bellow's fiction and those who didn't get him: 'It's an infallible test of character,' he announced. He was always telling me how the girl in Mexico City who disliked his hero – but nevertheless had an adobe full of Bellow's books – was somehow small of soul; fusty even: 'As if she hadn't been circulated in the outside air enough... she was dingy on the interior.' If there was one thing Bellow wasn't it was fusty – and Larry had done his fair share of circulation in the air of different continents in his wide-roaming thirties. He could even recite whole paragraphs of *Humboldt's Gift*, something that might not have improved his love life, I went on to tell him, as gently as I could.

At the circular table of Au Chai de l'Abbaye, I took a quick glance around me. It was almost too hot for consecutive thought. The red-gold wicker chair had stuck the shirt to my back. The café was beginning to draw its scanty lunchtime traffic, and I gave up on the idea of attracting the waiter for another *crème*. He was standing some way up the quiet side street, using his phone. Yes, Larry was his own creation, and he needed to go back now and find out who he really was. To rip it all up and start again. He was the opposite of what the French call *bien dans sa peau*: happy in his own skin. I was well aware that, while I had problems, Larry underwent *crises*. And there was nothing I could do but help him through them, one after another.

Gathering my thoughts, the sweat of midday nearly intolerable, I considered returning to the cool white interior of La Hune. On the main road, the purple shadow of the shops made me think of visiting a church; the nearby Église Saint-Sulpice, perhaps. However, that's where all the Americans would be hiding. Throwing down a couple of fifty-centime pieces (I still couldn't use the term 'euro cents'), I decided to trek back to the fifth and seek out L'Église Saint-Étienne-du-Mont. I had been meaning to go for some time – for reasons that were obscure to me – and it would certainly be quieter than the grandiose arches of Sulpice, as salving as they might be for my temperature.

As I began the long walk back – along the six-laned highway of the plane-dappled boulevard Saint-Germain – I thought about how forgiving Larry was of the Levines when it came to their wealth. To him they were like the Rothschilds or the Camondos of the 1870s: philanthropic entrepreneurs. The former family was the Paris wing of a dynasty that had started off in the Frankfurt ghetto. Once established in the capital, they had set about transforming France into an industrial superpower, building the Gare du Nord and developing the railways. The Levines of the nineteenth century had been industrialists too, and, like the Rothschilds, who had lived in a palatial pile on the rue de Monceau, kept a place on the rue de Rivoli, educating their children in the exclusive Lycée Louis-le-Grand in the fifth. This tradition had extended to François himself, though he had chosen law and politics, rather than business. The old Levines had seen France as a country where Jews could forge ahead, and do much good. Only after the Prussian victory did nationalism narrow to anti-Semitism. There was a financial crisis, which the country blamed on the Jews. Back then, the average Frenchman saw the Jewish people as a race who stuck together and supported each other, rather than the economies in which they worked. To them, Jews were all bankers, with secret affinities under their hats. One of the bestsellers of the decade had been *La France Juive* – Jewish France – and it had contributed to *l'affaire* and the rest. Yet the Levines had seen out this storm relatively unscathed. In the eyes of most of the country they were now viewed as part of France's magnificent heritage. In the twenty-first century, the threat very definitely came from radical Islamism, not a few Jewish plutocrats keen on expanding the economy for the glory of the Gallic people.

Turning off onto the rue de la Montagne-Sainte-Geneviève, a precipitous gradient perfect for time travel, I felt the temperature decrease by a couple of degrees centigrade. The narrow ascending street took me up past the deserted rue Mouffetard, providing, at last, some welcome shade. From here I could see the spire of the church, which always gave the Étienne-du-Mont an asymmetrical look from the front, and I followed this landmark up the hill. I wanted to commune with the souls of Pascal and Racine, both of whom had their tombs there. It was also where Rastignac paid for the desolate funeral of Goriot before they carted the old man off to Père-Lachaise, leaving him to view Paris from its elevation, exclaiming bitterly, 'It's between the two of us now!'

The tall spire was calling me on, though my ankles and calves were urging me to stop and rest. Perhaps I merely needed to take the hand of deep history once more; to escape the shallow trough of modernity.

Once inside the church, the marvellous air-con provided by the medieval stone cleared my head in seconds. The tall, perpendicular ceiling of the nave, with its tier of gothic windows, took me up into its clean white heaven. I felt as if I could think straight for the first time in weeks. I walked reverently along the aisle, noting the bowed crowns of a few faithful women; grave, entirely in black. Nuns most probably. For five minutes I wandered aimlessly, then, under the *coupole* of the Chapelle de la Vierge, a semicircular vault behind the altar reserved for prayer, I took a seat and looked up. It was a wonderful sight. The simple stained glass in the pointed arches, or ogees, transformed the fierce sunshine outside into cool shafts of crimson and blue. To the left I noticed the stone plaque commemorating Racine, with its partner plaque on the right – a brazen slot for entering your €1 piece. It had been years since I'd sat here, and I wondered why I didn't pay it a visit every week now I was resident for a year. The tall windows in their perfect dome had the effect of steadying me within, calming the motion of the soul. Hugo, whose own tomb was not far away in the Panthéon, linked these gothic architectural points with his humanist philosophy. For him, they were congruent with humanity's ascent from the gutter of poverty and crime to a state of grace and enlightenment. Unsure whether this was a tenuous connection too far, I decided the pristine light of the dome's eyes – gentling the cold stone pietà beneath it – at least had the effect of sharpening my thinking. Everything was clear now. Larry was right about one matter: the Levines certainly knew who they were. Whether this was a good thing or not, I wasn't yet sure. Maybe a little uncertainty was necessary to propel one through life. To be too convinced of one's place in the world might invite complacency. At any rate, Larry needed to go to Vienna with Lotte's letters and find out where he belonged in the universe. And soon – before he had a nervous breakdown.

I did in fact get to see my cousin again after we talked. A few days later, on the Friday before he and Ariel left on their travels, Rube had his art show opening at the Yvon Lambert gallery in the *sixième*, and we all went along to check it out. This prestigious location was actually very close to the café Au Chai de L'Abbaye where I had endured the heat of the deserted city. I mention this outing, because a certain thing Larry admitted to there has since gained in significance.

It was a febrile night in late July, and luckily the building's wintry white exterior, which admitted us under a nineteenth-century ironwork awning still containing its original glass, was as frigid inside. It took about an hour, walking the air-conditioned rooms with Larry and Ariel, flown with the complimentary *vin rouge*, before we were granted an audience with the show's star artist. In the end, we decided to take our time; examining and discussing the exhibits. And very strange and compelling they were too. I knew Rube integrated African colour and street art into his electronic installations, but these had a Richterian simplicity and directness. A gaunt minimalism I hadn't anticipated. Giant screens behind mysterious gauze hangings projected the same images over and over. Some were accompanied by loops of music, no doubt concocted by Rube in his home studio. These were mainly bursts of ironic distorted calypso, or what I imagined to be sluggish dub or trance. The big screens were hard to see, as groups of fast-chattering, ultra-hip *intellos précaires* in skinny jeans had monopolised the clean white floor space. A couple of passing poseurs in gold lamé shirts and handlebar moustaches had actually caused Larry to laugh out loud, until Ariel quelled him with a finger to his ribs. And she looked incredible, as usual, though dressed more conservatively for the evening – all in *noir*; sheer black tights and calf-length dress, a diamante clutch bag; her hair up in a delectable chignon.

While my cousin and his squeeze patrolled the aviary of the gallery, I employed the viewing method that had worked at the many London exhibitions I had attended in my twenties, ravenous to dig deeper into European history and its art. Instead of trying to take in everything, the trick was to spend time with a single picture or sculpture. Twenty minutes if necessary. This often had the effect of opening up the whole show; the key to its secrets. I tried this in one of the more deserted rooms.

There, on the floor in the corner, dwarfed by the space, sat one of those eighties ghetto blasters that boasted every knob and function, many of which were probably superfluous. At its centre was a mini TV screen (which had been fashionable for about five minutes, until people realised you couldn't see the ball during a Wimbledon final), on which glowed the same footage running on the larger panels in the other rooms. It featured a woman's face, a black African face, emerging from flickering darkness; very stern, though modulating until the faintest slope of a smile appeared on her lips and in her eyes, before returning into the gloom again. This had been playing everywhere on a loop, and it made me ruminate on how micro-incremental human expressions were. Leonardo knew this, of course, but we were exposed to hundreds of them – and were tasked with reading them – every day. No wonder we were all, as a species, exhausted. The point of Rube's exhibition, if it had one, was maybe its injunction to stop attempting to read the expressions and minds of everyone you meet, and just concentrate on one. A loved one, perhaps. To slow right down. Despite my scepticism over much modern art, I found myself unexpectedly moved by this face; emerging, disappearing, then re-emerging with her ebony features, until being dragged back into the darkness.

I had been expecting Rube to be morose, as a number of posters for his show (featuring the same mahogany female visage) had been disgracefully defaced with racist graffiti the week before. But when Larry and I finally cornered him in the main gallery, he was in fine spirits. Dressed in a loose red T-shirt under a black suit jacket, his robust hands stained with putty or clay, sipping from a full glass of Château Barreyres, he had shed his slightly solemn persona for the evening. His joy at having the whole exhibition to himself showed in his fluttering eloquent eyelashes as he talked. It was only after a moment that I realised the two fawning blondes at his elbow were not curators or galleristas, but the art world's equivalent of groupies. Fortunately, Ariel (who might have taken a dim view) had chosen that moment to talk to the Yvon Lambert's august patrons, and we hoped they would detain her for some considerable time. These men were both friends of her father's, and they stood like two parentheses around the black exclamation mark of Ariel's figure at the far end of the room.

'You guys okay for wine?'

Rube seemed suddenly taller before us; his forehead higher and nobler; the faint line of a 'tache on his upper lip, trimmed in a fastidious arc.

'I'm good,' I replied, both of us having taken a third glass from a passing silver tray a moment before.

'I love all this, Rube,' began Larry, expansively, his hands outstretched, 'I just wish I understood what it all meant.'

'You're not going to ask an artist to explain his art, now, are you?' I nudged my cousin.

'I don't mind,' shrugged Rube, 'I have been doing it all night. But only to people who want to buy.' And he smiled, showing us the teeth of different sizes. Tonight, Rube was towering, handsome, elated; at the very peak of his brilliance or capability.

'You're out of my price bracket, man!' cried Larry. He was being the warmest I'd seen him with Ariel's ex – perhaps due to a combination of booze and the fact that the two of them rarely got to speak together. The three of us felt immediately like a good combination. Larry was wearing what appeared to be an approximation of a Hawaiian or Florida short-sleeved shirt, mango-coloured, and vented to the third button. His impressive chest, with its central pelt of hair, had confronted the Parisian art elite at every turn, like an accusation. He had even garnered the glances of a couple of Saint-Germain-des-Prés hipsters, unsure as to whether Larry's get-up was the new look, to be slavishly copied at the next opening.

'You must be immensely proud,' I interjected, hoping it wasn't a patronising observation.

As we were talking, the two girls – bird-like things with platinum hair and PVC jeans – turned to each other and began chattering very fast in French. I was glad of their retreat, and leaned forward the better to hear what Rube had to say.

'This is my dream, guys,' said Rube, shaking his head slightly, as if in disbelief. 'You don't know how hard I've worked to get here. *Et voilà – maintenant*, they come after me. And not the other way round.'

They, as we all knew, were the French art establishment. Not quite welcomed yet into the upper echelons, like a Steve McQueen or a Chris Ofili, Rube was getting there. He had stormed the barricades, using the art mafia's bourgeois fascination with street *tagueurs* as a tool of entry. There was a great light of vindication in his glassy eyes: a sense of triumph that a black man could go – in a resistant, rebarbative society – from a two-bed tower-block flat in the twentieth to the sleekest of galleries in the sixth. It radiated from his fiery, emancipated brow. He had long held no truck with the notion that poor beginnings kept you back or turned you bad, and had scorned the media apologists who claimed as much for the *Charlie Hebdo* killers.

'Have you sold anything?' Larry enquired, suitably impressed.

'Almost all of it! I am surprised. And relieved, *c'est sûr.*'

My cousin whistled. As with 'man', only Larry could get away with this corny reaction. It was true, there was money for art again in the new economies of Europe, where for a decade it had been the Chinese and Americans sucking up everything in sight. Russian oligarchs were investing in young, emerging artists once more, and Rube had had his eye on a couple of shadowy patrons patrolling the spaces. I'd heard back in London that these money-bandits from the Urals went for only four things, which had acquired an apt acronym: SWAG. Silver, wine, art, and gold. There was even a pleasing hierarchy in this order, although Larry and I would undoubtedly have placed art at its zenith. Rube's vigilant eyes understood all this well, and he looked for these men over Larry's shoulder while we talked.

'Have you said hello to Ariel yet?' asked Larry.

'Ariel?' Rube replied, as if surprised to hear her name. 'No. I don't think she likes me tonight.'

'Whatever gives you that impression?'

Rube shrugged. 'Maybe *mes deux amies,*' he said, gesturing to the chirruping girls. 'I do not know. Or care.'

A certain fierceness entered Rube's expression and left as quickly as it arrived, to be replaced for a moment by his default-state moroseness.

'What is it about women,' ventured Larry, fishing for some male solidarity, 'that they give you the push, and yet still want to exercise all their rights of possession? Pure irrationality.'

Rube nodded in a way that suggested he both agreed and disagreed. 'She's young, *c'est tout*.'

'You can't just ascribe it to that,' my cousin persisted, 'it's an infallible rule. Across the board, regardless of age.'

I turned to Larry, and was dismayed to see he was employing his grimacing smile, as if he'd just been hit by a spike of neuralgia. 'So you're saying every woman who's been out with you has regretted giving you the push afterwards? Has wanted you back?'

'Well, most of them might have regretted going out with me,' he laughed, his shirt collar trembling. 'And not all of them gave me the push.' Here he fixed Rube with his deep-set eyes. 'You're still very protective of Ariel, I see.'

'I was her first boyfriend, so yes. Of course.'

We all knew this wasn't strictly true. Like most ex-Bobos from wealthy families, she had been drawn to the seamier side of life from a young age. Larry had told me Ariel had lost her virginity at fourteen, and that by sixteen she was seeing an Italian promoter, a certain Mario Gigliotti. The great Mario, a man whose name, according to my cousin 'even sounded like a hard-on', loomed large in the pantheon of his imagined love rivals. Even though Ariel only went out with Mario for a month, this stud was someone he felt to be in active competition with, probably nightly, in the bedrooms of the Place des Vosges. Ariel had let slip that Mario Gigliotti could keep it up for hours on end without Viagra, and this had penetrated deep into Larry's psyche. He even suggested that he'd like to run some tests on Mario, to see if there wasn't anything science could learn from the unique way his nerves and blood vessels were configured. I advised Larry that Mario being a full decade younger than him probably had much to do with it, and to cease any further mention of him. The one thing a woman doesn't want is to see her current partner writhing on the hook of envy. Larry, being an *ingénu* or a novice at long-term relationships, even at his age, would have to learn this. The dicks of lovers past figured big in his mind – much bigger than in Ariel's, most probably. I remember one day asking him what it meant to be well read in the twenty-first century, and he replied that he'd rather be well hung than well read. I told him the ideal, of course, would be to be both. But he insisted the animal advantages were more important in terms of human survival.

'Can I ask you a question?'

'*Bien sûr.*'

I girded myself within for what Larry was about to say. He was hungry for all sorts of knowledge now he had got Rube alone. Across the room, I caught sight of Ariel giving the three of us the briefest of glances. Even from that distance, I could make out the hot molasses pools of her eyes, accusatory in that pert French fashion; eyes perhaps too big for the petite oval of her face. Undoubtedly, she knew we were talking about her.

'Are you still in love with her?'

At this, I felt a sense of panic.

Luckily, Rube found Larry's vulnerability touching. He showed us his teeth again, laughing loud, shaking his head in a loose gyration.

'I'm serious,' my cousin continued. 'She won't tell me. But you can. You must. We're all guys here together, I mean... I have to know.'

'I am her friend!' exclaimed Rube, his greatly sympathetic face alive with animation, with extended human warmth. 'We had a good time together and then she moved on. Now we are buddies, *compris?*'

'That's all I need to know,' fired back Larry, although I knew he wanted much more.

'Why are you so uptight, man?' demanded Rube, with genuine concern. 'She loves you – *elle t'adore*, as your Beatles sang. Enjoy it! Bask in its glow.'

Larry smiled uncertainly. 'I've got five weeks to do that. She's very hard to get through to – she finds it hard to open up. She's like this shell that won't open.'

'I know. *Je m'en souviens!*' agreed Rube. 'Her nickname at school was *Devine* Levine, because nobody knew what she was thinking.' And for the first time I felt the invisible handshake of mutuality between them. They had both been through the vicissitudes of dating a beauty; a woman all of Paris would have sold relatives for; a demanding cynosure of male desire. It came at a price, as they both knew. Even when stalking the flea markets of the Puces de Montreuil in the *vingtième*, Larry had told me Ariel had been propositioned three times by the vagabondish stallholders, 'Men not fit to shine the windscreen of her Citroën.'

'I suppose I just had to ask. It's the first time I've been in love myself.'

I reacted to this by swaying back on my heels, and clearing

my throat. This was news to me – he had never made such a frank admission. I knew he had been serious about a whole host of women in the past, but the knowledge that he had waited until the grand old age of thirty-seven to give his heart was a revelation. Before things became too candidly Californian, I said: 'Only in Paris could you admit to that, Larry. It's the spirit of the capital, osmosing into you. Doing its time-honoured work.'

'No, I'm serious, man.' There was a childlike look of appeal across his open face. He was whirling the index finger of his right hand, looking for the right words – words that wouldn't embarrass us all further. But one look at Rube's steady grin told me he wasn't embarrassed. He was full of swift admiration.

'Larry, I'm happy you are with Ariel. I'm happy for you both. I know you think otherwise. *Elle est jeune, c'est tout.* She needs a teacher like you to show her the world.'

My cousin's chest expanded. 'Thank you.'

But Rube hadn't finished. He wasn't going to get too sappy, not just yet anyway. 'And I know you are trying to belong with her people – to fit in. But maybe it is not such a good idea…'

'No, no,' protested Larry. 'It's not like that.'

'She has her people, you have yours. When I dated Ariel, she did not try and fit into black culture like all the other white girls I went out with. She was her own person.'

'Of course, don't I know it! But you have to understand – I fell for her before I knew she was part of any particular culture. I mean, I had no idea her father was from this prestigious French family. I had no idea she was even Jewish.'

I felt myself wanting to defend my cousin, but kept silent.

'You cannot *become* Jewish, any more than Nick can become black.'

'I know that very well, Rube,' said Larry, glancing at me, the smile reappearing on his face.

At this absurd notion, a détente appeared to spring up between the two of them. For myself, I was still reeling from Larry's admission. An instance of what I believe is currently known as 'oversharing'. I knew, of course, that he and Ariel were much in love, but not that Larry was a virgin when it came to such emotions. He had left it so late! Admittedly, I'd never asked him, but it only reinforced how the closest to us are like locked medieval books of hours. Their intricately illustrated pages remain pressed shut, facing one another; their secrets safe for years. Perhaps because I'd been through the mill of love, I imagined everyone else had too. Balzac rightly said true love resembled childhood, in its prodigality and its tears. Thinking of this, it struck me that the hill overlooking Père-Lachaise must have been the old master's favourite in Paris, as it was also where Lucien in *Lost Illusions*, after the death of his teenage actress lover, laments, 'Who will love me?' It was a question I had turned over recently, during my sweating nights on the balcony: whether I would ever fall in love again. This is always our panic; why we stick it out with unsuitable people. Love is one of the few things in life that can't be coerced, contrived or planned for. You either get lucky or you don't. As true for the mud-spattered heroes of the nineteenth-century novel as it is for their counterparts in the technology-crazed twenty-first century.

At that moment, Ariel appeared in our orbit, causing Larry to come volleying forth in greeting, his hands in motion. Only before he had a chance to speak, she stopped his mouth with a big ostentatious kiss. I checked Rube's reaction to this – a genuine smile – and knew all would be okay.

'*Messieurs*,' she exclaimed in her subterranean tones, bending forward to receive the gentle visit of Rube's lips to both her cheeks.

Larry was still speechless, and it didn't seem to bother him that the love of his life went and put her arm around the star of the show. After all, she was doing it as much for the loitering blondes as for Larry.

'What do you think?' Rube demanded.

'*Magnifique*,' she answered immediately. 'I am so proud of you.'

With her hair up, Ariel's face had lost a lot of its immobility, and I noted the stirring dark hairs at her nape, stray and somehow precious. It was only when you saw a human close-up (and it was a while since I'd seen a woman other than Mme George in such close proximity) that you realised how delicate and defenceless human life was. At such moments, I always thought inadvertently of the diggers at Auschwitz and their tumbling human cargo; the bodies still of infinite value, despite their desecration. Just the notion that each individual had once been loved by another fellow human sealed them with some kind of permanence in the universe. There were things evil could never eradicate.

'I adore the big screens,' advanced Larry, not even the slightest bit envious now, it seemed, of Ariel's arm around Rube's waist.

'Yes, Papa's friends think they are the best thing they have had all year.'

'They said that?' asked Rube, his eyes straining wide.

A blast of ska, which had been coming forth periodically from the installation next to us, relayed a snatch of a chorus. The words sounded very much like 'the bitterness of life is causing us strife', but I could have been wrong.

'*Oui, ils sont très heureux*. It is such a shame about the posters.'

'*Bof*.' Rube shook his head. 'They can do what they want to them, as long as they do not touch the art itself. Or me...'

The defiled posters for Rube's show were a subject I hoped wouldn't come up. I had only seen a single advert for the Yvon Lambert – on the rue Pierre-et-Marie-Curie – and had almost missed it among a run of adverts for a new Monoprix. Thankfully unadulterated, it showed the same ancient African face that appeared in the installations. Passing rapidly on the way to the Sainte-Geneviève library, it had taken a split second to connect the name Rubens Xavier to Rube. Larry had told me earlier that it was posters further out in the *vingtième* that had received swastikas, and other unforgivable slurs in illiterate French.

'*Certainement*,' insisted Ariel. 'But I have asked my father to get Franck to raise it with Les Républicains.'

'Ah, *ma chérie*,' said Rube, forgetting Larry was standing next to him. 'He doesn't have to do that.'

'Who is Franck?' I asked.

'Franck Riester. The Mayor of Coulommiers,' interjected my cousin, answering for Ariel. 'When a mosque in his district was defaced a couple of years ago he made a big campaign for it. Condemned it in the strongest terms.'

'What happened?'

'No one listened, as usual,' said Ariel, deploying her best sangfroid.

'I mean, what happened to the mosque?'

'They left a pig's head outside it, and covered it in swastikas. The building hadn't even been finished.'

'That's awful.'

'Franck came over, didn't he?' said Larry.

'*Oui*,' Ariel replied, with her scarlet pout. 'It's a shame you weren't there that night. He and Papa stayed up all night, how you say – *hatching* plans. They are militantly against such rubbish.'

As indeed François would be, I thought, knowing how even before the Hyper Cacher siege, France's recent surge in far-right nationalists had targeted his community too. Especially high-profile Jews. A vague memory of a kidnapped businessman from a few years back presented itself. But before I had the chance to bring it up, Rube broke free of Ariel.

'*Mes amis*,' he started grandly, throwing up his hands, reclaiming some of his earlier bonhomie. 'Let us not talk of such shit tonight!'

At this we all laughed, especially Larry, who, I imagined, might one day become good friends with Rube if he allowed himself.

'And now,' announced the artist, 'if you will excuse me, I am going to sniff down some Russian dollars.'

'Do such things exist?' asked Ariel.

'I will make them exist,' and he kissed his old girlfriend goodbye.

To our surprise, Rube came forward to Larry and me, and embraced us both in turn. We received the full Gallic farewell. Catching his cinnamon scent, strangely enjoying the warmth of his muscular arms, I found his gesture very moving.

'*À tout à l'heure!*'

And then he was gone.

At the end of the summer, Larry returned, full of his customary tales, his face and chest like golden oak; untraumatised by being in Ariel's company for so long. Quite the opposite: he was gentler, more open to ideas; big with travel confidence. His exceptional gifts were even more apparent. It was quite a surprise to see him again. I had become used to his absence. I, meanwhile, had stayed in the oven of the city and made much headway with the book. Europe was having a hot summer everywhere, the type it gets every ten years. Even a couple of years back, many had died in the August heatwave. Then the world had been in uproar over Syria. The regime there had used chemical weapons on its own citizens, and Hollande alone among the Western leaders was backing America in a possible military intervention. The American vice president had even gone so far as to call France its 'oldest ally', a queasy volte-face after the insults regarding cheese and surrendering monkeys from a decade before. But I was able to work, despite the heat, and missing Ed too. There had even been a couple of afternoons of sweet rain that had redefined the *douceur de vivre* for me – like tasting the very best, the most succulent meat of the lobster. Life had suddenly appeared superabundant again.

With *Elysian Fields*, I had gone back, after my breakthrough in La Buvette des Marionnettes, to the fundamental questions. Why do societies precipitate revolutions – more pertinently, why do certain factions within them see them as panaceas, when history teaches us the opposite? I had returned to the writings of the *moralistes*, the unique French tradition of thinkers from Montaigne through to Camus – men, in the words of the late, great Tony Judt, with no pejorative nuance in their writing. It was only with *J'Accuse* that the political intellectual was born. I felt privileged to be able to savour the ideas of these men – like enjoying the complex notes of a Margaux at a series of wine tastings – rather than doing hack work over the summer, like many of my colleagues back in London. With successful publication comes certain advantages. For the last few years I'd managed to avoid the commitments of the professional historian that drain time from actual research and writing: the conferences, the professional associations, the reviewing, the endless terms of teaching. I was also able, at last, to charge through many contemporary works that had been weighing heavy by my bedside. It seems I've always had an insatiable capacity for accumulating knowledge, much of it without any utilitarian value. I'd often wondered why Louis XVI, incarcerated in the Temple, read up to twelve books a week despite the certainty that his head was about to roll. What was he trying to prove? It was only on the morning of his execution, when Cléry helped him to dress and offered to brush his hair, that he said, sadly, 'No, it's not worthwhile.' I recall being struck by this utterance as a boy, when immersing myself in all things French. I see now that it's at the core of why being a historian appealed to me. The revelation of how great men and women acquit themselves at crucial junctures in a nation's progress is of much importance. This is what we look for. It instructs us about life and how to live it – or at least how to die well. Many monarchs, or would-be rulers, were surprisingly graceful moments before getting the chop: Charles I and Mary Queen of Scots for two. They behaved as we would want mortals who felt they were divinely anointed to behave. Many of the stories have the ring of truth, too, not of apocryphal fables. At moments of high symbolic value – the execution of a king – the human details are what linger, not the brutal, but apt, report that Louis' neck was so fat it took more than one go for the guillotine to sunder his head from his body. It's the king's quiet outrage at having his hands pointlessly bound before he took the scaffold ('What are you doing?' he is alleged to have protested) that lingers. Also his final magnanimous words, which were to be cut short by the sound of drummers and cries of '*vive la République*': 'I forgive those who are guilty of my death, and I pray to God that the blood you are about to shed may never be required of France…'

As a boy, too, it was the bewildering factions of Revolutionary France in the 1790s that held me spellbound. The Girondists, the Jacobins, the Enragés, the Fédérés, the Montagnards, the Feuillants, and (a taxonomy which always, to a history-hungry twelve-year-old, sounded like a race of space invaders) the Thermidorians. Yet, after a couple of decades spent among these strange breeds, I had come to think their distinctions and their struggles didn't matter so much. It was what individual acts meant in the long perspective that engaged me now. Making sense of it in the twenty-first century was the job. As Zhou Enlai said wittily of the Revolution's significance after almost 200 years: *It's too soon to tell*. This comment, I felt, summed up the challenge facing the modern historian. When, with world events ever-evolving – with the Middle East grappling with the aftermath of its own series of revolutions, and the spread of Islamic State – was it ever soon enough to tell?

To explore all this further, I began an email correspondence with a Sorbonne professor (safely at a distance in his holiday home in Nantes), Pierre Serma, who asserted that the Revolution should simply be seen as an anti-colonial struggle, one of a series, from the sixteenth-century rebellion against Spanish rule to the post-war independence movements of the twentieth century. I concurred with much of his thinking, and wanted to take his stance a step further in my book, and make a link to the twentieth-century 'colonialism' of money – of globalisation, and the dominance of the banks and the transnational corporations. All our coming revolutions, I posited, would be directed against fiscal misdemeanours, something Professor Serma thought worthy of pursuing (though I got the feeling he would rather be at the beach with his family than discussing the link between the global financial crash and the roots of social unrest). I put it to him, grandly, that my book might conclude by linking the English riots of 2011 and the Parisian riots of 2005 with the uprising of 1789. All, I insisted, were closer in cause than you might think. All were sparked by economic and social disenfranchisement. In this sense, it was astonishing the Revolution didn't explode a century earlier, during the Grand Siècle. The London riots were condemned as an ugly shopping spree, a materialist orgy, with nothing political attaching – but look at when they occurred, I urged Professor Serma: in August, when the ancient regime of public schoolboys Cameron, Clegg and Mayor Boris were sunning themselves in Barbadian hideaways. They had left the denizens of the inner cities to eat their metaphorical cake, and had paid the price. It was a line of thought I was eager to pursue, and had received the thumbs-up from my new editor in London. Professor Serma, it had to be said, was yet to reply to my last email.

During the final weekend of the month, in the dog days, I caught up with Larry and Ariel for lunch at the chaotically busy Chez Hanna, a falafel joint in the Marais. The restaurant – with a frontage open to the deep, narrow street, painted a fire-engine red, with an enticing takeaway counter at the far end – was where Ariel came to meet her Israeli friends, many of whom she had met at a kibbutz. We were seated at the back of the tiny dining room, in the cool, watched by globular evil-eye pendants; the two of them babbling about travel. They were thin and very brown; happy, full of energy. Larry, especially, had lost much weight. Whether this was from stress over the Levines or conscious dieting it was hard to tell. *Très mince*, as the French say.

During a lull in their talk, it struck me not only how little I knew about Ariel's daily life, but how little I knew of those around me. Self-involvement; terminal, most probably, at my age, but I decided on making it a project to rectify the situation.

'Your life is admirably compartmentalised,' I suggested, as Ariel bit down on her aubergine and chickpea pitta. 'I never see you at the Sorbonne. Where else would you recommend around here?'

Ariel put a hand to her mouth. She couldn't talk for a moment, and we both smiled at this. It was lovely to see her smile, a rare occurrence, as I have said. Larry had his arm draped protectively around the back of her chair, and was looking around at the kvetching young men and beautiful, dark-eyed women. He had polished off his falafels before us, and was taking in the ambience. The whole room was flooded with the ever-beguiling smell of herbs and roasted vegetables. I was confident the ancients had felt the same about this odour – some things are ineradicable from human experience.

'*Ça va mieux*?' I asked.

'Yes,' Ariel said, when finally she could. 'Let me see. We go to Le Merle Moqueur, or the Le Requin Chagrin. How you say – roar-cous places?'

I'd never heard of either, but I imagined they were student bars in the Quarter, where old men in roll necks still tried to pick up young women. Those *dragueurs* we'd all read about in *A Certain Smile*. It was astounding that the older man-student combination was still going strong. I didn't want to include Larry in this category, but perhaps that's where he belonged.

'Le Requin Chagrin?'

'The depressed shark.'

'Yes,' I mused over my steaming plate. 'That's quite a concept.'

'*Oui. Quelle rigolade.*'

Ariel was a lusty eater, and I'd sat across from her while she devoured roast chicken with what appeared to be fangs. I liked this characteristic: for some reason, it spoke not of bad etiquette but of a greedy appetite, vitality, youth. And a great lack of self-consciousness. Eating was a bodily function we performed in public, and there was no point bringing dainty manners to the table when the food you were about to eat made them redundant. I had gone for the aubergine and couscous with tahini sauce, and was taking it steady.

'Why,' asked Ariel, still chewing, pointing at my plate, 'do the Americans insist on calling that an eggplant? How can they ignore such a beautiful name?'

They had been to America on their travels, and I imagined she had encountered the word there. 'I have no idea... It's their cultural loss. Like many.'

'*Au-ber-sheen,*' repeated Ariel in her husky tones, making the word beautiful.

Larry swivelled in his chair, to join the conversation, his brown arms rippling. 'It's not the only variant. Every time I asked for hash in a diner, she thought I was scoring drugs.'

'I did not!' Ariel cried, indignantly.

'Yes, you did, your little face went white.' And before she could reply, he kissed her on the lips.

'*Tu es insupportable!*'

Still in love, then. Over the last half hour, they had told me how they had begun their travels in Delhi, then went on to Tibet, and Beijing. It had been monsoon season, and Ariel had wanted to go home almost immediately. But Larry had talked her round, taking her to mist-shrouded temples, teaching her words in Mandarin, introducing her to noodle dishes with chicken he neglected to tell her was locust. From Tokyo they had flown to San Francisco for a week, then to Mexico City before coming to Europe. I liked Larry's travel tales and wanted to hear more.

'What did you do in San Fran? I've never been.'

Larry warmed to his subject, his hands already shadow-boxing. 'We spent an incredible week there. You know, just checking out the bay and the bridge, going to the markets, the bookshops – you'd love City Lights, Nick. Plus I did a lot of talking to people from the medical community. Those who are promoting transparency in the drugs industry, that is.'

'And you did all this on holiday?'

'I still had my laptop, my phone. We weren't cave-dwelling.'

'Although,' began Ariel, careful of offending Larry, 'some of the places were less than *génial*.'

'How do you mean? *Pensions* with broken windows and cockroaches?'

'*Bof* – worse than that. Mexico was rough.'

'Everywhere is rough for you, darling, after where you grew up.'

They had developed a ribbing, gently competitive style over the summer. That's what five weeks of seeing each other's face for twenty-four hours a day bequeaths, I decided. But somehow, I liked it better than their previous tentative reverence. The honeymoon period was over. It suited them to bitch like this – they had broken each other's ice irrevocably. I tried to remember what it felt like to be that close to anyone and gave up after a moment. Cass and I had never broken each other's ice, or into each other's inner sanctum. There was an acre in our hearts where we had both stayed free.

'Tell me about Mexico,' I demanded. 'I haven't been there either.'

Larry took a slug on his full-strength Coca-Cola (in the classic green bottle I remember so well from childhood visits to Paris), and said: 'As mental as I remember it. And as fantastic. I think it's my favourite country in the whole world. When I was there last it had all the Zapatista unrest going. Now it's Los Zetas – the gangs and the warring drug cartels. Have to watch your back. But we didn't go to the north. Just bussed it down into the Yucatán.'

'Those buses!' cried Ariel, crossing her legs and forcing me to ignore an expanse of succulent thigh inches from my own legs. She was wearing a simple, white orchid-print dress, and a pair of ballet pumps, and looked almost edible. How did Larry manage most of the time? I would be in a state of perpetual arousal.

'Oh, man,' said Larry, 'You were terrified.'

'Before they head off into the jungle,' continued Ariel, 'the drivers cross themselves.' And she demonstrated a *signum crucis*.

'That's worrying,' I said.

'And they have this light – how you say?'

'For the speed limit,' picked up Larry. 'It goes on when they exceed it.'

'*Mon Dieu*,' gestured Ariel. 'The fucking thing never went off!'

'Hey,' interjected my cousin, 'since when did you swear in English?'

'I can't think where she got it from...' I ventured. 'But listen. I'm envious of you both. I can't remember when I last got away.'

I could remember, and had in fact been thinking about it all the time while they regaled me with their adventures. It was a bad habit of mine, never to be fully present in conversations. My mind was always elsewhere, dawdling in the past, or speeding ahead anxiously into the future. I could never just *be* in the moment. The last time I had stepped on a plane was when Cass and I flew to Florence. She had been six months pregnant with Ed, and imagined it was the last time she would go anywhere for a while. We had flown over the Alps at ten in the morning. It had been spectacular. I recall the mystical ascent to the ice field above the clouds, the sense of privileged access to a kind of atmospheric Champs-Élysées. I had bagged the window seat, and later, with the intensely hot sun producing mist-shafts, I remember thinking the surface below the silver wing resembled the top of a giant blue brain. An earth brain. Later still, a pristine Antarctica of cloud had arrived; the dominant colours piercing white, cream, grey, cobalt, ice, ultramarine. If I looked down, the parted cumuli revealed the snow-sheeted mountains many thousands of feet below, like viewing the bottom of a shallow pond. I had been dazzled by the strange blue suspension after the soaring ascent, and remained looking out of the window for most of the journey. Usually, I like to read on planes, but the vaulted dome of the troposphere on that sunny morning was too good to miss. Coming in to land over northern Italy, the smoke of heavy industry mixing with the drifting atolls of clouds, I experienced a pang of regret that we were descending, leaving the magical world behind. Up there, I had registered a transcendent feeling of being closer to the spiritual, the minute-by-minute action of the soul. Perhaps it was the love of elevation again. Perhaps it was just love. Why did I find it so pleasing? That wonderful panoptic point of view; the sudden reveal of a larger pattern; the streets and enclosures and motorways unaware of their own intricate design. We had a happy few days in Florence, suffering in a pleasant way, as all do, from Stendhal's syndrome after an overdose of art. And both of us looking ahead to the new baby, my hand on her stomach all the while; linked and in love in a way I thought I would never experience, and probably never will again.

'It's incredible now, the global reach of the campaign…' my cousin was saying, bringing me back to earth.

'Sorry, run that once more, Larry.'

'His *projet nouveau*,' beamed Ariel.

'The Transparent Trials Campaign. Something I put up on the website back in June. Just from sheer frustration, really. No one was lifting a finger to effect any change. But now it's gone viral.'

'What do people have to do?'

'Well, there are two tiers of subscription. The public and the medics. You register your support for the campaign, and when we have enough names we take it to parliament to change the legislation. I mean, half the drug trials from 06 to 09 have no results published *anywhere*.'

Larry had told me all this already, but it was useful for him to rehearse it again. He'd been invited onto TV a couple of times and his performance had been less than slick. All conviction, without much finesse.

'I thought you said trying to change legislation was pointless.'

'Okay, maybe I did, but we can't just sit on our hands. Information is going missing every year. Doctors are being misled! Trials have been suppressed and no one's taking any action. No one knows which treatments work or which are safe any more. True clinical data is never disclosed and we're all prescribing blind. It's extraordinarily dangerous!'

Ariel was looking admiringly at Larry as he made his rant. There was a zealot's intensity in his face; his curly hair grown out into an almost Dylan bouffant over the summer, adding to the effect.

'And how have the big pharmaceutical companies reacted?'

Larry shook his head. 'They're protecting their commercial interests, the same as they have over the last twenty, thirty, forty years. But public awareness is another thing. Public shame is very powerful, and they don't want to be seen to be killing anyone.'

'That's very bad for business,' agreed Ariel, drily.

'Abaddon-Blix almost killed me.'

'Now that the website is getting so many hits,' continued Larry, side-stepping my personal gripe, 'the pharmaceutical community is campaigning very hard against us – or me, specifically. They've gone to the Central Court of the European Union to try and close me down.'

'You mean your website?'

'Same thing.'

I hadn't been on Larry's site for a while, and wanted to see what I had missed. Recently I had been feeling very removed from public life; stuck, as was customary for me, in the eighteenth century. I was becoming static – people's lives had moved on, morphed into new shapes, while mine had remained inert.

'Tell me where to sign up, Larry. And I'll send a link to Cass back home. Actually, Ed might be better – he'll canvass his whole class.'

'Thanks. Spread the word.'

My cousin looked around for the single waiter and caught his eye almost immediately; a harassed man in the trademark black waistcoat, pencils and pad in his pocket. He bore an uncanny resemblance to Norman Mailer. '*Un express, s'il vous plaît*,' hollered Larry. Then he turned to us.

'Have you got time?'

'Yes,' Ariel and I answered simultaneously.

'*Trois*,' shouted Larry at the man's retreating bulk.

'So,' I began, 'you both look great. Going around the world is good for the waistline, obviously.'

'Well,' said Larry. 'It was hard work for me, but not Ariel.'

She shrugged indifferently and began playing with the high-capped sleeve of her dress. 'I just eat what I like. I do not see the point of starving myself.'

For a moment, I regretted bringing the subject up. A memory from the spring of Ariel pouring scorn on the 'fit models' used in the top designer ateliers and workrooms came back to me.

She had told me about the girls with scars on their knees from fainting and falling over, or those who resorted to eating tissues instead of food. Voluntary starvation was rife in the fashion world. Her mother, as style editor, had been outraged when size-four clothes had been delivered to one of her shoots, as if they were intended for children. Rivka was always looking for the telltale signs of anorexia in her daughter, but none of them appeared to be present in the bountiful creature sitting opposite me.

'How did you get through Italy eating what you liked?'

Ariel laughed. 'I had pasta every night. It was wonderful. While he went At-keens.'

'She means I just had the antipasti. And water instead of beer. Cutting out the carbs.' Larry turned to Ariel. 'Fucking nuts is what I went.'

'And then you even developed a craving for matzo. Which proves you're not Jewish – as no one Jewish likes them.'

At this, Larry looked suddenly affronted, so I quickly questioned them further about their adventures.

They told me that after Mexico they had flown to Milan, then journeyed down to Florence, Pisa, Rome, and finally to Pompeii. They had only spent a couple of days in Vienna on the way back to Paris. The thought of this made me suddenly remember my cousin's mission.

'Hey – what happened with Lotte's relatives?'

Larry took a deep intake of breath; considered his words: 'We couldn't find them.'

'They didn't exist,' admitted Ariel.

'Well, I wouldn't go as far as that...'

'Sorry,' I persisted, 'but I don't understand. You did take along her letters?'

'All of them, yes. And we went straight to the district where Lotte grew up and they stayed on their visits.'

'The Hietzing,' added Ariel. 'The thirteenth.'

'It's a big suburb on the western outskirts. Up until 1955, it was half occupied by the Russians, half by the English. Luckily, the Bergs were in the English sector, according to Grandma, so she and Edward had easy access when they returned to the family.'

'So what happened?'

'We went to the town hall, where Otto worked, and there was no trace of him. Admittedly, there was a reluctance there to talk about lives of families in the post-war period.' And here Larry eyed Ariel to check she was still listening. 'You have to remember, sixty-five thousand Jews were deported; one hundred and thirty thousand fled, so it's not exactly a point of pride. Vienna had the third largest Jewish population in Europe at one time.'

'I thought Otto was some big bureaucrat.'

'He was a pen-pusher, really, according to Lotte's correspondence with Mother. A man with ideas above his station. I can see why the animosity was mutual – there she was, returning with her handsome husband, while he was stuck signing off on municipal documents, year after year.'

'What about their house?' I asked. 'The family home?'

'The whole street had been demolished,' sighed Larry. 'Which was not unusual, given post-war reconstruction. I wasn't really expecting to find it.'

'We ended up,' said Ariel drolly, 'in a graveyard.'

'That doesn't surprise me,' I volunteered. 'What about Ottilie and Elise? I know you were hoping they might still be around.'

'Nothing. No school records, or marriage or death certificates. This was all available online at the town hall. It's not as if we had to dig. It's just possible that if the Bergs had Czech or Hungarian blood, the two nieces might have returned to Prague or Buda after the Occupation Zones were dismantled in fifty-five, so their records might be there.'

'But we did not fancy more sweltering cities,' grumbled Ariel, her voice pleasingly gruff.

'And what about the cemetery? Was there no family tomb?'

Larry shook his head impatiently. 'As I said, they were too poor for anything like that, even if they had wanted one.'

'We walked everywhere, looked at every stone...' Ariel lamented, theatrically. 'The only good result was that we found the grave of Klimt.'

'He was there?'

'Yeah,' said Larry briskly. 'But not in person.'

I knew Klimt was a big hero of Ariel's, one of the reasons she was so enthusiastic about going. She probably felt disappointed that they had spent more time at his graveside than at the Klimt Museum.

'So what next?' I asked, slightly afraid of Larry's reply.

'There is no next... Back to square one.'

I took a look around the cramped room as Larry admitted sadly to this impasse. Chez Hanna had emptied out since we sat down, and a post-lunch clientele, mainly made up of solitary businessmen, had begun to take tables near ours. However, it was somehow still noisy. The complex compound smell of coriander, parsley and many other herbs was still going strong from the takeaway counter, enticing customers from the bustling rue des Rosiers.

'*Tiens*,' announced Ariel. 'I have an idea. How about this? Your website gets how many hits a week?'

'Ten thousand,' shot back Larry, 'especially now the Transparent Trials Campaign is up and running.'

'How about you post something there?'

Larry's brow furrowed; deep plough-lines that would soon need no sudden facial expression to be permanently visible. 'No. It's not a forum for personal stuff.'

'But we have gone all around Vienna,' she said gently, 'in search of your family. Your,' and she chose the word with precision, 'heri-targe.'

'What would I put?'

Ariel pouted. '*N'importe quoi*. Say you are looking for anyone who knew your relatives in Europe after 1945. Because they have vanished in a puff of air.'

We were both grateful she didn't say 'smoke'.

Larry shook his head at this, but I could tell he was giving it serious consideration. I looked around for the long-awaited coffee, but could see no sign of our man.

Ariel sat back and smiled; triumphant, almost, at her suggestion. Norman Mailer had forgotten our espressos, but I could see my cousin didn't care. He was already writing the post in his mind.

*

It's a truism to say that life will pull the rug from under your new brogues just when your feet are getting used to the resistant leather, but that's exactly what Cass did at the end of August. On the last day, to be precise. A sun-basking morning, I had walked Larry down to the Institut where we had spent a rare half an hour over coffee. He seemed healthier and happier than I'd ever seen him, though he still griped about his appearance when we whizzed through his travel photos on his phone. Larry was one of those unfortunate people for whom weight shows in the face. His girth had actually narrowed considerably over the summer, but his face still bore the old meat, tanned and furrowed and characterful though it was.

After saying goodbye, I stepped out onto the wide boulevard Montparnasse to make my weekly call to Cass and Ed from one of the capital's remaining phone boxes. These chrome and glass-enclosed cabins allowed one an unimpeded view of one's surroundings, and, while talking with my son, I took pleasure in the tableau of a Paris slowly filling with cars after the summer break. Looking northwards, the great cambered road was arrow-straight, with dusty planes shedding their first leaves; the newer trees imprisoned in green protective cages. To the south was an even longer stretch of road; the red awnings of the pavement cafés far back from the traffic. This view afforded a wonderful sense of perspective – intentional, of course, Haussmann building thoroughfares that were revolution-proof. Over this urban highway hung the inescapable tower. It had been a while since I had seen it close up, and it seemed less dowdy than I recalled. Perhaps they had cleaned it over the summer. It was still somehow sinister in the morning sun, with its graphite striations soaring upwards. It continued to give out an inescapable impression of imposture. Paris's one attempt to Manhattanise loomed friendless and vulnerable over the elegant balconies, like a man exposing himself.

It was only after I had talked to Ed for five minutes about his (to my mind) unfortunate new obsession with Chelsea football club, that Cass came back on the line and dropped her bombshell. I will try not to exaggerate here. I'm just relating the facts as they happened.

'There's something we should discuss,' she began, 'and now seems as good a time as any.'

'Go ahead,' I said cheerily, the sun warming my face through the prisms of the Perspex and glass. 'If it's about Ed's new head teacher, then I can sympathise. He's just told me all about her.'

'No. It's more significant,' she said, her voice small and coiled. 'Harvard have offered me a fantastic opportunity, and I've decided to take it.'

'Really?' I said, my intestines clenching. It was too late, I told myself, for them to have offered her a teaching post, with term almost upon everyone, but I feared the worst.

'As you might know,' she continued carefully, 'they're digitising the Emily Dickinson manuscript archive, and they've asked me to go over and help with the project.'

I had read somewhere that there was a feud between Amherst and Harvard over the ownership of many documents, Harvard having been given the Dickinson family manuscripts in the 1950s. But I didn't think of Cass as someone they might call on to help. Though an expert, along with Margaret Homans, on new feminist and deconstructionist theories regarding the poet's linguistic strategies, I doubted whether Cass had ever been near an actual letter or poem.

'You're going to America?'

'Yes…'

'Permanently?'

'It's a two-year project.'

'And after that?'

There was a silence in which I heard the draw of cars along the boulevard behind me.

'Most probably we'll stay, yes…'

The turmoil in my stomach became a sharp stab.

'But… Hey. Listen a minute. Slow down a bit and think of the implications here.'

She sighed. 'I have thought everything through, from what it means for my career to Ed's future, too. I believe I'm making the right move.'

'When are you going?' I pleaded, attempting to suppress the panic in my voice.

'Oh, not at once,' she said with a horrible calm matter-of-factness. 'I'm still tying things up in London. Harvard say they can wait until December.'

'What about UCL?'

'They're fine with it. Wolff said I can teach my seminars and lectures this term and keep my post here indefinitely. A number of professors have done the same. They have strong links with Columbia, as you know.'

Jonathan Wolff was the head of the faculty, someone who

I knew had marked Cass for a professorship, sooner rather than later. The Dickinson archive job could only work in her favour. This, however, was far from my mind at that moment.

'So, effectively you and Ed will be in London until Christmas. And then you'll just disappear?'

'Nick. I'm sorry to have to tell you all this so suddenly—'

'What does Ed think about it?'

She paused, though not for long enough, to my mind. 'He says he will miss his friends, but he's excited.'

'And why, may I ask, did he not mention this crazy caper to me over the last five minutes?'

I looked at the antiquated LED screen of the phone where my euros were fast diminishing. I had a mere five left.

'It's not a caper,' Cass said, trying to master her voice. 'I wanted to tell you myself.'

'You can't control him like this,' I protested, my temper suddenly roaring forth from the back of my throat. This, as I well knew, was a disastrous move.

'Don't tell me what I can or cannot do.'

'He'll be without a father!'

I could tell what my ex-wife was doing as we spoke; how she was sitting, if not where. Her mahogany bob would be trembling with righteous power and decisiveness. To her mind, there was nothing wrong with this decision, as far as Ed went. Secretly she had always wanted him to grow up an American, and now she had the opportunity.

'You're getting hysterical,' she slurred, sounding more Bronx than Boston.

'Don't you want our son to have a father?'

'Please, Nick, don't get melodramatic at this hour.' And, banally, she added, 'We are an hour behind, remember.'

'What can I say to change your mind?'

'Nothing,' she said, 'as far as I'm concerned.'

'Okay. So when can I see him again?'

Cass cleared her throat, taking time I didn't have. 'Well… There's more chance of us going over there than of you coming over here, if that's what you mean.'

At this I registered something seismically strange. She had long since vetoed any trip I might make back to see Ed in London for arcane reasons of her own. And, of course, since the spring, she had always shown a reluctance to get on a Eurostar herself and make a visit with him – the easiest thing in the world. No, something had changed over the summer with Cass, of that I was sure. Everyone's life was changing rapidly, except mine, I thought, with a hot flush of panic and self-pity. I was now to languish for the rest of my life in the dungeon of familial isolation and chronic pain.

'Are you seeing someone?'

There was a lengthy pause. 'I'm not going there, Nick.'

'You are, aren't you?'

'It's simply none of your business.'

I looked with despair at the cars whipping past, barrelling into futures I didn't have. Futures where families stayed together and loved each other.

'It *is* my business if Ed starts to look on another man as his father!'

'That's unlikely,' she said robotically. 'Listen. We will have to discuss this another time.'

I sensed I was about to groan or cry out loud, but pulled back from the brink at the last moment.

'So… your mind's made up, then?'

'Yup,' she replied briskly. 'It's done and dusted, I'm afraid.'

And then, before I had the chance to say another word, my money ran out and we were cut off.

FOUR

September. The Parisian *rentrée*, when children dash through leaf-lined streets in their red scarves on their return to school. When the whole metropolitan machine begins to hum once more. These carefree children I watched from my balcony over the coming weeks. It goes without saying that every one of them, in my eyes, was Ed.

When I spoke to Cass again, calmly this time, she was just as adamant about her decision. The question of my own ostracism was redundant in her eyes. She had her own life to lead, her career to follow, and, if such a move was inevitable (as she so obviously thought it was), then better Ed go to America before he was of secondary-school age. Or 'high-school age', as she termed it. And, when I finally got to speak to Ed, all I could register was his supreme state of impatient excitement. What kid wouldn't be blown away at the prospect? He seemed to think I would be coming to visit him in the States every weekend. He had no idea what a final and conclusive severance this might prove to be. My own parents were understandably upset by the prospect of not seeing their grandson for a very long while, if not for ever, given their age. It was out of my control, I told them. How else could I explain the situation? In the past, post-divorce, there had always been a rueful quality to my father's voice whenever Cass was brought up, as if getting involved with her had been an error of manly judgement. At the time, naturally, they had professed to like and admire her – it was only after our split, predictably, that they confessed to finding her an uphill struggle. This is often the case, of course. We put up with the partners of our friends or relatives in the spirit of support or camaraderie, or even masochism. They have made their choice, and we must stand by them. We must suppress any scintilla of a suggestion that they have made a terrible mistake. To do so would be an act of treason towards either friendship or consanguinity. And now, talking with my father, he couldn't disguise the fact he thought I was reaping what I'd sown. This was less apparent when I spoke to my mother. She wanted to know whether the scarf she had knitted her 'favourite boy' would reach him for Christmas. Her guess was as good as mine, I told her.

Call me old-fashioned, but I've never played a tactical game when it came to love. Cass must have long planned all this, and such a thought made me feel hopeless and unmoored within. My problem was always that I never thought ahead enough in relationships; never schemed, now if I do *this* or *that*, then the outcome might be the *other*. Fantastic though it might seem, I have never knowingly manipulated another, but have laid myself bare to receive manipulation in return. Is this outright stupidity in this day and age? Or a touching innocence, as Larry likes to think? Having said that, I wasn't entirely blameless in the collapse of my marriage. I wouldn't be honest with myself if I claimed otherwise. There was the temper for a start. Then the time spent deeply immersed in many books and projects. And then this significant fact: though I admired Cass for her intellect – and, it has to be said, her virtues of pragmatism and efficiency in bringing up Ed – I long ago realised I didn't actually like her. About six months into our relationship, in fact. This felt like pulling a girder out of a building under construction. It was bound to collapse in the end. Once something is admitted to the inner self, it becomes fact very quickly. It's impossible to hide in the eyes. And Cass, sharp as a tack as she was, would have registered it at once. Why, then, did I waste everyone's time by going ahead and having a child with her? During early September, no other question resonated more strongly. My sense of remorse over this notion grew to unbearable proportions.

In the mornings and evenings on the balcony, watching the Jardin turn brown, the stately avenues of chestnuts dropping their hand-sized leaves onto the oatmeal gravel, I felt as if I had lost a limb. Or that one was earmarked for amputation. The white Paris skyline, never without a crane, and the washed-out pearly skies above it, mirrored back my sense of vacuity, of imminent loss. In the cafés I heard 'September Song' at least twice. You could almost detect the forlorn Parisian accordion playing on street corners as I tramped back and forth to the library. I took to eating alone, consciously avoiding Larry and Ariel, as well as Rube and Professor Singh. This latter evasion I regretted, as I'd got to know and like Nadir over the summer. My novelist friend was in the capital for a week, and I met him for a quick drink at the rough-and-tumble Le Crocodile opposite Le Pantalon, but I laid low for the rest of his stay. In the evenings, at my restaurant table for one, usually near the door or the toilets, the white paper cloth stained with the gravy of my *poulet pommes frites*, a *petit pichet* of wine at my elbow, I contemplated the future. It didn't look good, that was for certain. The flat was too oppressive to stay in most nights, so I would spend hours in cheap local places like La Gueuze, or Le Gay Lussac, half-heartedly lingering over printouts of my day's writing, pen in hand. The waiters were convinced I was working on a book to rival *La Recherche*, and approached my table nervously to ask if I wanted *l'addition*. No, I would tell them, just another *pichet* – wine being favoured over spirits or their potent bottled beers, as I didn't want to get drunk; indeed, Hemingway didn't even consider wine to be 'proper liquor'. La Gueuze, a *moules marinières* joint at the foot of the rue Soufflot, was my favourite of these haunts, with many young men alone at early-evening tables, lingering over soup with sops of baguette. With its stained-glass windows bearing the Stella logo, wooden chairs and banquettes, stone floors and a busy bar playing techno, it was the kind of Paris I had long avoided. But it made me feel anonymous, which was the intention. Later, when the tourists, or *les jeunes* turned up, frantically sending 'textos' while their food went cold, I would repair to somewhere quieter. Often, I'd end up in the melancholy Pizza Odessa – which also doubled as a bar, the nearest to me on the boulevard Saint-Michel – where I would think up vain plans to make Cass see sense.

I also returned, on an almost daily basis, to the place Paul Painlevé, which I had for some reason neglected over the summer. As the days and weeks wore on, as the leaves imperceptibly began to fall, I made my morning visits. I must have sat on every bench in rotation. The gradient of the nearby rue Saint-Jacques gave the place a pleasant sense of unevenness or dislocation, with the green benches at the bottom staring up at the rue des Écoles and the imposing Sorbonne, while the ones at the top allowed, through thinning trees, a view of the turreted Thermes de Cluny. And everywhere the lulling, rolling, aquatic tumble-hum of the fountain, located under the monument to Octave Gréard, reformer of the baccalauréat. This stone frieze, with its simplistic teacher and child, had never pleased me, but now I found it oddly moving to contemplate. On the many occasions I visited the rue des Écoles in my twenties, it had been a statue of Montaigne – with its famously polished right foot, the result of so many hands hoping it might impart wisdom – that had fascinated me. Now I liked to gaze on a bronze she-wolf, under which sat a suckling Romulus and Remus. But the sound of Gréard's fountain was essential – almost like a drug I had to score every morning. Sitting on one of the benches, overlooked by the towering tree of heaven, oblivious to the necking students or mysterious resting men in sunglasses, I would think about that other factor in the new domestic equation. Cass's resistance to me coming to see my son before they left. All I could conclude was that she had some sort of romantic situation going on there that wasn't conducive to me paying a visit. I was pretty sure, from talking to Ed, that she hadn't moved some man into the Rosebery Avenue apartment, but then I sensed he was sworn to some kind of silence, or vow of omission. I wasn't about to push him on the matter, and anyway, our time was so limited on the phone, I didn't want to spoil his sense of excitement.

Inevitability theory is a nice concept – the monkeys and their labour over the keys – but nothing should ever be inevitable, given the random collision of atoms. Cass's move to Harvard had always been on the cards, but for ever accompanied by an Augustinian sense of deferral. And now she was going ahead. And maybe with some man in tow. What else could force her to give up the life and career she had made for herself in London? The thought of returning next year to find them departed from London filled me with a cold dread. Almost as if the city, despite its 10 million inhabitants, would suddenly be empty. During those mornings in the park, I even considered staying in Paris permanently. The currents of change were shifting under my feet, too. There was always the ULIP, I told myself – the University of London Institute in Paris – which had asked me to teach there a few times. But I had always resisted because of Ed. What was to stop me now?

All this I debated inwardly on the way to and from work. Up the long, dragging hill, past the block-like slab of the Sorbonne with its implacable cornices, the Lycée Louis-le-Grand on the opposite side of the road. Usually into a strong headwind, the breath of decay now upon the city. With my legs giving me grief, it came to feel like a daily penance; for what, I wasn't sure. The descent to the place Paul Painlevé was ever a joy in the morning, while the return was always a downer, now that the colder weather had arrived, with its autumnal whip. And the blue-uniformed security guards at every door, with their silly peaked policemen's caps, most of them impertinent, had started to cause me irrational annoyance. I had seen them hassling students who obviously had valid passes. One particular girl in a black polo neck (of all things) had given back, in Parisian style, as good as she had got. In March, they had even caused me trouble, suspicious of my accent, until I had come to know the pair on the Sorbonne's north doors.

In my free time away from the book I took to aimless flâneuring, of a type I hadn't undertaken for years. I covered a lot of ground. It seemed imperative that I look upwards, too, at the buildings I had always taken for granted. Up at the shuttered balconies where I imagined myself into possible domestic situations of my own. What was to stop me making a life for myself here? Apart from the physical ailments, Larry was always telling me I still had a lot to offer. Ariel, also, had seconded this, on our nights out together. Like I said, as three only children together, there was never the sense that I was intruding on the happy couple. We were all secretly glad of the companionship. However, a Paris without them might be as intolerable as a London without my ex-wife and son. Loneliness creeps up on you, compounded by age. I had never felt myself particularly afflicted with it, though I was never a very successful solitary. I was always better off in a relationship than out. But in one's forties, everyone has very definitely coupled up or started families of their own. Only the mad and the very brave lit out alone. As Larry's literary hero said, the conditions were tough. You wouldn't make it without love. And these units of exclusive love, these families, were impossible to break into; with invitations for nights out, or get-togethers between toiling parents, made weeks in advance, involving many complicated bouts of rescheduling, like a dental appointment. This was why Paris had been so freeing, with Larry and Ariel present. The experience resembled being a teenager again, meeting up at bars, or wherever one happened to be. But their absence over the summer had been like a melancholy farewell to youth. You get to a certain age when you realise you've had your future: it's called your past. During the dog days I had listened to Britten's *Sea Interludes* over and over, and now, come September, found I couldn't face them. They reminded me too freely of my overheated August isolation.

The streets I walked followed no pattern. It was enjoyable to get lost in the maze around the rue de la Huchette, near to the river. There were many secretive alleys, with well-tended window boxes high above the winding, shadowed cobbles. Also sordid pick-up cut-throughs, like the rue Xavier-Privas, with its ranks of parked motorcycles, and *Je suis Charlie* tags painted over by swastikas, or the FN logo. If I found myself out near the green barrows of books, I would descend to the *quais* and walk along by the turbid water. I sauntered past the sad capstans, over the difficult stones, communing with the fast-flowing water on its unstoppable course. The trees, too, were just beginning to show their October palette of mustard, mauve, biker-jacket brown. They swayed in the wind over the taupe river. It pleased me to contemplate them for minutes at a time. Above them, on the other side, soared the august limestone of the Palais de Justice; a great classical dignity in every line, interrupted by the conical lead-tiled towers. And the silent herons of the spring were nowhere to be seen. They appeared to have been replaced by seagulls; gabbling and kvetching on currents of air. Even these Paris birds – constantly alighting or floating hopefully – possessed an elegance, a dignity, a suavity, compared with their greedy London cousins.

I also ventured north of the river, hoping I wouldn't bump into Larry or the Levines. Up the rue des Archives, with its imposing walls of medieval stone, past the Musée de la Chasse and its unexpectedly serene courtyard. Here, in the north Marais, I found myself in what resembled an Italian city, a welcome escape from the babbling bars of the Quarter. A Milan or a Turin. The narrow streets led me in bewildering circles – something I desired, of course. My walks there always reminded me of the time my father and I had tried to find the Picasso Museum; him standing frowning on every street corner, turning the map upside down, trying to appear confident and in control. I only passed the *musée* by accident myself, on a morning when piercing light made me squint into the shadows of arched doorways. The place was marked by a plaque on what looked like a residential row of houses at the bottom of the rue de Thorigny. For such a towering figure so minuscule a monument. That morning, I stopped in the little cobbled square at the road's termination, which was split by a zigzag on which rampant *vélomoteurs* tore past. There, with the freshness of September in my nostrils, the smell of warm bread from a patisserie or the Café Thé opposite, I had an unwelcome revisitation of the Sartrean tremors. With the young on their bikes sailing off to work in elegantly arranged scarves, the leaves scattering in the gutters, I was met again with the sweet and terrifying knowledge of my own existence, pressing in unwontedly. Totally destabilising, and the last thing I needed. The passage of air in my throat, the cold in my hands, causing them to bloom like mottled chunks of liver, sent waves of panic over me. It had never slipped my mind that Roquentin had been a historian, and, over the weeks I spent trying to rationalise my reaction to Cass's move, I recalled that Sartre also stated it wasn't a profession that fits a man for psychological analysis. I was beginning to agree with him. I had no idea what any of anything meant.

Leaving my bench – and the beech on the corner, whose green, going-gold leaves had unsettlingly resembled an ageing male head – I went straight to the rue du Parc-Royal and sat in the square watching the mothers and their children. Only there did I begin to get a grip. But then another, more familiar, malaise assailed me. It is ironic how, when one's heart is strung out on one's own family situation, tableaux of other people's become nigh on unbearable. And so it proved that morning. The sight of mothers setting free their charges to run along the gravel paths, in their mittens and buttoned-up pink and blue duffle coats, was destroying. A stinging sense of unfairness, too. Where were the fathers of these children? Not living in another country, working pointlessly on books they barely believed in any more, soon to be many thousands of miles away.

If there was a place I returned to as October approached it was the Jardin; opposite me every morning on opening the shutters, and a solace within reach. It had been pleasurable to watch the avenues of chestnuts thin and turn brown from my elevation across the road, and now I wanted to be closer to them; to touch the bark of the trees, as it were. Scoring my English papers from the kiosk opposite Le Petit Journal, I would enter through the gold-tipped gates and walk the stately paths, which always appeared to be covered with sand rather than gravel. Like a beach with trees. There I would contemplate the fat busts of Stendhal and Flaubert – the former, with his sideburns, putting me in mind of Larry. On sunny mornings, depending how early I arrived, the light would throw long shadows from the benches and single chairs, an impermanent grid that was pleasing to walk through. And everywhere the coming decay, with the trees russet and weeping, was offset by evidence of thriving life – the boys playing with their boats in the fountains; the lovers who hadn't gone home yet, kissing on the benches. Walking past the figure of Sainte Geneviève, with her idealised plaits, sometimes resting at the Pavillon to read the headlines and see if Britain was still standing, I would be drawn inevitably to the Medici fountain. This secluded trough of green water, perfect for contemplation, surrounded most days by watercolourists of dubious talent, was now in early autumn some kind of oasis. With its statue of supine Galatea – the sexiest sculpture in the world, as everyone knows – it held me in its elegant grip for hours.

Obviously, I couldn't wander in the park all day – the Sorbonne was still paying me to write a book. Yet when I wasn't in the Jardin, I would visit the cinemas, many familiar from my youth. My favourite was Le Desperado on the rue des Écoles. One afternoon I slipped in to watch Sorrentino's dazzling, baffling *The Great Beauty* – full of unforgettable images of giraffes and dwarves and a society obsessed with surfaces. Fellini, yes, but deeply moving all the same, with its ageing writer who finds the boat marked 'family' has long since sailed without him. After my trips to the Desperado, it was good to sit at the café Le Rostand and watch the world dance past. A few times there, I would see the ominous arrival of the CRS – the Compagnies Républicaines de Sécurité – the notorious riot police in their sinister blue buses. They would always congregate before any whiff of expected trouble, just as they had in '68. Indeed, the rue Soufflot opposite had been at the very epicentre of insurrection during *les journées de Mai*. The thought of this made me a little more forgiving of the uptight security guards around the corner. Given France's political situation, there was always the chance it could kick off again at any moment.

On my way back from the Rostand one day, I received a jolt that perhaps put my coming separation from Ed into perspective. Passing the École Maternelle at going-home time, I saw briefly, through an open doorway, one of the black marble plaques put up to commemorate the deportation of Jewish schoolchildren during World War II. There were over 300 of these grim reminders installed in Paris over the last decade; and while the word Vichy never passed anyone's lips, as Larry found out to his cost, it was only right and just that there was some kind of memorial. The black square itself was like a death; a black abyss, held in abeyance only by civilised codes of conduct. Stopping there by the railings, dry-eyed but with my heart pounding, I reflected that, as bad as things were, the severance from my son at least wasn't terminal.

When I finally saw Larry again it was already October. He had been walking across the river once a week to keep fit, and we met one lunchtime on the Place des Vosges. He had been for a heavy night on the cocktails with Ariel, Ana and Delphine, and as a result was only putting in a half-day at the Institut. I shook hands with him by one of the fountains and sensed at once that he was annoyed with me for lying low. It was cold, one of those dry, brittle days, with custard-coloured sun pulsing through every now and again. My cousin was in a black Puffa jacket and a beanie hat. My one concession to the weather was a scarf, worn like Tom Baker's Doctor Who, and thus not much of a protection against the temperature. The big surprise, however, was on Larry's face.

'You've grown a beard,' I said, stunned.

'What of it?' Larry returned tersely, indicating that we should walk.

We set off in a southerly direction, heading for the exit that led to the rue de Birague. The park was looking slightly threadbare and windswept; the four fountains, one in each corner, toiling away like maids scrubbing steps.

'Well, it's been a while since—'

'And whose fault is that?' he interrupted, rubbing his growth, which bore a few barely visible threads of grey. 'It's not a new phenomenon. I've had it for a month.'

'Has it been that long?'

'About that, yes.'

While still in its early stages, Larry's beard was on its way to the full Victorian. And why not? I wanted to say, but his bullish mood foreclosed any further comment. It had been the fashion for a couple of years for young men to go bravely full-beard – and of course they could, confident that not a whisper of grey would intrude. Nothing more Poseidon-like, more Herculean, than a big black beard on a young man. But at our age, I reflected, it was harder. Still, when I looked around Paris, it appeared only openly gay men under forty-five were clean-shaven. I had even considered growing one myself, now I wouldn't be seeing Ed much again. But over the phone he had categorically refused to speak to me if I attempted the look, saying I was trying to get down with the hipsters or some such nonsense. Larry's beard had, for the first time in his life, the curious effect of making him seem vain. Which was strange, as while my cousin was intellectually vain (me more so, probably), he had never been physically self-regarding. I suspected that he had gone for the bardic or heroic look, or the self-consciously alpha; a signification of the man who wants to attract a woman for the purpose of child-rearing. Or just impressing her with his vitality and masculinity. His Hellenic virility. All of which my cousin had in mind when it came to Ariel.

'You're outrageous, man,' Larry was saying as we walked under the medieval arch that led to the one-way rue de Birague, and so downhill towards the busy rue Saint-Antoine.

'Why's that?'

I realised now that, until he shaved it off, Larry's gaucheries would have their focus in the tangled growth of hair on his chin.

'You know your trouble? Your lifelong trouble?'

'I thought we were going for a friendly catch-up lunch, Larry. I'm still trying to get my head around events. A bit of sympathy might not go amiss.'

'Your trouble is that you go to ground when things take a

turn for the worse. It's the worst thing you can do. You need the support of friends and family.'

'I know. It's a hard habit to break.'

'You're too insular.'

'I admit it, yes.'

'What's with switching your phone off?' Larry's shoulders were hunched, and he was looking around for somewhere to score a *baguette fromage-jambon*. He had told me earlier there would be no time to sit down and chat. The only shops I could see were high-class boutiques and a Chilean bar, Le Cap Horn, where we had gone to get wildly drunk when I first landed in Paris. Somehow, those days seemed quite far in the past.

'Larry, I had to have time to think things over.'

'And did you reach any conclusions?'

'Well, not really... Part of me wants to let them go with good grace and humility. And another part wants to punish her for being so selfish.'

Larry nodded his head at this, assimilating stances I was only just understanding myself. I hadn't really thought there was anything I could do about the situation, not practically, anyway.

'Are you going to see them?'

'Cassie said they would try and get over here at half-term. I know Ed wants to.'

I told Larry about my fears that Cass had embarked on a serious relationship, and he merely shrugged, as if it was the most natural thing in the world. He had always referred to the Sorbonne as the 'Sore Bore'; now he had started calling me by that name. He told me to be realistic – I had married a foreign national (just as he hoped he might), and I should, at my age, know they always had a homing instinct back to the old turf. He fully expected to end his days in France – hopefully in the chateau in the Loire. 'Yes,' I told him. 'But you have to figure in the fact of a child. You have to take account of it. Emotions – blood ties – don't follow logic or known rules.'

'How you react to this is a test of character,' Larry was saying now. 'Of mettle.'

'You don't have kids, Larry. You wouldn't understand.'

He huffed and puffed at this; throwing his hands into the air, nearly gubbing a passing tourist in the mouth. 'Why have I always hated that phrase? As if no one ever possessed a sense of empathy or imagination.'

'She's taking away the only thing that has meaning in my life!'

I didn't know I was capable of such phrases. As I might have mentioned, Larry always had a strange galvanising effect on people – as if he were some kind of truth drug.

'But you will be separated by geography only! Just like you have been for the last five years. Even when you lived round the corner in London, Cass never wanted you there.' And here my cousin mellowed as we left the noisy flow of the rue Saint-Antoine and headed up the quieter passage of the rue de Sévigné. 'You know, as he grows, he'll come to see your importance as a parent. What you've provided for him. You'll become closer, as father and son. You only get one dad.'

Both of us looked warily at each other at this unstable statement. 'Not if there's another man whom he thinks of as his father.'

'You don't know that.'

'I've got a pretty good idea who it might be.'

'Really? From the English department?' asked Larry, indicating that we should step inside a patisserie.

Relieved to be off the street, I immediately realised how hungry I was. At the counter I feasted my eyes. Before us was a banquet of saucisson and tiers of cheese. It was unusual to find a non-kosher place in the Marais. For some reason, I lowered my voice to a whisper.

'No, social and historical sciences.'

'Not Professor Scheanshang?'

'Yes. She could never stop badmouthing old Scheanshang. He touched her up apparently, at a departmental drinks night.'

'Amazing,' Larry remarked, wide-eyed. The beard had certainly altered his face. He looked at once younger and older. It was terribly disconcerting.

'Yes, he put his hand on her behind as they stood in the drinks queue. Left it there in a proprietorial fashion for a few seconds, as if they were already a couple.'

'Wow. And she told you this?'

'Yes, but only to make me squirm, most probably.'

'Then you know it's not him.'

'Why's that?'

'Because it's never the obvious ones who've been using your shaving foam when you've been away…'

Larry scored us both the freshest-looking baguettes from the tumbling pile in the window, and we left the shop for the street once more. As we walked he became less angry with me.

'Do you think she's serious about the Dickinson project?'

'Without a doubt. Amherst have a good claim on the ownership of many of the manuscripts, so they need someone neutral to arbitrate.'

'But with a Harvard background?'

'Absolutely. It's a two-year digitisation project. Cass and Ed won't be living with her parents; they'll be on campus.'

We were heading for a square I had never been to before, a secluded raised platform of cobbles, dotted informally with benches, bowered with limes. It was off the beaten track, studded with those bistros and faux-rustic restaurants that certain gourmands probably swear by as being the best place in Paris.

'Never been here before?' asked Larry. We had stopped and were scanning the square for somewhere that might sell us coffee.

'No. Where are we?'

'The place du Marché-Sainte-Catherine. I come here a lot when I want to escape the Levines.'

'I thought you were in a state of bliss.'

'There's been a bit of – how shall we say? – friction lately.'

'Oh, do expand,' I said, looking around for a bench, all of which were unfortunately colonised by packs of female foreign-exchange students, singing and swaying along to a tune that seemed to be playing simultaneously on their iPods. These kids were everywhere in Paris just now. And like everywhere, there was nowhere to sit.

'Maybe later. I wanted to talk about your situation. The one that's kept you a stranger for over a month.'

We passed the terrace of Chez Joséphine, an upmarket place

where the wealthy ate stonily, like gobies in an aquarium, behind a polythene rain-screen. It looked vaguely familiar, for some reason. Perhaps I had eaten there with my parents thirty years ago, when such places were affordable.

With a sense of regret, we left the square and hung a left up the rue de Jarente.

'There's nothing more to say about it, Larry. Except I'm heartbroken.'

'I can see that…' he nodded. 'I'm sorry this is happening to you. But people's lives evolve in unpredictable ways. You can't control anything. You have to let people go. Even your son. He's a good kid, Nick. He'll be okay. You should have a little belief in him… Who knows, at half-term you might be able to outline some sort of functional situation for the next few years.'

'I don't think Cass has thought that far ahead.'

But the fact that Larry *had* surprised me. There appeared to be new gravitas evident in him, or maybe he'd just been at the Kabbalah again. Indeed, with the beard there was something Greek, or Byzantine, about Larry's face; the jut of his profile. Despite his sallow skin, its tan still memorised from the summer, the facial hair had ennobled his features. It struck me that he might have only grown it because he was self-conscious about his bulky chops, but I was getting more used to its novelty by the minute.

As we walked up the taxing gradient of the rue Mahler, I asked: 'What have you been up to, then?'

'You mean last night?'

'All of it.'

'Well, to cut a long story short, we all got scandalously drunk on Ariel's credit card. We kicked off in the rue Vieille-du-Temple and hit the bars. I want to live on that road.'

'Maybe you will. One day.'

'No seriously, I've got it all planned, my friend. It was a pre-birthday night for Ariel. We started in this tiny speakeasy called Au Petit Fer à Cheval, then moved on to L'Étoile Manquante. A crazy place — just the toilets are worth a visit. There's this hidden camera that films you there as you wash your hands.'

'I'd forgotten about Ariel's birthday. When's the big day?'

'November the first. Twenty-one, can you believe it! She was born in 1994, Nick. That fact still worries me.'

'What can you give the girl who's got everything? Twice.'

We were on the rue des Rosiers now, passing patisseries with gold menorahs in their windows. There was a close, convivial feel to the street, as if everyone had shared purposes or secrets. Packs of young boys wearing baseball caps queued for falafels, speaking in racing French; inflected and hard to catch. There was also a strong presence of gendarmes, armed with the type of heavy-duty machine-guns I knew I would never get used to. In a moment we would pass Chez Hanna, where I had last met them both.

'Her folks are planning this big thing at the apartment, but she just wants to hire a boat on the Seine. Get all her DJ friends down there.'

'Couldn't she do both?'

Larry shot me a look. 'They're a strange family, Nick. They have all these rules and codes of conduct I'm only just becoming aware of. Everything has to be *comme il faut*.'

'It's always the way with those old clans. *La discrétion* is paramount.'

After a while debating this, we exited the hustling cobbled thoroughfare and found ourselves at the site of Larry's big night out.

'And here we are. La rue Vieille-du-Temple. Doesn't look much – but one day, all this will be mine.'

'Are we going to walk for ever, Larry?' I demanded, stopping to massage my knees. 'Only, I'm not sure I can go on much longer.'

My cousin pulled an admonishing grimace, made severe by the beard. 'Like Diderot says, no one secretly likes walking more than a man with a limp.' And he clapped me on the shoulder. 'Come on. I know the perfect place.'

In a moment we were sharing a bench in a sequestered workers' park on the rue des Blancs-Manteaux. It was quiet, overlooked by the back of a Catholic church and a spreading copper beech. The wealth of a few streets away appeared to have vanished, replaced by a *banlieue* feel. Construction men in dusty boots, chowing down on baguettes, sat on adjacent benches, their legs planted far apart. Pairs of black and Asian shop girls were similarly picnicking, the park's tatty gravel punctuated only by what looked like a broken roundabout and a children's slide, on which a girl of three in a red mac forlornly played. I was glad, however, to rest my legs, and was even strangely reassured by the crowd of Algerian toughs wearing hoodies who seemed to be guarding the iron, green-painted, two-way gate.

Larry had been telling me that the Transparent Trials

Campaign had been going from strength to strength. The website traffic had increased considerably, just in the last month. He had even been interviewed by BFM, the French twenty-four-hour news channel, something that I was sorry to have missed. Then I recalled Ariel's suggestion.

'Did you post something about Lotte up there?' I asked, mildly ashamed that I hadn't visited his page to find out myself. I couldn't believe any of his votaries had any relevant information to impart.

'Yeah, but so far no luck,' Larry said, the formidable baguette forcing him to chew and speak simultaneously. 'Only a couple a cranks have responded so far. But that's par for the course. It's like I've reached a total impasse.'

'What kind of cranks?'

'Incredibly, they both left anti-Semitic slurs. And I didn't even mention the word "Jewish". Just "Vienna" and "relatives".'

He looked sad as he delivered this information. Larry was increasingly being made aware that a Jewish identity didn't come without certain caveats – such as the possibility of receiving verbal or physical abuse on a daily basis, for your whole life. Or even live in constant fear for your life. Not something the average goy is familiar with.

'Dismal,' I muttered, looking across to the little girl who was sliding repeatedly down the silver chute, but without much joy on her face. I wondered where her mother was, and worried that I couldn't locate her on any of the benches.

'There's a phenomenal amount of that kind of crap on the internet now, you know? Even hoary old hoaxes like the

Protocols of the Elders of Zion are coming back in. Europe's in a mess at the moment. Nationalism is resurgent; the far right are on the rise... It's as if everybody's memory banks have been wiped.'

'What does François feel about all this?'

Larry paused. 'He's horrified! On top of that, he spends half his time fending off accusations from Jewish journalists that politicians like him have lost their identity and become too French. Then he's attacked from the right for being too Jewish. The secularist ideal of the Republic was never to be self-effacing about your Judaism. It was about finding a balance between loyalty to your background and to the state.'

'What are you going to do? About Lotte, I mean.'

'I don't know,' he shrugged. 'Sit and wait, I suppose. None of it makes sense. To think that we tramped around the Ringstrasse for two days and found nothing... A total aporia.'

Larry's use of the recondite word took me back instantly to our youth – to debating Hegelian dialectics and Kant in his sulphur- and potassium-reeking teenage bedroom. Now he too was staring straight ahead at the lost girl in the crimson mac, wondering perhaps, like me, where her mother might be. Aporia. From the Greek meaning 'impassable'. No way forward. For now, at least.

'But Nadir had a breakthrough, of sorts,' said Larry brightly. Always a swifter eater than me, he had finished his baguette and was dusting off his hands.

'Oh, yes?'

Larry checked himself momentarily, as if realising he'd stumbled into a faux pas; then reconsidered, figuring I could take whatever it was he had to say. We knew each other so well, I could detect these things at once.

'He got to see his kids again. Sorry to tell you that now.'

'No, no. Don't worry. That's marvellous. I'd been wondering how he was doing.'

'There's always the invention called the telephone,' said Larry, drily.

'Did he go out to Bobigny?'

'God, no. There's no rapprochement with Jaspreet. Not just yet, anyway. No, they moved him from that hellhole on the rue André Gide.'

'Really? The Institut have given a learned professor an upgrade?'

'Well, if you want to call it that. It's a proper apartment now. On the rue de Vaugirard itself. Bit tatty – you know the type. Where every balcony has window boxes and washing hanging out.'

'So the kids came to visit? All three?'

'Yeah, as a kind of house-warming thing.'

I looked around to see if the toughs on the gate had vamoosed, but they were still there. Coming from London, I had always found the French equivalent of young hardmen laughably unthreatening, and this bunch were proving no exception. I was in no doubt they would part politely as we left.

'He's invited us both for a beer next week, if you're up for it.'

I turned to Larry, happy things were back on an even keel with us. 'Certainly. Count me in.'

Then my cousin nodded to the *fromage et jambon* monster I

had barely made a dent in. 'You know, if something does come up with my research, you won't be eating many more of those.'

I smiled at this. At least his confrontational humour had made a reappearance. 'Perhaps not,' I said. 'But it was your choice. There's no shortage of bagels around here. We didn't have to dig on swine.'

'Shit, I suppose not,' he said, as if weighing up some internal contradiction. 'I forgot about that.'

One of the literary observations that sparked my Francophilia as a teenager was Henry Miller's assertion that Parisian women, unlike their English or American counterparts, didn't look away when they caught your glance; instead they held it fearlessly. And these were not just the streetwalkers of Les Halles, but respectable women with their Dior bags, returning to their duplexes high above the rue de Rivoli. When I finally tried this theory out on my next visit as a callow, hormone-raging young man of fifteen, I was amazed to find Miller was correct. They really did return one's stare, and with a look of brutal pragmatism, too. When it came to matters of the body, French women knew how to handle the reins.

Thirty years later, as I walked in the nasty drizzle on the way to meet Larry and Nadir, the yellow Parisian twilight fast descending on the boulevard Pasteur, I found Miller's rule still held. Every woman I passed, despite the blowy weather, returned my look. Why I was practising this now, I had no idea. Maybe I felt the time for such flirtations was fast running out.

Late for our rendezvous, though not imagining they minded

much, I eventually found the dingy Café Mont-Saint-Michel up a side street off the rue de Vaugirard, and nowhere near where Larry had described it. Not that the walk had been wholly unpleasant. I had gone to La Hune to pick up my book of essays on the black Jacobins (I had forgotten about it after Cass's bombshell), and decided to hoof it all the way down the rue de Rennes to where it meets Vaugirard. There at the busy intersection, hampered by rain and late shoppers, I was startled to see the ebon chip of the Tour Montparnasse looming distantly at the end of the road. There's a similar experience provided by the Eiffel Tower – one that Parisians know and love – of looking up suddenly to see the tower gracefully erect and in full view through a gap in the buildings. Even more special to look up again, around 5 p.m., when the famous lights flicker on, transforming it into a Christmas wonder. But the old black Tour wasn't welcome as I pushed my way south, waiting for the speedy pedestrian-crossing lights to slip to green. Behind it pulsed immense atmospheric disturbance, blue and grey rainclouds mushrooming at a considerable pace. I tried to take my eyes off it, but it proved hard. I concentrated instead on the reflections of yellow car headlights in the puddled boulevards, suddenly evocative and poetic at rush hour. Maybe it was the fact I had no idea what they did in the damn building that irked me so. Was it occupied by the money fiends? In which case, why didn't they move it lock, stock and barrel to La Défense? Undoubtedly, the effect of its appearance at the end of the vista was what the planners of the Gherkin had in mind – the same thing happens when you hit the Kingsland Road in London. There the thing is: fat and silver and almost touchable. But the

Tour hung over my walk, attempting to bedevil my mood, an endeavour in which it wasn't quite successful. I wanted to be positive around Nadir, both of us being in roughly the same boat, paternity-wise.

When I shoved through the tatty red doors and into the roar of the sports bar, I found my cousin and the good professor propping up the zinc; both a couple of beers down. It was over an hour before I caught them up and they stopped talking Institut business; complex science of which I had no comprehension.

Abruptly, Nadir said: 'You know, La-ree, I have been investigating your Bobby Dylan – a very brilliant commentator on politics and the human heart. It's rare to find the two combined.'

With his silver scrolls of hair and dense beard, Nadir was looking very distinguished. This hair, I imagined, warmed his neck. There was a chilly breeze blowing in from the street; the café now full with workmen hollering away at a match on a fuzzy screen in the corner. With both Nadir and Larry bearded, I felt a masculine deficit immediately.

'So you got around to him?' enquired Larry, his right foot up on the brass rail. I had gathered he had lent the professor most of his Dylan and Woody collections to help ease his passage into the new apartment. 'It takes a lifetime to get really acquainted.'

'Undoubtedly. It is the same with many eminent cultural figures. One takes away a distorted view from the media.'

'What was your favourite Woody movie?'

Like a good academic, Nadir had studied them all.

'Allen has fallen off of late,' said the professor seriously, as if passing judgement on an eminent colleague who everyone knows is showing the first signs of Alzheimer's.

'So you like the earlier, funnier films?' I pitched in.

'No. In my opinion his best is *Husbands and Wives*. To that I could relate.'

'A fine choice,' remarked Larry.

'And I also particularly like the line in *Love and Death* about not wanting to commit suicide in despair at a Godless universe, just in case you read in the papers a couple of weeks later they've found something.'

At that moment, there was a cheer from the whole bar as a goal was scored, as if everyone was laughing at Woody's one-liner.

'And favourite Bob?' asked Larry hopefully, like the Jehovah's Witness who feels he has just made a convert.

'*Nashville Skyline* has been on rotation in the new flat since I moved in. "I Threw It All Away" is his best lyric. By far. So shrewd an analysis! Of my own life, in fact. It is as though Mr Dylan has already lived it all before me!'

'How is the new place?' I enquired, not wanting to spend the entire evening discussing my cousin's obsessions. God knows, I'd had a lifetime of that.

'It will *do*,' said Nadir, non-committally; and I saw there was much he didn't want to go into. Much privation and humiliation that he still had trouble assimilating, considering himself, as he did, to be a family man, a paterfamilias. 'As Larry will attest – nothing can beat the last apartment for squalor and depression.'

Nadir's eyes were up on the ceiling now, as if examining the greenish patina – the result of a million packets of Gauloises – for answers to life's conundrums. The very paintwork was cured. Larry had raised his finger to the barman a moment ago, and three Kronenbourgs, their golden bodies crowned with foam, appeared on the bar before us.

'So,' I began, 'how was it for Ajooni, Geena and Nanak when they came over?' I surprised myself at how hungry I was for information about his family. I had learned the names of his three children over the summer. Ajooni, the eldest, and born in the Punjab, was apparently most like her mother; while Geena, the middle child, was fifteen and starting to rebel. The boy, Nanak – his father's joy, and about whom Nadir couldn't talk without knobbles of emotion erupting on his forehead – had just turned thirteen.

'It was an amazing thing to see them again,' Nadir smiled, his face brimming with feeling. 'Ajooni is like a grown woman now at seventeen. I hardly recognised her. But Geena is the ringleader.'

'How do you mean?' asked Larry, taking a pull on his new beer.

'She organised the mutiny, as it were. Told her mother they still had a father, that he lived in the same city and they were all going to visit him in his new abode.'

'You said she was fearless,' I added.

'A total firebrand! God knows where she gets it from.'

'Her mother?' suggested Larry.

'Not even from Jaspreet, no. Maybe her grandmother. Granny-*jaan* has been over to visit many times in my absence.

She even insisted they go to the Gurdwara more than once a week.'

Nadir had told me that Paris, incredibly, only had one place of Sikh worship, the Singh Sabha, a blighted-looking place on the last stop of the Métro out near Charles de Gaulle airport. Also hard to believe was that it doubled as a Hindu temple too.

'I can't imagine they enjoyed that much,' said Larry.

'No, no,' insisted the professor, turning to Larry. 'You would be surprised how much they do. They told me they have been singing *kirtan* and helping out in the kitchens. It is hard for you to understand how we thirst for a sense of community here, a sense of belonging. It is, as they say, *très difficile* to belong in Paris. And now the school is telling Nanak to cut off his hair…'

'What did they think of the new pad?'

'Very much like where they live now,' laughed Nadir. 'The same crummy balcony that's too small to dry your clothes on. The sounds of the neighbours and their *amours* all night.'

'At least there are no murders or gambling,' I suggested. The professor had told me how both had been features of the Bobigny estate where *les flics* were a constant presence, pulling bodies from wheelie bins, busting terrorists, or breaking up illegal poker dens and dog fights.

'True, true,' nodded the professor in his considered fashion. 'It is quieter here. You probably passed my block on the way. It's next door to Montparnasse Expression.'

'Ah, I think I know where you mean…' I remembered this little shop, a few hundred yards from the amber-lit Institut itself. A sad electronics and photocopy place that appeared days away from going out of business, offering *façonnage* and *tous travaux d'impression*. The whole district in fact had a frayed, peripheral feel to it – as if central Paris had given way to Clichy. The street where the bar stood, the rue des Volontaires, was a dirty, climbing cut-through behind the station, only frequented by the donkey-jacketed workmen who were stamping their feet at a missed penalty on the TV screen.

'But home is where one's children are,' said Nadir, attempting profundity through the fug of alcohol. 'So for a night – when they joined me – it was home.'

'You really believe that?' asked Larry. 'I mean, many times you've told me about taking them back to Bathinda. Isn't the Adesh Institute always offering your old post back?'

'Yes, that is true,' said Nadir, his thriving pewter beard dabbed with foam, something about which neither of us wanted to inform him. 'But my children have grown up French. They are more French than Indian. And when they came to visit I felt I was at home.'

Stirred by this notion – feeling many unwelcome fears myself – I said: 'I'm hoping that will be the case when Ed comes and sees me.'

'I hope so too, Nick. Although I don't know how good he is in the kitchen. As you know, I am incompetent in culinary matters, so Ajooni cooked us a biryani. All in all it was a magnificent evening.'

Behind the mild spectacles there was a force to Nadir's eyes – what I imagined to be the intense gaze of the patriarch, now neutralised by his ostracism, but still present and waiting to assume righteous control. His hands too, turning and turning his beer on its cardboard mat, were powerful hands, brown with tufts of spiderish hair.

'Now my three are almost grown,' he said in his temperate but firm way, 'you see how the children you have helped to create suddenly have their own spontaneous lives; plans and thoughts and emotions you cannot control. This might not be so easy to observe in your son because he is still small.'

'Oh, it is.'

'Sure, sure. But as they get older you will observe they have a vitality that is out of their parents' jurisdiction. And this is only correct. Nanak-ji will one day see that I did not abandon him, even though I can see he is beginning to turn against me.'

'Really?' asked Larry.

'Yes, La-ree-ji' Nadir replied, sadly. The more the professor drank, the more this affectionate suffix surfaced. 'But I must let him feel his resentments. Let him live his own life.'

'I can see the same thing happening with Ed,' I added, my chest constricting uncomfortably at the mere thought.

'The thing is, gentlemen,' said Nadir. 'Families go on for ever, despite their members dying. I can see now that ending a family has consequences that those who end it never envisaged. The repercussions keep returning to your door. My three will never stop thinking of me – or wanting to see me, hopefully – until the day they die. And when they visit again, I will once more feel as if I am at home. You have to create home where you can find it.'

Larry and I nodded at this, almost furiously in my case.

'It must be a good sign, surely,' I said, 'that Jaspreet sanctioned their visit after all this time.'

'*Peut-être*. Maybe she doesn't have a stony heart after all. And she can see where it's heading. A broken family is an entropic system.'

'That's a fine way of putting it,' I smiled.

Miraculously, another three beers had appeared before us. It was shaping up to be quite a night. Despite the subject of our conversation, I was feeling oddly high or transcendent – connected somehow to higher energies; free of the cerebral yak that academics usually indulge in when together. It was as if this was an exchange all three of us had needed for a long time.

'And even she,' Nadir continued, 'hasn't had it so easy. Despite taking all my money, around Bobigny they have long called her a *randi rona*.'

'What's that?' broke in Larry, his annoyance at things he didn't know showing itself in his frown as usual.

'A discarded woman, euphemistically speaking.'

There was a moment's silence between us; all three of us lost in our own contemplations.

Then Nadir said: 'How are you gentlemen with death?'

It was a startling question, one at which I almost laughed.

The professor continued, 'Only I am a few years older than you, and it seems to be my constant companion. I was wondering, quite idly, whether you two had reached that stage earlier than me.'

'I reached it long ago, Nadir,' I smiled. 'Maybe not every third thought—'

'Only now I cannot help but feel life is like a diving board. You inch along it for years, confident there is much distance to go before you reach the edge. And then suddenly, one day, the whole board is behind you, and you are face to face with the deep water below.'

'That's an image I will try to forget the moment we leave this bar,' said Larry.

'Me too,' I assented, 'though it might be hard now.'

'Anyway, I've always thought one's attitude to death depends on what you do or don't believe.' Larry knew Nadir wasn't an observant Sikh, and they had long ago given up debating the possible existence of an afterlife. For two scientists, such conversations always seemed to be premised on absurdities from the start.

'Yes,' nodded Nadir, finally wiping the foam from his beard in a big swipe. 'Kierkegaard said belief begins where thinking leaves off.'

'I still have naïve notions of spiritual connections,' I ventured. 'We leave indelible imprints in each other, so why not the cosmos?'

'I am too drunk to answer that coherently, Nick,' said Nadir, probably glad that not many of the surrounding Frenchmen could understand a word of our conversation. 'But in the Sikh religion we have a phrase, used when someone dies, that brings me comfort.'

'What's that?' asked Larry, eager, as only an atheist can be, to have his convictions proved wrong.

'*Pura ho gaya*,' said Nadir, but with no spin of reverence. 'It simply means someone had completed their span of life on this earth. And, if you believe in such things, that their soul is ready to begin its gradual transmigration.'

'So, it's like saying someone had a good innings?' I offered.

'Not quite,' Nadir said, turning to me sharply. 'In fact, the distinction is fairly considerable. Your phrase is for old-timers who kick the bucket. *Pura ho gaya* means that, even if one dies relatively young, there is an acceptance that this was your allotted time on earth. That is what brings me comfort. It applies to any passing.'

'Ah,' said Larry in his high facetious tone, 'but who does the allotting?'

'God, of course!' Nadir roared, the volume of his voice taking us both by surprise. His outburst had the effect of foreclosing the subject. We all knew not to get into such debates now.

'Yeah, who else?' grinned Larry. 'The Big Boss.'

'You know,' Nadir said, light from the glittering bar in his spectacles, making it hard to read his eyes, 'when I first began work in Paris, fifteen years ago, I was assigned as an assistant consultant, one day a week, to the old Hôtel Dieu on the Île. The name was a constant source of not amusement or wonder, but stimulation.'

'Why's that?' I asked, naïvely. The name of the oldest hospital in Paris had long since lost any philosophical spin for me.

'Because,' Nadir said with maximum gravitas, 'it made me realise – whether you're a believer or not – that we are all staying in God's hotel, and we must remember to pay the bill before we leave…'

The drink was certainly bringing out the homespun wisdom, though Larry and I could do nothing but nod in agreement at this. I took a quick glance around the place: it was steeped in drink and lives most definitely more difficult than our own – like something out of Zola. Soon the match would end and all the men (I couldn't see a single female among them) would trudge back home to their womenfolk, and deal with whatever situations they had to deal with... Yet, after our talk, I was certain I didn't want any of it to end. I didn't want the match to end. I didn't want the three of us to return to our several existences. I didn't want our lives to end – I dreaded the day when we would all topple over the edge of our own diving boards. I wanted us all to remain there, at that beer-sticky bar, for ever.

The day after Ariel's birthday, I received a frantic call from my cousin very late at night. It was only after I sat up in bed, squinting at the illumination from the screen of my mobile, that I realised it was in fact the middle of the night – 2 a.m., to be precise.

'What's the matter?' I asked urgently. 'Is something wrong?'

'Yes, Nick,' came Larry's voice, very high. 'You could say that. And I'm sorry to wake you.'

'For Christ's sake, Larry, it's two in the morning.'

'I know, I know.'

I could hear ambient noise in the background and thought for a moment he might be on the street.

'Where are you?'

'I'll tell you in a moment.'

'You're not at the Levines'?'

'No, I'm not.'

'Larry, if you're going to be fucking cryptic, I'm really going to lose it with you.'

Since our drink with Nadir I hadn't been sleeping well at all. Not only was the work on the book not holding me, but Cass and Ed, at the last moment, had cancelled their half-term visit. I had been mortified by this, though tried not to show it when talking to my son. Pressure of work and preparation for moving to the States had been blamed – she simply didn't have the time, she informed me, to take a week's holiday in Paris. Whether I would see them at all before Christmas was still up in the air. Never having been an advocate of sleeping pills – and now, of *any* pills – I had taken to willing myself to sleep every night, trying to forget about the whole fiasco. It had been hard, but most nights I made it after reading something involving but not too heavy. Maurois' fleet-footed biography of Balzac had done the trick earlier that evening, but now Larry's intrusion had put me into the red. Zero to 100 mph in a matter of moments. I tried to collect myself as he explained.

'I've had a day you wouldn't believe, Nick. A great many things have changed and I'm just trying to get my head around them.'

'Okay,' I said, mentally counting to ten. 'Start from the start.'

'I had an extraordinary meeting with François and Rivka this morning.'

'Meeting? Sounds like you're in business together. Where?'

'Hold on – I'll get to all that… I'm still trembling, from the implications.'

'Implications of what?'

'Of what went down. Listen, this is hard for me…'

'Harder for me.'

'Ariel came along too.'

'Where?' I demanded, tugging the bedclothes, my eyes acclimatising to the light. The white-painted walls of the bedroom, which I usually found so relaxing, were failing to calm me down. I felt as if I was talking to Larry from inside a sensory deprivation tank, or a dream. For some reason, turning on the bedside lamp was not an option. Perhaps I thought it might be impossible to get back to sleep if I did.

'To the Institut.'

Baffled by this, I said. 'Okay, so they all came to see the world-famous labs. You're going to have to tell me what this is all about soon.'

'The upshot, Nick,' and his voice constricted at what he was about to say, 'is that I am now persona non grata in the eyes of Ariel's parents.'

'That's pretty serious,' I said, sitting up even higher, fully alert now.

'You're telling me, man.'

'What precipitated that?'

Larry paused, then said: 'I asked her to marry me.'

'Jesus!'

'I know.'

'When?'

'Last night, at her birthday party. Everything was going so well – we were on the boat by the Quai Malaquais. You couldn't imagine a more romantic setting.'

'I can picture it… But what happened?'

'Well, to cut a long story in two, she told her folks in the morning—'

'And they came to discuss the matter with you.'

'Correct.'

In a pause, I heard the wailing sirens of Paris's police vans, no doubt tearing down the underpasses near the river. In my surprise at his revelation, I forgot to ask what Ariel's reply had been.

'Larry,' I asked tentatively. 'Where are you calling from?'

With a terrible, heaving sigh of irony, he said: 'My old place.'

'On the rue André Gide? You're joking.'

'Nope. Not joking. They let me have it back.'

'Don't tell me – it was empty after Nadir moved out?'

Through gritted teeth, my cousin said: 'Yes.'

I let this sink in for a moment, and allowed Larry to have his say. Such a reversal was hard to comprehend all at once. We talked for another hour at least. I know it was about that long, as it was ten past three when I finally reset the phone's alarm to give me an extra hour's sleep in the morning.

Let me reconstruct Larry's showdown with the Levines for you. I will try to be as truthful as possible. Usually, if I'm awake enough, I have a good ear for the telling detail; though as he gabbled on, I needed to read deeply between the lines regarding much of what he said.

The way he told it, he had just put on his lab coat at half ten, and was on his way down the corridor on the sixth floor when he was startled to see the lift open at the end of the passageway, disgorging François, Rivka and Ariel. He said he'd been so hung-over, he thought for a moment he was hallucinating. I remembered this corridor from my visit. High over the rue de Vaugirard, it afforded, through smoked glass, a view of the bleak tower blocks of southern Paris – of Bagneux and Malakoff, with planes taking off distantly and soundlessly from Orly Airport.

'My goodness...' Larry exclaimed, stopping dead in the corridor, unprepared for any contretemps, let alone the coming onslaught. He hadn't seen them at breakfast, which wasn't unusual, and had gone straight from his guest bedroom, where Ariel usually slept, to the shower and so to the RER for Pasteur. But it was surreal, he said, to see them suddenly transplanted there, *en famille*, for the first time. 'What brings you all here?'

'Monsieur,' began François, and from where Larry was standing he could detect the *citron* cologne, at full morning strength. 'We must discuss this matter urgently. Before it goes any further.'

Once they were all face to face, Larry noticed at once that Ariel had been crying, and that she was there under considerable duress.

'Shall we go somewhere more private?' Larry asked cautiously, attempting to usher them along. And this was the part that surprised him the most; that sent him the widest curve. No, insisted Rivka, who was smiling with her even-lipped mouth – like a smile painted on to an egg, as Larry had described it – the corridor would do, and anyway they both didn't have time as they were off to work. For such a private man as François – and one so much in the public eye – to stage such an intervention in the corridor of a public building was extraordinary to Larry. But that's exactly what happened. The parents and defiant daughter had stood their ground in front of him.

'Monsieur,' François had repeated, as if getting something off his chest that had long weighed heavy. 'It is not possible for you to marry my daughter.'

The sentence had hit my cousin like a punch to the sternum.

'I see,' he said slowly, looking to Ariel, who appeared struck dumb by the situation herself – a little girl, really, savagely overgrown into carnal womanhood. 'I was going to ask your permission, formally, of course.'

'Well, n-now there is no need,' the father stammered in English, towering over him, a deranged look appearing in his avian eyes.

'Care to tell me why you have reached this decision?' asked Larry, crestfallen and more than a little angry.

'Monsieur, surely it is obvious,' and he paused for maximum effect. 'She is Jewish, and you are a Gentile.'

For some reason, Larry hadn't thought being a goy top of the Levines' list of possible objections. Not belonging to the same *beau monde* of François' family he imagined as his main impediment. That, along with the age differential, and his wild and woolly ways. Afterwards he had lamented to me that he should have just blurted out, 'But *I am* Jewish!' Though he couldn't provide anything in the way of conclusive proof. 'And anyway,' he said, 'we always forget to say the most important things in arguments.'

There had been a stunned silence in the corridor. The very walls seemed to reel from this explicit statement of what the Levines assumed to be a prosaic fact. *You are a Gentile.*

Rivka broke the pause.

'*Nous sommes désolés*,' she said, moving forward as if to touch him; her dignified seashell earrings trembling in her earlobes, 'but we cannot accept our daughter marrying *out*, Law-rawnce. It is completely unacceptable.'

'I'm sorry,' Larry said uncertainly. 'I didn't think that was going to be such a big deal…'

This was clearly the wrong thing to say. All of François' proud talk about French *laïcité*, of his staunch secularism, had suddenly vanished into the chemical-pungent air of the Institut.

'Yes, *docteur*,' the father rejoined, with imperious sarcasm, as he enunciated my cousin's title, 'to us it is a big deal.'

Then Rivka added: 'A *very* big deal, I am afraid.'

At this moment, Ariel turned on her mother venomously: 'And you, *Maman*, would know all about that.'

The daughter spat the words with a cold accuracy.

'*Chérie*,' insisted Rivka, with a faux insouciance, 'that was the nineteen-seventies.'

'As if that excused anything!' Larry had said later. He had told me long ago that Rivka's first husband, Bernard, had been a non-Jew who had in effect saved her from perpetual obscurity when she first arrived in Paris. A designer, he had taught her the perfect French she now deployed with such style, and then taken her to New York. Which, of course, is where she met François when he was still a lawyer. To Rivka, the question of whether she upheld tradition had seemed irrelevant in that laissez-faire decade. But now it appeared to be of supreme importance.

'*Nom de Dieu!*' continued the daughter. 'Your first husband is a goy, but I am not allowed to marry one.'

'We will not discuss this now, in this situation,' said Rivka evenly, still smiling.

Here Ariel pointed at Larry: 'Who cares if he is not a Jew!'

Which caused my cousin to say, inanely: 'I'm sorry. I can't help it.'

'You are both such hypocrites!' Ariel continued, causing François to physically take her right forearm in his huge grip. Perhaps he thought she might make a bolt for it. Everyone's temperature was rising uncontrollably. The father was insistent that they clear the matter up once and for all.

'*Ça suffit!*' he snapped.

But Ariel hadn't finished. '*Alors*. What is okay for you is not okay for me, yes?' There was a husky force to her voice that gave it authority.

'We are a family, and we will do things in the tradition of that family,' announced François pompously. His daughter was trying to break away, but he held her firmly.

'Your father is correct,' added Rivka. And then, quick as the jaws of crocodile: 'The matter is closed.'

'No, *Maman*,' exploded Ariel. 'It is far from closed!'

Larry's sense of despair, of hallucination, was now overwhelming him. He had looked down six floors and seen a slurry of gold from the mulched leaves in the gutters below. All through the confrontation he had been looking over the Levines' shoulders in terror that the lift doors would open. He had never witnessed a domestic scene like this – even when his father had been exposed as a philanderer, there had been no open vituperation. As they continued to fight among themselves, Larry had told me his mind had returned with high sadness to the previous day. He had visited the flower market on the Île de la Cité and bought up the most exquisite peonies and tulips he could find. These he had distributed around Ariel's room, which already heaved with gifts and cards. In his pocket had been the sapphire engagement ring, secreted like a revolver, that he had purchased only the week previously. Until he produced it later, on the deck of the clamorous boat – the lights of the Louvre sending impossibly romantic yellow threads over the swell of the Seine – Ariel had thought the blooms were her only gift. She had been overwhelmed. To be proposed to on her twenty-first birthday by the man she loved had rekindled all her girlish dreams, the type that modern women like her were supposed to scorn. She had said *Oui*, to Larry's offer. *Oui*, a hundred times over, and he had slipped the ring onto her slim third finger, where it had glittered enchantingly in the freezing Parisian night. It was significant that she wasn't wearing it in the corridor of the Institut. Rivka, no doubt, had banished it the moment she laid eyes on it at breakfast. To go from such happiness to such plunging despair in the space of a day! It was all intolerable to Larry. He could see his dreams dying before his eyes, almost as if they were laboratory animals, determinedly being put to death under the vivisectionist's coldly callous gaze.

'You cannot insult us like this!' François was raging at his daughter. 'And in public too!'

'No? Well, you cannot control me,' returned Ariel. 'You just cannot!'

'*Tais-toi, maintenant*,' intervened the mother.

And then Ariel deployed the heavy artillery, something

Larry had feared from the start. In a low growl she turned on her father: 'You may control Solange, your *petite poule*, but you cannot force me to do something I do not wish… I am in love with Larry and I am going to marry him!'

With the mention of Solange, François let go of her arm. She had apparently committed a cardinal sin, one never ventured in French families. Mitterrand might have made his wife and his latest squeeze into best friends, but, as a rule, you didn't bring up the mistress. This was something you never did. She was a secret to be kept hidden in plain sight. To refer to her by name was pretty much the opposite of *comme il faut*.

There was suddenly no rancour in François' voice as he spoke. 'That is my business.'

'*Vraiment*? Well, your little Solange is why you are *un hypocrite aussi*!'

'*Arrête, maintenant*!' said Rivka.

Ariel ignored her. 'Is Solange a Jew?'

'Ariel!' reprimanded her mother.

Both Rivka and François were now silently at boiling point, wishing, perhaps, that they had never come – that they had curtailed Larry's crazy marriage scheme by email. Indeed, my cousin had spent abundant time on the phone with me wondering why they had chosen to follow him to the Institut and have it out there. It was still baffling. Certainly they wanted to nip his proposal in the bud, but why hadn't they waited until he returned in the evening? Perhaps – and this was the most convincing explanation – they hadn't wanted such a soiling exchange to take place on the hallowed parquet floors of the Place des Vosges apartment.

But Ariel wouldn't let it go, as Larry helplessly watched the rusty leaves fall in the street below.

'Tell me, Papa, is Solange a Jew?'

'Ariel!' Rivka exclaimed.

Larry now held his hands up in defeat. 'François, Madame – I can accept what you have come to tell me…'

'Is she a Jew?'

'*Ariel*!'

François raised his distinguished nose to the fluorescent strip lighting, unwilling to lower himself to this level of debate.

'So, it is okay for you to *fuck* a non-Jew, but not for me to *marry* one?' She was raging, her cascades of black hair shimmering with a kind of righteous power.

'*Ça suffit*!' Rivka hissed.

Larry felt she might have slapped her daughter if it wasn't for the look of triumph now on Ariel's face. She had made her point. Whether it would change anything was doubtful. Larry by this time was almost fainting, not just from the startling reversal of his fortunes, but from the potency of François' cologne.

'Listen,' he began unsteadily. 'I – we,' and he indicated Ariel, 'should have discussed all this with you long ago.'

'*Certainement*,' nodded Rivka, calmer now.

'It was wrong of me to make certain assumptions…'

Ariel glowered at this. There was no doubt, according to Larry, that she would remain defiant to the end.

'It is not that we do not like you, Law-rence,' advanced the mother. 'Quite the opposite.'

'Thank you,' managed Larry, relieved, but still hopeless inside. 'One never knows until one is told.'

'We have enjoyed having you in our home for the last few months...'

The use of the past tense was a fresh shock to Larry. For the first time that morning he began to realise the full implications of the Levines' visit.

'And vice versa,' he said.

'You have broadened our horizons immensely.'

François, with a look of shame barely concealed on his finely etched face, added, 'You have been an impeccable guest...'

'But now?' asked Larry, willing them to come out with it.

'But now, I am afraid, it cannot be.'

The words kicked Larry in the shins. 'I'm sorry. What cannot be? Your daughter's hand in marriage. Or me continuing to stay under your roof?'

There was a silence in which Larry looked back and forth between the parents. Ariel stood to one side, a sulky look of indifference on her face – careless of the whole silly scene, but nonetheless aware that there were matters over which she had no jurisdiction.

'*Malheureusement...*' stated François. 'Both.'

'So... you're saying I must move out?'

François nodded, causing Ariel to sigh, and mutter, '*Putain de merde...*'

Rivka stepped forward, and here she stunned Larry by taking up both of his hands in hers. He remembered how warm they were, and how cold and lifeless his felt in her gentle grip.

'*Tout a une fin,*' she said, with genuine regret. '*C'est dommage*, but we will have to say goodbye to you.'

Larry was poleaxed. Still with Rivka's hands in his, he managed, 'I see.'

'We are sorry,' Rivka went on, 'but there are certain things that cannot – how do you say – be count-en-*nornced*.' And she pronounced the last word with a slithery finality.

'Thank you for your hospitality,' Larry muttered stupidly. 'I have valued it… and enjoyed it… more than you know.'

'Ariel will help you collect your belongings, but now…' and Rivka looked grandly at her husband, 'we have many things to attend to. *Au revoir*.'

And she leant forward and delivered the full *trois baisers*.

In seconds they were gone – François sheepishly, but deliberately, avoiding a handshake. They disappeared into the lift, and so off to their high-powered jobs; leaving Larry alone with Ariel, the black kohl from her earlier tears caked and cracked under her defeated brown eyes.

It certainly was an extraordinary scene. The long and short of it was that Larry spent the rest of the day organising accommodation with the Institut (his old dump was all they had to offer), and ferrying his stuff from the Marais to Montparnasse in Ariel's Citroën. I asked him if he had been on the balcony when he first called, then remembered his old place didn't have one. The street noise I imagined was indeed the street – he had just bidden a sad farewell to Ariel, who had driven home across the river, while he went indoors to open a bottle of whiskey that François, ironically, had given him earlier in the year. Understandably, he was in pieces. There was no denying the bald facts of his situation. To them, he was an English goy from a modest background, while she was an adored daughter from a swanky Parisian family who was still studying for her degree. What were the chances of the Levines supporting their engagement? There was no way they'd sanction their daughter marrying out. I felt strong sympathy for Larry, and hopefully managed to impart this despite my anger at being jolted awake in the middle of the night, thinking someone had died. Who were these stuck-up *gens chics* to reject my cousin? He had plenty to offer, damn them! He was still young and vigorous, with a brilliant, if wayward, mind. The mystery of ethnic bonds was something I would never fully understand. Surely if two people were in love, in this day and age, this sanctioned the union? I thought – as had Ariel, evidently – that we had moved on from such prohibitions. The Levines still played by the old rules, quite obviously. Larry had told me that their lecture – before they got going on Rivka's ex-husband and Solange – had been all '*il faut que* this, *il faut que* that…' He hadn't realised that, in life, there were so many things that were *necessary*, either to remember or to do.

The fact was, the rebel angel was now in descent at a considerable rate of knots, and had no idea about its next move. Ariel had said she would stick by him, would marry him and love him through eternity, et cetera, but she didn't fancy her chances of survival if she wore his ring again under François' roof. She was sure she would bring them round in the end. But my cousin wasn't so certain. After she had gone, halfway through the bottle of absurdly expensive single malt, Larry kept repeating a single phrase to me: *quel plouc*. What a mug. What a mug he had been not to see all this coming. '*Quel plouc!*'

Towards the end of our conversation, clutching at straws in order to provide Larry some comfort, I asked: 'Did the Levines actually know about your research into Lotte?'

For the first time since we began speaking he became cagey. 'I'd mentioned it... a couple of times. As did Ariel. But they maintained this kind of lofty silence every time I brought it up, so I didn't push it.'

'Might it change things if they knew?'

Larry laughed drily. 'François would want a full DNA test proving I was related to Adler and Freud to be convinced. Followed by me dropping my pants for a final inspection. But hey – I live in hope.'

'One would have thought your status as a scientist counted for something. Rube's a great guy, but imagine their bourgeois *horreur* if he had proposed and not you.'

'Oh sure,' said Larry. 'They would have had a collective brain haemorrhage. Of course, they would love *un médecin dans la famille*, just not a Gentile one.'

'What are you going to do?'

'I'm not sure, Nick. I'm up to my eyes at work. There are reports and articles stacked up that I haven't attended to... And now this. It's thrown me the widest curve. I don't think it's all sunk in yet. You know, I had become used to their place, their old-world manners, their...'

'Say it.'

'Jewishness.'

Larry went on to tell me that in September, without the aid of a chef, Rivka had cooked a Rosh Hashanah dinner, of which he was invited to partake. Not just the gefilte fish and pickled herring he had grown used to, but a grand feast. She had slaved all day to recreate a nostalgic Eastern European meal, but 'zhuzhed up', to use her phrase. Starting with blini canapés, followed by a *zakuski* – a spread of small hot and cold Ukrainian Ashkenazi dishes – they had been startled when a giant curd-cheese flan had appeared from under a silver cloche as the *pièce de résistance*. It had been sumptuous, and he had sat reverently while the food had been blessed. He had felt truly welcome in their home for the first time. But now he had crossed an invisible line by asking for their daughter's hand, and they had done their utmost to push him back behind that line, where he could be of no further threat.

'You know,' he began again, his voice trebly and mournful. 'I kept thinking how little Ariel resembled her mother as they spoke. It's not often you find that with mothers and daughters – there's always some telltale gesture or behaviour or verbal tic, even if the physical resemblance isn't that much apparent. Her plump little hands had been so warm, as if she had been heating them for me… Ariel has her father's hands. And the way Ariel went at him about Solange. Almost as if *she* was the spurned woman, the wife who had lost him. There was that note of sexual betrayal there—'

'Larry?'

'What?'

'Tomorrow's another day.'

He sighed. '*Today's* another day.'

'We'll talk about it again in the morning. When you've got your bearings.'

'Cool,' he said, and I remembered at once how he used this

word all through his teenage years. It made me emotional just to hear it again. *Cool.*

Once I reset my alarm, I had to practise a kind of mental confidence trick to get back to sleep. As I finally drifted under, terribly concerned for Larry's future, I realised that listening to him had taken my mind off my own troubles with Cass and Ed for the first time in weeks. It was a relief; a deliverance, even. You might think all this is about me – my humiliating tribulations and trials – but it's not. It's about my cousin, in the end. It's about Larry.

The following day I took my coffee at an outside table of Le Bac Saint-Michel, which can be found on the boulevard if you continue in a southerly direction past the florists and the comedy theatre. The morning was a wonder of spangling autumn sunshine, and, despite my sleep-deprived weariness, I lingered on the way down to look in at the Rim Librairie second-hand bookshop, which had just begun to put out its stalls of old editions of Rimbaud and tomes on African art.

At my table, dipping my croissant into my *crème*, I obsessively went over what Larry had told me. He was in deep trouble, of that there was no doubt. Keeping pace with the twenty-first century was hard enough, let alone the setbacks and reversals of one's own private life. Sometimes just entering into the motion of any given day felt like jumping into rapids. I had begun to keep a journal again, or diary, after Cass's decision – partly just to record what was said at what point, just in case things turned litigious – and I had intended to write down much of what Larry said on my MacBook. But the pristine morning, the lulling rumble of the traffic, argued against this act of dry documentation. It was certain there weren't to be many gems like this for the rest of November. It felt oddly paradisal. The sun actually felt hot on my neck after I had removed my scarf. It was glorious to sit there, *sans* newspaper, in the golden haze of the low sun, imbibing the gasoline and rubber smells of the early traffic, just thinking.

In a strange sense, I could see that the Montague and Capulet hysteria of yesterday's scene – the high drama of love across divided clans – had been exciting to Larry. He still felt there was a way around the Levines, of course – persuasion had been his weapon of choice from infancy. Not only did he have an urgent need to belong, to claim an ethnic identity, he was in love with the whole package. For Old World manners, read luxury beyond his wildest dreams. Though not materialistic in any sense, Larry had been seduced by the goose-quill eiderdowns, the Louis XVI *fauteuils*, the Chagalls and Daumiers dripping from the walls. He liked being around it – so antithetical was it to the Formica-fest that was the house on Northolt Road. There was no warmth, or history, or sense of belonging there. He had become acclimatised to what Ed would term its *bling* – a word that had gone out of fashion ten years ago, but was seeing something of a revival. And more seriously, Larry believed in love. He wanted to devote the rest of his life to Ariel. He was ready to settle down with her and relinquish all others. He was feeling intensely all those heroic, oceanic yearnings that hit a man in his late thirties. And her parents were preventing him from putting any of it into action on grounds of his ethnicity. It was all very saddening, and I checked that my phone at my elbow had enough battery left, just in case my cousin sprang another epic call on me, as he had threatened.

Staring up the long perspective of the street, the sun glancing off the iron balustrades and double-backed benches, I pondered the truism that involving oneself in another's troubles is always richly therapeutic. As I told you, Larry's new situation had cooled me down over Cass's refusal to visit with my boy. It was true that I desperately wanted to see him again. To think they could be enjoying this Parisian sunshine – and were missing it in favour of drizzly London – was crushing, but perhaps not the chest-compressing sadness it had been. I knew now I would have to play the long game when it came to Ed. One can become too monothematic, especially living on one's own.

As I thought about all this, a gentleman in an old-style overcoat – too hot for the freakish weather – sat down a few feet away on one of the café's wicker chairs, which were all printed with the legend *Le Bac*. Slowly stripping the gloves from his hands, he laid his hat (yes, he was wearing a homburg, of all things) on the table and stared off down the street. It was one of Paris's joys, this silent communion at the outdoor café table – the covenant that you didn't need to have any other business in mind other than just sitting and watching. The man was in his seventies, heavy and tall, *distingué* – though not one of *les beiges*, the corduroy-wearing professors from the Sorbonne. He resembled a retired banker, one of many who had bought duplexes in the sixties – those pads with great views high over the boulevard Saint-Michel – and, for obvious reasons, had seen no need to leave. I watched as in seconds this man was joined by the wide-smiling maître d' – who seemed to know him well – to whom he nodded a regular order. After this he sat composedly, like me, allowing the sun to warm his old and angular face.

'*Le Monde, Le Monde... Libération!*'

The cry of a man on a bicycle made us both turn in its direction. A Korean-looking old-timer, wearing thick glasses, was locking his bike to a caged sapling, and smiling hopefully in our direction.

'*Les journaux, messieurs?*' he called out, as he advanced on us, pulling from his *sac* a wadge of periodicals and dailies.

He was on to the old man first, bending forward over the gold-rimmed circular table. Very genial and cheeky, he displayed his wares; though there was no sense of intrusion or hawking. They seemed to know each other and greeted each other warmly. He was on handshake terms – and with the *patron* too, who came out with the old man's *café* and exchanged a few words, which were lost to me under the grind of the traffic. I felt a pinch of regret at this scene – maybe it was just the legendary French bonhomie in action, but it had always been mysterious why I was unable to make easy friends with the locals and *vendeurs* like this. The old man bought his *Le Monde* and flattened it out before him with a serious expression. Though I had deliberately chosen not to buy my usual *Guardian* from the kiosk, I decided at once that I would do the same if the superbly genial Korean made his way over.

'*Libération! Le Monde,*' he hollered, as he caught my eye.

'*Pour moi, aussi,*' I said, indicating the old man's choice.

As he bent forward, placing the paper before me, I realised I only had a €10 note. But this was no trouble for the paper-seller: no trouble at all. Now that I could see his face close up, I saw his eyes, behind the lenses, were surrounded by raised webs of wrinkles, like the boles on a cherry tree. He was as old as the distinguished gentleman, and still doing a paper round.

'*La monnaie, pas de problème!*' he announced extravagantly, placing a €5 note and a column of coins carefully on top of the paper.

And then he was off, wobbling down the wide road. The old man and I had been the only pavement-dwellers at Le Bac, and without further customers the happy Korean had been forced to unchain his bicycle after a mere couple of minutes. I felt strangely sorry for him.

As I watched him disappear into the distance, towards Denfert, still calling, '*Le Monde, Le Monde,*' I recalled a similar man from my Parisian youth, who used to do the rounds of the cafés in the afternoons, selling next day's editions early. There was even a possibility it was the same guy.

I peered down at the paper – and how comforting and familiar was *Le Monde*, with its gothic typeface and tiny subheadings – to be confronted by a big picture of Camus. Only the French could place a photo of an Algerian philosopher and literary genius that prominently in a national newspaper. The *Guardian* had been favouring inert pictures of food or gurning celebrities for the past year – something the marketing gurus probably told them shifted copies. A couple of years ago had seen Camus' centenary, and he had been everywhere. The British press hardly followed suit for Dylan

Thomas the following year. Sarkozy, of all people, had wanted the author of *L'Étranger* interred in the Panthéon, but he had been blocked by *l'extrême droite*. The main headline was a piece about Christiane Taubira, France's black Justice Minister, who had been the focus of recent racist abuse. She was back in the news again. Two years previously, *Minute*, a so-called satirical magazine, had printed a headline that read: 'Clever as a monkey, Taubira gets her banana back'. Of course, the journal had pleaded innocence – the disgraceful headline was predicated on the fact that banana also means 'smile' in French slang. Now it was fresh abuse from the Front National. I read on for a few lines, shaking my head in disbelief. *Icône de la gauche et exécrée par la droite...* always the same implacable lines of attrition. Then I noticed that even the cartoon at the bottom of the page featured Camus, causing me to grin, and only just rescuing my admiration for all things French.

Scanning further down the front page, wondering if there was time for another coffee before I had to drag myself out of the scintillating sunshine and into a dusty library, I saw there was more about the mysterious male body dragged from the Seine a few days previously. A thin column, not meriting many of even *Le Monde*'s words, it wasn't a story that had exactly gripped Paris, as the man had been black. But Larry and I had discussed it before his showdown with the Levines. There was the famous case of a body found in the 1880s that had never been identified – *l'inconnue de la Seine* – whose death mask was later said to resemble Greta Garbo. There was no chance of this case, we agreed, reaching such levels of poetic notoriety.

Then, as I read further, I felt my heart arrest itself in mid-beat.

For a moment I couldn't believe the evidence of my own eyes. A sick medulla, heavy as a paperweight, gathered instantaneously in the pit of my stomach. The body taken from the Seine at the quai du Louvre on Monday night, the article stated, had been formally identified as that of Rubens Xavier, an emerging artist from the *vingtième*, Paris.

FIVE

While one could have foreseen Larry's situation – and perhaps mine with Cass – no one could have predicted what happened to Rube. Never the tragedy of Rube.

For days afterwards, everyone was numb with shock. Ariel went to stay with Larry on the rue André Gide, as she couldn't stand being around her stony parents in the aftermath of such a disaster, such a body blow. It was her first bereavement: her first fresh and startling experience of death, and Rube's murder – and it turned out it very definitely had been a murder, not a suicide, as some of the right-wing papers initially claimed – brought her and the man she still insisted on calling her fiancé even closer.

The facts were chilling. Post *Charlie Hebdo*, everyone knew racist attacks were on the rise in Europe, as were extremist right-wing positions in mainstream politics – indeed, two years previously, there had been the worrying launch of a pan-European alliance of far-right parties, and the sinister Pegida was currently on the march in Germany. Then there was the continued dismal and depressing electoral success of the FN – the Front National. But the racist murder of a rising artist was a new and shocking development. No one knew the exact location where Rube had been stabbed, but it hadn't been at his studio, or the flat in Belleville where he still lived with his mother. The most likely location was on the boulevard Masséna, after his regular Monday-night slot DJ-ing at the Petit Bain, a green barge under the new Bibliothèque Nationale that was fast becoming the hippest multimedia nightspot in Paris. His murder had immediately been linked to the JNR – the self-styled Young Revolutionary Nationalists, a Paris-based neo-Nazi group. Apparently, Rube had said something about them in an interview; a rant about how disgraceful and ludicrous they were, intimating they were responsible for the death in 2013 of Clément Méric. After reading this they had evidently come after him. Before the Hyper Cacher siege, the attack on Méric – an eighteen-year-old anti-fascist activist – was the one that had really jolted Paris awake. Out shopping in the Forum des Halles for Fred Perry and Ben Sherman shirts – both, curiously, favourites among skinhead and left-wing culture in France – he had apparently been involved in a verbal altercation with five members of the JNR, after which he had been punched with a knuckle-duster. The head of the fresh-faced youth had made contact with the concrete when he went down, and, as a result, he had died the following day. The anti-fascist group of which Méric had been a member – the Antifas – had a militant history going back to the 1920s, but he had been causing no trouble that day. His murder had precipitated rallies calling for the dissolution of all fascist organisations. I had briefly been in Paris that summer, and I recalled one that had gathered at the top of the boulevard Saint-Michel, near the fountain, with the Parisian Left, young and old, out in force; carrying placards with slogans scrawled hastily onto cardboard. The FN had distanced themselves from the Méric affair, and had themselves blamed the smaller, loosely organised groups of radical fascists, such as the JNR, who were in opposition to seemingly everything: gay marriage, Islam, Jews. And immigration, of course, especially from black and Asian populations. The demonstrations had been largely peaceful, but there had been some clashes with the police – intimations of things to come, perhaps. Indeed, Rube, Larry and I had discussed Méric and *Charlie Hebdo* back in July, sitting on upturned paint cans at the ultra-cool Andy Wahloo, drinking slaking pints of *blonde*. Rube had been disparaging about the paper, saying it occasionally carried racist and anti-Semitic cartoons, along with depictions of the Prophet. The fact that it had come to this was all very hard to believe.

The funeral was held seven days later, at the Église Saint-Germain de Charonne, very near Père-Lachaise, in the district where Rube's mother had brought him up as a good Catholic. A sad, rain-misty morning, with buffeting wind; the sky drained of light until it resembled a grey gruel.

I travelled there with Larry and Nadir, and our cab had moved slowly and gravely in heavy traffic up the rue de Bagnolet, with its trashy shops and fast-food outlets, just south of the imposing walls of the cemetery. We passed La Flèche d'Or, built into the old Charonne station, where Rube had DJed many times. And the streets where he had run as a young *tagueur*, no doubt. Finally we arrived at the church. With its red conical spire and austere white stone, it looked like something from the twelfth century, the kind of church we used to stop at in the sleepy *villes* while motoring through the Midi in the old Renault 4. As the back doors of our taxi were flung open to the wind and the rain, I had a sudden memory of the old car. I saw clearly – in detail only a child can gather – the choke, and the gearstick that resembled a plumbing tool; the rearview mounted on the dashboard in which I used to make faces in an attempt to make my father laugh while driving. It was a wonder any of us ever returned alive.

As we gathered ourselves by the kerb, I saw there were many figures in black already walking up the steep stone steps, like iron filings drawn by a magnet. Most had their heads bowed under glistening umbrellas. Rube had pulled a big crowd to his final show, quite clearly. There were all kinds here: artists, musicians, bohemians; but also black faces from the neighbourhood, ranging from seven to seventy. All were moving respectfully through the church's dark, medieval portal.

'*Ça va?*' Nadir shouted into the wind. He was wearing a grey Astrakhan hat, in lieu of his turban.

'Yes,' I replied, overwhelmed by the bleakness of the scene.

Larry, hollow-eyed; his big beard blown about his face, merely nodded in assent.

And the three of us, in our hired charcoal suits, followed the other mourners up the difficult steps.

I hadn't expected an hour-plus Catholic Requiem Mass, but that's what we got. Much of it was very moving, and not a little surreal. Under high walls of whitewashed stone, overlooked by statuettes of the Virgin and John the Baptist, we were ushered into a pew behind a woman I took to be Rube's mother.

Younger than I expected, she sat very still, her copper-brown hands gathered in her lap. Glancing to the left, across the nave, I saw the figure of Ariel, her head bowed intently, flanked by Ana and Delphine. It was a moment before I noticed the coffin – oiled pine with a cascade of gladioli on the top. I thought, stupidly, how lonely Rube must feel in there. As lonely as his mother in front of us; attentive in prayer, dry-eyed and enormously dignified. And Rube inside his box, dead for all eternity.

There were many hymns and readings, and we were up and down relentlessly for the solemn hour; reciting 'Hail Mary, full of Grace', and managing to sing along only by following a *basso profundo* from the pew behind. I had expected a black pastor, but we got a monkish, almost Amish figure out of a Bergman movie, who delivered a sermon that terrified us all – rich in obscure theosophy and quotations from Genesis; about the human as dust, or as so many piles of ashes. There was no reference to the manner of Rube's death or how his life had been taken as a result of bigotry and violence. A couple of his artist friends gave moving readings before we had to turn to our neighbour for the odd ritual of shaking hands with a stranger. Finally, we were all asked to walk up for the Eucharist – Larry, Nadir and I thankfully being given the opportunity to cross our hands over our chests to be blessed, rather than take the full blood and body of Christ in the form of the wafer and wine. Filing out under the papal curtain, past the shining coffin, thinking of Rube's body in the last moments it would remain *intacto* before it was taken to the crematorium, I experienced the full drama and mystery of the soul; the great question of its final destination. And all this to the accompaniment of one of Rube's favourite ska tunes: the rousing 'Freedom Day'. I wanted very much to hug his mother as we passed; but something in her eyes, just dots surrounded by spoilt mascara, naked in their solitary grief, advised me against it.

It was only when we were on the steps again that we talked to Ariel. It was her connection, after all, that brought us here – though we had all grown to love Rube. She told Larry that she was ditching the modelling to concentrate on her studies. Life was too short, she said, for *frivolités*. Lining the stone staircases, there were also many figures who looked like they belonged to the press, some photographing the coffin as it was laid into the rear of the hearse. We had anticipated them, but Ariel began looking with brutal intent in their direction.

'*Les cons*,' she said, her black veil flapping in the gale.

Larry went to hug her, and she burst into tears over his shoulder. I wanted to look away, or say something in support, but I could do neither for a moment. The service had been so unexpectedly stirring I felt speechless.

'Why do the beautiful ones always get it?' she was saying in muffled French. 'It's always those who die first.'

We all saw that her grief and bitterness had been intensified, somehow, by the attack on her own people at the start of the year.

'*Je sais, je sais…*' Larry comforted her.

'And why must they photograph him now?'

With her unstoppable tears, I suddenly saw her as Dylan's woman who breaks like a little girl. She might ache and make love like a woman, but I perceived at once how young and innocent she still was. There was her first boyfriend, now in a patiently waiting coffin, brutally murdered on account of the colour of his skin. This, and the Hyper Cacher siege, were certainly her personal introductions to a world where terrible things occurred, and daily too. Before January, nothing remotely like this had touched her own life during her sheltered upbringing on the Place des Vosges.

Ariel broke the embrace with Larry, and went to corral Ana and Delphine, who were walking slowly down the steps, arm in arm, like Pound's petals on the black bough.

Nadir talked with us for a moment, and then pointed to Rube's mother, who was standing strikingly alone at the top of the steps.

'There's not much family, is there?' he murmured.

'Rube's father left when he was two,' said Larry, numbly, his voice hampered by the drizzle. 'I think his mother forced him to go…'

At this, I thought, *Just like I was forced to*, and regretted at once the self-indulgence on such a morning.

'You know,' said Nadir, 'I think I shall go and offer *mes condoléances*.' And he turned back up the steps to talk to her.

This left Larry and me alone with each other. None of us except Ariel had been invited to the crematorium, and this was only correct. We hardly knew him. Even the director of the Yvon Lambert gallery, who had sat behind us in church, didn't know his artist that well, I imagined. Rube had been a loyal, almost noble presence. With his solemn, profound, immoveable aura, he had always come across as a man who had seen a lot – who knew the interiors of hidden, forbidden rooms; in the psyche as well as the thirteenth *arrondissement*, most probably. At that moment, all I could think of was the way his eyelashes had trembled with emotion as we talked to him at his big show in the summer. He had been a lovely, sensitive guy, and I wanted to engage some of his friends, hear their memories of him, before he became just another statistic of racist violence.

However, there wasn't to be the opportunity, as after five minutes reminiscing between ourselves about our nights with Rube, Larry said: 'You know, sorry to change the subject, but I had a message on the website that looks interesting.'

Over the last ten days since Rube's body had been found, and the police investigation had taken over, I had thought of little else other than his gruesome tragedy. For a moment I had no idea what my cousin was referring to.

'What do you mean?'

'You remember the post about Lotte?'

I noticed, on the street below, our cab had arrived, its driver pulling smoothly to the kerb. But no one was going anywhere until Rube did.

'Is this really the time, Larry?'

'No,' he said urgently. 'I need to tell someone. I can't discuss it with Ariel at the moment.'

'Obviously.'

'I think I might be on to something. There's this guy who says his mother knew our grandmother…'

I turned to Larry and saw the brimming concern in his eyes. It's strange how a beard curtails none of the emotion in a face. As with the niqab, the eyes do all the work. I had a sudden memory of being in a shopping mall in London with Ed, and asking directions of three women covered entirely in black except for thin vents revealing their eyes. When they started cooing over my son, I didn't need to see the whole face to tell they were genuine. It was there under their glossy Middle Eastern lashes.

'Someone from Vienna?'

'No. In Amsterdam, of all places.'

'Really? Was there more information?'

'I've emailed him back. But I'm still waiting for a reply.'

At that moment, there was a solid clunk from the street as the brutal boot of the hearse was slammed shut. Everyone turned. The car looked like a giant stag beetle there on the road; crouched in readiness to scuttle off – horribly glossy and slick.

'We'd better get Nadir,' I said, as people started to move. I looked up towards the church door and saw the professor, the wind battering his Red Square hat, talking gravely with the thin figure of Rube's mother. It looked as if he, alone of us gathered there, was providing some comfort.

'He'll catch us up,' Larry said, and we began to walk towards our car. 'But listen. Take a look at the website. See what you make of it.'

'I will,' I said, a gust of rain stinging my eyes until I was almost blind. 'I will.'

And then, inconceivably, things got worse.

Three days later, on Friday – the thirteenth, of all days – a meteor of hate hit Paris. Islamist gunmen, inspired by so-called

Islamic State, armed with Kalashnikovs and suicide belts, went on a rampage of killing in the tenth *arrondissement*, beginning with two blasts at the Stade de France, where Hollande had been watching a friendly between the national team and Germany, and then on to a series of seemingly random attacks on bars and restaurants along the rue Voltaire, culminating in the worst massacre seen on French soil since World War II. The Bataclan, a venerable, pagoda-like music venue I had often passed over the years, was attacked by the terrorists as a concert was in progress. Ninety young fans of a cult American band, ironically named the Eagles of Death Metal, were executed as they tried to escape, the killers reportedly shouting '*Allahu Akbar*' as they fired, blaming their actions on Hollande's recent airstrikes in Syria, until the police finally stormed the building.

The atrocity brought the city to its knees. If the *Charlie Hebdo* attacks in January had terrified Paris, there was still the lingering sense that the cartoonists had been culpable in satirising the Prophet; goading, almost, the snake of a blind, militant death cult to attack it. That assault was perceived as a political assassination, while the senseless siege and killing at the Hyper Cacher supermarket a few days later was viewed, as Larry had been the first to tell everyone, as a return of old-style anti-Semitism, the like of which Europe never wanted to see again. But the horror of Friday the thirteenth was on a different scale, and aimed at a different target. The snake that Hollande had failed to stamp out had returned to bite the city again, killing ten times as many people. And on this occasion, the targets had been a football stadium, a concert hall, three bars and a restaurant. Indeed, the reliably scuffed and bohemian Carillon, where fifteen were massacred as they enjoyed an al fresco drink on the unusually temperate November evening, was where I had been for a cognac with Larry after Rube's funeral. It was an attack not on a perceived political target and the Jewish community, but on the softest underbellies of a democracy; on sport and music, on the Parisian culture of *la terrasse*; on eating out, on drinking, friendship, laughter; on love itself.

The gloating, blood-drunk ISIS warlords in Syria had immediately taken time off from building their caliphate to pronounce the assault on Paris 'the first of the storm'. According to them, their so-called 'soldiers' had targeted the 'capital of prostitution and obscenity'. Yet, far from attacking the brothels and crack houses of the *dix-huitième*, they had targeted the *dixième*; the cool, multi-ethnic home of liberal, educated, creative Parisians; the young people most likely to oppose military intervention in the Middle East. And then they had blown themselves up, or slipped away to the *banlieues* of Saint-Denis, or across the border to Belgium. Undoubtedly, a new warfare where the enemy couldn't be identified by the colour of its uniform had been underway since 9/11. The world knew that well, and had fought vainly to combat it. But these attacks perhaps marked the horrific culmination of such warfare. Its masterpiece of destruction. Despite early paranoia that the terrorists had slipped into France with the streams of refugees fleeing Syria and North Africa, the majority of the attackers had in fact grown up and been radicalised in the mother country, until they had turned viciously against it with unimaginable brutality. And these amped-up, macho puritans had got it wrong, just as Puritans had done over the centuries. It wasn't an attack on degeneracy they were making, but on freedom: on *liberté, égalité, fraternité.*

The following day, Paris woke up in a state of trauma. My son called me breathlessly to check if I was okay, and I spoke to him for half an hour, reassuring him I was. How to explain such slaughter to a child? Impossible, so I didn't try. I even had a call from Birkbeck, enquiring after my safety. The previous night I had quickly phoned Larry and Nadir to confirm they were all right. It took longer to get hold of Ariel. She had been out with friends in a bar very near to La Belle Equipe, where nineteen people, many in the same party celebrating a birthday, had been gunned down. It turned out that a couple of her friends had been injured, but mercifully not killed, at the Bataclan. For my part, at 9 p.m. on the Friday, when the shooting started, I had been on the way home from a Paris Photo exhibition of fine-art photography at the Grand Palais. Once back in my apartment, I had stayed up most of the night, drinking beer after beer, glued to CNN; listening to the endless undulating wail of sirens along the Seine as they took the many hundreds of injured to the hospitals, which had, Paris learned later, been on a high 'white alert' for an attack such as this since January. Only Hollande seemed taken by surprise, declaring 'war' on ISIS the same evening, putting the city under a state of emergency that forbade people to gather in large numbers. To me, as a historian, this declaration seemed extraordinary – France had never even admitted it was at war with the Algerian FLN in the fifties and sixties, merely saying that it was locked into a struggle against 'outlaws'. When I met Larry later on the Saturday to lay flowers outside Le Carillon, whose pavement *terrasse* still bore carmine stains and shards of shattered glass, he told me war was exactly what ISIS wanted: a chance to engage with France's 'crusader' soldiers on what it deemed its own soil. He also told me that certain colleagues at the Institut had heard rumours that its American research students were already talking of leaving the city and heading home. 'Who are the surrender monkeys now, then?' he growled, through his big beard.

Rube's murder, and then the unthinkable terror of what happened a few days later cast the darkest of shadows over November. Far from taking our focus away from our grief over Rube, the orgy of violence in Paris's streets and venues intensified it – it seemed to close down the light and hope in our souls. Unlike Rube's racist stabbing, Friday the thirteenth appeared to be a random attack on the free people of a Western democracy as they went about their leisure pursuits. Anti-Semitism had again reared its head in an under-reported attack a few days later in Marseilles, where three young thugs in ISIS T-shirts had stabbed a Jewish schoolteacher on the street. Thankfully, the man had survived. But 130 did not, during that dark November night in Paris. On that Friday, as I had wandered with a glass of Malbec in my hand, between the tasteful shots of New York architecture and Delhi slums in the Grand Palais, the young of Paris had been losing their lives. The following day, their faces were everywhere, on the covers of *Libération*, *Le Monde*, *Le Figaro*. And on the ground too, amidst the candles and flowers. In the soft evening light outside the Carillon, they had all appeared incandescently beautiful; their hopeful smiles illuminated by wavering flames. And the fact didn't escape me that the vast majority had been younger than me – men and women in their twenties, early thirties: just starting out in life. None would see middle age, let alone old age. The world had shifted on its axis yet again; and, not for the first time, the young and blameless had forfeited their lives in the convulsion. Nobody knew what was coming next.

Balzac, in a letter to his sister, spoke of taking a walk in Père-Lachaise to 'cheer himself up'. We might take a different attitude to death these days. Held at such a distance, it's too earth-shattering when it crashes in on us now, as it had done in January, and again on Friday the thirteenth. It was easier, perhaps, in days when it was more ever-present. The atrocities, along with Rube's murder and windswept funeral, continued to shut out the light throughout November. The police investigation into his killing, we were assured, was still going ahead in earnest, despite the chaos. But thus far no one from the JNR – or from any fascist organisation – had been arrested. The cops had global terrorism to counter now, so I didn't hold out much hope that they ever would.

It was a full fortnight before I remembered to check Larry's website page, and it took a while to find the comments thread to his post. For ten minutes I had been waylaid by his last article, written before the discovery of Rube's body, about the phenomenon known as the December Effect. Apposite, he probably felt, in the run-up to the festive period, this was an exposé on how, for over a decade, the FDA's performance was measured by how many drugs it managed to approve in a single year. 'A large proportion were rushed through in a panic around Christmas,' the piece read, and I could hear my cousin's cajoling voice as I read on. 'No way was it believable that over half the assessments passing new drugs as safe and marketable could be completed during December alone. And these were substances people would be putting into their bodies by the following December. By the late eighties this practice was endemic, but thankfully, due to a long and embarrassing process of exposure and regulation, they've knocked it off.' Larry always did have an eye on an American readership, and I noticed his pieces were full of stateside inflections. Scrolling down, it took a further few minutes to find Larry's post about Lotte in a sidebar.

And there, alongside it, was the response he had told me about, on the comments thread, under a number of posts 'removed by the moderator'. *Dear Doctor Frost, My mother knew your grandmother,* it read, baldly. *Let's talk.* Followed by a name: *Jacob Bloom.* And that was all... But the name Bloom caught my eye at once. I immediately thought of *Ulysses*, as only a Gentile would. Short, and maddeningly cryptic – and quite possibly the work of another Judeophobic crank – I immediately phoned my cousin to find out if he had heard any more. He had. That very morning, he had received a belated reply from Mr Bloom. The email had been very polite, gracious even, but it had refused to expand; to go over anything, in fact, in cyberspace. No, the mysterious Jacob had insisted, they would have to meet and talk face to face. There was too much to say – and of too much import – to set down in an email.

Larry had invited him to Paris, promising to pay the fare, but this had received an even more negative response. He was an old man in his seventies, he complained, with many ailments, living alone in Amsterdam. His days of taking trains to foreign cities were over, even if the city in question was Paris. And anyway, in the light of recent events, it was too dangerous. Larry, of course, was unequivocally eager to follow this invite up, and he immediately asked me if I wanted to join him. It must be something significant, my cousin said, if he required they talk face to face.

I was evasive at first, and – to be frank– not keen in the slightest about following my cousin on another fruitless caper. The day at the CDJC had been enough. But I changed my mind when he told me why Jacob had been on his site in the first place (and this was a question that had been at the back of my mind from the start).

A lifelong sufferer from high blood pressure, Jacob had experienced an adverse reaction to a new statin his doctor had prescribed him. Over the past year, he informed Larry in very good written English, he had found the near-complete indifference to his plight from the Netherlands medical community 'quite staggering', and had been reduced to surfing the net to find testimony from fellow sufferers, or any kind of professional help or advice at all. And so he had stumbled on the page of Dr Larry Frost, the fearless campaigner, whose Transparent Trials initiative was gathering pace by the week. I felt immediate sympathy and concern for old Jacob. How could I not? We were already connected in adversity. Indeed, my legs seemed to ache with an odd empathetic spasm when

I heard about his plight (not an unusual phenomenon: I can't look at acrobats or footballers exerting themselves on TV without feeling a strange pain in my own limbs while they punish their bodies).

When Larry asked me again about accompanying him to Amsterdam at the end of the conversation – using his pre-emptive sceptical tone, anticipating categorical resistance – I immediately assented.

'I'm in,' I said.

'You're in? You mean you'll come with me?'

'Yes. I'll clear the decks. Just let me know what he says.'

'Nick, you won't regret this.'

'I'd better not…'

Our talk had filled me with a vague sense of euphoria, and this, I knew, was because it had hatched another significant plan in my mind. In the weeks after Rube's funeral I had been making a last-ditch attempt, under the Perspex hairdryer surround of the payphone in the lobby, to get Cass and Ed to come out and see me before they disappeared to the States at Christmas. God knows, I told them, I would return to London at a moment's notice if she gave the word, but as ever she was strangely obdurate. They would come, she said, even if it was for the day – she just didn't know when. I was familiar with this characteristic deferral of Cass's – it was as enraging as *it's your decision*. Efficient as she was, paying every bill on time the moment it slithered through the letterbox, she had a habit of burying her head in the sand when it came to her emotional life. That's if I still figured in it. The plan I was now cooking up was to invite them over to Amsterdam when

Larry and I went to visit Jacob Bloom. Neutral ground for us both, it was where we could both say our farewells. The ace up my sleeve was that I happened to know exactly why Ed would want to go. He told me he had been studying America at school – had filled a project book with cuttings on New York – and had become obsessed with the city's heritage, the Dutch settlers, and the Big Apple's former name. If my plan came off, he would get to hit old Amsterdam before he made it to New Amsterdam. Sitting there, surrounded by the white erasure of my apartment's walls, Jacob's bare message before me on my laptop, I almost rubbed my hands together in triumphant anticipation. Whoever this old-timer was, he would be helping out both cousins, and in ways he could never be aware of.

My scheme wasn't without setbacks, however, some of them immediate.

The following morning, I talked to Cass at length, while Mme George looked sullenly and soundlessly on from her den; the top of her head, with its antimony hair tufting from under her black sewing cap, like an insolent rebuttal in itself. Talk is perhaps the wrong verb – plead is more like it. Cass had no intention, she told me, of 'dragging Ed all the way to Holland'. In that gratingly refined Boston accent that I would never get used to, she dug in her heels like an intelligent mule. I was hamstrung by the fact that I didn't have a firm date for the trip with Larry, as Jacob had told him he would be staying with his daughters and grandchildren in Rotterdam until early December. It would be a weekend, I told her, but I couldn't be certain as to which weekend. Always astute and acute, as if she never needed sleep, Cass asked me to call back when I knew. This I took to be another deferral tactic, and my temperature rose steadily until I felt my mobile give a single buzz in my coat pocket. A text message. Taking it out and scanning it with the receiver under my chin, Cass's needling voice in my ear, I saw it was from my lawyer back in London. It read: *Gallagher to settle out of court. Assets free by end of year. Rest easy.* My heart leapt up. It had been so long, I had forgotten about my absconded accountant. 'Cass,' I interrupted bluntly. 'Ask Ed if he wants to go to Amsterdam before Christmas, and we'll talk again in a couple of days when I know more.' And then I hung up on her, which I knew she wouldn't like one bit.

And then I called my lawyer. Ten minutes later I left the lobby with my brown satchel of books and headed over the road for the Jardin. I felt like kicking my heels in the air, à la Gene Kelly. All the heaviness of the past few weeks lifted momentarily. It was the outcome everyone had wanted. Old Moon Face had evidently seen sense. Either pay up, he had been told, or face a lengthy stretch of hard time. He had gone back to Ireland and had been skulking around, but they had pinned him down in Donegal. It turned out his missus had been informing the prosecution of his whereabouts from the start. When the lawyer had told my novelist friend that Barry had been found, he apparently hadn't been bothered either way. 'That's because he had no money to steal,' I said, with a wry smile. I then thanked him profusely and explained I had to get away to make sure I was allocated a place in a reading room. He had made my day, but I didn't say so, just in case lawyers charged extra for that.

Walking the paths of the Luxembourg, heading towards l'Odéon, a definite spring in my step, I had already decided what I would do with the money. I would give the majority of it to Ed for Christmas. It might be my parting gift to him. There was money and money, of course. He would be growing up around the deeply indifferent wealth of Cass's parents – old dough that allowed her father to be a painter and her mother a professor and minor poet. But a father's bequest was special. I would put it into an account that he could access when he was eighteen. Goodness knows, if I didn't do that it would be sucked into paying off debts and be gone in six weeks. I had heard from my Ph.D. student in London too. She would be moving out in the New Year, and I might have to pay rent on the place myself for the indefinite future. She had sounded mentally healthier than in the spring, however, for which I was pleased. I recalled seeing one of her texts lying around as I packed for Paris, and had opened the introduction up to see she had run a blue biro under every line. Not just apposite paragraphs and quotations, but *every line*. For page after page. If that wasn't a sure sign of impending madness, I didn't know what was.

So I would be able to get myself straight, financially, at least for the foreseeable future, and then set up an account for my son. The decisiveness of this gave me a great sense of satisfaction. Tramping the damp gravel, stretches of which were puddled and impassable, I noticed the tobacco-and-amber leaves of a few weeks back had turned to a black sludge, swept up against the balustrades. Despite the brisk temperatures, the Luxembourg wasn't deserted, and many of the benches were occupied by scarf-wearing couples or solitary men. I glanced back over my shoulder and saw, with fresh immediacy, the Montparnasse tower lording it over the central lake. Had it always been that high? No, it was perhaps an illusion caused by the stripped trees: the lack of foliage had revealed it. Its black shape seemed impossibly near and intrusive. The few chestnuts that had any leaves left were wicker cages; claret-coloured tatters fluttering from their branches. The *trompe-l'œil* of the Jardin's trees from early summer, an illusion I had so delighted in, had disappeared, replaced by a bare reality. I shivered and walked ahead.

Hurrying now, I pressed on into the fighting wind and exited onto the busy main road that led to l'Odéon. I knew I had to make the Bibliothéque Mazarine before 10.30 in order to get a seat. Located up near the river, it was the oldest library in France, a place I had somehow neglected this time around. I needed to visit its ornate reading room to look up certain notes on Paine's *Agrarian Justice*. Overlooked by placid busts of Rousseau and the rest, I had always enjoyed its ambience. Professor Serma had finally got around to reading the first two chapters of *Elysian Fields* and had responded positively. It had given me a new burst of energy. I remembered the Mazarine fondly from my twenties, and I was looking forward to its special atmosphere of civility and charm. It hadn't escaped mine and Larry's notice that Rube had been murdered in the shadow of a library. There was something terrible about this fact that I couldn't quite put my finger on.

I walked quickly past the tapering Doric columns of the Odéon theatre, where Hitler had apparently strolled on his one visit, and headed down the descending street that led onto the boulevard Saint-Germain. My mind clamoured with plans

— for Ed; for Larry, now that his own plans were in tatters; for everyone's future. I couldn't wait to see my son, and was certain I could talk Cass round once my cousin had come up with a definite weekend to visit Jacob.

Though running very late, I found it hard to resist stopping at the window of the Librairie Guénégaud, with its distinctive deep-purple frontage and plaque informing the passer-by that Paine, no less, had lived in a house on the site for five years. Even this seemed apposite. The accident of passing the second-hand shop where the subject of my current chapter had once broken bread and drunk vinegary *vin rouge* told me the stars were coming into alignment. I peered in, past the scuffed woodwork around the windows, into the deep interior, epidemic with books. First editions from 1840, doorstoppers on Picardy Chateaux for the tourists; pamphlets, esoterica and occultism. I wasn't sure I had ever been inside. I had always loved its window, though, and the painted legend by the door: *Folklore; Erudition; Régionalisme*. And the chiselled plaque above it, of course, which I strained my neck to read, as I had done as a young man, full of my own plans and dreams, which had somehow become derailed. Thomas Paine: *Anglais de naissance, Americain d'adoption, Français par décret*.

Well, I thought, as I headed off down the street: if my own son was to become American by adoption, I couldn't think of a better avatar than old Tom himself.

Just as I had schemed it, Ed was ecstatic when he found out he might get to see Amsterdam and meet his father before

Christmas. December arrived in Paris – like a sombre visitant priest – and, once Jacob finally got back to Larry, a date for the meeting was set for the second weekend of the month.

In the days leading up to our trip, I worked very hard on the book, and saw little of Larry, paradoxically. He was deeply involved in his campaign and the backlog of work at the Institut. And Ariel, too, was occupying him, as she went through her stages of grief. Paris itself was busy grieving, and burying its dead. Staying with him when she could at the rue André Gide, she was also seeing a part of Paris she wasn't accustomed to. The tatty parks and smeary cafés as the city sprawled its way south. I kept myself to the Sorbonne, hiking back up the hill every day – in the dark now – brooding on what might await us in Holland. Not just Jacob's 'significant information', something that he assured Larry would be worth his trouble hearing, but how it would go with Ed and me. The plan was to take the first Thalys high-speed train via Brussels on the Saturday morning – leaving very early, to give us all the more time together. Cass and Ed would be arriving mid-morning, and we would have most of the day to explore the city. Larry would go off and hit the bars, undoubtedly, but that was fine, as Jacob could only see us on the Sunday anyhow. One thing was for certain: I needed to remain dry-eyed – for who wants to see their own father cry? I had never witnessed mine weeping, though that wasn't to say he was without emotion. He was Welsh, after all. And I needed, for everyone's sake, to keep my temper.

On the evening before the trip, back at the apartment after packing for Amsterdam and drinking what must have been a whole six-pack of stubby Kronenbourgs, I decided to take in the view from my balcony.

Yanking the lever and stepping out into the noise of the street, abundant even from five floors above, I tried to welcome the cold rather than resist it. The night was too icy to stand outside for long, but I felt I needed to clear my head, to wake up. I tried to focus my eyes. The jewel tray of nocturnal Paris glittered sensationally before me. Down below, a black Peugeot taxi had mounted the kerb and was trying to park on the pavement, reversing and grinding its gears. Cries from groups of *jeunes filles*, scarfed up and in mittens, breathing steam and singing drunkenly on the way home, reached me over the traffic noise. All of Parisian life, still going on, as I hoped it always would. Fear was still in the air after the November attacks, no doubt about it – indeed, the Sunday afterwards, firecrackers had been set off among mourners in the place de la République, causing mass panic. But the city refused to be beaten. The Friday following the thirteenth had seen a social-media initiative to drive everyone out into the bars and restaurants as normal; with people texting and tweeting *Je suis en terrasse* to demonstrate their defiance. A reckless defiance perhaps, but one somehow glorious, in the face of those who dared to attack the liberal, cosmopolitan, multi-ethnic West while they were merely having a drink, or at the match, or watching a concert. Freedom, and the Enlightenment values so beloved of the French, had come under a terrifying assault from barbarity and ignorance. Yet the citizens of Paris were determined the twisted ideology of so-called jihadism wouldn't prevail. Reason itself seemed to be at war with intractable belief, and, in the eyes of the West, the latter was doomed to lose.

With my last beer in one hand, the other on the heavy black iron balustrade, I toasted the city I had grown to love more than any on earth. '*Santé*!' I shouted over the blue Jardin and coldly twinkling boulevards. Feeling I should go inside before I caught pneumonia, I drained the bottle and took a final glance. Paris was all before me, in all its elegant, elaborate, enchanted sensual glory – and my future was, too, if I could find the courage to go out there and grasp it.

A few miles out of Brussels, the train having picked up speed again, Larry turned to me and said:

'To go back to what you were saying, I can only see this as a win-win situation.'

It was still early. In fact, it hadn't been light for long. Larry and I had grabbed a coffee and a croissant at Paris-Nord and wordlessly boarded the Thalys high-speed express. It was only as we approached the Belgian capital that both of us had felt like making conversation. Anxious as I was about seeing Cass and Ed for the first time in almost a year, I might have grumbled something about there being no point to the trip – indeed, might have even said that seeing my son was the only reason I was going along at all.

'How is that so, Larry?' I muttered, and leaned my temple against the window. I had made sure I had the window seat, as I always found the aisle, with its distractions and toe-stubbings, nigh on impossible.

'Okay, even if Jacob's mother was only Lotte's playmate in

Vienna and their involvement goes no further into adulthood, there's a lead there…'

'That's assuming he's not a crank. Anyway, you'd be going back to the twenties. The Great War, even. Grandma was born in 1910.'

'And then there's the question of how Jacob ended up in Amsterdam.'

'I'm sure all will be revealed.'

Reflected in the smoked glass of the train I could see Larry's face: the beard was even bigger now, more mountain-man, and his eyes shone with excitement despite the early hour. I knew where this gleam emanated from, and it was tiring me out already. He had projected much into the future, counted his *poules* well before they were hatched. The very name Jacob had excited him from the first moment the old guy had made contact. Earlier, I had said sharply, 'Just because this fellow's mother was Jewish, doesn't mean Lotte was at all. You're still clutching at straws. Children of many ethnicities mixed and played innocently with each other before Hitler came to power in thirty-three.' But I could see he had already convinced himself that Jacob had a great revelation in store. I was certain it would be more along the lines of Douglas Adams's 42. 'Remember as well,' I had counselled, 'that he has something to gain from you hiking all the way to the Netherlands for a one-to-one. As with me coming to Paris thinking you could cure me, he's probably labouring under the same misapprehension.'

In the window I could see Larry's hand movements were restricted by the tight seating; though he was running a forefinger along the middle ridge of his brow as he thought things through. Of course, much in his personal life was riding on this too. He held out a wild hope that he might be returning to Paris with unexpected news regarding his provenance; a gift to hand Ariel's parents on a silver dish. I could tell he still hoped they might overlook the disparity of age and class and agree to his offer of marriage if he proved beyond doubt that he was one of them. All very unlikely. In one sense I was grateful that he was fired up, however. The squalid aftermath of Rube's murder, and the massacre of the thirteenth, had cast a pall over everyone's spirit. Leaving Paris had freed us from having to contemplate it, and it struck me that this was my first trip out of the city since my summer jaunt to Nadir's toxicology conference in Chantilly.

'But like I say – it's win-win. You get to see Ed, and I finally get to make some progress. Hopefully.'

'You shouldn't raise your hopes, Larry. I'm serious.'

'I just know this is important, Nick. I can feel it in my water. I only hope we have enough time with him. Do you think Sunday is enough?'

'It depends on what he has to say,' I said neutrally.

Flying by outside was the curious emptiness of the Low Countries; flat as a coin, cut with irrigation channels; the spare trees appearing and disappearing out of the early mist. All of it drained of colour, except for a pale, insipid green left over from the fertile months. There were farm buildings and construction yards; sudden levees and canals neatly lined with equidistant planes; grey ghosts of towns on the distant horizon. The main impression was of a people-less landscape that was nevertheless not a wilderness. It had been mysteriously and meticulously cultivated. But where had the population got to? Some of the flat fields resembled the waterlogged broads of Norfolk, though they were undoubtedly the location of great battles in both world wars. Earlier, I imagined we had passed the scene of the Battle of the Bulge, far away on the German border. I had no idea where we were in actual fact. Only once there were windmills would I be confident we had crossed into Holland.

'You've been to Amsterdam before, Nick?'

It was odd we had never discussed this while making preparations for the trip.

'Yes. But only once, for a weekend. Years ago.'

Or had it been twice? I remembered the first time for certain. It had been during one of the summer terms at Cambridge – I couldn't recall if it was the first or second year – with friends I hardly knew, doing the usual things; smoking hash in the cafés (which I didn't much care for). Then walking along the canals by the incomparable black-brick seventeenth-century townhouses, and later seeing some band at the Paradiso, which was an even worse experience than the marijuana. But I loved the fresh, open feeling of the streets (derived from their proximity to the sea); the little humpback bridges and the bicycles; the novelty of getting everywhere via trams – or the Yellow Death as the locals called them. Also the rare occasions when I heard Dutch spoken – a vigorous, Germanic language that delighted my ear strangely after so much immersion in French. The atmosphere of gentle liberalism had reminded me of the Quarter, and I had made up my mind to return, though in different company. On the last night I had lost my friends, who later told me they had all gone to listen to blues at the Last Waterhole, and then taken a walk past the famous windows. If I remembered correctly, I returned to the pension, after a couple of solitary Amstels, to read La Fontaine.

'I've been many times,' said Larry. 'But this is special. You want to take them to the Van Gogh Museum, by the way, if there's time. Oh, and the Museum of Torture for Ed. He'll love that.'

I turned to him and saw, next to his heavy book – Walter Benjamin's *Theses on the Philosophy of History* – a crumpled cache of envelopes tied with a red elastic band. Lotte's letters. It struck me that it was the first time I had seen them, and I felt vaguely ashamed I had never asked to take a look. I leaned over and said, 'May I?'

I reverently slipped off the band and opened the first envelope. The paper felt impossibly brittle; the sepia ink forming a looping hand over page after densely written page.

'Her handwriting is so like my mother's...' said Larry.

'And mine,' I said in wonderment. 'Mind if I have a read of these later? In the hotel?'

'No, take them, by all means. I've read them so many times, I'm blind to them.'

'Even the ones without a Vienna postmark?'

'I've been concentrating on those recently, actually. They knew many, many people, all over Europe.'

'Not surprising, given Grandpa's profession.'

I reflected, as I had before, that the rise of email had destroyed more than just the intimacy of another person's presence on the page – it had proscribed the language in a crucial respect. Looking down at Lotte's letters, certain passages were incomprehensible, but others were bell-like in their clarity. With a letter, one could see where a correspondent had speeded up under duress or emotion, or slowed down to pick a particularly pertinent noun or phrase. All of this was lost on a computer – not to mention the larger loss resultant from possible electronic breakdown. Wipe a hard drive, and all is gone. But these crumbling letters – only sixty years old, but seemingly from another century – would last a lot longer than me and Larry. I felt very close to Lotte; this woman I hardly knew, and my cousin not at all.

'Thanks,' I said, gathering them up. 'I'll take care of them.'

I looked around for the drinks trolley, and then remembered there wasn't to be one on this wonder of French engineering. I would have to hike to the bar for another coffee, which I felt badly in need of. Glancing at Larry's book, I smiled. He had Benjamin's essays open now on the flip-down table, and was reading with a pained concentration. I myself had tried to tackle the *Arcades Project* in my early twenties, and parts of it had sprung to mind when I flâneured around Paris back in September. The bit of Benjamin that I did remember was one of his Thirteen Theses of Writing. It warned of attempting the conclusion of a work in your familiar study, 'as you would not find the necessary courage there'. They were wise words. Though I was some way off employing this maxim for *Elysian Fields*, I had used it when completing all my previous books, and could report that it worked.

I glanced down at my own book, sitting unthumbed before me. Larry had long urged me to read *Daniel Deronda*, in order that I could tell him whether it 'was worth the Herculean effort,' and I had taken him up on the challenge in the dead days while we waited to board the train. My Oxford World's Classics edition sat before me like a rebuke. I was only 300 pages in, but I had been secretly enjoying the immersion in nineteenth-century fiction that wasn't French. It had also forced me to think hard again about identity, what it really meant in the end, and what might be waiting for us among the genteel canals of Amsterdam.

'Hey,' said Larry, turning to me. 'He's a poet, by the way.'

The gleam hadn't diminished one jot in his eyes. How did he manage it at this hour?

'Who?' I asked, perplexed.

'Jacob Bloom.'

'Really?'

'Yeah, I googled him. Quite well known and respected. Translated a fair amount, too. He's just done a new edition of Levertov's complete works for the Dutch market.'

It was another pincer of shame that I hadn't even taken the step of investigating Jacob myself on the internet. 'I'm looking forward to meeting him more and more.'

'Me too, man,' said Larry, and went back to his book.

Though I knew, before we got to Jacob, that there would be much emotional terrain I would have to clamber over first.

When we eventually hissed into Amsterdam's Centrum – still early, at only 10.30 in the morning – there was a surprise waiting for me. Standing in the aisle as sleepy passengers hauled their baggage from the racks, I checked my phone. There was a voice message I hadn't picked up, sent over an hour beforehand. It was from Cass. There had been some kind of trouble with their tickets at St Pancras, but her signal had been so bad that her message had been machine-gunned and fractured by break-ups until she had been cut off.

It was only when Larry and I made it onto the main concourse – a wide expanse aswarm with tourists and Saturday traffic – that I was able to call my ex-wife.

'What do you mean they wouldn't let you through?'

'I'm telling you, Nick, I've never been so sore in my goddamn life!'

'You sound it. Just explain what happened. We've only just got here ourselves.'

In the background I could hear Ed importuning, *Mum, Mum, Mum, tell him what happened!* and it melted me within to hear his voice.

'For what this has just cost me, we could've come to see you in goddamn Paris, stayed at the Crillon, and had the oysters!'

'Cass – just tell me what's going on…'

'With a case of champagne thrown in!'

After five minutes – which were expensive for me, on my mobile bill, and on my soul – all became clear. She explained in furious tones that when they had arrived at the barriers to press their barcoded tickets against the glowing red terminus, they found they were refused entry. Chaperoned over to the Eurostar customer-service desk, she discovered to her horror that their outward-bound tickets 'inexplicably' had the wrong date printed on them. Cass told them categorically that when she booked them online, she had put in the correct information. It must have been computer error, she yelled, and I knew Cass was too efficient to make a mistake of this sort. It wasn't in her nature. But the 'cheeky Uriah Heep' on the desk, to use her phrase, was having none of it. He was obdurate, unsmiling, superior. The date was wrong, so they couldn't travel. They could, of course, purchase replacements, as their return tickets for the Sunday appeared to be correct. And how much were these? she demanded. Since they counted as emergency last-minute bookings, they would be £250, unfortunately, madam. *Each*. All this Uriah informed them without a flinch. At that moment, Cass had freaked out, demanding, in her American way, to speak to someone; to be 'handed a fucking phone, pronto!' But this being England there was no one to speak to, much less someone to hand her the telephone with which to do so. The Eurostar personnel just surveyed her stonily, while Ed, no doubt, dissolved with embarrassment in the background. She told me she would've called off the whole 'cockamamie visit', and put their eighty-quid tickets in the shredder, if Ed hadn't resisted this plan. Apparently, he had kicked and barked and cried in protest. They had to go, that was all there was to it. At this point, Uriah informed them in tones of oleaginous ingratiation that the tickets reduced to £200 if they travelled the following day, but they would have to book them now to ensure the reservation of two seats. And this is what Cass had done in the end. She had booked two tickets for the Sunday, but only to placate Ed, who wanted not only to see Old Amsterdam, but to see his father for what even he felt to be a significant farewell. 'So you'll only be here tomorrow afternoon?' I had asked urgently. 'That's when we're seeing this old guy...' 'Well – go figure,' she had hollered, still full of high indignation. 'You'll have to work around him. It's the best I can offer, I know that much. To have come today would have meant the whole trip costing me nearly a grand...' I felt momentarily lost for words. And then sorry for her. This was the situation, and we would all have to deal with it.

Thus a one-day visit to Amsterdam had set her back close on '800 bucks', and that was before Ed had even squeezed his first tube of mayonnaise onto a cone of chips.

'That's not like Cass to mess up,' said Larry, stroking his beard. 'Maybe her subconscious made her book the wrong tickets, given how little she wants to see you.'

We were standing like stranded fish on the beach of the station, unsure of our next move after this reversal.

'Thanks for that insight. I think it's fated I never see them, Larry.'

'Listen,' said my cousin, hoisting the rucksack he'd seen circumnavigate the globe more times than Jules Verne, 'let's get to the hotel first and worry about all this later.'

'What are we going to do all day?'

Larry stopped and smiled: 'We'll think of something...'

Negotiating what could be one of the most difficult or significant days of your life with a full Amstel hangover is not to be recommended. But that's what I was contemplating as I sat opposite my cousin the following morning, in the Dampkring coffee shop on the Southern Canal Belt, buttering a scone with trembling, geriatric fingers.

Larry had certainly thought of something – too many things – to amuse ourselves with. After Cass's turnaround, our Saturday had started with a full cultural overload. Our hotel, The Eden, backing on to the Rembrandtplein, with the river flowing in front, was central and expensive. But, I told myself, it was only for two nights, and Friday had seen the startling restoration of my funds to my bank account, courtesy of a repentant Barry Gallagher. So I didn't mind spending big. We had freshened up and headed straight for the museum quarter, taking in the Van Gogh before a lengthy lunch, then the spectacularly overhauled Rijksmuseum. After this we had headed east to wander the still bohemian Pijp, talking incessantly – about Cass, about his situation with Ariel, and, of course, about Jacob. Larry was in such a state of high anticipation I wondered if he was still in his right mind. But then that was always a hard question to answer when it came to him. It seemed possible to share anything with him. Donne said no man was an island, but he was as wrong about that as he was about death not being proud. I wasn't sure I had ever told Larry so much about my ex-wife over the years, and this surprised me, as we walked at sunset through the Sarphatipark, with its ponds and bare branches. It diminished my sense of isolation to know I could broach the subject with my friend – and I considered Larry more a friend than mere relative now; one I had become closer to over the course of the year. With the light rapidly fading, feeling we were far out on the periphery, my planned family day in tatters, Larry decided there was only one thing for it: go out and get drunk.

I didn't resist. We went first to the Zeedijk, where Chet Baker had met his end, in the manner of Clément Méric, as it happened, though probably self-inflicted in his case. Then on to a terrible Irish-themed pub in Dam Square, followed by a hazy tram south to the Leidseplein, and on to the Last Waterhole (still going strong, I was happy to see). Finally, after countless beers on an empty stomach, we ended up in the Melkweg – or the Milkbar – another Kubrickian haunt I recalled from my undergraduate visit. There, against a backdrop of beats we didn't like or understand, we raised our glasses to the Paris dead, and toasted the memory of Rube. Rube especially, we decided, deserved to be counted among the noble and the noteworthy. As with Degas, we had heard a quantity of secret sculptures – mostly in wood – had been found in his studio. We hoped his installations and carvings would live for ever, as imperishable visual art, taking their rightful place next to the Van Eycks and Ruisdaels in the gleaming galleries of Amsterdam. Somehow, we found our way back to The Eden, past the blurred gables and white-framed windows; the lights sparkling prettily in the treacherous, bike-swallowing canals.

'I used to come here all the time,' said Larry, leaning back with his coffee cup, looking around at the café's tiled, vaguely deco interior.

'I know,' I groaned. 'You've told me.'

'No. I don't mean Amsterdam. I mean this coffee shop.'

'When were you here?' I enquired, wishing my cousin's voice were quieter.

'Ten years ago, man. They used to have a famous cat named Bowie…'

I took a fuddled glance around myself. There was no sign of Bowie this morning. But there were plenty of stoners. Some, incredibly, were already pulling on pipes.

'When did you arrange to meet Mr Bloom?' I asked, taking a mouthful of scone and washing it down with coffee.

'Midday.'

Still chewing the gluey dough, feeling abysmal, I looked at my watch. 'That only gives me two hours.'

'Have they called yet?'

With much anxiety, I was awaiting a phone call from Cass, who had told me their train would be pulling in around now. 'No. Not even a text from Ed.'

Larry tugged at his beard. 'Hey, Eurostars are delayed all the time. I wouldn't sweat it.'

Despite his maddening pragmatism, Larry was one of those ready-for-anything travelling companions, and this made me want to take more trips with him. It would have been good to have gone around the world when we were both still in our thirties and in good health. He had the crucial gift of spontaneity. Whereas I always had to plan everything to death; was cautious of talking to strangers, of jumping from the train and walking away from the beaten track.

'Do I look like I'm sweating?'

'You do, actually.'

'That's the beer, Larry…' I shook my head. 'Never again.'

'Listen, they're probably stuck in the tunnel under the Channel.'

'Please don't say that. I'm going to have to cut away from the meeting if they're significantly delayed.'

I had planned to make the short walk to the Centrum to greet Cass and Ed, spend a couple of hours kicking around the shops and streets, then return to find Larry. And, of course, to meet them later for dinner. Or the Last Supper, as I kept referring to it the previous night.

My cousin took stock of me. 'You look troubled, my friend.'

'Well, none of this is adding to my sense of well-being.'

I massaged my temples, hoping very much that I would stabilise in time to meet my son. I had felt half-cut earlier, in the shower, and sensed at one point that I might pass out. And this would never do. For Ed to meet his father and find the breath of alcohol on him was something I had never envisaged. Cursing Larry, whose extra body mass meant he could put more away, I decided I shouldn't drink any more. After so much gradual weight loss I couldn't handle it any longer. And now my whole frame felt fractured after so much walking – my knees and ankles aching with a valetudinarian rebuke; the stinging nerve damage nipping me and making me grit my teeth.

'You should stick to wine like a good Frenchman,' Larry smiled. 'Hey, I forgot to tell you with all the confusion yesterday. Jaspreet let Nadir back.'

'Well, well. That's terrific news,' I said, sitting up, my mind beginning to work with something approaching clarity.

We talked on for a while about Nadir, medicating ourselves with strong coffee. While I had been standing on my freezing balcony, Larry had gone for a drink with the professor; to the Volontaires – a slightly more salubrious bar than the Mont Saint-Michel – just down the street from the Institut. There Nadir had said with some pride that following his children's visit his wife had since made peace with him. Larry had doubted this was a good move, and it was only after an hour that Nadir persuaded him that separation and divorce was next to being cursed in his culture. He would move back, take up his rightful role at the head of the family once more. Despite the privation of living in the Wild West enclave of Bobigny, he would find his place in the world again. Jaspreet had punished him enough, he had said. His lessons, many and various, had been learned. I was very happy for him, though I could sense Larry felt abandoned, washed up on the rue André Gide by himself now: back where he began.

As we talked on, and I started to feel gradually more human, Larry also reminded me of everything I had said the previous night. After the best part of an hour, a kind of drinker's remorse set in, cementing my resolve to stick strictly to a single glass of Côtes du Rhône with dinner later, like *un homme français*. According to my cousin, I had become unbearably emotional about my son before we had raised a tankard to Rube. Tearful, almost, about my imminent separation. I realised then that, as a species, we weaken as we get older, rather than become tougher. And this is a terrible surprise! There's no worse feeling than recalling the things one said the night before, as if a curtain has been pulled back, revealing one's psyche with all its clamouring needs and neuroses. I remembered Larry, too, confessing how sky-high he felt the stakes to be now – how this visit could save his relationship with Ariel. I recalled telling him to shut up at once, but also admitting to myself that I had never felt closer to him.

'Shall we do it?' Larry said, inclining his head towards the door.

It was now half-past eleven, and there had still been no reply to my texts. 'We've got half an hour.'

'That's okay. We can wander. The sun's come out.'

'Are you sure…?'

Once we stepped outside, I could see Larry was correct. In the dim coffee shop I hadn't been aware the day had any weather at all. I found it was even too warm to wear my trench coat, which I took off and slung over my shoulder.

We began walking in silence along the Leidsestraat, towards the address Jacob had given us. It was like a spring morning all of a sudden, with couples out doing their Sunday stroll; or *ochtend wandeling,* to use the phrase Larry took pleasure in teaching me. It resembled a March morning from youth, one of those where you notice everything. The tall elegant houses, with their closely packed windows, had a crispness to their outline. The bicycles tied to lamp posts were arresting in their detail. Many of these were old, broken things, but they had been personalised somehow; loved by their owners, without a doubt. Certainly, the trees were bare, but the sunshine lilted along the canals, sparkling in the turbid water. For December it was almost hot. Every face had a supra-reality as we passed; the windowbox flowers powerfully purple and yellow. It was a strange, surreal walk – and not just because of the quality of the sunlight, or the hangover, which I mercifully felt to be diminishing. No, there was something more. It might have been post-alcohol euphoria, but I felt something was ending in me. A tide had gone out to its furthermost point – had receded until it vanished to a barely visible line of foam on the horizon – and now it was coming back in once more.

Larry pressed a button on a brass entryphone panel and waited. I stood next to him, staring up at the five-storey building; a slim and leaning wonder, with an attic room under its gabled Dutch hat. One thing was certain: the enigmatic Jacob lived in a beautiful house.

Or part of a beautiful house. Once we were inside, we couldn't find him. We anxiously climbed the creaking stairs, which were uneven and slanting as if the foundations were suffering from subsidence. Outside, a small voice had merely said, 'Third floor,' when it had crackled from the console, and we were obeying it, though without much luck.

As we doubled back and descended from what was probably the fourth floor, my knees complaining like troublesome twins, we saw an open door at the end of a dim hallway. Natural light was flooding a room at the back of the house, but there appeared to be no one around. Unsure of how many apartments there were, Larry turned to me, about to speak.

But before he could, a figure appeared in the light.

A voice reached us from a distance of fifteen feet. A strong voice, capable, when it wanted, of projection. It was full of friendly surprise. Though with a very slight, albeit humorous, topspin of indignation.

'There are two of you…!'

I turned to Larry. 'You didn't tell him?'

Larry ignored me and said: 'Jacob Bloom?'

At the end of the corridor was a small man with white hair and spectacles catching gleams from a light source behind him. As we approached, I could see he was wearing a houndstooth jacket with pens in the top pocket. A shirt collar, open, perhaps a light green, gave him the air of an academic greeting students for a tutorial. As we drew near, I could see that behind his round glasses lurked watchful, walnut-coloured eyes, with hawk-like lids. On his chin was a grey stubble, or an attempt at a beard; and his forehead, high, many-lined, seemed a little too big for his body.

'Yes, yes,' said Jacob impatiently as we stopped in front of him. 'Which one of you is Dr Frost?'

'That's me,' said Larry, extending a hand with almost trembling eagerness. 'I'm so very sorry. I forgot to tell you, this is my cousin, Nicholas.'

'Ah, a cousin. That makes sense...' The stooped old man took Larry's hand and surveyed us both in turn. I tried to take him in. He really was small close-up, curled and snail-like with age; the receding hair pure white and kinky, with filaments of red in the strong sunshine from what I could now see was a large sash window in the room behind him. A detailed, sallow face, like a Rembrandt. But there was something fierce about him too. A hard, calloused, surviving thing.

I took his hand, which was surprisingly delicate, and said in an apologetic tone: 'I'm very pleased to meet you, Mr Bloom.'

As I shook his hand, I saw, to the right of the doorway, a Mezuzah scroll in its tubular decorative case. The Hebrew letters were somehow comforting, a feeling I found quite unaccountable until the old man let go of my hand.

'Please, do call me Jacob,' and he smiled for the first time; a gentle, wise, rare thing to behold. The smile of a man who had thought deeply, had given up on the easy explanations, but still found the world grave and ironic and absurd all at once. 'And please, don't stand on ceremony, gentlemen. Do come in.'

'Thank you,' returned Larry.

'It's not much, but you have come a long way, so make yourselves at home.'

He offered us inside with a wave of his arm, and it was only then I noticed the characteristic gnarls and boles of arthritis on his fingers.

The apartment was big and book-filled. In the window was a long desk with a green leather blotter and, of all things, an electric typewriter, which squatted formidably like a museum exhibit. Next to it was a cup of tea or coffee steaming in the December light. There was a faint smell of beef stew and boiled cabbage – not unpleasant – also the yeasty odour of bread. And dust, too. I took a glance around as Jacob pulled an armchair across for Larry to sit in. Every available inch of wall space was shelved, with hardbacks and journals packed tight against each other until they almost burst their banks. There was also a tall, heavy bookcase, flat to the far wall. It was orderly, however, with no stacks of texts rising like stalagmites from the floor, as in my parents' cottage. At the back of the room was a doorway into a dark corridor, which I imagined led to the kitchen and sleeping areas. Beside this, like an afterthought, was a dining table with four chairs, scattered with papers and candles; and framed photographs, too, in dim corners, mostly black-and-white and faded. On a low surface was a record player, next to which sat a tumble of vinyl; the classical canon, with Arcadian scenes on their covers, some in just their paper inner sleeves. All in all, it was lived-in, erudite, old-fashioned, cosy – the home of a poet, in fact.

'Please, take a seat, both of you,' implored Jacob. 'I only

returned from Rotterdam yesterday, so the place is in a bit of a state.'

My cousin sat in the tubular-steel armchair provided for him, while I took a dining-room chair from under the table.

'We're honoured you found the time to talk to us,' Larry said, in awed tones, looking into every corner at once.

'Not at all,' said Jacob. 'I have many questions to ask you. And vice versa, I am sure.' Then, using the projection of his voice he had employed in the hallway: 'Tea?'

'Yes, please,' we both assented.

With his hands on his hips, Jacob surveyed the two of us. 'It's only herbal. I make it in a big samovar, which belonged to my aunt Hannah. She used to live here.'

'This was her apartment?'

'No, no, no,' and he waved away the notion with an air of vague regret. 'In this house. In the basement…'

And with that he disappeared into the tenebrous corridor, where we heard clankings from what I supposed was the kitchen.

Larry and I looked at each other. We didn't need to say anything. There was a sudden sense of privileged access; of expectation and excitement – and in us both, for once.

I glanced across at the long, book-piled desk – where Jacob laboured over his translations, no doubt. The first cover I saw was a hardback of Rosa Luxemburg's letters, published recently, if I remembered correctly from the review pages of *Le Monde*. Despite owning the monolithic electric typewriter, he was obviously a man who liked to keep up to date.

Before I could pick up the volume and take a look, Jacob

was back with us; bearing a tray with a steel teapot, two small china cups and what looked like a plate of little jellies and fruit preserves. These he placed on the only remaining space on the desk.

'Please,' he said, sitting down in the rotating chair, which looked as if it had been orthopedically customised, 'help yourself. I would serve you, but my hands aren't what they were.'

Larry looked over at Jacob, with his sympathetic physician's gaze. 'I'm sorry to hear that. Arthritis?'

The old poet held up the crooked fingers of his right hand.

'Unfortunately, yes.'

'Not a convenient affliction for a writer,' said Larry, with a doctor's maddening talent for stating the obvious.

Jacob passed over this swiftly. 'So, do tell me. Did you have a good journey?'

'Yes, thank you,' Larry replied, with a strange strangled deference, as if Jacob were a relative; his father, even. He always seemed to convert senior males into father figures in a flash. As I pondered this oddity, my cousin continued: 'The train is just so fast from Paris now. I remember doing the same distance Interrailing. There was time to finish a novel. And, of course, we had yesterday to get reacquainted with the city.'

'Excellent,' said Jacob, steepling his fingers; assessing Larry quietly. 'And how is the health of Paris?'

'It's wounded, but it's still the City of Light.'

'Have all the Jews left for Israel yet?'

'Not the last time I looked,' Larry said.

'That's as it should be. We must be free to live wherever we like, without harassment. Or worse.'

For a fleeting moment, I could see my cousin was including himself in Jacob's 'we', until the old man continued: 'And your email tells me you work at the Institut Pasteur. You wouldn't know it from your website.'

'Yes. I have a day job,' Larry grinned, wanting to make a good impression. 'Neuropharmacological research.'

'So you are not merely a firebrand campaigner?'

Jacob was looking with unusual penetration at my cousin, as if trying to fathom what he was really about, or why this intense, vaguely embattled, bearded man had agreed, at the drop of a hat, to come all this way on the most tenuous of threads.

'God, no! That's all extracurricular. An obsession of mine...'

'I'd like to clarify a few things you have written there, about drugs trials and accountability, if that is all right with you?'

'Sure,' Larry smiled, and my heart sank. If the old man was thinking of suing whichever corporation had damaged his health, he might experience the same expensive and intolerable wild goose chase that I had. I made a note to advise him properly if the conversation came around to it. My cousin continued: 'But do you mind if we do it later? There's always email if you want me to expand in detail.'

'Yes, of course...'

Jacob settled himself into the headrest of the chair; the light from the impressive, white-framed sash window revealing every etched line on his face in geographical relief. A map of some interest and distinction, undoubtedly; his nose describing a noble parabola over the mesh of wrinkles on his cheeks, his raggedy beard. In this light he looked closer to eighty than seventy. He appeared to be momentarily lost in thought. As Larry poured me a cup of the weak, almost translucent tea, I observed Jacob's hands. His fists lay twisted in his lap, the thumbs wedged in tight under the knuckles, between the second and third fingers; the nails yellow, like big toes. They recalled for me Dennis Potter's hands in his last interview.

'I have just started on a new translation of the *Paradiso*,' Jacob began, without prompting. 'I'm too old for it now, without a doubt. I'll probably never finish, but I find the terza rimas strangely comforting to work on.'

'Are there many rhymes in Dutch?' I asked, taking a cup of the hot tea from my cousin.

He turned to me full of gentle amusement, and I saw he could be a wry, waspish character too. 'Virtually none! But it is the Aristotelian underpinning that is giving me the most pleasure. The *Commedia* was very popular during the war, not that I remember...'

'Did you find the Catholicism a, erm, problem?' asked Larry, gaining in boldness. It was obvious a discussion of Dante was breaking the ice for us all.

Jacob shook his head, his high, hairless brow a pistil whose petals had been blown away.

'Not at all. Virgil's theological vision must have stood for civilisation, in the face of everything that was going on in the early 1940s... However, I couldn't face the *Inferno*. I shall start at the end and work backwards.'

'It's the only way to understand life,' smiled Larry, and I worried for a moment he was going to say something jejune and embarrassing. We were back in his teenage bedroom again. 'As Kierkegaard said—'

I jumped in and enquired: 'But your own verse? Are you still writing?'

Jacob took a deep sip of air between his plump, mauvish lips, as if the matter was full of much vexation. 'When I can. My last collection came out over a decade ago. It all takes so long... Tell me, Nicholas, what do you do? I know your cousin's work from his very brilliant website, but I didn't expect two visitors today.'

'I'm a historian. Revolutionary France. I'm back with Paine at the moment.'

Jacob nodded, and I could see he was a man who relished high discourse, who would be bored by small talk. Larry and I, as I've said, were suckers for this kind of exchange, too, but I checked myself, knowing there were more important matters to get to in the time we had. I recalled, also, that at any minute my ex-wife or son might ring me and explain where on earth they had got to.

'Ah, Thomas Paine. I love that line of his. How did it go?' And he searched the bright window as if the answer were to be found there. 'France, despite all her massacres, had not slain the mind of her country. It is what I feel about Europe as a whole, especially now. The intellectual life is still strong – and that is what will save us in the end.'

'Hear hear,' said Larry, taking one of the coloured jelly sweets from the plate and putting it experimentally into his mouth.

'It's a great line. But I think you'll find it's Burke.'

'Really?' exclaimed Jacob, full of a sudden avid surprise.

Larry now was looking at me, almost warning me not to contradict the venerable, sage-like poet. 'So who said that the more perfect a civilisation is, the less occasion it has for government?'

'Now that *was* Paine. For certain,' I replied, and took a sip of tea.

'I would like to read some of your work,' continued Jacob, his hooded eyes alighting on me.

'And vice versa,' I said, with due reverence.

There was a pause where we all registered how much there was to say, and how little time we had. I thought I heard the ticking of a distant clock; bicycles from the street outside. Clearing my throat, I began: 'Tell me... because I have an interest – a vested interest – what was the nature of your adverse reaction? Because I suffered one too, though with a different medicine, I understand.'

Jacob nodded, the filaments of his hair dancing and silvery in the light. 'I had to stop with my new statins because they gave me a peripheral neuropathy.'

'Where, if I may ask?'

'Unfortunately in my hands.'

Larry shook his head, and I was extremely worried he was about to say *bad luck*. If Jacob already had arthritis, the last thing he needed was nerve damage that afflicted his hands. I looked across again at his twisted fists, and felt the familiar empathetic twinge in my legs.

'I had the same thing happen to me, though it was with an antibiotic.'

Jacob raised his eyebrows. 'I am sorry to hear that. You know there is no cure for a neuropathy – isn't that right, Dr Frost?'

Larry nodded, not wanting to discuss any of this, I could tell. At least not before he asked the old man about Lotte.

'We expect everything to be curable these days, don't we?'

'Yes,' I smiled, 'we certainly do.'

Larry butted in: 'There's no medical procedure that doesn't have the potential to kill you, I'm afraid. Sad, but true.'

Disregarding this, I asked, 'Are you in much pain?'

'Yes, constantly. I can barely type now. I have to draft everything in longhand. The medical community over here have been next to useless.'

'Same as in England,' I submitted, and sensed a warm pulse of feeling expand in my chest. I felt as if I had found a friend for life. It struck me that he was the first person I had actually met who had suffered in the same way I had. Another brief silence arose in the room.

'Well...' announced Jacob, breaking the poised quiet. 'It's good to discover shared interests.'

At this we all laughed. Mainly because of Jacob's delivery – it was a Jewish delivery, it had to be said; the ability to turn a mildly funny line into a wisecrack that sets the table on a roar. Also, to convert tragedy into comedy without any loss of seriousness. There was a dactylic rhythm to his speech; didactic at certain points, but emphasised and authoritative. As we settled down, Jacob went carefully to pick up his own cup, which was still steaming in the wintry glare. I noticed immediately, next to a pot of pens, scissors and pencils, many of which looked recently sharpened, a pile of envelopes not dissimilar in character to those Larry had given me in the train, but which I had thus far been unable – shamefully, since last night – to take a glance at. They appeared to be old: wartime letters, by the looks of them. They held my attention until Larry said, 'So. Tell me about your family. I'm dying to know this connection between yours and mine...'

Jacob nodded in silence for a moment.

'The family that is still alive, or those who have left us?'

'Both,' answered Larry, unguardedly.

'Well... as I told you in my email, my daughters live in Rotterdam. Hannah and Deborah.'

'Named after your aunt?' my cousin interjected.

'Yes. Hannah is the eldest. She's an arts therapist – the visual arts. Spends her days with paints and glues and dyes. And Deborah is, I suppose, a housewife. They both live around the corner from each other, though why they have chosen to live in an area that resembles a concrete jungle, or a financial district, defeats me. What can I say? I have four adorable grandchildren, who I have spent the past few weeks spoiling. And Hannah and Deborah seem very happy, now both are in their forties. They have nothing to complain about. And neither do I, really. They have enough money, and husbands I can tolerate.'

Larry and I chuckled at this, though I was feeling a burn of envy, as I always did, when people's perfect domestic situations were described to me. None were ever that perfect, I told myself, and it had taken many years to understand this. Still, only Holland, with its platonic perfection of lifestyle and human being, could offer something so close to the idyllic.

'You're very lucky,' I found myself saying. 'I'm supposed to be meeting my own son and my ex-wife later. At the Centrum. That's if they ever get here.'

'Really?' exclaimed Jacob with sudden interest. 'Don't let me keep you.'

'No, no. Please do go on. You're the reason we came to Amsterdam, after all.'

Or the reason Larry came, I thought, but didn't say.

'So what about *their* mother?' Larry asked tentatively. 'I mean your wife?'

Jacob sighed and nodded his head, seemingly gathering words. He rotated a few degrees left and then right in his chair, and I could tell this motion pleased him. I looked down at his feet and saw how worn the carpet was under his desk. He had sat here for years, most probably, devoted to the production of literature, to real composition, not just the collation and interpretation of historical facts. Next to his feet was a wastepaper basket full to the brim with balls of paper. It reminded me, momentarily, of the National Lottery draw.

Eventually, Jacob said: 'Esther died in 1989. Of breast cancer. Unfortunately, she never got to see her grandchildren. I didn't have her for long. She was a child of the 1960s. We both were.'

'That's really very sad…' Larry murmured, but with due conviction that Jacob registered. 'I'm sorry.'

I had to conclude that Larry, as a scientist, was actually quite simple and straightforward in his emotional life. He wanted conventional things, and I could see this with the whole Ariel saga. Only now, after so many years, was I beginning to understand it. We expect the brilliant to be many-layered, in every respect, but it was only Larry's analytical mind that was unconventional.

'We had a good life in Rotterdam for a long time.'

'So you didn't live here?' Larry said with surprise. 'In Amsterdam?'

'Not at all. I grew up here, but moved to Rotterdam when I was a teenager. I was an English teacher and translator there for a couple of decades before I published anything. It was only after Esther died and my children married that I returned. This place,' – and he gestured to the book-filled walls that were sparkling now in the wintry light – 'has only been my home for the last fourteen years. My old age. And my dotage, too, most probably.'

'You say you moved as a teenager. Were you an only child?'

Jacob fixed Larry with a sudden steeliness. 'No. I had two brothers. But I never got to meet them.'

Before we could both react to this strange statement, the old man announced: 'Gentlemen. Have you had lunch?'

Larry and I looked at each other. Certainly, I was hungry, and my hangover stomach was demanding that I eat. And I knew at a glance that Larry was too. It was past one o'clock, and neither of us had factored in anything so quotidian as food.

'No,' my cousin replied. 'We haven't.'

'Would you like some?'

'Yes,' I said instantaneously, another gust of feeling rising in my chest at Jacob's hospitable offer. 'That would be terrific – if it's not too much trouble.'

'Then let me fix something up! I have some beef bratwurst

and sauerkraut in the kitchen that has been boiling for hours. I can't eat it all by myself. I hope you don't mind simple fare.'

And with that he rose with some difficulty, and headed for the back of the room. There was evident pleasure in this act of sharing, we both knew, and weren't about to say no. Without prompting, Larry and I stood up and walked after him into the dark annexe that led from the corridor.

Thus, for the following two hours we broke bread and drank more tea with old Jacob at the dining table. We must have covered every topic available, from Larry's work, to the situation with the Levines, and the Jews of Paris, to Revolutionary France, even our mothers and fathers, and the prospect of losing my son to America. Jacob listened to all this with a rare attention, as befits a man for whom words, the nuance and tone of language, are his living. He seemed to be logging it all for later use. As the light sank in the sash window, he lit candles, and we sat in a kind of peasant-kitchen glow – reminiscent of Van Gogh's early paintings – finally easy in each other's company. And, mercifully, I felt my mobile buzz once in my pocket with a text message from Ed. They had been stuck in a tunnel, as Larry predicted, but were on their way. I texted back immediately: *Phone me the moment you arrive, I will come and meet you. Love Dad.* I replaced the mobile in my pocket, finding I was marginally more relaxed, though still not fully in the moment with Larry and old Jacob.

As my cousin swabbed the last cabbage from his plate with what must have been his fourth buttered roll, he said: 'So… Tell me about your early life in Amsterdam.'

I knew he wanted to say, *your mother and Lotte*, but was too shy to get to the point. He was waiting – as we both were – for Jacob himself to bring the subject up. To reveal his secrets. Indeed, the name Lotte hadn't been mentioned once since we arrived, though I sensed it was about to be.

'Well, my mother's family were originally from around here,' began Jacob, dabbing his bristles with his handkerchief. 'The Keizersgracht, in the Southern Canal Belt. But I didn't grow up here. I grew up in a house opposite the Portuguese synagogue in the Jodenbuurt, the Jewish area. My mother, Mimi, married a Hassid, you understand, a man named Amos Liebegold, and he insisted they move. You see...' – and here Jacob leaned back, his head of scanty hair almost making contact with a Russian-looking oil-lamp affixed to the wall – 'I never knew my mother and father.'

'How come?' demanded Larry, his expression baffled. 'I don't understand.'

'I was brought up by my aunt. Hannah Bloom.'

'So you took her name?'

'Yes.'

'And you lived here with her? In the basement?'

'Goodness, no!'

'I'm still a little confused, I must confess, Jacob.'

The old man shook his head, as if girding himself to go over territory that had long proved too arduous for repeated visits. 'Let me start at the beginning. My mother's family were the Kleins. Tailors from around here, very successful from the beginning of the last century. When she married Amos, she had to get used to a different kind of life. Okay, she was observant, but not devout. Mimi had many friends here, but Amos disapproved of most of them. Then, in the late 1930s, my mother had the first of her children. Two boys: David, born in 1936, and Aaron a year later, give or take. And after that—'

Here Jacob broke off, emotion rising in his voice. But Larry finished his sentence.

'The war came.'

'Correct. The war came. I, of course, was not yet born. My mother and father and their sons were forced to stay in the ghetto… You cannot imagine – I cannot imagine – what it is like to live a life that is not free. With proscriptions that forbade you from travelling by tram, from riding a bicycle, from seeing a movie, from sitting in your own damn garden, or a public park, after eight o'clock in the evening.'

'And having to wear a yellow star,' my cousin offered.

'Indeed. But some Jews even wore that with pride. In the beginning.'

'How long were they in the ghetto for?'

Jacob evaluated Larry's question as if it had been asked by a child. Part of a foolish, naïve catechism. He scratched the white stubble on his chin with his distorted right hand.

'The Jodenbuurt became a ghetto in January 1942, Dr Frost. It was all cordoned off by barbed wire, with signs declaring *Juden Viertel*. And the bridges were patrolled by armed guards, as if the population there were contagious. A leper colony…'

'And then?'

'And then the whole family, my mother, father, David and Aaron – who were only little boys, remember – were transported to Westerbork. This was in the spring of 1943.'

'I see,' said Larry.

The light had sunk to almost nothing in the room now, December darkness coming on so swiftly. Larry exhaled, causing the flame of one of the low-burning candles to flicker, then recover.

'My mother was already pregnant with me by then… From Westerbork – which was a holding camp, like Drancy in France – they were taken to Poland.'

Larry was now staring fixedly at Jacob's hooded eyes. These appeared small behind their lenses; circles of glass in which the candle flames danced.

'Whereabouts in Poland?'

'Auschwitz for my father and the boys…' elaborated the old man. And then, with a great heaving motion, as if a hand were helping him inflate the lungs from inside: 'Where I presume they were gassed immediately… My mother was taken to Birkenau, because she was pregnant, you see. There she gave birth to me, in August 1943.'

'So… you were born in a concentration camp?'

My own mind was reeling at the revelation of these facts. We seemed to be a long way from our earlier conversations about Tom Paine and the pharmaceutical industry. A long way from civilisation, in fact.

'That is correct. I was born in a concentration camp. Mimi and I survived, almost until the camp was liberated in early 1945. But before the Americans could reach us, we were put on a forced march. A death march, in fact, during which, I am sorry to say, my mother died.'

I had read about these, of course, as had the whole world, in Primo Levi's books. I recalled a passage from *The Truce* in which he states that the Nazis were well aware that sometimes 80 per cent would die on these exodus marches. It was just another form of mass slaughter. Only one more cruel, perhaps.

Jacob sat back, still as stone for a long moment.

'So…' advanced Larry, shakily. 'What happened next? How did you survive?'

'You are right to ask. The odds on me surviving were unreal. Infinitesimal, you might say. As a child of not yet two years of age, I was taken care of by the women. Polish, most of them. Gipsy women, or so Hannah told me. They managed to get me back to Holland with the few remaining Dutch prisoners. There, through a process I neither remember nor fully understand, was I delivered into the hands of my aunt.'

'But if the ghetto was empty, how come Hannah was left behind?'

'She wasn't left,' exclaimed Jacob, with fresh energy. 'She was hidden!'

'By whom?'

'Okay. Let me tell you the whole story… Hannah was my mother's elder sister. She had made a bad marriage in her early twenties to this fellow Bloom. She divorced him after about a year, apparently – no one ever knew why. But as a result, she was a bit of a family disgrace, or a black sheep – even to the Kleins, who were liberal and had many Dutch friends. So, she was an outcast already. When the war broke out, my mother was already a mother of two in the Jewish district. Whereas Hannah remained around this area, with all her bohemian acquaintances, many of whom were communists, and who formed the core of the resistance. Hannah was single and childless – which was unusual for a woman of thirty back then. Plus, she had radio communication skills. She had a certain mobility – or invisibility – that made her perfect for the underground movement. And before you ask, what she really contributed she would never tell me. Thus, when it was time for the whole Jewish population to be shifted like cattle to the ghettos, she decided to remain behind.'

'Where?'

'Here,' replied Jacob, ingenuously.

'In this very house?'

'Yes. In the basement, as I said. The family who sheltered her were Dutch communists. They owned this place. Many of them were eventually put to death for circulating illegal newspapers. There was a great trade in false identity papers, ration cards – you name it. All of which my aunt may or may not have played a part in. Many spied for the Allies, or took part in armed raids, sabotage. She never told me her exact role…'

'That's unbelievable,' murmured Larry.

'No,' countered the old man. 'What is unbelievable is that she survived the *Hongerwinter*.'

'What's that?' my cousin demanded, with mild irritation.

'The great famine in the winter of 1944. Here in Amsterdam, twenty thousand died of starvation or related diseases. A few who came back after the camps even said they counted themselves lucky to have been under the Nazi cosh, and not to have lived through it. At its worst, people were eating dead rats and taking the joists and rafters of their own houses to burn as fuel. Many buildings collapsed as a result. It almost happened to this place. You could probably tell as you came up the stairs.'

Larry and I exchanged a brief glance. 'That would explain much,' I said, and realised I hadn't spoken since Jacob began his tale.

'So...' the old man continued, his chest concave, defeated somehow, 'I don't recall my mother whatsoever. What I know about her, my aunt Hannah told me. Mimi was a lovely woman, I gather. Less harsh than her sister, who could be brutal. I remember a good few hidings from her over the years.'

'So where exactly did you grow up after the war?'

'Ironically, in the Jodenbuurt. The place Hannah scorned my mother for moving to, with her devout and devoted Amos. My aunt was strict, but fair. She loved music and books, and bequeathed the love of both to me, as you can see. And she remained a single woman. I don't remember a close male friend or a suitor for the whole of my boyhood and adolescence. It was only as I grew older that I registered this as in any way strange. In retrospect, there were any number of women who might have been her lover. But even now I still know very little about her. You have to realise, here in Amsterdam after the war, what was a population of eighty thousand Jews was reduced to five thousand. When I was returned here, every living relative except my aunt was dead. There was no one to ask about family history. And before you enquire, my aunt's first husband disappeared too. There was no trace of Solomon Bloom after 1945, just as there was no trace of so many others. It was as if they had never lived... But Hannah was a good surrogate mother to me. Of course, we had our differences, and I couldn't wait to get out and go to university. In fact, it was while I was there that she died. The doctors said she had a heart defect. I was only twenty... And very quickly after that, I met Esther. We moved to Rotterdam to start a new life, and that was that.'

'But when you moved back here,' advanced Larry, 'you managed to find a place here. Where Hannah was hidden.'

'Yes. It took a while before something came free. But here I am. It feels right somehow.'

There was a long silence while Larry and I took all of this in. Then he braced himself before asking the question he had been straining to ask from the beginning.

'That's an incredible story, Jacob... I'm moved. And greatly saddened. I think we both are... But I'm still wondering – I'm still in the dark, as it were – just how Mimi, your mother, knew our grandmother, Lotte. Were they penpals or something? Before the war?'

'No!' cried Jacob, startled by the very notion. 'Lotte was Dutch. She grew up right here, just around the corner!'

Here, almost in slow motion, I imagined my cousin actually levitated, his feet leaving the ground, while holding on to the edges of the dining-room table, as if in imitation of Caravaggio's *Supper at Emmaus*. The moment was that surreal and arresting; that heart-stopping.

'What? – you mean – *she can't have been...*'

I stepped in, as Larry appeared to be having trouble speaking. 'Are you saying our grandmother wasn't from Vienna?'

'Yes.'

'How can you be so sure?'

Larry was shaking his head, far from gathering his

composure. Though his mind was evidently working at the speed of light. A billion neurons trying to find connectivity.

'I am sure. Trust me.'

'And was she…?'

'Jewish?' returned Jacob. 'Why, of course.'

At this, Larry seemed to freeze in his chair.

'Gentlemen,' Jacob said, his voice suddenly projecting with great force, 'I am certain. Please trust me… Although, for a moment, when you both turned up earlier, I had a brief second of doubt.'

For a while, Jacob's speech, his very presence in the room, was tuned out by my own thoughts. He was talking, but I was simultaneously unable to understand what he was saying. If Lotte was Jewish, then of course it meant our mothers were too, which in turn… The ramifications of what Jacob had revealed were working on me – through me – on a physical level; like a hot, liquid ore osmosing from the stomach into the bloodstream, and so into the rest of the body.

Then Larry's voice broke in. 'How can you prove it?'

'I have her letters,' the old poet barked, with a note of triumph. 'The correspondence between Lotte and Mimi.'

'Where?'

Without another word, Jacob climbed unsteadily to his feet and headed over, in the virtual darkness, to the desk. There was barely time to look into Larry's bewildered, imploring eyes, before the old man was back with us. He let drop the sheaf of letters I had spotted earlier onto the dining table.

'Here. Be my guest… but be careful. Like me, they are very old.'

With fingers that I could plainly see were trembling, Larry slipped the string holding the pile of faded envelopes together and took out the first to scan. We both saw at once, without having to read a word – and it looked as if they were written in Dutch, anyway – our grandmother's distinctive looping hand. This only added to the quiet uproar inside me; the physical revolution going on in the pit of my stomach. To see Lotte's handwriting here, in this context, was compellingly surreal.

'I imagine you're wondering how I have them?' said Jacob, sitting himself back in his chair, a vague mixture of excitement and sorrow in his eyes.

'It's definitely Lotte...' Larry managed, his head bowed, reading intently words he couldn't understand.

'When I was a teenager,' Jacob commenced, 'an early teenager, maybe barely thirteen, I went snooping around my aunt's bedroom, like young boys do... And I discovered what you are reading now. Of course, I had asked Hannah about my mother and my wider family as I grew up, and she had told me everything – including the rivalries, the falling-outs and making-ups. And of course, she told all about my mother's friends when they were both girls themselves. My mother's best friend from the age of three was Lotte Guttenstein—'

'*Guttenstein?*' snapped Larry, impatient of every detail.

'Little Lotte Guttenstein, from the Keizersgracht also. Her family were a clan of tailors too, but wealthier than ours. Lotte and Mimi were inseparable friends all the way through school and into their early twenties. Of this, my aunt was jealous, she freely admitted. Despite having her own friends, she was envious of the special bond between them. And Lotte was vivacious and rebellious in a way my mother could never be. They were a perfect match. She had one brother, Isaac, who was well educated, but was eventually forced to work in the family shop, which was situated at the bottom of this very street. I will tell you where you can find it, if you care to take a look later. Of course, Isaac hated this, as did his sister when she, too, was inveigled into the family trade. Then, one day when Lotte was twenty-six, in walked a handsome Englishman – or Scottish man, I understand – over here on business, by the name of Edward...'

'This is unbelievable...' broke in Larry.

'And Lotte and Edward fell in love. This was 1936, bear in mind. People were under no misapprehension about what was coming. There was great debate about what to do. If you were Jewish, it was an impossible dilemma. To flee and lose your livelihood? To start again in another country? Or to stay and take your chances? Well, for Lotte there was no question. She was in love, and she decided it was too risky to stay. She came to the conclusion that it was safer to return to England with Edward. Mimi was heartbroken, of course. As was everyone. Understand that Lotte and Edward weren't yet married – and, of course, with him being a goy, you can imagine what a stink that caused in the Guttenstein family.'

'I can imagine,' said Larry, drily, watching Jacob in a kind of transcendent daze.

'So, Edward takes her away, back to England. But Lotte promises my mother she will write. And here,' and he indicated the letters, 'is proof that she was as good as her word. They wrote letters to each other for four years, up until 1940, when the Nazis arrived and made it impossible to do so. But here's the interesting bit – though I can see you are both fascinated by all of it, understandably – before they made it to London, Edward whisked Lotte off to Paris. And not for a weekend, but the best part of a year. They lived in the Pigalle district. This is what my aunt told me, and it is corroborated in these…'

'To Paris?' I asked, still stunned by it all. 'Why?'

'To de-Semitise her, if I can put it in those clumsy terms. It was very, very common at the time. To be Jewish in Europe then was to find yourself in great danger. Like living on the edge of a volcano. Even in England it was safer to assume another identity. Many Jews married Gentiles to reinforce the process. It stopped the questioning. The *Judenfrage* was still a great threat. Paris is where they – your grandparents – married, and where Lotte Guttenstein from Amsterdam became Lotte Berg from Vienna. She took the surname at random – from the composer, I think. It's all there in the correspondence. There are many letters from Montmartre, which are wonderfully romantic; and the process they describe is fascinating. With Edward, she learned how to walk and talk like a young English lady, or a Viennese lady. And then they sailed to England before the outbreak of war. The remainder of the letters date from after 1938. They were sent from an address off Russell Square.'

Larry was smiling now, as if a great current, an electric charge, were flowing through him. It was as if a circuit board that had lain broken for years had finally had the last missing connection fixed with soldering iron and tweezers. 'This explains why,' he said, almost laughing, 'when I went to Austria, out of the twenty-five Lotte Bergs born in Vienna around 1910, not a single one had anything to do with us...'

'You were on a wild goose chase!'

'Yes,' Larry said, ruefully, though commingled with a strange effervescence. 'But it was worth it,' he smiled.

Jacob had begun looking with mild consternation at my cousin's sudden and eccentric hand gestures, and this caused me to smile too.

'When I saw on your website that you were looking for relatives of a Lotte Berg from Vienna, I knew instantly who you were really after...'

'So why did she only change half her name?' my cousin asked, suddenly perplexed.

Jacob nodded to himself at this question, not at all sure of the answer. However, all this seemed very familiar territory to me for some reason, as I had read much about the Kindertransport over the years. I knew there was a reluctance for Jewish immigrants in Britain to keep any German-sounding name during the war, but I figured Lotte put her foot down when Edward tried to persuade her. She had wanted to keep one last vestige of her identity intact. She had wanted to remain a Lotte. Without that, there was the danger of being effaced within. Of total erasure...

'Who knows?' Jacob eventually replied. 'But I do know Edward insisted she legally change her surname. She told my mother this, not with sadness, but with a great sense that she was doing the right thing. In every letter she begs Mimi to leave Holland herself. But, of course, by then, it was too late. In the last letters, Lotte describes the progress of her first pregnancy. She says that, if it's a girl, they will call it Natalie. It was only earlier, over lunch, when you, Nicholas, told me your mother's name, that I knew for sure you were really Lotte's relatives...'

'Goodness,' I exclaimed. Like Larry, I was now eager for more information. 'So why would Lotte, in the nineteen-fifties, send these bogus letters to Larry's mother from Vienna and all over Europe?'

Jacob shrugged. 'To reinforce the lie. Children are inquisitive, as you can see by my example. All it takes is one rumour to get around a school. The so-called Jewish Question still lingered long after the war.'

'But why be ashamed of her Jewish identity?' said Larry. 'Why lie to her own daughter? Why make up a bunch of false relatives: Otto and Ottilie and Elise and the rest?'

'You would have to live through the war to answer that. Even in Britain, after your Immigration Act, Jews were seen as undesirable aliens... Anyway, one tells a lie so many times it becomes truth. It's harder than you think to live under a false identity. Though, of course...' – and here his voice became harsh and slightly mechanical, originating from the back of his throat – 'it makes it easier if your whole family has been wiped off the face of the earth.'

The full gravity of this statement seemed to hit Larry and me gradually, like a slow-motion punch. The reasons for this were formulating simultaneously in both our minds.

'So the Guttensteins were...'

'Yes,' Jacob said. 'All destroyed in the camps. People thought for a while that Lotte's brother Isaac had escaped, but it was a different Isaac in the end, after the family money. People did such sordid things, believe it or not, even after what they had been through...'

'Did your aunt ever see Lotte again?' I asked. 'I mean, did she ever return to Amsterdam?'

'Apparently, yes, but only once. In 1948. But it was too sad. Everyone was gone, as I explained... Lotte didn't even leave my aunt an address to contact her in England. Which was a shame, because on every visit I have made to London, I have gone to the house off Russell Square and looked up at the windows to see where my mother's best friend once lived. There was no trace of her there. I even sent letters there myself, hoping they would be forwarded. Indeed, I have been meaning to ask you: do you think the other side of the correspondence exists?'

I turned to Larry. 'It's probably up in your parents' loft, along with everything else Beverley has taken a lifetime to get around to.'

'I'll call my mum tonight,' my cousin said instantly. 'She might be interested to find out who she really is.'

'As might mine,' I added.

'If they do turn up, I would love to read them,' said Jacob slowly. 'It would be the only thing I have left of my mother's, except...' – and here he reached to the shelf behind him and took down one of the faded black-and-white photos – '... for this.'

Jacob looked down at it with obvious pleasure.

'My mother is on the left, my aunt is on the right. It is the only photo I have of either of them.'

He showed it to us. It was tiny, in a miniature frame, a shot of two young women with nineteen-thirties' roller-curled hair under stylish hats – teenagers only, perhaps – with the strong force of their incipient lives beaming from their dark eyes and voracious smiles, transmitting their vitality in a direct line from the past to the present. Knowing what happened to Jacob's mother, it was an intensely sad tableau. It reminded me of nothing other than the snap of my mother with Larry's, posing as two burgeoning young lovelies at the fairground.

Larry was staring as intensely as I at the picture. 'She was beautiful.'

'They both were!' urged the old poet. 'Though I can see why Amos chose my mother.'

While Jacob was showing us the photo, a sharp sense of pure sadness had begun to spread through my very being. It seemed to reach a maximal peak of melancholy, and then just keep on getting deeper and blacker by the second. Not just sadness for his family who – his aunt notwithstanding – he never got to meet, but for us; for the wider family that Larry and I now knew to be ours, but who had been exterminated along with so many others. Now it was all horribly and pressingly personal. I saw in a giddy rush the terrible fate of those who didn't escape; who didn't get free. Rather than being the tragic others they had been in the morning before we set foot in Jacob's apartment, a certain number, it was clear, had been our ancestors. Our flesh and blood, our kin. The Holocaust was suddenly unbearably close to home. It had always been a benchmark in human depravity since the camps were liberated in 1945; an affront, a vile insult to the whole of humanity, but finding out that my own kin had been among its victims made me feel the shock of it anew. With this realisation, too, came a fresh and surprising sense of responsibility; of seriousness, and of fidelity to the past. An imperative to learn the real facts, no matter how long it took. And above all this was the stark realisation that Jacob's survival – the very fact of which had just made the mass extermination of 6 million fellow human beings personal for us – was as near to a miracle that an atheist such as Larry, and a suffering agnostic such as myself, could admit.

Just then, while these thoughts were tearing around my mind, my phone went off. It hammered in my pocket, unignorably.

Snatching it up, I saw that it was Ed calling. Larry and Jacob stopped talking abruptly.

'You're here?' I spoke breathlessly into the receiver. My son's voice was small but excited on the other end.

'We've just got here, Dad! But come quick or we'll have to go back without seeing you!'

'Okay, okay. I'll be right with you! I'm in the middle of something. Yes, ten minutes!'

And I closed the phone without even hearing his goodbye.

Before any of us could say anything further, the phone burst into life again, but I cut it short.

Jacob was looking at me wistfully. 'You have to go? It's a shame we cannot all speak further.'

'I do, I'm afraid, but my cousin doesn't have to.'

'It would be good to talk some more...' said Larry, tentatively. 'If that's okay with you?'

The old man looked between the two of us. 'Certainly, you are welcome to.'

There was a silence during which I decided what to do. 'It's okay, I'll stay for a moment longer. I just wanted to ask a couple more things, and then I'll go.'

My phone gave a little throb on the dining table indicating that a voice message had been left. But before I could pick it up, the damn thing rang again. I saw at once that it was Cass, and brutally stopped the call dead; feeling, absurdly, like Peter denying his master.

'You'll have to go, Nick,' urged Larry. 'I'll see you back at the hotel.'

'I know, I know,' I said, gathering my trench coat. Then I turned to Jacob. 'Is there any way we can thank you for this? For keeping the letters so diligently – for taking the time to talk to us? For lunch, even?'

'Just stay in touch,' the old man smiled, the flesh on his cheeks as thin as onionskin. I could see in the candlelight that his hair had once been brick-red and fulsome, reduced now to mere wisps of white. 'I would like to know you both a little more. If nothing else, you are my only link to the past. As well as both being charming gentlemen. And I would like to read your work. Maybe we could even talk further about our afflictions.'

'I'll get your email from Larry...' Then I took a glance over at the electric typewriter on the desk, shrouded in darkness. I hesitated before I asked: 'Have you got a computer?'

'Does it look like I have one?!' exclaimed Jacob. 'No, I go to the library. I use theirs. That's where I communicate with my daughters and do my research.'

As I made to go, Larry asked the old man a question that I first thought knuckle-headed in its stupidity.

'Have you got any advice for us?' my cousin enquired gently. 'Now that we're officially, well…'

It was only a matter of time before he said something like this, I ruminated, as I did up the coat's belt.

'Now that you both know you're *Jewish*?' asked Jacob, raising both eyebrows over the rims of his spectacles.

He settled back in his chair while the full absurdity of my cousin's query filled the room. Then he leaned forward intensely.

'Write poetry.'

'I'm sorry?'

'Like I said. Write poetry…'

'I don't understand. What if I can't?' puzzled Larry.

'Adorno said there could be no poetry after Auschwitz, but he was wrong. There *has* to be! There *must* be! Or we are all lost. Eternally…'

Larry was nodding in agreement at this, while I stood motionless in the centre of the room, listening to the old poet. I knew I might have to do some running in order to catch up with my wife and son, and this was giving me much anxiety.

'That's great advice,' my cousin finally managed.

'I haven't finished yet…' said Jacob, becoming almost stern. He had both our attentions once more. 'There's this to remember also… If you can help it, *don't be*. Because in this century, and in the many centuries beforehand, stretching back for millennia, it's been a life-threatening condition.'

Now he had both of us puzzled.

'You will have to explain yourself, I'm afraid. You mean *don't be Jewish*?' Larry asked, incredulously. He might have even attempted an uneasy smile to test if Jacob was joking.

'Exactly. If you can help it, don't be Jewish. Because history tells us you will spend your whole life running – and for most of that time, in fear of your life. But if you find out you *are*, then... Let me put it like this. Anyone listening to our conversation for the past few hours would think it is my great misfortune to have been born Jewish, and in the last century. However, there are certain things to be regretted, but that fact I cannot. There is a difference between misfortune and calamity. I am alive, and so many left this world by the chimney, as the expression goes. I have my poetry – the verse I dared to write in defiance of Adorno – and the whole of Europe has poetry to write, not just the Germans, believe me. What's more, I also have Hannah and Deborah, and my grandchildren. So, I have been lucky in many ways – and in ways that perplex me.'

Here Jacob paused as Larry and I took in what he had just said. The candles, still burning miraculously, were throwing our three giant shadows against the far wall; the whole room glowing with a strange intensity.

Then he continued: 'Yes, my friends, you have no idea of what you wish for, coming to me and asking after your deceased relatives. And now you have proof positive of a Jewish identity. At one time, my advice would have been to keep quiet about it. But not any more. Take it on board, and be proud of it, gentlemen. Because not so long ago you would've had to have kept moving along in shame, in the darkness, with a quick step and a pair of sealed lips…'

And maybe again now, I thought – but didn't say – in the twenty-first century.

Jacob blinked at me. I stood watching him, stranded in the centre of the room. Larry and I were momentarily without redress following the old man's speech. It was impossible to add anything to what he had just said.

'But I see I am keeping you! Please, it won't be rude if you go…'

I went over to Jacob, my heart thumping in my chest. I wanted to say many things, but knew I wouldn't be able to. I would have to save them for our correspondence.

Instead I said, simply: 'Thank you,' and held out my hand.

Jacob took it, and to my surprise enclosed it in a double grip; the grasp weakened by his rigid fingers.

'Like I said, stay in touch… And don't forget, as a great writer once wrote, to go east, and become better acquainted with the conditions of your race.'

'I will,' I said, wanting to ask who he was quoting; transfixed by the moment until he released my right hand.

'*Shalom*,' he cried as I headed for the door. 'And careful on those stairs.'

I turned around to give a wave, only to see they weren't looking in my direction. Jacob was already talking with my cousin, who resembled, in the quivering candlelight –which held every tone of green and gold – some kind of bearded Methuselah.

*

Two minutes later I was running.

Two minutes after that, I was still running, as if in pursuit – or being pursued.

Two minutes after that, I was running even faster, flat out; my heart racketing between my ribs, along what seemed like endless and confusing stretches of canal; the lights from the black houses pooled in exquisite amber bands across the water.

Ten minutes after that, I was running still, but by this time I was hopelessly lost.

It was now fully dark, and the streets looked very different after nightfall. Each began with a nexus of bridges, then gave way to long tranches of heterogeneous – though admittedly beautiful – canal-side houses. It seemed I had streaked past every building and chained bicycle at least twice.

Gulping down the icy night air deep into my lungs, the change jangling like an alarm in my pocket, I glanced at my watch. It was already five. We had talked for so long! I was still reeling – physically so – from what had been disclosed. What on earth could Larry be thinking now? It felt wholly wrong to leave them both there. It was scarcely believable that he had been correct all along in his wild assumptions. And now, he most probably imagined, there was no real prohibition against him marrying Ariel; though perhaps nothing would be so simple. It was indeed momentous... Sprinting, I meditated on it all with a rare intensity. The revelations seemed to sear the very synapses. I was who I was – who I had always been – except now I felt myself to be someone else entirely; someone extra, with an added component... Yet how could this be, when I was who I had always been from the start!

It was also strange, I managed to register, as I forged ahead blindly, how focused the mind can be when the body is in fast motion. Marathon runners must know this. Paradoxically, it's only when we are stationary at our desks that the imagination flits about. Running, one could achieve a great deal of concentration. I wanted to think about little Lotte Guttenstein and her dashing Edward for a moment, as I knew I wouldn't have the chance later. They had fooled everyone, even their own children. Everyone except my cousin, it seemed. Only Larry – that man of ardent zeal – had felt the blood bond with another race, and through art, of all things. Yet that had been enough. Meeting Jacob via the internet had been, if not a miracle, then a triumph of his beloved connectivity... So the refugee and the Scottish pharmacist had made a quiet life in suburban Ruislip, living unobtrusively, as Lotte had wanted. But still harbouring great pain within, no doubt. I tried to imagine my grandmother once more, tried to piece her together from fractured memories of our visits, and she appeared vividly before me for a few seconds, as I raced through the very streets she might have walked as a young girl with her best friend, Mimi. Though I could only picture her as a benign old lady, transmitting the love she felt for her grandchild without ever explicitly saying so, she was still alive in my mind. She was smiling and laughing, nodding rhythmically in her Eastcote living room; her hot-blooded colour high in her face, saying something controversial to shock my father, while winking at me...

The vision of my father caused another vivid tableau from the past to appear before me. After Rube's murder, Larry and I had had a long discussion about the persecution of the Jews, and how what had happened to European Jewry over many centuries, the Paris supermarket siege, and the murder of the promising black artist, were part of the same malaise. It was merely hatred of *the other*, or what the French would call *la différence*, he had insisted. He had pointed out that one of the heroes of the Hyper Cacher attack had been a young Muslim shop assistant, who had helped hide Jews in the basement; the one ray of hope in the whole incident. I had had a similar discussion with my dad, though when I was much younger. I was thirteen. We were sitting in the garden of Spring Cottage, on the slatted benches, towards dusk. I was drinking wine, which wasn't surprising, as my father had always provided wine at dinner, mixed with a little water, as far back as I remember. A French affectation, and one my school friends lavished with much envy. We had been arguing about the danger of ascribing national or ethnic characteristics to any given people (like I said, he was ever eager to initiate me into high-flown talk). He warned me against tarring any population with the same brush, something I have never forgotten: 'See, it works both ways if you do that. If you claim the Germans exhibit one set of stereotypes, then you have to admit other nationalities and ethnicities have their own, too. And you wouldn't want to do that, would you?' I recall nodding my head in fierce agreement, the midges of evening swarming in the luminous air. He went on to explain that he didn't see Hitler as particularly emblematic of any nationality – he wasn't

Austrian, or German or Teutonic, he was a recognisable type, one belonging to every race and country on earth. Without pause I had asked, 'What type is that, Dad?' Blinking for a moment, my father had replied: 'A *twat*.' I was shocked by the harshness of the word, the actuality of him having said it, the absurdity of it, especially given that his voice had suddenly slipped into the Welsh register, accentuating the word's resonant vowel. *A twaaht*. He continued: 'Hitler had a *twaat-ish* personality, see. He was a failed artist; an inadequate; a bitter, hateful, ludicrous, power-mad little gimp, who only fooled people for a few years, yet somehow became this unstoppable bacillus. History is full of them, as you will find out. Nero, Attila the Hun, Stalin. But none so poisonous and deadly as old one-bollock Adolf...'

Dubious as a piece of historical analysis, perhaps, but as psychoanalysis it had been spot on.

As I hammered the pavements, attempting to keep up the pace, still worryingly lost, my father and grandmother dominated my thoughts with a strange insistence. But I also pondered Larry's question to Jacob, and the whole subject of advice. A lifelong giver of advice, my cousin had asked it of the old poet. Extraordinary! And what a reply he had been given. I hoped he would take it to heart; as I hoped I, too, would be equal to it. Advice was available everywhere, it seemed, and for free. Larry had ignored his parents' advice and gone into pharmacology with much success, while mine had given me no advice at all, allowing me to take up a job that, for the most part, I loved. But then I had ignored my father's advice when he said I should be wary of marrying Cass, even after she fell pregnant; just as Ariel had ignored her father when she announced Larry had put a ring on her finger. Such headstrong creatures! And yet so easily led by the nose too. I had taken my consultant's advice and swallowed his damned medicine, when a little independent thinking might have saved me from a lifetime of pain – pain that was now shooting up my legs and into my pelvis in imitation of a medieval torture.

Out of breath, my knees screaming, fearing I would at any moment rupture both Achilles tendons, I came to an exhausted stop before a familiar-looking bridge.

I creased over from the waist, wheezing bronchially, like an Olympic sprinter coming to a staggering halt. It had been five years, I realised, since I'd had to do any running. Though I had the advantage of resting my hands on a bollard, I felt I might pass out. There was a livid moment as I sensed consciousness slip away, my vision full of glitter. Then I seemed to stabilise…

But where on earth was I? Before I set off, I had called Ed to tell him I was on my way, yet now the very layout of the streets seemed incomprehensible. I had asked in bars, consulted tourists, and those whom I thought were native Amsterdammers, but had been directed, most probably, in the wrong direction. The Centrum was only ten minutes from Jacob's house, but it might as well have been located in another country. And for this to happen now, of all evenings!

But there was no time for such reflections.

I set off again, blindly, towards a bank of houses I imagined to be the beginning of the Old Centre. Above me was a clear December night sky of plush navy; the first stars Van Gogh whorls, an effect produced by my velocity. Every person I passed was bundled up in scarves and padded jackets, breathing ostentatious quantities of steam as they talked. Quite suddenly, I decided to take to the middle of the road, for increased speed. Volleying through a phalanx of angry cyclists, I tried to find the express momentum, the forward propulsion I would need to catch them in time.

So delayed had their train been, Ed had told me they would only have a mere forty-five minutes before it would be time to check in at security for their return. And after the king's ransom the whole expedition had cost Cass in the first place, I didn't like to guess at her temperature... Yet there was no reason to be so baffled by the geography. I had walked the route from the station to the hotel with Larry only the day before. I should've recognised it all. But nothing seemed friendly. Amsterdam was like a time machine at night. You really felt you were back in the seventeenth century, with gabled Dutch Renaissance classics on every corner; whereas in Paris, you were never far away from the insistent lime-green of the *pharmacie* cross, leaving you in no doubt as to which epoch you belonged. Sweating into my trench coat, dazzled by the austere beauty of the reflected lights, I admitted to myself that I really had no idea where I was.

And now I was running, with a fresh sense of purpose, through a warren of tiny streets. This had to be the Old Centre, surely. At a tight bend I caught a clutch of tourist signposts, but none gave any indication of the station. Anne Frank's house, yes, but the Centrum, no. And over there were the famous streets of shame, with their neon windows and bored sex workers. I recalled, with a burst of hope, that the Red Light

District wasn't far from the station. The tawdry landmark at least indicated I was nearer my wife and son. Taking a guess on a left turn, I peeled off down a street full of glittering Amstel signs. But where was everybody? The bars were empty. It was a Sunday, sure, but compared to the previous evening the streets were strangely deserted. And where were the cabs? I had decided a moment ago I would have to find one to make what would be a two-minute journey, but I couldn't see a single taxi... The stinging burn in my ankles and knees was becoming nigh on intolerable as I neared the end of the road. I exited a cobbled thoroughfare, and found myself face to face with another canal.

A nightmare!

Jogging on the spot, enveloped in my own steam, I cursed myself for not investing in Euro sat nav on my phone, then considered calling Ed one more time. But he would only see me as a useless father for getting myself so lost. And Cass would be more than scornful if I dared to call her number.

However, there was no time for such self-reproach.

I was off once more; the black abyss of the canal cancelled in a trauma of determination. Off like a blue streak: barrelling through the night air; vaulting over traffic islands; barging into tourists. 'Hey, mister...' called out a six-footer in a North Face jacket, his accent Dutch. But his cry was lost with my velocity.

And mounting by the second, a sure sense of panic gathering in the pit of my stomach. There was a real danger now I would miss them completely, and that would never do. No, that would be inconceivable.

Without thinking twice, I gambled on doubling back through the Old Centre, and tore back into the lurid lights. After a couple of limping minutes, harassed by stinging tendons and head pressure – which had returned, making me feel an aneurism was surely only seconds away – I sighted landfall. A street sign. *Centrum straight ahead*. And I had been so close all along.

Leaving the tight maze of shops, bars and brothels, I abruptly saw the grand frontage of the station, rising like a Bavarian town hall; monolithic in the glare of its poetic uplighting. So that's where it had been hiding!

Crossing the road, I made towards it; taking the long esplanade in painful strides. It still seemed a long way off, somehow. But this must have been an illusion caused by the station's turrets and sheer scale. I was there in a matter of moments. Finally dodging the blue-lit trams, which were pulling up one after another, I tried to compose myself. I sensed I was sweating and wheezing chronically. There was a feeling of delirium behind my eyes, and I thought for a moment I was about to pass out properly. I felt the inside pocket of my trench coat to check the bulge of the scarf my mother had knitted for Ed. She had posted it to me in Paris, and I had brought it along with the passbook for the bank account I intended to give my son as a Christmas gift. Not much compared to the continued presence of a loving father, but it was the best I could do.

I raced into the main entrance, and headed straight for the Eurostar desk. Glancing up at the big eye of the old clock, I saw I might be too late. Then, still jogging, I noticed that all the passengers for the next departure had gone. In the distance was a queue of people, all checking their tickets in at the barriers for the airport-style security that would see them stripping their belts and jewellery and putting them on a conveyor, while they themselves walked under the arch of the X-ray machine.

I *was* too late. I had missed them. They had gone home!

Then, in despair, my legs about to give way underneath me, I heard a voice.

'Daaaddl!'

I slammed to a halt and looked frantically around to locate the familiar sound. And there, twenty feet away, by a coffee chain outlet, holding paper cups and napkins, were my ex-wife and my son.

The boy ran towards me, his arms outstretched. In seconds those arms were around my waist, my own legs palpitating. I pulled him closely into the folds of my coat in a tight embrace, my hand stroking his hair. He seemed so new, somehow, like a coin minted that morning. Looking down, he appeared to have shrunk, as if time had stopped, or gone backwards, since I last saw him. Under my fingers, the pelmet of his dark brown hair seemed impossibly moist and glossy. All at once, I felt the unbearably reflective sheen of his boyish moptop to be of infinite value. I didn't want it to disappear off the face of the earth, like everything must. I desperately wanted every light-catching fibre of my son's hair to outlive me, to outlive everything. I felt overcome by the moment. The unfathomable bonds of blood.

Ed pulled away, blinking, taking in his father with wide eyes – with *my* eyes. Then he said, ''Sup blud?'

'I beg your pardon?'

I knew the sweat was running down my face in runnels. Despite the December cold, it was trickling down the back of my neck and past my shirt collar. I must have looked like a madman. He repeated his question, which I could barely understand.

'I said, "'Sup blud?"'

'You will have to translate, Ed.'

'What took you so long?'

'I'm sorry. I got held up. Then I got lost…'

'Oh, that is *crump*, Dad!'

At that moment, I became aware of Cass entering our orbit. She was dragging one of those wheelie cases I always disliked, the ones that caused anyone following behind to trip over them on busy concourses. Hers was a teal blue, gripped by a wiry hand. In her other hand she brandished a steaming cardboard coffee cup, almost as a weapon. She also seemed miniaturised and new. Her hair was different, the bangs longer; her sharp little features smaller, accentuated by make-up. There was something muscular about her walk and her stance when she reached us, as if she'd been spending a lot of time in the gym. I could tell she was far from happy.

'What the hell happened to you?! We almost went home…'

'Yeah. Look, I'm sorry, okay? Something came up during the meeting. Something that… I couldn't get out of.'

'You'll have to do better than that, Nick!'

Ed was hopping from foot to foot, occasionally taking his ankle up in a leg-stretch exercise, like a sprinter about to take off. Sometimes he would perform a long slide, as he used to do in the flat, in his socks. All of this was exciting to him, I could tell. Even the prospect of his folks having a row on the concourse of a foreign station.

'I was with Larry... We've had the most extraordinary afternoon.'

She cut me off. 'And so have we. But for different reasons, I imagine!'

'Listen, let's not get into this,' I said, lamely. 'I'm just glad I caught you in time.'

'Until we saw you running, I swear, we were just about to join that queue.'

I looked across and saw more people checking through the ultra-modern chrome barriers. These seemed out of place next to the station's red-and-white stone columns, which put me in mind of Granada's Alhambra, for some reason.

'Are you going to miss the train?'

Cass shook her head, and her bob vibrated. 'We've got a couple of minutes... I can't believe we came all this way just to have coffee. And lousy coffee, too.'

And here she tossed the majority of her cup onto the platform. Ed jumped back just in time to miss the splash.

'Mum, you can't do that!'

'I just have, okay?'

The breath still raw in my throat, in an attempt to calm her down, I asked, 'Didn't you even get the chance to look around? I know Ed wanted to.'

'For less than an hour, yes, while trying to call you.'

'It was proper hectic, Dad!' beamed Ed, who had now gone over to his mother's side, taking the wheelie trolley off her in order to play with it.

Cass faced me now, her arms folded.

I locked eyes with her. It was a sad moment. I felt it to be terminal. The sort of moment I would remember for ever; though to my son, it was just another day in the pageant of youth.

'Are you all set for the States?'

'Yes,' Cass replied. 'All packed and ready to roll.'

'Andrew's gonna come, too,' piped up Ed, then he put his hand across his mouth, instantly aware he had said something wrong. He looked up at his mother, guiltily.

I found Cass's eyes again.

'Who's Andrew?'

There was a silence, a fairly intense pause, despite the noise of commuters and tourists all dragging their cases and jabbering around us. Before Cass could answer, Ed said: 'Mum's new boyfriend.'

As I had guessed! Yet the sure confirmation didn't stop what felt like a mild electric shock delivered to the heart. For a horrible moment I imagined I could smell this Andrew on my son from the moment I hugged him. A queasy intimation that this other male had left his organic residue on my own flesh and blood.

'Oh, yes?' I asked, holding Cass's steady gaze. 'And what does Andrew do?'

'He's in finance, if you must know.'

'A banker?' I demanded, incredulous.

'Yes, he works in the City. He has links with Wall Street, so he's going to be joining us. Initially, at least.'

I turned to Ed. 'So, do you like this Andrew?'

'He's safe, bro... but he ain't you.'

At this I smiled inwardly, but tried not to show it on my face.

Good old Eduardo! I knew his comment would go straight to Cass's heart, just as the revelation of her new man had jolted mine.

'Well, it's really none of your business, Nick.'

All at once I felt my temper rise in me, like a blood vessel about to pop. I tried to quell it helplessly.

'You say taking my son to live in another country, maybe indefinitely, with another man in tow, is *none of my business*?'

'Oh, come on! America's not the moon!'

'It's starting to feel like it. To me at least!'

We were squaring up to each other now. Cass glanced over at the departures board, and I knew she was about to say it was time they went. But before she could, Ed butted in: 'Okay, you olders go off and have a bitch-fight, yeah? I'll just stand here and film it on my phone.'

'Don't be insolent!' Cass yelled.

And I knew, in that moment, she had lost control of him, somehow. On some fundamental level, Ed had slipped the apron strings. I had always firmly believed that children needed two parents to lay down the law. To back each other up, to corroborate the strange and confusing litany of blandishments and stringencies that constitutes a childhood. If it's just one parent giving the orders, those reasonable demands quickly become the whims of a tyrant, living deludedly in a dictatorship of one.

'Hey,' I said, knowing their time was fast running out. 'I've got something to tell you too. I found it out this afternoon with Larry.'

'What's that?' asked Cass, uninterested.

'I'm Jewish.'

I looked at my ex-wife and saw her expression almost imperceptibly drop, modify itself, then return to normal. All in a fraction of a second. Had I had married an anti-Semite? Who knew?

'You're kidding?'

'Would I joke about something like that? No, Larry's correspondent proved beyond doubt that our grandmother was a Dutch Jew. Can you believe it?'

'I thought she was Austrian.'

'So did we, this morning.' And then, thinking of all the recalibrations this new condition would bring, I said: 'I may have to give up shellfish.'

I could see out of the corner of my eye that Ed was curious about this revelation, though not quite sure what it meant. Relieved, too, that his parents weren't about to kill each other. He had done world religions in school, very briefly, so he knew roughly what we were talking about.

'Does that mean I'm Jewish as well?'

I meditated on this for a moment. I could see Cass's features had become even more inscrutable. As I pointed out before, her face always seemed to darken, almost perceptibly, when something didn't go her way.

'Not technically, no. But it does mean you've got Jewish blood… So as good as.'

He looked abruptly crestfallen. 'Aw, that's dred, Dad. Why can't I be properly Jewish too?'

I felt a bubble of laughter well up inside me. I was glad I had mastered my temper of a few minutes ago. It was something I'd never managed with my ex-wife. Now I had never felt more in control of a situation.

Strangely high or euphoric from this, I said: 'Well, I'm afraid not everybody gets to be. It's a shame, but there you go...' And then, without quite knowing what I was saying, I addressed my son directly: 'Listen. Who do you really want to live with, Ed? Me or your mother? Because I have to know...'

I had no idea I was going to say these words. They just tripped spontaneously from my lips.

My son looked instantly lost at this most serious of all questions. I regretted asking it at once, of course, there in the noisy confines of Amsterdam's Central Station. But where else could I have raised it?

Cass scowled at me with fresh exasperation.

Ed was looking between the two of us, unsure of what to do. With his mother about to speak, he went over to her and demonstrated, by a physical action, his reply. Something I had been scared of all along. He put his arms around his mother's waist, causing her legs – sturdy pillars in black jeans – to stand even more firmly and defiantly on the cold concrete of the platform. Ed then stared over at me, almost coyly, apologetically. All his street bluster of a few minutes ago cancelled. He was just a little boy, all of a sudden, in need of his mum.

Well, I had my answer, and unequivocally. Of course he would choose his mother. And what a fool I was to have asked! It was selfish to have put Ed on the spot like that. It was choking to the heart, undoubtedly, to get this learnt, but learn it I must. I must have been out of my mind to ask him to make such a choice. But at least now I knew. Any mad hopes of my son coming back to Paris with me (and I had, I knew, on the deepest, most animal level, entertained these hopes), lay dashed alongside the spew of cold coffee on the concourse.

At that moment, a thundering voice came over the station's tannoy, announcing the last call for the Eurostar to Brussels and London St Pancras.

'We're going to have to go now, Nick,' said Cass, almost gently; sensing, perhaps, a scintilla of how I was feeling.

'Okay, then. Have a safe journey.'

And Ed flew from his mother's side to give me a last hug. It seemed to dissolve me into the concrete.

'Ciao, Dad,' he smiled, pulling away. 'I'll Skype ya!'

'You do that…'

And then I remembered. I had forgotten to hand over the presents. Fumbling in the trench-coat pockets, I pulled out the gift-wrapped scarf, and with it the envelope marked, simply, *Ed*.

'From your granny. And from me, too. Happy Christmas.'

As Ed thanked me, Cass gave me a weak smile; half of apology, half some indefinable emotion, which I was too tired to evaluate at that moment. It struck me then that it took talent to love another human being. Perhaps I had always lacked it, or had learned it too late. I had a tin ear for female subtlety, that was for certain.

Taking up the wheelie trolley, Cass ratcheted up the handle in preparation to leave.

'Goodbye, Nick. We'll let you know when it's time to visit.'

'Thanks,' I said, and then for some reason using the American locution, 'so long.'

And then they were off, hurrying towards the burnished chrome barriers.

As they went, Ed span around, and gave me the briefest of waves. I returned it, with what I imagined to be my biggest, most fatherly smile.

As I watched them go, getting smaller and smaller, I decided Larry was right. Ed was a good kid. I should trust in his future more. He would be okay over there in the States, despite all my fears. In fact, I wanted very much for Larry to be here with me now, to reassure me of this. In light of the day's revelations, I badly needed to talk to him, to look upon him. Of course, the person I really needed to look upon was myself, given what had arisen. I knew I wouldn't be able to put off this strenuous task for much longer. After all, Larry and I had a whole lifetime to talk about it all – to assimilate it – and I couldn't wait to begin.

Wanting my son to turn around again so I could see his face one last time, I could only think about how Larry had been set free by Jacob's words. Emancipated, rather than chained, in a new identity. A final self. To know you were definitely someone was liberating, not confining. Definitely who he was at last! Not just Everyman, but one man. And a Jewish man, at that. Descendant of Abraham, Isaac and Israel, and the Twelve Tribes themselves. Free now that he had found a place for himself. A place of spiritual belonging; a community where he might be embraced; and a community, he hoped, that would one day be embraced by all the fellow inhabitants of the planet he loved.

As I watched Cass and Ed disappear onto the distant train, I needed to believe my cousin's advice to me. Believe that things would always turn out well for the good kids. Like he said, I should have a little more faith in my own son. Yes, Larry had been right about everything, in the end. Just about.

ACKNOWLEDGEMENTS

Thanks, firstly, to all the subscribers of this book – *Jacob's Advice* would not exist without your generous support. Secondly, thanks and praise to John Mitchinson, whose vision got the ball rolling again, and who made my year when he said he'd be proud to publish my novel. Thanks also to the many great people at Unbound: Fiona Lensvelt, who commissioned the book, and whose energy and ideas gave it wings; Georgia Odd, who saw it through a crowdfunding campaign at the height of summer; DeAndra Lupu, who kept a tight rein on its production; and my judicious and rigorous editor Rachael Kerr, from whom there is no hiding place, in the best sense of the phrase. Special thanks to Mark Bowsher for getting us over to Paris to make a sparkling campaign video without getting arrested by the gendarmes. Also, thanks to Amy Winchester, Anna Galbraith, Mathew Clayton, Alex Eccles, Lucy Lawson, Catherine Emery, Jocelyn Nguyen, Lauren Fulbright and all at Unbound. Lastly, thanks to Mecob for the brilliant sunlit cover.

Many editorial eyes passed over the book as it developed over the years, and the advice I received was invaluable. Abundant thanks to Samantha Ellis, James Cook and Dan Jenkins in this department. Special thanks to professor Mark

Bannister for advice on all things French. For the sections of this novel that address pharmaceutical research, I am indebted to Ben Goldacre's excellent book, *Bad Pharma*.

For commissioning book reviews that kept me afloat during writing, thanks to Alice Jones, Justine Jordan, Sam Leith, Toby Lichtig, Tom Fleming and Houman Barekat. Thanks to the Zen Writers Group – Elise Valmorbida, Roger Levy, Anne Aylor, Gavin Eyers, Oana Aristide and Annemarie Neary; and to The Prime Writers, especially Antonia Honeywell for bringing so many talented forty-plus authors together in the first place.

My gratitude also to the following good people for their support: Aki Schilz, Joe Sedgwick and Nelima Begum at The Literary Consultancy. Also Matt Morrison, Ben Musgrave, Monica Germana and Michael Nath at the University of Westminster. Thanks to Alex Preston, David Flusfeder, Patricia Debney and Dorothy Lehane at the University of Kent Canterbury for their good advice. Gratitude also to Andreas Loizou, Andrea Bennett, Richard Skinner, Lee Haven-Jones, Meena Ayittey, Sam Mills, Neil Griffiths, Monique Roffey, Amanda Craig, Helen Brocklebank, Benjamin Markovits, Keren David, Marina Benjamin, Amy Rosenthal and Alice Allan.

For their time, guidance, understanding, love and support, thanks to my mother, Yvonne Enright, Ian Tuton, Amanda Ellis, Ezra Ellis, Edmund Ellis, Hannah Ellis and Aida Hakim. Finally, love always to Samantha and Benjamin.

This book is dedicated to the memory of Becky Swift (1964–2017), founder of The Literary Consultancy. The

Rebecca Swift Foundation is a UK-registered charity established in support of women in poetry, and home to the Women Poets' Prize.
rebeccaswiftfoundation.org / @FoundationSwift

Unbound is the world's first crowdfunding publisher, established in 2011.

We believe that wonderful things can happen when you clear a path for people who share a passion. That's why we've built a platform that brings together readers and authors to crowdfund books they believe in – and give fresh ideas that don't fit the traditional mould the chance they deserve.

This book is in your hands because readers made it possible. Everyone who pledged their support is listed below. Join them by visiting unbound.com and supporting a book today.

Debby Accuardi
Alice Allan
Hephzibah Anderson
Oana Aristide
Odelia Aslan
Meena Ayittey
Jason Ballinger
Mark Bannister
Zena Barrie
Eveline Bechor
Marina Benjamin
Matthew Blakstad
Simon Booker
Robin Booth

Karen Bradley
Jack, Jude & Erin Brayley
Stephanie Bretherton
Helen Brocklebank
Stephen Brown
Christina Browne
Ben Butler-Cole
Clare Carlin
Zoe Chapman
Andrew Chesshire
Lisette Chesshire
Sue Clark
Jason Cobley
Bunny Cook

James Cook

Mike Corder

Isabel Costello

Amanda Craig

Emma Curtis

Patricia Debney

John Doyle

Amanda Ellis

Carolyne Ellis

Ed Ellis

Ezra Ellis

Rebecca Ellis

Samantha Ellis

Yvonne Enright

David Evans

Gavin Eyers

Charles Fernyhough

Caroline Franks

Claire Fuller

Nicole Gallop Mildon

Guinevere Glasfurd-Brown

Aaron Goldstein

Emma Grae

Oli Grant

Christopher Greenland

Josephine Greenland

Mike Grenville

Neil Griffiths

Haydn Hades

Daniel Hahn

Michelle Hakim

Richard Hassall

Jonathan Heawood

Elise Zen Hilton

Antonia Honeywell

Rivka Isaacson

Andrea James

Amy Jenkins

Dan Jenkins

Alice Jolly

Ariel Kahn

Ann Kennedy Smith

Dan Kieran

mildmanneredarmy Laird

Bernice Landry

David Lascelles

Ewan Lawrie

Alison Layland

Garth Leder

Max Liu

Andreas Loizou

Alan Mahar

Benjamin Markovits

Linda Martin

Kate Mayfield

Kevin Mcgeary

Ali Mercer

Sam Mills

John Mitchinson

Matt Morrison

Jeremy Mortimer

Ben Musgrave

Michael Nath

Carlo Navato

Annemarie Neary

Joc Nguyen

Sue Nieland

Ben North

Mick Paulusma

Matt Peover

Justin Pollard

Alex Preston

Emily Rhodes

Lorraine Rogerson

Richard Rose

Cari Rosen

Amy Rosenthal

Arup Sen

Heloise Senechal

Anita Sethi

Laurence Shapiro

Rebecca Sharkey

Richard Sheehan

Ofer Shemtov

Richard Skinner

Hazel Slavin

Rachael Smart

Toni Smerdon

Alison Souter

Helen Southworth

Alexander Spears

Dov Stekel

Gillian Stern

Terry Stiastny

Jon Stoker

Ashley Stokes

Neal Sussman

Emma Sweeney

Ewan Tant

Louisa Treger

David Turner

Ian Tuton

Jan Tyson

Lindsey Tyson

Paul van Heyningen

Laura Vaughan

Sarah Vaughan

Debora Maria Vila

Tom Ward

Venetia Welby

Jayne White

Isobel Wohl

Jeff Wood

Sharon Wright